D1480250

MEDALON

MEDALON

—◆—

Book one of the Hythrun chronicles

—◆—

JENNIFER FALLON

TOR®

A TOM DOHERTY ASSOCIATES BOOK • NEW YORK

This is a work of fiction. All the characters and events portrayed in this novel are either fictitious or are used fictitiously.

MEDALON: BOOK ONE OF THE HYTHRUN CHRONICLES

Copyright © 2000 by Jennifer Fallon

Originally published in 2000 by Voyager, an imprint of HarperCollins*Publishers*, Australia

Map by Ellisa Mitchell

A Tor Book
Published by Tom Doherty Associates, LLC
175 Fifth Avenue
New York, NY 10010

www.tor.com

Tor® is a registered trademark of Tom Doherty Associates, LLC.

ISBN 0-765-30986-6

EAN 978-0765-30986-0

First Tor Edition: April 2004

Printed in the United States of America

0 9 8 7 6 5 4 3 2 1

for
Adele Robinson

ACKNOWLEDGMENTS

I always threatened that my acknowledgment would read something like: I would like to thank my children, without whom this book would have been finished several years sooner . . .

In fact, without their unwavering faith, it might never have been finished at all. I would particularly like to thank David, for his endless supply of coffee and for turning out so well when his mother spent so many of his formative years lost in another world. My heartfelt thanks also to Amanda, for her excellent proofreading and for naming the God of Thieves, and to TJ for being such a good listener—although I wish she had not waited until I was halfway through the final draft before asking, "What would happen if R'shiel was Joyhinia's daughter?"

I would like to thank Irene Dahlberg and Kirsten Tranter for seven pages of insight that pointed me in the right direction and Lyn Tranter at Australian Literary Management for her patience.

My heartfelt thanks go to Dave English from the Alice Springs Yacht Club, for his expert advice on sailing. Nor can I forget to mention Toni-Maree and John Elferink MLA, for their unwavering support when I needed them most and for putting up with my eccentricities on a daily basis.

Last but not least, I must thank my good friend Harshini Bhoola, whose relentless enthusiasm and endless reading of draft after draft of this series earned her an entire race of people named in her honor. She deserves a place with the gods.

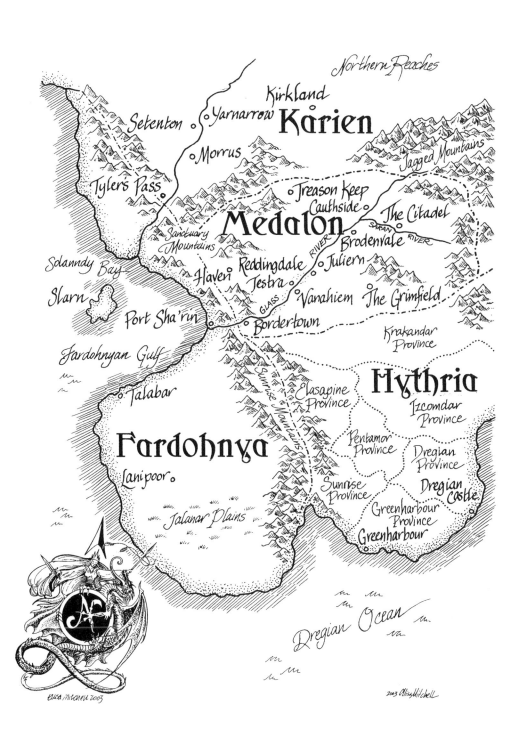

part one

—w—

THE CITADEL

chapter 1

The funeral pyre caught with a whoosh, lighting the night sky and shadowing the faces of the thousands gathered to witness the Burning. Smoke, scented with fragrant oils to disguise the smell of burning flesh, hung in the warm, still air, as if reluctant to leave the ceremony. The spectators were silent as the hungry flames licked the oil-soaked pyre, reaching for Trayla's corpse. The death of the First Sister had drawn almost every inhabitant of the Citadel to the amphitheater.

R'shiel Tenragan caught the Lord Defender's eye as she pushed her way through the green tunics of the senior Novices to take her place past the ranks of blue-gowned Sisters and gray-robed Probates. Feeling his eyes on her, she looked up. The Mistress of the Sisterhood would have her hide if he reported she'd been late. She met the Lord Defender's gaze defiantly, before turning her eyes to the pyre.

Out of the corner of her eye she saw the Lord Defender take an involuntarily step backward as the flames seared his time-battered face. Surreptitiously, she glanced at the ranks of women and girls who stood in a solemn circle around the pyre. Their faces were unreadable in the firelight. For the most part they were still, their heads bowed respectfully. Occasionally, a foot shuffled on the sandy floor of the arena. *How many were genuinely grieving*, she mused, *and how many more had their minds on the Quorum, and who would fill the vacancy?*

R'shiel knew the political maneuvering had begun the moment Trayla had been found in her study, the knife of her assailant still buried in her breast. Her killer was barely out of his teens. He was waiting even now in the cells behind the Defenders' Headquarters to be hanged. Rumor had it that he was a disciple of the River Goddess, Maera. The Sisterhood had confiscated his family's boat—and with it, their livelihood—for the crime of worshipping a heathen god. He had come to the Citadel to save his family from starvation, he claimed, to beg the First Sister for mercy.

He had killed her instead.

What had Trayla said to the boy, R'shiel wondered? What would cause him to pull a knife on the First Sister—a daunting figure to an uneducated river-brat? Surely he must have known his plea would fall on deaf ears? Pagan worship had been outlawed in Medalon for two centuries. The Harshini were extinct and with them their demons and their gods. *If he wanted mercy, he should have migrated south*, she thought unsympathetically. They still believed in the heathen gods in Hythria and Fardohnya, R'shiel knew, and the whole of Karien to the north was fanatically devoted to the worship of a single god, but in Medalon they had progressed beyond pagan ignorance centuries ago.

A voice broke the silence. R'shiel glanced through the firelight at the old woman who spoke.

"Since our beloved Param led us to enlightenment, the Sisters of the Blade have carried on her solemn trust to free Medalon from the chains of heathen idolatry. As First Sister, Trayla honored that trust. She gave her life for it. Now we honor Trayla. *Let us remember our Sister*."

She joined the thousands of voices repeating the ritual phrase. It was uncomfortably warm this close to the pyre on such a balmy summer's eve and her high-necked green tunic was damp with sweat.

"Let us remember our Sister."

Small and wrinkled, Francil Asharen was the oldest member of the Quorum and had presided over this ceremony twice before. She was Mistress of the Citadel, the civilian administrator of this vast city-complex. Twice before she had refused to be nominated as First Sister and R'shiel could think of no reason that would change her mind this time. She had no ambition beyond her current position.

Harith Nortarn, the tall, heavily built Mistress of the Sisterhood, stood beside her. R'shiel grimaced inwardly. The woman was a harridan, and her beautifully embroidered white silk gown did nothing to soften her demeanor. Generations of Novices, Probates, and even fully qualified Blue Sisters lived in fear of incurring her wrath. Even the other Quorum members avoided upsetting her.

R'shiel turned her attention to the small, plump woman who stood at Harith's shoulder: Mahina Cortanen. The Mistress of Enlightenment. Her gown was as elaborate as Harith's—soft white silk edged with delicate gold embroidery—but she still managed to look like a peasant in a borrowed dress. She was R'shiel's personal favorite of all the Quorum members, her own mother included. Mahina was only a little taller than Francil and wore a stern but thoughtful expression.

Next to Mahina, Joyhinia Tenragan wore exactly the right expression of grief and quiet dignity for the occasion. Her mother was the newest member of the Quorum and, R'shiel fervently hoped, the least likely to be elected as the new First Sister. Although each member of the Quorum held equal rank, the Mistress of the Interior controlled the day-to-day running of the nation, because she was responsible for the Administrators in every major town in Medalon. It was a position of great responsibility and traditionally seen as a stepping-stone to gaining the First Sister's mantle.

R'shiel watched her thoughtfully then glanced at the man who was supposed to be her father. Joyhinia and Lord Jenga were coldly polite toward each other—and had been for as long as R'shiel could remember. He was a tall, solid man with iron-gray hair, but he was always unfailingly polite to her and had never, to her knowledge, denied he was her father. Considering the frost that seemed to gather in the air between her mother and the Lord Defender whenever they were close, R'shiel could not imagine how they had ever been warm enough toward each other to conceive a child.

The fire reached upward, licking at Trayla's white robe. R'shiel wondered for a moment if the fragrant oils had been enough. Would the smell of the First Sister's crisping flesh sicken the gathered Sisters? *Probably not,* she noted darkly.

Behind the members of the Quorum and the blue-gowned ranks of the Sisters, the Probates and Novices were ranked around the floor of the amphitheater, their eyes wide as they witnessed their first public Burning. Some of them looked a little pale, even in the ruby light of the funeral pyre, but tomorrow they would cheer themselves hoarse with glee when the young assassin was publicly hanged. *Hypocrites,* she thought, stifling a disrespectful yawn.

The vigil over the First Sister continued through the night. The silence was unsettling. Another yawn threatened to undo her, so R'shiel turned her attention to the first ten ranks of the seating surrounding the Arena. They were filled by red-coated Defenders who stood to attention throughout the long watch. Lord Jenga had not spared them a glance all night. He did not have to. They were Defenders. There was no shuffling of feet numbed by standing all night. No bored expressions or hidden yawns. She envied their discipline.

As the night progressed, the crowd in the upper levels of the tiered seating gradually thinned. The civilians who lived at the Citadel had jobs to do and other places to be. They could not afford the luxury of an all-night vigil. In the morning, the Sisters, Probates, and Novices would still expect to be waited on. Life went on in the Citadel, regardless of who lived or died.

The night dragged on in silence until the first tentative rays of daylight announced the next and most anxiously awaited part of the ceremony.

As a faint luminescence softened the darkness, Francil raised her head. "Let us remember our Sister!"

"Let us remember our Sister," the gathered Sisters, Probates, Novices and Defenders echoed in a monotone. Every one of them was tired. They were beyond being reverent and wished only that the ceremony were over.

"Let us move forward toward a new future," Francil called.

"Let us move forward toward a new future," R'shiel repeated, this time with slightly more interest. Finally, the time had come to announce Trayla's successor, a decision that affected every citizen in Medalon.

"Hail the First Sister, Mahina Cortanen!"

"Hail the First Sister, Mahina Cortanen!" the crowd chanted.

R'shiel gasped with astonishment as Mahina stood forward to accept the dutiful, if rather tired, cheers of the gathering. She could not believe it. *What political scheming and double-dealing had the others indulged in? How, with all their intrigues and plotting had the Quorum actually elected someone capable of doing the job well?* R'shiel had to stop herself from laughing out loud.

As the cheers subsided, Mahina turned to Jenga. "My Lord Defender, will you swear the allegiance of the Defenders to me?"

"Gladly, your Grace," Jenga replied.

He unsheathed his sword and stepped forward, laying the polished blade on the sandy ground at the feet of the new First Sister. He bent one knee and waited for the senior officers down on the arena floor to follow suit. The Defenders up in the stands placed clenched fists over their hearts as Jenga's voice rang out in the silent arena.

"By the blood in my veins and the soil of Medalon, I swear that the Defenders are yours to command, First Sister, until my death or yours."

A loud, deep-throated cheer went up from the Defenders. Jenga rose to his feet and met Mahina's eyes. R'shiel watched her accept the accolade. Never had a woman looked less like a First Sister.

Mahina nodded to Jenga, thanking him silently, then turned to the gathering and opened her arms wide.

"I declare a day of rest," she announced, her first proclamation as First Sister. Her voice sounded rasping and dry after the warm night standing before a blazing bonfire. "A day to contemplate the life of our beloved Trayla. A day to witness the execution of her murderer. Tomorrow, we will begin the next chapter of the Sisterhood. Today we rest."

Another tired cheer greeted her announcement. With her dismissal, the ranks of the Sisterhood dissolved as the women turned with relief toward the tunnel that led out of the arena to make their way home. They muttered quietly among themselves, no doubt as surprised as R'shiel was to learn the identity of the new First Sister. The Defenders still did not move, would not move, until every Sister had left the arena. Mahina led the exodus. R'shiel studied Joyhinia and the other members of the Quorum, but they gave no hint of their true feelings.

The sky was considerably lighter as the last green-skirted Novice disappeared down the tunnel and Jenga finally dismissed his men. R'shiel waited for the others to leave, hoping for a moment alone with the Lord Defender. The pyre collapsed in on itself with a sharp crack and a shower of sparks as the Defenders broke ranks with relief. Many simply sat down. Many more flexed stiff knees and rubbed aching backs. Jenga beckoned two of his captains to him. The men rose stiffly but saluted sharply enough for the Foundation Day Parade.

"Georj, keep some men here and keep the pyre burning until it is nothing but ashes," he ordered the younger of the two wearily.

"And the ashes, my Lord?" Georj asked.

"Rake them into the sand," he said with a shrug. "They mean nothing now." He turned to the older captain. "Tell the men they may only rest once their mounts are fed and taken care of, Nheal. And then call for volunteers for the hanging guard. I'll need ten men."

"For this hanging guard you'll get more than ten volunteers," Nheal predicted.

"Then pick the sensible ones," Jenga suggested, impatiently. "This is a hanging, Captain, not a carnival."

"My Lord," the captain replied, saluting with a clenched fist over his heart. He hesitated a moment longer then added tentatively, "Interesting choice for First Sister, don't you think, my Lord?"

"I don't think, Captain," Jenga told him stiffly. "And neither should you." He frowned, daring the younger man to laugh at his rather asinine comment. "I am sure First Sister Mahina will be a wise and fair leader."

R'shiel saw through his polite words. Jenga was obviously delighted by Mahina's appointment. That augured well for what she had in mind.

"The expression 'about bloody time' leaps to mind, actually," Nheal remarked, almost too softly for R'shiel to make it out.

"Don't overstep yourself, Captain," Jenga warned. "It is not your place to comment on the decisions of the Sisterhood. And you might like to tell your brother captains not to overindulge in the taverns tonight. Remember, until tomorrow, we are still in mourning."

Jenga turned from the pile of embers and noticed R'shiel for the first time. As day broke fully over the amphitheater, bringing with it a hint of the summer heat to come, he walked stiffly toward the exit tunnel where she was standing.

"Lord Jenga?" she ventured as he approached.

"Shouldn't you return to your quarters, R'shiel?" Jenga asked gruffly.

"I wanted to ask you something."

Jenga glanced over his shoulder to ensure his orders were being carried out, then nodded. R'shiel fell into step beside him as they entered the cool darkness of the tunnel that led under the amphitheater.

"What will happen now, Lord Jenga?"

"The appointment of a new First Sister always heralds a change of direction, R'shiel, even if only a small one."

"Mother says Trayla was an unimaginative leader, lacking in initiative. Actually, she used to refer to her as 'that useless southern cow.'"

"You, of all people, should know better than to repeat that sort of gossip, R'shiel."

She smiled faintly at his tone. "And what about Mahina? Joyhinia calls her an idealistic fool."

"Sister Mahina has my respect, as do all the Sisters of the Blade."

"Do you think her elevation means a change in the thinking of the Sisterhood?"

The Lord Defender stopped and looked at her, obviously annoyed by her question. "R'shiel, you said you wanted to ask me something. Ask it or leave. I do not want to stand here discussing politics and idle gossip with you."

"I want to know what happens now," she said.

"I will be called on to witness the Spear of the First Sister swear fealty to Mahina. It will undoubtedly be Lord Draco."

"He's supposed to be the First Sister's bodyguard," R'shiel pointed out. "Yet Trayla died at the hand of an assassin."

"The position of First Spear is a very difficult one to fill—the oath of celibacy it requires tends to discourage many applicants."

"So he gets to keep his job? Even though he did not do it?"

Jenga's patience was rapidly fading. "Draco was absent at the time, R'shiel. Trayla fancied she was able to deal with a miserable pagan youth and ordered him out of the office. Now, is that all you wanted?"

"No. I was just curious, that's all."

"Then be specific, child. I have other business to attend to. I have an assassin to hang, letters to write, and orders to issue . . . "

"And banished officers who offended Trayla to recall?" she suggested hopefully.

Jenga shook his head. "I can't revoke the First Sister's orders, R'shiel."

"The First Sister is dead."

"That doesn't mean I can rearrange the world to my liking."

"But it does mean you can rearrange the Defenders," R'shiel reminded him. She turned on her best, winning smile. "Please, Lord Jenga. Bring Tarja home."

chapter 2

arja Tenragan lay stretched out on the damp ground, looking out over the vast empty plain before him. The earth smelled fresh from the morning rain and the teasing scent of pollen from the myriad wild flowers tickled his nose, daring him to sneeze. Nothing but the distant call of a hawk, lazily riding the thermals, disturbed the early afternoon. The rain had increased the humidity but done nothing to relieve the heat. Sweat dampened the linen shirt under his soft leather jerkin and trickled annoyingly down his spine.

The border between Medalon and Hythria lay ahead. It was unmarked—merely a shallow ford across a rocky, nameless waterway that everyone, Medalonian and Hythrun alike, simply referred to as the Border Stream. Tarja listened with quiet concentration. After four years playing this game he knew that out there, somewhere, was a Hythrun raiding party.

Suddenly, the silence was disturbed. He looked over his shoulder as Gawn marched purposefully toward him, his smart red coat stark against the brown landscape. *He might as well have a target painted on his chest*, Tarja fumed. As soon as he reached Tarja's position, he grabbed Gawn's arm and pulled him roughly down to the ground.

"I told you to get rid of that damned coat!" he hissed.

"I am proud of my uniform, Captain. I am a Defender. I do not skulk through the grasslands in fear of barbarians."

"You do if you plan to survive out here," Tarja told him irritably. His own jacket was tucked safely away in his saddlebag, as were the red coats of all his men. He was wearing an old shirt and comfortably broken-in leather trousers and jerkin. Hardly the attire for a ball at the Citadel but infinitely preferable to being shot by a Hythrun arrow. Tarja absently brushed away a curious beetle come to investigate his forearm and turned back to studying the ford, cursing Jenga. Gawn was only one of many stiff-necked, brand-new officers that Jenga had sent south over the last four years. He sent them to the border for combat experience. Most of them even survived. He had his doubts about Gawn, though. He had been here almost two months and was still trying to cling to the parade-ground traditions of the Citadel.

"What are we waiting for?" Gawn asked, in a voice that carried alarmingly on the soft breeze.

Tarja threw him an angry look. "What's the date? And keep your damned voice down."

"It's the fourteenth day of Faberon," Gawn replied, rather confused by the question.

"On the Hythrun calendar," Tarja corrected.

Gawn frowned, still annoyed and rather horrified that the first task Tarja had set him to on his arrival at Bordertown was learning the heathen calendar.

"It's the twenty-first . . . no, the twenty-second day of Ramafar," Gawn replied after a moment. "But I fail to see what it—"

"I know you fail to see what it means," Tarja interrupted. "That's why you won't last long out here. Two days from now it will be the twenty-fourth day of Ramafar, which is the Hythrun Feast of Jelanna, the Goddess of Fertility."

"I'm sure the heathens appreciate the effort you put in remembering their festivals for them," Gawn remarked stiffly.

Tarja ignored the jibe and continued his explanation. "Our esteemed southern neighbor, the Warlord of Krakandar, whose province begins on the other side of that stream, is traditionally required to throw a very large party for his subjects."

"So?"

Tarja shook his head at the younger man's ignorance. "Lord Wolfblade thinks that it's far cheaper to feed the ravening hordes on nice, juicy Medalonian beef than cut into his own herds. It happens every Feast Day. That's why you need to learn the Hythrun calendar, Gawn."

Gawn still looked unconvinced. "But how do you know they'll come through here? He could cross the border in any number of places."

"The farms over there don't get raided much. The families are probably heathens, or they're too close to Bordertown. The farms to the north and further east, however, get raided on a regular basis."

"Heathens! If you know that, why don't you arrest them!"

Tarja scanned the ford as he spoke. "I don't *know* that they're hea-thens, Gawn, I only suspect it. The last time I checked, the Defenders needed a bit more than suspicion to arrest otherwise law-abiding, hard-working people. We're here to guard the border from the Hythrun, not persecute our own people."

"To place the law of a god above the law of the Sisterhood is treason," Gawn reminded him officiously.

Tarja didn't bother to reply. There was a line of trees southeast of them which could easily conceal a raiding party. There was no telltale glint of metal to alert him to their presence, no betraying nicker from a horse, or even the soft lowing of stolen cattle on the breeze. But they were out there. Tarja trusted his instincts over his eyes. He knew the Hythrun Warlord was waiting, as he was, for his chance to cross the stream.

Tarja had been on the border long enough to develop a grudging respect for Lord Wolfblade and kept an unofficial score in his head. By his calculation he was currently one up on the Warlord. The day before Gawn's arrival, he had foiled a raid on a farm not far from the ford a few days before the Feast of Kalianah, the Goddess of Love. Tarja thought wryly that if the Hythrun did not worship so many gods, his life would have been very boring indeed.

Gawn fidgeted impatiently, uncomfortable with the waiting, and no doubt concerned that his uniform was getting dirty. Finally he stood up, disdainfully brushing dirt and grass seeds from his red coat.

"This is pointless!" he declared loudly.

The black-fletched Hythrun arrow took Gawn in the left shoulder. Tarja let out a yell as Gawn screamed. Gawn clutched at the protruding arrow, blood seeping through his fingers. Tarja glanced at the young cap-tain and quickly judged that the wound was not fatal, so he left him where he fell. Tarja's troop of forty Defenders broke from the trees behind him with a savage war cry. From the tree line he had been watch-ing so closely, the Hythrun raiders broke cover, driving a dozen or more red spotted cattle.

Tarja quickly judged the distance to the border and realized it was going to be a close call. He turned back to his men, waiting impatiently as his sergeant, Basel, led his mount toward him at a gallop, hardly slowing as he approached. Tarja began to run forward as they neared him. The sergeant dropped the short lead rope as he grabbed at the pommel of the saddle. He let the horse's momentum carry him forward and swung up into the saddle on the run. He could barely keep his seat as his feet searched for the flying stirrups and he untied the reins from the pommel.

The Warlord's raiding party was cutting across the open plain toward the stream, riding at a gallop, stampeding the stolen cattle before them. Tarja and his men, leaning forward in their saddles, rode diagonally at a dead run to cut them off. The Hythrun knew that the Defenders were forbidden to cross the border. The stream represented safety and the fifty or more Raiders had only one aim in mind—to reach it before the Defenders could intercept them.

Tarja caught the tail end just as the first of the Hythrun were splashing over the ford to safety. The cattle ran blindly, too spooked to stop for anything as insignificant as a shallow stream. As soon as they were safely across, the Raiders in the lead ignored their booty, and wheeled their mounts around in a tight circle. They plunged back over the ford to hold off the Defenders while their comrades made the crossing.

The opposing forces were suddenly too intermingled for them to risk their short bows. Steel rang against steel as Tarja plunged through the melee, looking for Damin Wolfblade. He spied the fair head of his adversary at almost the same time as the Warlord caught sight of him. The Hythrun turned his mount sharply and galloped to meet the Medalonian captain.

Tarja ignored the battle around him as he raced to engage the Warlord, although a part of him realized that more and more of the Hythrun had reached the safety of the ford. Damin came at him with a bloodcurdling cry, wielding his longsword with consummate skill. He dropped his reins, guiding his magnificent golden stallion with his knees, as Tarja blocked the blow, jarring his arm to his shoulder. He parried another bone-numbing strike and quickly countered with a killing stroke that Damin barely deflected at the last moment. The Warlord was laughing aloud and Tarja knew his own face was set in a feral grin as he traded blows with him. They were so evenly matched, had done this so many times before, it was as much a part of the game as the cattle raids.

"You lose this time, Red Coat!" Damin shouted, as he suddenly steered his mount from under Tarja's blow, which would have taken his arm off at the shoulder had it connected. Tarja glanced around and realized that almost all the Hythrun were over the ford, although several were nursing bloody wounds. His own men milled about in frustration, just as weary and bloodied, as they watched the enemy escape. Wolf-blade wheeled his horse around, before splashing over the stream to safety, and saluted Tarja impudently with his sword from the other side.

"That makes us even, Red Coat!" Apparently Tarja was not the only one keeping score.

The Hythrun raiders wheeled around and galloped away from the border to gather their stolen cattle, whooping victoriously, taunting the Defenders.

Tarja let out a yell of frustration as he watched them ride away. If only that parade-ground fool had kept his head down. He cursed Gawn under his breath as the Hythrun disappeared into the trees on their side of the border.

"Why in the name of the Founders can't we follow them?" Basel demanded as he rode up to Tarja. His sleeve was torn and soaked with blood from a long, shallow cut, but the sergeant appeared too angry to notice he had been wounded.

"You know the answer to that, Basel," Tarja reminded him, his chest heaving. "We're under strict orders not to cross the border."

"A stupid order given by stupid women who sit in the Citadel with no idea what happens outside their bloody sewing circle!"

In anyone else's hearing, such a comment would have earned him a whipping, but Tarja knew how he felt. He shared the man's frustration. All the border troops did.

"Be careful Gawn doesn't hear you voice such sentiments, my friend," he warned.

Basel scratched at his graying beard and glanced back toward the red-coated figure stumbling through the waist-high grass toward them. Gawn clutched his arrow-pierced shoulder calling out for assistance.

"One could almost wish the Hythrun were better marksmen," the sergeant remarked wistfully.

"I suspect they'll get many more opportunities to use him for target practice. In the meantime, you'd better get Halorin to take that arrow out of his shoulder. The last thing I need is Gawn whining about a festering wound. Then we'd best see how much damage Wolfblade did to the farmsteaders."

The trail left by the Hythrun was not hard to follow. Tarja led his men along the raider's path for several hours before they reached the small farm that had been the target of the raid. The Warlord never raided the same farm twice in succession—he preferred to leave his victims time to recover before he struck again.

Tarja urged his horse to a canter as the smell of burning thatch reached him. Damin Wolfblade was not a particularly vicious man. He was certainly an improvement on his predecessor, who had been known to crucify his victims. If the farmsteaders offered no resistance, he rarely did more than destroy a few fences and take his pick of the cattle.

As they rode into the small yard surrounding the farmhouse, Tarja was shocked by the devastation. The house was gutted. In the smoldering ruin only the stone fireplace still stood. Where the barn had been was nothing but a forlorn, blackened framework that threatened to topple at any moment. Tarja dismounted slowly, shaking his head.

"We didn't have no choice, Cap'n."

Tarja turned at the sound. Leara Steader, the owner of the farm, walked toward him from the gutted house. Her homespun dress was torn and filthy, her face soot-streaked, her eyes dull with grief. Her arms hugged her thin, shivering body, despite the heat of the late afternoon sun.

"You know better than to fight them, Leara," he said, handing his reins to Basel. "What happened? Where is Haren?"

She stared at him blankly before answering. "Haren's dead."

Tarja took Leara's arm and led her to the well. "What happened?" he asked again, as he carefully sat her down. The normally tough farmsteader looked fragile enough to break.

"Haren fought them," Leara told him in a monotone. "Said we couldn't let them take the cattle this time. Said we wouldn't be able to pay our taxes if they took the cattle." She took the ladle of water he offered her and sipped it mechanically, as if it was an effort to swallow, before she continued. "He met them at the gate. Told them to go away, to leave us alone. Told them he'd fight them. He cut one of them with his sickle. They laughed at him. Then they killed him."

Tarja urged another sip of water on her, wishing he had something stronger to offer the woman. He called Ritac over, leaving Leara by the well staring numbly into the distance.

"See if you can find Haren's body. We'll burn it before we leave." Ritac nodded without a word and went off to carry out his orders. Tarja returned to Leara and squatted down in front of her. "Why, Leara? You know we never tax those who've been raided. Why not let them take the cattle?"

"Last patrol that came through told us it weren't the law. Told us we'd have to pay, no matter what. Said things would change, now that there was new officers here."

"Who said that?" Tarja asked curiously. The practice of not taxing victims of Hythrun raids was one that predated Tarja's posting to the border, and he had never thought to question it. Strictly speaking, the victims were not exempt from levies due to hardship. It was just that the Defenders chose not to enforce that particular law. These people suffered enough from the Hythrun, without making it harder for them by taking what little they had left for the Sisterhood.

Leara looked up and pointed at Gawn, who still sat on his horse in the middle of the yard, holding his wounded arm gingerly. "It were him."

"Ritac!" Leara jumped at Tarja's sudden shout.

The corporal hurried over to them. "Sir?"

"Go with Mistress Steader and see if anything can be salvaged before we leave." Ritac's eyes widened at the anger in Tarja's voice. He helped the woman to her feet and led her toward the house. Tarja crossed the yard in five angry steps. He grabbed Gawn by his red coat and jerked him out of the saddle.

"What the Founders—" Gawn cried as he hit the ground with a thud, jarring his already wounded shoulder.

"You stupid, miserable, son of a bitch," Tarja growled, reaching down to pull Gawn to his feet. The captain cried out as his shoulder wound began bleeding afresh. "Verkin sent you out to familiarize yourself with the border farms." He slammed his fist into Gawn's abdomen. The younger man stumbled backward with a cry, doubling over with the pain.

"How many more, Gawn?" Tarja punctuated his words with another blow, this one to Gawn's jaw. The punch lifted the captain off his feet and he landed heavily on his back. Sobbing with pain and outrage, he scuttled backward along the ground to escape Tarja's wrath, crying out with every movement of his wounded shoulder. "How many more farmsteaders will die because you decided things were going to change, now that you've arrived on the border?" Tarja bent down and hauled Gawn to his feet. "What gives you the right—"

"The right?" Gawn sputtered, stumbling backward out of Tarja's reach. "It's the law! What gives you the right to flout it? You're the one who lets these people off paying their taxes! You're the one who lets heathens go unpunished! You're the one—"

Tarja did not wait to find out what else he was guilty of. He smashed his clenched fist into the young captain's face with all the force he could muster. With an intensely satisfying, bone-crunching thump, Gawn dropped unconscious at his feet. Shaking his hand to ease the sting, Tarja turned back to his men, who had all suddenly found something else to do. Ritac hurried to him and glanced at the unconscious captain, before looking at Tarja.

"Did you find Haren?"

Ritac shook his head. "Mistress Leara says they threw him into the house before they set it on fire. He's had his Burning at least."

Tarja frowned. It was a measure of the Warlord's anger that they had burned Haren's corpse. Hythrun considered the Medalonian practice of cremation a barbaric and sacrilegious custom. Wolfblade must have been in a rage, if he ordered a body burned.

"Let's get out of here then," Tarja announced, flexing his still-aching fist as he walked back toward the house.

"Er . . . what about Captain Gawn, sir?" Ritac called after him. "He appears to be unwell."

He glanced over his shoulder at the corporal. "That arrow wound must be worse than it looks," Tarja replied calmly. "Tie him to his saddle."

Ritac didn't even blink. "Aye. Nasty things, those Hythrun arrows."

It was another four days before Tarja and his men arrived back in Bordertown. They had taken a detour to deliver Leara to her sister's farmstead, before heading home.

Gawn regained consciousness and had barely spoken a word to anyone, although he was obviously in pain. He now had a broken nose and two rather impressive black eyes to accompany his arrow wound.

Bordertown was the southernmost town in Medalon, located near the point where the borders of Fardohnya, Hythria, and Medalon met. Their detour meant entering the town by the North Road, past the busy docks on the outskirts of the town.

Harsh shouts, muttered curses, and the sharp smell of fish permeated the docks as they rode by. Sailors and traders, riverboat captains, and red-coated Defenders swarmed over the wharves that were lapped by the broad silver expanse of the Glass River.

To Tarja, the docks were about the worst thing he had ever smelled in his life, and every time he rode past them, he wondered at those who found so much romance on the river.

They rode toward the center of the town past wagons and polished carriages clattering and clanking along the cobbled street lined by taverns and shops. The buildings were almost all double-storied, with red-tiled roofs and balconies that overlooked the street below, festooned with washing hung out to dry. Rickety temporary stalls with tattered awning covers were set up in the gaps between the shops which sold a variety of food, copper pots, and even exotic Fardohnyan silk scarves. There were beggars too—old, scabby men and pitifully thin young boys, missing an arm, a leg, or an eye. Occasionally, he caught sight of a Fardohnyan merchant with his entourage of slaves and his gloriously exotic *court'esa* dressed in little more than transparent silk and a fortune in gems.

Tarja forgot how much he disliked Bordertown every time he left it, and was surprised that after four years, he had still not grown accustomed to it. He preferred the open plains—even the dangerous game he played with the Hythrun Warlord.

Tarja led his men to the center of the town where the market was in full swing. There were stalls everywhere selling just about anything Tarja could name and quite a few things he could not. The smells and sounds of the wharf were replaced with more familiar animal things. Raucous chickens stacked in cages, bleating sheep, evil-eyed goats, and squealing piglets all vied with each other to attract the most attention. A stand selling exotic colorful birds drew Tarja's eye, where a large black bird with a tall red crest yelled obscenities at the passersby. Tarja could feel the undercurrent of the town's heartbeat, like a distant thrumming against his senses.

The town square was dominated by a tall fountain in the shape of a large and highly improbable sculpted marble fish which spewed forth a stream of water into a shallow circular pool. A crowd had gathered to watch as a small man dressed in ragged clothes stood on the rim of the pool. He was yelling in a high-pitched, animated voice.

Tarja glanced at the man with a shake of his head, then turned to Basel. "I thought old Keela was sent to the Grimfield?"

The sergeant shrugged. "They can't keep locking him up forever, sir. He's crazy, not a criminal."

"The gods seek the demon child!" Keela was yelling fervently. "The gods will strike Medalon asunder for turning from them!"

Tarja grimaced at the lunatic's words. "He'll be wishing he was back in the Grimfield if he keeps that nonsense up for much longer." He turned his horse toward the fountain, and the crowd parted eagerly for him, expecting a confrontation. *Hoping* for one.

Keela stopped ranting as Tarja approached and stared at him with his one good eye. The other eye was clouded by a cataract which made the wizened old man seem even crazier than he really was.

"Go home, Keela," Tarja told the old man. His words brought a disappointed murmur from the crowd. They wanted a fight.

"The gods seek the demon child," Keela replied in an eminently reasonable tone.

"Well they won't find him in the Bordertown markets," Tarja pointed out sternly. "Go home before you get into trouble, old man."

"Father! What are you doing?" A young woman dressed in poorly made homespun pushed through the crowd, alarmed by the Defenders confronting her father. She glanced at the old man and then hurried over to Tarja and looked up at him desperately. "Please, Captain! You know he's not right in the head. Don't arrest him!"

"I wasn't planning to, Daana," Tarja assured the young woman. "But I suggest you take him home before someone takes exception to his public speaking."

"I will, Captain," she promised. "And thank you."

Daana hurried over to the old man and pulled him down from the fountain. As she dragged him without resistance past Tarja he looked up and grinned crookedly.

"You've been touched by the demon child, Captain," Keela told him with an insane chuckle. "I can see it in your aura."

Tarja shook his head at the old man. "Well, I'll be sure to give the demon child your regards when I see him."

"Mock me all you want," Keela chuckled. "The demon child is coming!"

Daana managed to drag her father away as the disappointed crowd dispersed. Tarja turned his horse toward the Headquarters on the other side of the square.

The Defenders' Headquarters were located in a tall, red-brick building. It boasted a rather grand arched entrance that led into a courtyard in the hollow center of the building. Another troop was preparing to depart as they rode through the archway. The captain, Nikal Janeson, waved to them as they entered. He finished his discussion with the Quartermaster, then walked over to Tarja as he reined in his mount. The Quartermaster raised a laconic hand in greeting before disappearing inside the building. It was hard to believe he was the Lord Defender's brother. Verkin claimed he tolerated him because he would rather have Dayan Jenga cheating the local merchants on behalf of the Defenders than have him cheating the Defenders on behalf of the local merchants.

"Let me guess. Festival of Jelanna?" Nikal asked, taking in the various bandages and slings Tarja's troop wore. It was Nikal who had made Tarja learn the Hythrun calendar when he first arrived in Bordertown four years ago.

"And thanks to Gawn, they got away," he told Nikal as he dismounted. Ritac stepped forward and took Tarja's reins, leading his mount through the crowded courtyard to the stables. "You heading out along the Border Stream?"

Nikal nodded. "The week after next is the Festival of Bhren, the God of Storms. Damned if I know how they get anything done in Hythria. They seem to spend an inordinate amount of time stuffing their faces in honor of their gods."

Tarja smiled briefly, then his expression grew serious. "While you're out there, you might want to reassure the farmsteaders that they won't be taxed if they're raided. It seems our young captain took it upon himself to instigate a few changes while he was out on his own."

Nikal glanced at Gawn. "Damned fool."

Gawn had dismounted and approached the two captains. His bearing was stiff and unyielding as he nodded to Nikal politely before turning to Tarja.

"I must inform you, sir, that I intend to make a full report to Commandant Verkin regarding your reprehensible actions. I imagine he will want to see you as soon as I have made my report."

"Reprehensible?" Nikal asked with a grin.

"For your information, sir, Captain Tenragan attacked me viciously for no reason!" With that, the young captain turned on his heel and strode toward the main building.

"Your mistake, my friend," Nikal said as he watched him leave, "was letting the stupid bastard live."

"Don't think I wasn't tempted."

"Well, he's right about one thing, Verkin does want to see you." Nikal gathered up his reins and swung into his saddle. "There's been quite a few changes since you left. Trayla's dead, for one thing."

"Dead? How?"

"Murdered by a heathen, from what I hear." Nikal glanced over his shoulder at his troop to assure himself they were ready to depart. "I'll let

Verkin fill you in. I have to get going." He leaned down and shook Tarja's hand warmly. "It's been good having you here, Tarja. I shall miss you."

"You'll not be gone for that long."

"No, but you will. You've been recalled to the Citadel, my friend."

chapter 3

'shiel hurried along the broad walkway to the Citadel's Lesser Hall, buttoning the collar of her green Novice's tunic as she half-walked, half-ran along the vine-covered brick path. She was late for Joyhinia's reception, and her tardiness was among the many unforgivable sins her mother frequently criticized her for.

R'shiel did not want to be at the reception for Sister Jacomina, the new Mistress of Enlightenment. She was not looking forward to an evening of standing around in the Lesser Hall being accosted by her mother's followers, who would ask her interminable questions about subjects she had no wish to discuss in public.

R'shiel was firmly convinced that Joyhinia had no friends, only followers. She hated being the daughter of a Quorum member. She often wished she had been born a boy. Then she could have joined the Defenders. It would be nice to be free from the shadow of her mother's overweening ambition.

She reached the entrance to the Lesser Hall just as the Citadel's walls began the Dimming. Some of the younger Novices whispered that it was magic that made the walls of the Citadel brighten slowly at the dawn of each new day and dim to darkness with the setting of the sun. The Probates simply considered it a unique architectural feature that was beyond the understanding of the Novices. R'shiel thought this a much more likely explanation. The Sisters preferred not to discuss it at all. Tarja told her it was because hundreds of years ago the Citadel had been a complex of heathen Temples. Whatever the reason, the glowing walls flooded even the deepest recesses of the huge white fortress with its hundred halls, both grand and humble, with soft white light. It also reminded R'shiel that she was late.

The faint sound of massed voices reached her ears as she eased open the heavy door to the Lesser Hall. Novices and Probates were required to gather each evening in the Great Hall, led by the senior Sisters, to give thanks to Sister Param and the Founding Sisters for their deliverance from the bonds of pagan worship. R'shiel had learned to recite the Daily Affirmation as a small child and knew well the punishment for not joining in enthusiastically. Harith's cane was accurate and painful. The only benefit of being ordered to attend this reception that R'shiel could think of was that she had been exempted from attending the Affirmation.

The Lesser Hall was lit with hundreds of candles against the inevitable Dimming, although the walls had only just begun to lose their radiance. It was about half the size of the Great Hall, which meant it could still accommodate five hundred people comfortably. The domed ceiling, supported by tall, elegantly fluted columns, was painted a stark white—no doubt to cover the licentious heathen artwork underneath. The walls were white, like all the walls in the Citadel, and were made of the strange, impervious material that glowed and dimmed with the reliability of a Defender's Oath. R'shiel glanced around and spied Joyhinia talking to Sister Jacomina and the Karien Envoy on the far side of the Hall as she edged her way along the wall. With luck, she would be able to convince her mother she had been here on time. R'shiel rarely defied her mother openly—she was not that foolish—but she was adept at walking the fine line between compliance and defiance.

Joyhinia looked up and caught sight of her with a frown. R'shiel gave up trying to hide and decided to brazen it out. She squared her shoulders and walked purposefully through the gathered Sisters and Defenders to greet her mother.

"Mother," R'shiel said with a respectful curtsy as she reached Joyhinia and her companions. "Please forgive me for being so late. I was helping one of my classmates with her studies. I fear I lost track of time."

Better that, than Joyhinia learn she was late because Georj Drake had been teaching her the finer points of knife throwing. R'shiel could not ever imagine having a need to use such a skill, but it was such an unladylike pastime that she couldn't resist the offer to learn. R'shiel sometimes worried about her tendency to do things that would deliberately provoke Joyhinia.

Her mother saw through the lie but accepted it. "I hope your class-mate appreciated your sacrifice." R'shiel knew that slightly sarcastic tone from long experience. Her mother turned to the Envoy and said, "Sir Pieter, I would like to introduce my daughter, R'shiel."

R'shiel dutifully curtsied to the Envoy. He was a solid man with lazy brown eyes and the weary air of a jaded aristocrat. He took her hand in his, kissing the air above it. His ceremonial armor creaked metallically as he bowed to her.

"A charming child," he said, looking her up and down, making her feel rather uncomfortable. "And a noteworthy student, so your mother informs me."

"I try my hardest to honor my mother's faith in me, my Lord," she replied, thinking that was almost as big a lie as her excuse for being late.

"Respectful and charming," Lord Pieter said with an approving nod. "No doubt she will follow in your footsteps one day, Sister Joyhinia. The Quorum will soon benefit from two generations of Tenragan women, I suspect."

"R'shiel will choose her own path, my Lord. I want nothing more for my daughter than her happiness."

R'shiel did not bother to contradict her. She had less say in her future than the average Hythrun slave, who at least had the advantage of *know-ing* he was a slave.

"You must be gratified to know that you have such dedicated students awaiting you in your new post," the Envoy remarked to Jacomina.

The new Mistress of Enlightenment nodded somberly, although the look she gave R'shiel was far from enthusiastic. Jacomina might use many words to describe R'shiel, but "dedicated" was unlikely to be one of them.

R'shiel had thought it odd that her mother had taken Mahina's pro-motion to First Sister so well, until she learned who had been appointed to fill the vacancy left by Trayla's death and Mahina's elevation. Jacomina was her mother's creature. She probably didn't have a thought in her head that Joyhinia hadn't put there.

For R'shiel, Jacomina's promotion was bound to prove awkward. As Mistress of Enlightenment, Jacomina would report even her most minor infractions to her mother, a situation that could only get worse when she graduated to the rank of Probate a few weeks hence.

A blonde Probate approached them bearing a tray of delicate crystal goblets filled with fine red wine, and Lord Pieter's attention was thankfully diverted to the ample cleavage of this new arrival. The Probate offered the wine with a polite curtsy, giving R'shiel a look of pure venom as the younger girl accepted a glass. Selected Probates had been ordered to serve at Joyhinia's soiree, but R'shiel, a mere Novice, was here as a guest. She would probably return to a room that had been overturned or to find all her clothes had been dunked in the garderobe. Being Joyhinia's daughter might get her invited to social functions, but it did not save her from the pecking order in the dormitories.

R'shiel sipped her wine and remained politely silent while Joyhinia and Lord Pieter resumed their conversation. The room gradually filled with the upper echelon of Citadel society. Lord Pieter answered in monosyllables, apparently more interested in eyeing the young women present. The man had an appalling reputation, particularly for one from a country that was so puritan it was rumored that even thinking impure thoughts was a sin.

Blue-gowned Sisters outnumbered the red-coated Defenders in the Hall, who, to a man, looked stiff and uncomfortable in their high-necked dress uniforms. They did not like these formal occasions. The Sisters of the Blade ordered them to attend so they could flaunt their superiority. At least that was what Georj claimed. R'shiel thought it more likely that they just didn't like all the bother it took to get dressed. A speck of dust, or a boot you couldn't use as a shaving mirror, would catch the attention of the Lord Defender faster than a man could blink.

A raucous, high-pitched laugh caught R'shiel's attention, and she turned toward the source. Crisabelle Cortanen was Mahina's daughter-in-law—a chubby, crass woman who had married Mahina's son Wilem when she was sixteen and had not managed to age mentally since that day. Crisabelle wore a frilly yellow dress that emphasized, rather than concealed, her bulk. Commandant Cortanen stood beside her, his expression one of long-suffering embarrassment. Refused a place in the Sisterhood as a child, Crisabelle was beside herself with glee now that her mother-in-law was the First Sister.

The main door was thrown open, and Lord Draco, the Spear of the First Sister, entered the Hall, followed by Mahina. Draco was tall, dark, and stern. To R'shiel, he epitomized the rank he held, but she found it hard to think of Mahina as the First Sister. She still looked more like a peasant than an autocrat, even in her beautifully tailored white silk dress with its seed-pearl bodice. Mahina accepted the bows and curtsies of her subjects with a maternal wave and approached Joyhinia, Lord Pieter, and Jacomina.

"My Lord. Joyhinia. Congratulations on your appointment, Jacomina. You honor us with your presence in the Quorum."

Jacomina replied with some inane comment that R'shiel did not catch. She had managed to step back out of the circle of people surrounding her mother and closer to the tall stained-glass doors that led onto the balcony, which had been opened to take advantage of the balmy evening. She was wondering what her chances of being able to slip outside and escape were, when the door opened and Lord Jenga, accompanied by a number of his officers, arrived.

As the men stepped into the room, R'shiel was stunned and delighted to see her brother among the officers walking behind the Lord Defender. Every eye in the room was on him and the Lord Defender as they walked through the Hall toward the First Sister. The Senior Probates stopped serving and stared at him openly. The others in the room gaped for a moment and then quickly looked away. R'shiel could almost see their ears straining to catch what was about to be said.

Tarja had been banished to the border by Trayla more than four years ago, although the reasons why had never been clear to R'shiel. When he was sent away, all Joyhinia had told her, in a cold and angry tone, was that he had offended the First Sister. Judging from the startled looks of the gathered Sisters, he had done more than just offend her. Even Mahina, who had always had a fondness for her brother, looked shocked to see him, which meant it was obviously not she who had recalled him. R'shiel wondered if her appeal to Jenga had been the reason for Tarja's recall, then decided it wasn't. Jenga was not the sort of man to be swayed by a smile and a heartfelt plea.

"Your Grace," said Jenga with a bow to the First Sister. "Lord Pieter. Sisters."

"Lord Defender," Mahina replied. She turned her attention to Tarja and gave him a long look. R'shiel glanced at her mother and was not surprised at her thunderous expression. Joyhinia was not pleased to see her son.

"Welcome home, Tarja," Mahina said.

"Thank you, your Grace," Tarja replied with a bow, then he turned to Joyhinia. "Mother."

"I wasn't aware that you'd been recalled, Tarjanian," she remarked coolly. "I trust your time on the border has taught you something useful."

"More than you could imagine," Tarja assured her. He caught sight of R'shiel, and his eyes widened with surprise.

"This is your son, Sister?" Pieter asked Joyhinia, as he took Tarja's measure. "You've never mentioned him before."

Joyhinia's expression did not change. "Tarja has been fighting on the southern border these past four years."

"Killing Hythrun, eh?" Pieter chuckled. "A worthy cause, Captain. And just how many did you dispose of?"

"More than I care to count," Tarja replied glibly. "Now, if you will excuse me, my Lord, I see that my sister is anxious to welcome me home. First Sister. Lord Jenga. Lord Draco. Sisters." Tarja walked through the small gathering to R'shiel, took her arm none too gently, and led her away. He didn't stop until they were through the stained-glass doors and standing on the balcony. As soon as they were out of the hearing of the gathering inside, Tarja let her go. "Founders, I was glad to see you! I don't think I could have stood being surrounded by those vipers for a moment longer."

"I can't believe you had the nerve to show up here tonight. Mother looks ready to burst something," she laughed. R'shiel was rather pleased at the disturbance his appearance had caused. Although it hadn't occurred to her when she'd asked Jenga to recall him, she realized now that with Tarja back, Joyhinia would have another focus for her disapproval. She stepped back and looked him up and down, thinking that his time on the border had obviously taught him some restraint. A few years ago, he would have started fighting with Joyhinia the moment he laid eyes on her. "When did you get back?"

"Yesterday. You know, I almost didn't recognize you. You're all grown up."

R'shiel pulled a face. "Hardly. I'm not even a Probate yet."

"Being a Probate is not what I would use as a benchmark for maturity," he laughed. "I suppose this means Joyhinia is still trying to mold you into the perfect little Sister of the Blade?"

R'shiel sighed. "I think she's starting to wonder if it's a lost cause. Somehow I get the feeling I'm not turning out quite the way she intended."

"I don't think either of us have turned out quite what Joyhinia intended."

R'shiel had always been close to her half-brother, despite the fact that he was ten years older than her and already a Cadet in the Defenders when she arrived at the Citadel as a baby. Joyhinia forbade her to socialize with him, but it had been a futile effort on her mother's part. As a child she had been spanked, on more than one occasion, for hanging around Tarja and the Cadets.

"Why do I get the feeling things are going to get rather interesting now that you're back?"

"Because he's a troublemaker," a voice joked from behind. Startled, R'shiel spun around and found Georj Drake, Tarja's best friend and her recent knife-throwing instructor, standing behind her. The young captain's hazel eyes were full of laughter. "You should banish him again before he can do any damage."

"Now there's a tempting thought," she mused. "Where shall we send him, Georj? Back to the southern border? Or maybe the Grimfield?"

"You are a cruel woman, R'shiel." She liked Georj. He was almost as much a brother to her as Tarja. "Maybe you should order him to the Arena."

"Georj!" Tarja warned. "I've already told you no."

R'shiel looked from Georj to Tarja and back to Georj again. "What?"

Georj took R'shiel's arm conspiratorially. "Well, you might be too young to remember, but back in the good old days, before Tarja publicly called Trayla a fatuous bitch, he was the undisputed champion of the Arena."

"I remember," she said, before turning to Tarja, wide-eyed. "Is that what you did? You called Trayla a fatuous bitch?"

Tarja glared at them but did not deign to answer. Georj tugged her arm to get her attention back. "Well now that he's back, he has a duty to regain the title. Ever since we heard he'd been recalled, Loclon has been bragging about how he can beat Tarja. He's issued a formal challenge, and your uncaring brother has refused it. The honor of every captain is at stake here."

R'shiel knew of Loclon, a slender young lieutenant with lightning-quick reflexes. He had been the talk of the Citadel all summer.

"I said no, Georj!" Tarja snapped. "Cajoling R'shiel isn't going to make me change my mind, either."

"Why not? Are you afraid he'll beat you?"

"No! I'm not afraid he'll beat me. I'm afraid I'll *win*, and then every half-witted, glory-seeking Cadet in the Citadel will want to take me on. I've done my time in the Arena, R'shiel. I don't need to prove anything."

"Why don't you just take the challenge and lose, if that's what you're

worried about?" she asked with somewhat contrived innocence, knowing full well the reaction such a suggestion would provoke. "Just let him
beat you."

Georj looked horrified. "Lose? How could you suggest such a thing,
girl?"

Before she had a chance to answer, the Probate who had served the
drinks earlier appeared at the doorway. She glanced coyly at Tarja and
Georj before turning her attention to R'shiel.

"Sister Joyhinia wants you to come inside, R'shiel," the Probate said
pleasantly, although her smile was meant for the Defenders. R'shiel was
surprised she had been allowed to spend even this small amount of time
with Tarja.

She glanced at the officers and shrugged. "I have to go."

"Poor little Novice," Tarja sympathized. "Can't ignore an order from
mother now, can we?"

"Do you think if I called Mahina a fatuous bitch, I could get myself
banished from the Citadel, too?" she asked under her breath.

The Envoy had moved away from the circle of women surrounding the
First Sister and her mother, and was standing, half-hidden by a column
on the other side of the room, fondling a rather startled-looking Probate.

R'shiel suspected her mother pandered to Lord Pieter's appetites for
her own reasons. Morality and sin were hallmarks of religion and the Sisters of the Blade never practiced anything that smacked of religion. The
hidden artwork throughout the Citadel was concealed because it
offended the Sisters to see the gods depicted, not because they cared
what carnal activities the heathens were engaged in. Good government
was based on law and common sense, not some heathen notion of morality. In R'shiel's opinion, Lord Pieter had crossed even that generous line,
and it was simply a sign of Medalon's fear of offending Karien that no one
remarked on the man's outrageous behavior.

R'shiel, with Tarja and Georj close behind her, approached her
mother. She was listening with interest as Sister Harith complained about
the growing number of heathens.

"It is time for another Purge," Harith was suggesting loudly.

"I agree they are getting out of hand again," Joyhinia remarked, which
made Jacomina nod enthusiastically in support. Joyhinia could suggest
running naked through the Citadel, and Jacomina would probably nod

enthusiastically in support, R'shiel decided. "The rumors of a demon child have flared up again, too. But a Purge?"

Mahina glanced at the Sisters and shrugged, unconcerned. "The demon child rumor has been around for two centuries, Sisters. We should pay it as much attention now as we have in the past."

"But this time it seems to be really taking hold," Harith remarked. "I wouldn't be surprised if it reached all the way to the southern border." She glanced past R'shiel at Tarja. "You've just come from there, Captain. Have you heard anything?"

"I heard a crazy man ranting about it. But nobody took him seriously."

"There! You see?" Harith announced, her point proved.

R'shiel wondered what rumor they were talking about. The goings-on among the few miserable heathens left in Medalon were not something that reached the ears of a mere Novice, even one as privileged as R'shiel. She leaned toward Georj and whispered, "What's a demon child?"

Mahina heard her and answered her question. "According to heathen legend, R'shiel, Lorandranek, the last king of the Harshini, sired a half-human child. They call him the demon child. He is supposed to have a great capacity for destruction."

"All the more reason to hunt him down and kill him," Harith added.

Mahina chuckled. "Hunt him down and kill him, Harith? This child was supposed to have been sired by a man who was last seen two hundred years ago!"

"But we don't believe in the gods; therefore logically, such a child cannot exist."

Mahina nodded in agreement. "Well said, R'shiel! And we are not going waste valuable resources sending the Defenders out to hunt down this nonexistent child. The rumor will die down as it always has."

"But you cannot deny that the number of heathens seems to be on the rise," Joyhinia pointed out. R'shiel recognized that feral gleam in her mother's eye as Joyhinia neatly maneuvered the First Sister into making a public blunder.

"I don't deny it, Sister. It is a matter of great concern to me. But I have to ask myself, what have we done to make these people turn from the Sisterhood? Does the fault lie with our administration? We should clean up our own house before we start looking at others."

Joyhinia bowed to the First Sister. "By your words you demonstrate the wisdom worthy of a true First Sister, Mahina."

The older woman nodded in acknowledgment of Joyhinia's eloquent compliment. R'shiel glanced at her mother and shuddered. She knew that look, knew that venomous, bitter gleam better than anyone. Joyhinia despised Mahina. R'shiel sipped her wine as she watched the elder Sisters and wondered how long it would be before there was another funeral, another public Burning, and another First Sister. She caught Tarja's eye and thought he was wondering the same thing.

chapter 4

'shiel straightened her tunic, checked that her fingernails were clean, and smoothed down her braid before she knocked on the door to her mother's rooms. The spacious apartment on the third floor of the Sisters' main residential wing had ceased being her home from the day she put on the Green. Not since she had been sent to the Novices at twelve had she returned without requesting entry. There was still a room referred to as her bedroom in the apartment, but it was bare of any personal touches. Visiting home was as warm and welcoming as visiting one of Brodenvale's well-kept inns. But she didn't really mind—one of the advantages of being a Novice was that it meant she didn't need to live at home. It was perhaps the only reason that she had never done anything serious enough to get herself expelled.

The door was opened by old Hella, Joyhinia's long-suffering maid, who stood back to let her enter with a barely polite curtsy. Joyhinia was sitting by the fire, an open book on her lap. The room was uncomfortably hot. Although the bitter winds of autumn had begun to swirl through the streets of the Citadel, today had been unseasonably warm. Joyhinia preferred the heat. She looked up, closing the book carefully.

"You may go now, Hella."

The maid curtsied and let herself out. Joyhinia studied R'shiel's new gray Probate's tunic for a moment before looking her in the eye.

"Well?"

R'shiel shook her head. This ritual had been going on for years now. Every Restday, when R'shiel arrived for their weekly dinner, Joyhinia met her with the same question. At first, when R'shiel was younger, Joyhinia had asked the whole question: "Well, have you had your menses yet?" As the years dragged on and nothing happened, the question had become abbreviated to a short, impatient "Well?" She had seen every physic in the Citadel, and none could give her a reason why she had not begun her cycle. All her friends had reached their time before they were fifteen. R'shiel had just turned eighteen, and although she had every other physical sign of womanhood, she remained amenorrheic. She wished Joyhinia would stop asking her.

Joyhinia shook her head impatiently at her reply. "Gray is not your color," she remarked, placing the book carefully on the side table. "You looked much better in the Green, with that red hair."

"I shall try to become a Sister as fast as I can, Mother. Perhaps the Blue will suit me better."

Joyhinia either did not notice the edge in her voice or chose to ignore it. "If you applied yourself, there is no reason you couldn't get through the two years as a Probate in one," she said thoughtfully.

"I was joking, Mother."

Joyhinia looked at her sharply. "I wasn't."

"Shall I pour the wine?" R'shiel walked to the long, polished table, which was already set with dinner, and picked up the decanter. It was time to get off the topic of her academic progress. That route could lead to awkward questions R'shiel did not want to answer.

"So, have you moved into the Probates' Dormitories yet?"

"Last Fourthday. I'm sharing with Junee Riverson."

Joyhinia frowned. "Riverson? I don't know the name. Where is she from?"

"Her family come from Brodenvale. They started out as fisherfolk on the Glass River. Her father's quite a wealthy merchant now. She's the first in her family to be accepted into the Sisterhood."

Joyhinia sipped her wine and shook her head. "I'll have you assigned to a room with someone more appropriate. The daughter of another Sister, at the very least."

"I don't want to be moved. I like Junee."

"I really don't care what you like, young lady. I'll not have you rooming with some river peasant from Brodenvale."

"We are all equal in the Sisterhood." At least that was what the Sisters of the Blade espoused.

"There is equal, and there is *equal*," Joyhinia replied.

"If you interfere with my rooming assignment, everyone will know," she pointed out, handing Joyhinia her wine. "There is already a suspicion that I've only succeeded so far due to your influence. If you change my room for a better one, that suspicion will become fact." To be more accurate, the suspicion was that were she not the daughter of a Quorum member she would have been thrown out of the Novices long ago, but Joyhinia did not need to be reminded of that.

Joyhinia glared at her for a moment, before relenting. "Very well, you may stay with your pet peasant. But don't come crying to me when you can no longer stand her screeching accent or her infrequent bathing habits."

R'shiel was not fool enough to gloat over this minor triumph. "I promise I shall suffer the consequences of my foolishness in silence, Mother."

"Good," Joyhinia agreed. It was odd how her mother only ever seemed truly pleased with her when she was able to outwit her. "Now let's eat before the roast cools."

R'shiel took her place at the table as Joyhinia lit the candles from a taper. The walls had dimmed to about a quarter of their daytime luminosity, and the candles did little to light the room. R'shiel waited until her mother was seated before she lifted the domed silver cover off her plate. It was roast pork, accompanied by a variety of autumn vegetables. The pork was tender and pale, and smothered in rich gravy. The sight of it made R'shiel's stomach turn.

"What's the matter?"

R'shiel glanced at her mother, wondering if she should say something about the meat. It smelled off, but then most meat did these days. Then again, she was probably wrong. She had warned her friends about eating meat that she could have sworn was rancid, only to find they considered it perfectly sound.

"Nothing," R'shiel replied, picking up her fork. "It looks wonderful."

"It should," Joyhinia grumbled. "It took enough effort to arrange. You would think I'd asked for some exotic Fardohnyan seafood dish, the way the cooks carried on when I ordered pork. You'd better eat every bite, or I'll never hear the end of it."

With a grimace R'shiel cut into her meat. They ate in silence, R'shiel forcing down every swallow. Joyhinia appeared to be enjoying the meal. If there had been even a hint of taint on the meat, she would have sent it back to the kitchens with a blistering reprimand for the cooks.

Finally, Joyhinia put down her fork and studied R'shiel across the table. "Jacomina says you missed class three times this week."

"I wasn't feeling well." Having her mother's closest ally as the Mistress of Enlightenment was proving rather uncomfortable. Mahina had never reported half the things she got up to. "I've been getting headaches. They seem to get better if I rest."

"Have you seen a physic?" Joyhinia had no patience with illness or invalids.

"I hadn't thought a headache worthy of a visit to a physic."

"Well, see Sister Gwenell if they continue. You can't afford to be missing classes."

"Yes, Mother," R'shiel replied dutifully. Missing classes was the only thing her mother seemed to care about—not if she might be ill. Annoyed, R'shiel pushed her unfinished meal away and said the one thing guaranteed to aggravate her mother. "Have you seen Tarja, recently?"

"Your half-brother does not choose to visit with me nor I with him. I suggest you adopt a similar policy."

"But he's my brother."

"Half-brother," she corrected. "However, that is irrelevant. Tarjanian is a troublemaker and you would do well to disassociate yourself from him."

"That makes it kind of awkward for you, doesn't it? A woman in your position? It's a good thing I toe the line." *Most of the time*, she added silently to herself, *and then just barely*.

Joyhinia's expression clouded with annoyance. "Don't presume to threaten me, my girl. I've no need to remind you what will happen if I hear of you misbehaving again."

"I'll make certain that the next time I misbehave, Mother, you don't hear about it," she promised with a perfectly straight face.

Joyhinia sipped her wine and studied her daughter critically. "You will push me too far one day, R'shiel. And I can assure you the consequences will not be pleasant."

R'shiel knew that look. A change of subject was in order.

"Why is the Karien Envoy here?" she asked. Politics was the one topic she could rely on to divert Joyhinia.

"I'm surprised you have to ask. He's here because we have a new First Sister. He wants the treaty between Karien and Medalon reaffirmed."

"Oh," R'shiel said. Any first-year Novice could have worked that out, but for the time being, her shortcomings were forgotten.

"He's also here to observe the Sisterhood," Joyhinia continued. "He wants to assure himself that we are not wavering on our policy of suppression of heathen worship. He wants Mahina to initiate another Purge. He's lobbying members of the Quorum to support him. Harith is already on his side. Francil won't care one way or the other, so long as it doesn't interfere with the running of the Citadel. If I can be talked around, Jacomina will follow, and he'll get what he wants."

"Isn't a Purge a bit extreme? There can't be that many heathens left. It hardly seems worth the effort to rid Medalon of a few scabby peasants secretly worshipping trees or rocks, or whatever it is that they hold divine."

Joyhinia frowned at R'shiel's impudence. "I see our new First Sister has her supporters. I hope you don't espouse such sentiments publicly, R'shiel. You must never forget that you are my daughter."

"Don't worry, Mother, there's no chance of me ever forgetting that."

"I'm glad to hear it. I've done everything I could to make your life as easy as possible, R'shiel. I expect you to return that consideration, one day." Joyhinia's face was hidden by the goblet, so it was hard to read her expression, but R'shiel had a bad feeling that Joyhinia already knew exactly how she expected R'shiel to repay her.

R'shiel also had a very bad feeling that whatever Joyhinia had in mind, she probably wouldn't like it.

chapter 5

The Lord Defender waited until the end of the month of Helena, three months after Mahina's promotion, before approaching the First Sister with the plans he had for some much-needed changes in the defense of Medalon. He unconsciously straightened his red coat as he and his officers strode the long hall that led to the First Sister's office. The sound of the officers' boots was muffled by the blue, carpeted strip that stretched with stark symmetry toward the large double doors at the end of the hall. The walls were at their brightest this early in the afternoon. On his left strode Commandant Garet Warner, the officer in charge of Defender Intelligence. A slender, balding man, with a deceptively mild manner, he had a soft voice which disguised a sharp mind and an acerbic wit. On his right, carrying a stack of rolled parchments, was Tarja Tenragan.

Sister Suelen, Mahina's secretary, rose from her desk as they approached. "My Lord Defender. Captain. Commandant. I'll tell the First Sister you're here."

The three men waited as Suelen knocked and then vanished inside the double doors. Jenga studied the plain, unadorned doors with curiosity. They were veneered with a thin coating of bronze to conceal, presumably, the heathen artwork underneath. There were many doors, walls, and ceilings like this one throughout the Citadel—covered with any material that would disguise the origins of their builders. Jenga had seen enough of the exquisite murals and delicate friezes to lament their camouflage. The Harshini who had built the Citadel were accomplished artists, but their subject matter tended toward the baser side of human nature and unfailingly depicted one god or another. Before the Sisterhood had taken possession of it, the Lesser Hall had been a Temple devoted to Kalianah, the heathen Goddess of Love. It had a ceiling that was, reputedly, quite explicitly erotic. It was whitewashed every two years without fail, to prevent the heathen images from ever showing through.

Jenga's musing was interrupted by the reappearance of Suelen. "The First Sister will see you now."

Jenga pushed aside the heavy door and entered the office first, followed by Garet and Tarja. Mahina stood as they entered. Draco remained standing behind her desk, his expression as inscrutable as ever. Mahina came around the desk to greet them, holding out her hands warmly. Jenga could not remember the last time a First Sister had shown him so much respect or had treated him so like an equal.

"My Lord Defender! Am I so daunting, now that I'm First Sister, that you felt the need for moral support?"

"Never, your Grace. I've brought these two along so that you can question them and spare me."

Mahina's brow furrowed with curiosity. "This is not a social call then, I gather? Well, let's be seated. By the look of that pile Tarja's holding, this is going to take a while."

The First Sister's office was a huge room, although Jenga had never been able to divine its original purpose. The walls shone with the Brightening, and large, multipaned windows that reached from floor to ceiling looked out over a stone-balustraded balcony. The massive, heavily carved desk sat in front of the tall windows, making the most of the natural lighting. Four heavy, padded-leather chairs, normally reserved for the Quorum, sat before the desk. Mahina indicated they should sit and took her place behind the desk, placing her hands palm down on its polished surface.

"So, my Lord Defender, what can I do for you?"

"I have a number of proposals, your Grace," he began. "Issues that concern the Defenders and the defense of Medalon."

"Such as?"

"The Hythrun Raiders. The treaty with Karien. The defense of our borders. The issue of internal unrest."

Mahina frowned. "That's quite a list, Jenga. Let's tackle it one at a time, shall we? Start with the Hythrun."

"As you wish, your Grace," Jenga nodded. "I want permission to allow the Defenders to cross the border into Hythria in pursuit of Hythrun Raiders."

Her matronly face was puzzled. "Jenga, are you telling me our boys simply stand on the border and watch the Hythrun ride away with our cattle?"

"I'm afraid so, your Grace."

"How long has this been going on?"

"A decade, or so," Tarja replied for him, making no effort to hide his contempt for the practice. "Trayla introduced the prohibition while she was visiting Bordertown about ten years ago. Her carriage broke down and she was stranded for the afternoon on the side of the road. She decided that if the Defenders had been closer to home, rather than across the border chasing the Raiders, she would have been spared an uncomfortable afternoon in the heat. She issued the order the next day and refused to counter it, despite numerous pleas by both the Lord Defender and Commandant Verkin."

"Is that right, Draco?" Mahina asked, looking to the First Spear of the Sister for confirmation. Draco nodded, his expression neutral.

"I believe it is, your Grace."

"Consider it countered," Mahina snapped, turning back to Jenga. "That is the most absurd thing I have ever heard. How much have we lost to the Hythrun in the last decade, because of her fussing? By the Founders, I wonder about my Sisters sometimes." Suddenly she looked at the three Defenders and grimaced. "I trust your discretion will ensure my remarks never leave this room, gentlemen?"

"You can rely on our honor, your Grace," Jenga assured her. Draco made no comment. He was privy to every secret of the First Sister and to Jenga's knowledge had never broken that trust in over thirty years.

Mahina glanced at Tarja. "Four years you were on the border, weren't you, Tarja? And forbidden to cross it? I'll send an order to Verkin today, countering Trayla's order." She smiled at Jenga. "See, that was easily taken care of, wasn't it? What was the next item you wished to discuss?"

"I want to strengthen the defenses on our northern border," Jenga told her, privately delighted at her reaction to his first request. "Or, to be more accurate, I would like to *implement* a defense of our northern border."

Mahina leaned back in her seat. "Our northern border is protected by the treaty with the Kariens, my Lord. It has been for nearly two hundred years. What need for defenses in the north, when the money could be better spent elsewhere?"

Jenga glanced at Garet and nodded. This was his area of expertise. "We don't believe the Karien treaty is as mutually beneficial as they would have us believe," Garet said carefully.

"I've just signed a treaty with them, assuring our protection for another twenty years," Mahina pointed out. "Are you suggesting the Kariens are not planning to honor that treaty?"

"Your Grace, I think we need to consider the history behind the treaty," Garet replied, " . . . what brought it about in the first place."

"I know the history of Medalon," Mahina reminded the Commandant. "I was Mistress of Enlightenment for quite some time, young man."

"I'm aware of that, your Grace, but I would ask that you hear me out." Mahina nodded and indicated that the Commandant should continue. "You need to understand the situation in Medalon at the time of the abortive Karien invasion, two hundred years ago. In those days the Sister-hood, although growing fast, was not yet a power to be reckoned with. Medalon was little more than a loose collection of towns and villages, most of which followed the pagan gods of the Harshini. The Sisterhood had evicted the Harshini and taken over the Citadel, but that was as much a sign of the Harshini aversion to confrontation, as it was to the strength of the Sisters of the Blade. Medalon had no military power to speak of."

"None of this is news to me, Commandant," Mahina told him.

"Bear with me, your Grace," Garet asked. "As I said, Medalon, as a nation, was nothing. They had no army. They had nothing that could be construed as a threat to Karien."

"But they planned to invade us, nonetheless," Mahina said.

"Actually, I doubt if they cared about Medalon much at all," Tarja added. "The Kariens were on their way south, to Hythria and Fardohnya. Wiping out the Harshini along the way was only *part* of their plan. They wanted the whole continent, from the Northern Reaches to the Dregian Ocean."

"But they failed," Mahina pointed out, obviously enjoying the debate. "They were turned back at our borders by a storm."

"They weren't just turned back," Garet said. "They were decimated. Incidentally, the heathens believe that Lorandranek called down that storm by magic and it was he who saved Medalon. But whether it was divine intervention or sheer good fortune, the end result was devastating for the Kariens. They had taken years to amass their invasion force, and King Oscyr of Karien had beggared the nation to do it. The failure of that invasion cost him the support of his Dukes and eventually caused the downfall of his whole house. But more significantly, it cost him the support of the Church of Xaphista. He was excommunicated and died in shame less than two years later. His half-sister's son inherited the throne, and it is from her children that the current royal house is descended."

"Commandant, I admire your grasp of history, but is there a point to all this?"

"Yes, your Grace," Garet nodded. "The point is, that when the treaty was first negotiated between Karien and Medalon, the Kariens were an impoverished nation, ruled by a fourteen-year-old boy. The Sisters of the Blade controlled the Citadel and a few villages surrounding it. Neither party to the treaty was in a position of strength, but both gained from it. Medalon earned a measure of security—with the treaty in place they need not fear for their northern border and could turn their attention to protecting their southern borders. Karien gained breathing space, but more importantly, they gained a measure of redemption from the Church, by making the eradication of the Harshini and all forms of heathen worship in Medalon a condition of the treaty."

"Which in turn," Tarja said, picking up the narrative, "led to the formation of the Defenders. The Sisters of the Blade supported the Kariens' demands because it suited their purposes to agree with them. The Church of Xaphista the Overlord is the most powerful force in Karien. It was safer to agree to their terms and keep them on their side of the border than to disagree and risk Karien knights on Medalon soil, or worse, their missionaries. The Defenders were created to rid Medalon of the Harshini and to crush all forms of heathen worship."

"A task they performed more than adequately," Mahina acknowledged. "And a philosophy we still hold to."

"And therein lies the danger, your Grace," Jenga said, deciding it was about time he added something to the discussion. "Just as the Sisterhood believes in the same thing it believed in two hundred years ago, so do the Kariens."

"Three years ago," Garet continued in his soft, deceptively mild voice, "King Jasnoff's son, Cratyn, came of age and was formally invested as the Karien Crown Prince. During the ceremony, he made his first address to the Dukes. He promised to finish the job Oscyr started. 'To see the Church of the Overlord stretch from one end of this mighty continent to the other,' I believe were his exact words."

Mahina shrugged. "The rhetoric of a boy newly come to manhood, surely? I cannot divert the sort of resources such an undertaking would consume on the idle boasting of one young man. Besides, as your very presence proves, we have the Defenders now. If the Kariens look like they are breaking the treaty, you are well equipped to defend us."

Tarja shook his head. "Actually, your Grace, we're not. We can defend the south, or we can defend the north. We can't do both."

Garet nodded in agreement. "Tarja's right. There are too many Defenders utilized for duties that can only be described as ceremonial. If the Kariens made a move on us, we wouldn't be able to stop them. For that matter, they wouldn't need to declare war on us. A foraging army the size of the Kariens' would strip Medalon clean in a matter of months."

Mahina held up her hand. "Slow down a minute," she pleaded. "You're getting way ahead of me here. Let's go back to the issue of whether or not the Kariens are even planning to break the treaty. You've given me nothing to suggest that they might."

"Correct me if I'm wrong, your Grace," Garet said, knowing full well that he wasn't. "But the treaty with Karien requires Medalon to stamp out all pagan worship and anything to do with the Harshini, doesn't it? In the past two years, we've uncovered more cults devoted to various Primal and Incidental Gods than were discovered in the thirty years prior to that. And rumors of the demon child are stronger than ever. Nobody has even seen a Harshini for over a century and a half, yet the cults continue to surface."

"The work of the Hythrun or the Fardohnyans, surely?" Mahina asked. "They still hold to the pagan beliefs. I hear that even after all this time, the Sorcerer's Collective in Greenharbor still keeps vigil over some lump of magic rock in a cave somewhere, waiting for the Harshini to speak to them again."

"It's called the Seeing Stone," Garet corrected. "It's in the Temple of the Gods in Greenharbor."

"Whatever," Mahina said dismissively. "Surely they are the ones encouraging the spread of the pagan cults?"

"I believe it is the Kariens who are encouraging the spread of the heathens," Garet replied.

"To what purpose?" Mahina asked. "They want to see the end of the pagans as much as we do. What possible reason could they have for encouraging them?"

"It's because they wish to eradicate the heathens. All of them, including every heathen in Hythria and Fardohnya. Far from being helpful, Medalon stands in their way now. Two centuries ago we were nothing, and but for a fortuitous storm, the Kariens would have marched straight through Medalon to reach the southern nations. But in a moment of weakness, they signed a treaty with us that they are honor bound to uphold. The only loophole they have is if we are not keeping our side of the bargain, which is the suppression of all heathen worship. The more cults that spring up in Medalon, the more reason they have for crossing our border to put them down. They don't have to break the treaty, your Grace. They can quite legally use it against us."

Mahina sighed, not totally convinced, but Jenga could see that she was not skeptical, which was a hopeful sign. "Lord Pieter was strongly suggesting another Purge, Commandant. Hardly the action of a man waiting to pounce on us for our lack of performance."

"A Purge achieves two things, your Grace," Garet told her. "It publicly acknowledges the existence of the heathen cults, which is what the Kariens need to legally cross our borders, and it ties up even more of the Defenders on internal matters. We cannot win. If you refuse to instigate a Purge, then you're not taking action against the heathens. If you start one, then you're admitting that the heathens are a problem. Either way, the Kariens can claim we have not adhered to the terms of the treaty."

"And if what you say is true, we have not the Defenders to repel an attack?"

"Not at present," Tarja agreed, "but we could establish a civil militia."

Mahina looked at the younger man steadily. "A civil militia?"

Tarja nodded. "A civilian force to take care of the internal policing of Medalon. Nearly half our military force is currently engaged in routing out small groups of heathens, who, for the most part, don't even know how to fight. It's a waste of men and training. We are a small nation jammed between three very large ones. We cannot afford to have our fighting force arresting farmers and confiscating chickens."

"How would this militia function?" Mahina asked. Tarja reached for one of the scrolls he had brought with him, but Mahina waved it away. "Tell me Tarja, in your own words. I've no doubt your figures are sound, but if you want me to sell this to the Quorum, I need to know how you feel about it."

Tarja put down the scroll. "Each town would have its own unit, commanded by an officer of the Defenders. The militia itself would be made up of volunteers—locals who would be trained by the officer in charge to undertake whatever action was deemed necessary to free the area of heathens. The Defenders would then be free to do something about our northern border. If necessary, you can claim the militia was established as a long-term alternative to a purge."

Mahina sighed. "Every now and then, Tarja, you prove you really are your mother's son. Or has four years of staring at the Hythrun from the wrong side of the border sharpened your instincts? I don't remember you being so astute."

Tarja did not like to be reminded that he might have inherited anything from his mother. "It's good common sense, your Grace."

Mahina shook her head. "Good sense is far from common, I fear, Tarja. However, you have given me much to ponder." She waved a hand in the direction of the scrolls. "These are your detailed plans, I assume?"

"And their estimated cost," Garet added.

Mahina smiled appreciatively. "A well thought-out battle plan, I see. If you attack our enemies as effectively as you have attacked me, Medalon will be well defended. I will study your proposal, gentlemen. And you'd best be prepared to defend it. I cannot take anything this radical to the Quorum without being certain."

"I will be happy to provide any other information you require," Jenga offered. His expression was stern, but inside he was filled with relief. For the first time since Garet and Tarja had approached him with their assessment of the Karien treaty almost five years ago, he had a woman in charge who was prepared to listen to him.

chapter 6

'shiel! Hurry up!"

R'shiel forced her eyes open and squinted painfully as the bright wall greeted her with its silent, glowing panels. Her pounding headache had abated somewhat, but she still felt groggy and listless. She rolled over on her narrow bed and stared sleepily at Junee.

"What?"

"Hurry up!" Junee urged from the open doorway. "We'll never find a good seat if we wait much longer."

Understanding came slowly to the younger girl. "Oh, at the Arena, you mean?"

"Yes, at the Arena," Junee repeated with an impatient sigh. "Come on!"

R'shiel swung her feet to the floor and gingerly lifted her head. With relief, she discovered she could move it without too much pain. She must have slept the worst of it off. Her headache was the third one this week. R'shiel had almost reached the point of doing what her mother ordered by seeking help from a physic. She slipped on her shoes and stood up as Junee tapped her foot impatiently by the door. She caught sight of herself in the small mirror over the washstand and grimaced. Her skin was waxy and there were large dark circles under her eyes. Even her gray tunic hung on her loosely these days. R'shiel tried to recall the last time she had eaten. Every time she neared the Dining Hall and smelled the meat, she found herself running in the opposite direction. The last time she had forced herself to eat, she had thrown up. Her tummy rumbled and complained, but she ignored it. Hunger was preferable to the alternative. She picked up her gray knitted shawl against the chill of the late autumn evening and followed her roommate down the corridor of the Probate's dormitory.

"Hey! Wait for us!"

R'shiel and Junee stopped and waited for the three girls who called after them from the other end of the hallway. Tonight was an event of some note at the Arena, and R'shiel was already regretting her decision to join Junee. Every Novice and Probate in the Citadel, every Defender not on duty, and probably a good many of the Sisters and civilians would be there. Georj had taken up the challenge that Tarja had refused. Everybody knew about it. Everybody wanted to be there.

Rumor had it that the only man Georj Drake had never beaten in the Arena when he was a Cadet was Tarja. Brash and good-looking, with a shock of golden hair, Lieutenant Loclon had been the undisputed champion of the Arena for months now. It would be a fight worth seeing, the other girls insisted—perhaps the best seen in the Arena for years.

Normally, R'shiel was not terribly interested in the fights in the Arena. She had grown up at the Citadel, and her brother was a Defender. There was little romance or excitement for her, watching men hack at each other with blunted swords. The fights had begun a century or more ago as training exercises. They were now the main form of mass entertainment and no longer restricted to the Cadets. Many officers and enlisted men continued to fight in the Arena long after they graduated to the ranks of the Defenders. Occasionally a brave civilian entered a bout, although the Lord Defender discouraged such rash bravado, even though the swords were blunted and the worst injury gained was usually a nasty bruise or the occasional broken bone. Tonight would be different, however. There would be no blunted swords and no quarter given.

The fight was to first blood. Loclon had formally challenged the captains and Georj Drake had accepted on behalf of his brother officers.

As she hurried along the street to the amphitheater with her friends, R'shiel worried about Georj. He had not been in the Arena for several years, whereas Loclon fought there almost every week.

By the time the five Probates reached the amphitheater, the crowd had grown considerably. A chill wind blew across the side of the small hollowed-out hill. With a shiver, R'shiel pulled her shawl tighter. Her headache had receded to a dull, throbbing pain at the back of her eyes, which she could ignore if she didn't think about it. Junee grabbed R'shiel's arm and pulled her forward, pushing through the crowd. When they reached the top of the grassy hill, she glanced around and then pointed at two red-coated figures leaning on the white painted railing.

"That's your brother, isn't it?" she asked.

R'shiel squinted into the setting sun and followed Junee's pointing finger. Tarja stood talking with Garet Warner.

"Where?" Kilene asked excitedly, pushing her way forward to stand next to R'shiel on the other side. "Let's go down there. Then you can introduce me."

R'shiel glanced at Kilene and shook her head, understanding now why she and her friends had been so anxious to join her and Junee. "I'm sure Tarja doesn't want a bunch of giggling Probates hanging around him. Besides, he's with Commandant Warner. The last thing you want to do is bring yourself to his attention."

Kilene looked uncertain for a moment, but her desire to meet Tarja outweighed her fear of Garet Warner. "Come on," she urged. "We'll never find a seat if we wait here."

R'shiel sighed and followed Kilene, Junee, and the other girls down into the amphitheater. As they neared the two Defenders, the other girls' bravery deserted them, and they stopped, waiting for R'shiel to catch up, before they approached the men. Tarja looked up as she neared him, his smile of recognition fading into a frown as he looked at her.

"Founders, R'shiel! You look awful."

"It's nice to see you too, Tarja."

"Sorry, but you're as thin as a hoe handle."

R'shiel could feel an impatient tugging on her shawl, which she loftily ignored. "I've been getting headaches, that's all."

"She won't eat, either," Junee informed Tarja, forcing the introduction that she could feel her companions itching for.

"Tarja, Commandant Warner, this is my roommate Junee. And this is Kilene, Marta, and Wandear," R'shiel said with a resigned shrug.

"Ladies," Tarja said with a gracious bow. Garet looked over the young women with vast disinterest, nodded politely, then turned back to the Arena.

"Can we sit here with you?" Kilene asked boldly, ignoring Garet as being too old and not nearly handsome enough to warrant her attention.

"You're more than welcome to sit here," Tarja told her. "However, I will be down below with Georj. In fact, we were just on our way there, weren't we, Commandant?"

Garet glanced at Tarja and then at the girls. "What? Oh! Of course! We'd better get a move on. Lovely meeting you all." Garet strode off without waiting for him.

"I have to go, I'm afraid, although I'm glad you found me, R'shiel. Georj wants you to wish him luck." He took her arm and before she could protest steered her away from the other girls toward the Arena. He opened the gate that led from the seating area to the sandy floor, then took her the short distance into the tunnel that led into the caverns that honeycombed the hill underground. R'shiel could hear male voices coming from somewhere to her left. As they entered the gloomy tunnel, Tarja stopped and spun her around to face him.

"You don't look awful, R'shiel," he said with concern, "you look like death. What's wrong with you?"

"I don't know, Tarja. I keep getting the worst headaches, and every time I smell meat I want to throw up."

"Have you told Joyhinia?"

"She told me to see a physic," R'shiel admitted, a little reluctantly.

"For once, I agree with her," Tarja grumbled. "Why not go home, R'shiel? You don't need to be here. Get some rest. Try to eat something." Then he smiled at her, and R'shiel understood why half the Probates in the Citadel wanted to be her best friend. "I'm sure Georj can redeem the honor of the captains without you cheering for him."

R'shiel frowned. "He will beat Loclon, won't he?"

"He'd better!"

"Can I see him before I go?"

"Of course," Tarja said, taking her arm. "I'm sure if he's planning to die tonight, the last thing he'd rather see is you, in preference to our ugly faces."

He led her into the cavernous rooms below the amphitheater, which had been built to house and train the fabled magical horses of the Harshini, who, like their owners, were long extinct and barely remembered, except for a few pitiful heathens who insisted on following the old ways.

The Sisterhood scoffed at rumors of magical horses, just as they denounced the idea that the Harshini were anything more than licentious tricksters. Their magic, according to the Sisterhood, was nothing more than clever parlor tricks, their horses simply the result of good breeding. She wondered, sometimes, how a race as morally bankrupt and as supposedly indolent as the Harshini had ever managed to build anything as impressive as the Citadel.

Georj was sitting on a three-legged stool in a large torchlit alcove, surrounded by several of his friends. They were all offering him advice, much of which, from the pained expression on his face, he considered useless. He looked up at R'shiel's approach and leaped to his feet, pushing away his well-meaning advisers.

"R'shiel!" he said, taking both her hands in his. "Has the thought of my glorious victory finally overcome your aversion to bloodsport?"

"I thought this was a duel, not a bloodsport, Georj," she scolded.

"Never fear, little sister," Tarja assured her. "Georj will give young Loclon a lesson in swordplay and a small scar to remember him by, that's all."

R'shiel leaned forward and kissed Georj's cheek lightly. "Be careful, Georj. And good luck."

"He'll need all the luck he can get, my Lady."

R'shiel turned to find Loclon standing behind her, flanked by two other lieutenants. She had only ever seen him from a distance before and decided that the Novices and Probates who spoke dreamily of his looks were, for once, probably speaking the truth. He was young, not much past twenty, and wore plain leather trousers, knee-high boots, a sword, and a blue sash tied around his waist. Georj was dressed identically, although his sash was red. Loclon moved with easy grace, his lithe body oiled and well muscled in the torchlight. Georj was taller and heavier than the younger man, who reminded R'shiel of a leopard feigning indifference to its prey before it closed in for the kill.

Loclon stepped forward. "Is this your sister, Captain Tenragan?"

Tarja did not appear too pleased that he had forced an introduction. "R'shiel, this is Lieutenant Loclon."

"Lieutenant," R'shiel said, with a barely civil curtsy. Something about this handsome young man set her teeth on edge. There was an air about him that spoke of arrogance, of cruelty.

"My Lady," Loclon replied. "I would be honored if you would wish me luck as well."

"I was under the impression you didn't need anything as mundane as luck, Lieutenant."

Loclon flushed as Georj and his friends roared with laughter. The young man's eyes blazed dangerously for a moment before he composed himself.

"Then you'd best wish all your luck on Captain Drake, my Lady. The old man will need it." With that, he stalked off toward the Arena.

R'shiel turned to the "old man," who was all of twenty-eight, her eyes full of concern. "Be careful, Georj."

"Don't worry about me, R'shiel," he declared. "Worry for all your friends in the Dormitories who will cry themselves to sleep tonight when I scar that pretty face of his."

Georj followed Loclon toward the Arena, his seconds in tow, full of laughter and back-slapping camaraderie.

R'shiel turned to Tarja. "Tarja, you can't let him do this."

He put an arm around her thin shoulders and hugged her gently. "I couldn't stop it R'shiel, even if I wanted to. Don't worry about Georj. Hard-earned battlefield experience will win out over parade-ground bravado."

"You're as bad as Georj. You aren't taking this seriously enough."

A muted roar from the stands reached them as the combatants entered the Arena.

"Go home, R'shiel," Tarja told her gently.

Suddenly R'shiel was no longer tired. "No, I'm coming with you. I want to watch this."

Tarja shook his head but did not argue the point. Together they walked back through the tunnel to the rectangle of light that was the entrance to the Arena.

The fight started slowly at first—a tentative clash of blades, each man testing his opponent. R'shiel could tell that Georj had the longer reach, but Loclon had speed and agility on his side. She stood in the entrance to the tunnel, watching the duel with Tarja, Georj's companions, and the two lieutenants who had accompanied Loclon. The crowd fell silent as the first blows were struck, the air charged with anticipation.

Loclon circled the sandy arena slowly, in a half-crouch, perfectly balanced on the balls of his feet. He flicked his sword out now and then, with a speed that seemed to take Georj by surprise. The captain was no longer smiling, his expression set in a mask of concentration. Georj was an accomplished swordsman. One could not rise to the rank of captain in the Defenders and be anything less, but he spent more time in the saddle than the Arena these days. He held his own easily enough. Loclon was unable to get through his guard, but he was fighting defensively. It was Loclon who had the initiative.

"Why doesn't he just attack?" the captain standing next to Tarja muttered impatiently.

"Georj never rushes into anything," Tarja replied, although R'shiel could tell he was wondering the same thing. "Give him time."

Loclon suddenly launched himself at Georj. His blade moved so fast it was a silver blur in the twilight. Georj held off the younger man, but he was being pushed backward, step by step. The roar of the crowd was thunderous as Loclon pushed the captain. The sound of metal on metal was lost in the din of the three thousand or more spectators who had gathered to watch someone shed blood. Their cries irritated R'shiel. They didn't really care who won. They just wanted to see a man bleeding.

Georj held off the attack well enough, but he appeared to be struggling a little. Loclon suddenly pulled back and turned to acknowledge the adulation of the crowd, a gesture that sent them wild. Georj recovered himself quickly, however, and the moment Loclon turned back to face his opponent Georj was on him, using his superior height and weight to push the younger man back. Loclon might have had speed, but Georj was as unstoppable as a rock in an avalanche. Loclon's face lost its smug expression as Georj bore down on him. The blows from the bigger man obviously jarred his sword arm every time he blocked a stroke.

R'shiel could feel the tension draining out of Tarja and his friends as Georj attacked.

And then, so quickly R'shiel hardy even saw it happen, Georj overextended himself and left Loclon an opening. With a startled cry, Georj lowered his sword and glanced down at his left arm where a long, shallow cut marked his forearm. Blood dripped slowly onto the sand. He looked stunned that Loclon had gotten through his guard. Loclon bowed to Georj raising his sword in salute.

The fight was to first blood.

And Loclon had won.

The crowd was quiet for a moment, shocked into silence, before it erupted into a thunderous cheer for the young lieutenant. Around R'shiel, Loclon's friends were laughing and congratulating each other as Loclon turned a slow circle, acknowledging the cheers of the crowd. R'shiel watched him with a frown, then glanced at Georj. Her stomach lurched as she saw the look on his face. She read murderous intent in his eyes.

"Tarja!" she cried, but it was too late. Georj raised his sword as Loclon turned his back to him, accepting the adulation of the spectators. With a wordless yell, Georj charged.

Perhaps he heard Georj's cry over the roar of the crowd, or perhaps he caught the movement out of the corner of his eye, but Loclon turned at the last minute, bringing his sword up to deflect Georj's blow. The crowd fell silent as the fight resumed, sensing the change in the combatants. This was no longer a fight to first blood, no longer an argument between two officers trying to prove a point of honor. This was deadly.

Loclon defended himself with the same blinding speed that he had shown the first time he had attacked, but he was no longer playing to the audience. Georj was intent on murder as much as victory. R'shiel's stomach cramped as she watched the men trade blows, watched cuts appear on both men go unnoticed in their frenzy.

"I think we should put a stop to this, Tarja," a quiet voice said behind her.

R'shiel glanced over her shoulder and discovered Garet Warner standing behind her. She wondered for a moment where he had been but found her eyes drawn back to the Arena. Both men looked tired and bloodied, but neither was willing to concede victory as blade struck blade hard enough to throw sparks.

"Georj will never forgive us if we stop this before it's resolved," Tarja replied, although to R'shiel he sounded more angry than concerned.

"Someone is going to get killed," Garet warned. "I'm sure Jenga would rather have a couple of peeved officers than lose a good man. It's gone on long enough. Besides, Georj lost. He should know better."

Tarja glanced back at Garet and then nodded. "You're right."

R'shiel held her breath as they stepped into the Arena, wondering if Garet's rank and Tarja's authority would be enough to overcome the bloodlust consuming both men. The crowd began to jeer as they realized what the appearance of the two officers meant. They were enjoying the spectacle. They didn't want it to stop. Not when it had just got interesting.

The Arena was huge, and Tarja was still about twenty paces from the pair when Georj stumbled and fell backward. Loclon was on him in an instant, swinging his sword in a wide arc, slicing his blade across Georj's throat in a spray of blood.

The crowd fell silent in horror as Georj screamed. R'shiel's stomach cramped again as she watched Loclon standing there, gloating. Tarja and Garet broke into a run, followed by the men who had been waiting in the tunnel entrance. Almost faint with disgust, R'shiel clutched at the cold stone wall of the tunnel as she watched Tarja run toward his fallen friend.

But he scooped up Georj's discarded sword, left his friend to the ministrations of his seconds, and turned toward Loclon. Garet was calling for a physic, in a voice that carried surprisingly well, considering how soft-spoken he normally was. As Tarja neared Loclon, the young man raised his sword again, preparing to take Tarja on. R'shiel bit through her bottom lip as another cramp seized her. Her fear was bitter enough to taste, mingled with the salty taste of her own blood.

Loclon crouched expectantly as Tarja walked toward him. The crowd held their breath. Georj had refused to cede the fight, and Loclon's act was unforgivable, but it might not be over yet. The only sound that filled the Arena was Georj's screams.

Tarja stopped just out of Loclon's reach. The young man was panting heavily. He was waiting for Tarja to move. Tarja hesitated for a moment then brought up his sword. Loclon blocked the blow easily, but before he could recover his balance, Tarja struck again. Lulled by Georj's deliberate movements, Loclon was unprepared for Tarja's speed or strength. This was no ceremonial Citadel captain fighting for his honor. This was an angry, battle-hardened veteran. Loclon was disarmed before he knew it. The sword flew from his hand as Tarja contemptuously flicked his blade, opening a savage cut from Loclon's left eye to his mouth. The lieutenant dropped to the ground screaming, clutching at his ruined face. Tarja left him there, turned on his heel, and walked back toward the tunnel, where Georj was being rushed out by his seconds and a blue-skirted physic who had run to his aid from the crowd.

R'shiel stood back against the cold stone wall as they hurried past her. Georj had stopped screaming. Carried by four of his comrades, he was unconscious now—from shock or loss of blood—and his head lolled backward as the blood spurted from severed arteries. Another crippling cramp seized R'shiel, and she realized that it had nothing to do with seeing so much violence. So much blood. Something else was wrong.

As Tarja approached the tunnel, she shrank back from the anger in his eyes. He did not appear to notice her as he strode past, too consumed by rage to notice anything. Another cramp, even worse than the last one, twisted her belly and she cried out. The sound must have cut through Tarja's fury. He stopped and glanced back at her.

"I warned you to go home," he told her.

R'shiel didn't answer him—couldn't answer him. Pain ripped through her like a gutting knife. She held out her hand, as she felt a warm rush between her legs. She looked down and was surprised to find herself standing in a puddle of bright blood.

"Founders!" Tarja rushed toward her as she fell. He caught her and scooped her up into his arms. The last thing she remembered before falling into a swirl of blessed darkness was Tarja holding her. Running. Calling for help.

part two

—⁂—

TRUTH AND LIES

chapter 7

The Greenharbor docks were a chaotic mix of sounds and smells, of tar and curses, of rank fish and screeching fishmongers, saltwater and damp sails. A forest of tall masts stretched around the harbor as far as the eye could see. There was a vibrancy that set this port apart from any other Brak had visited.

The crescent-shaped, natural bay was striped with different shades of blue, marking the deep channels that led out to the Dregian Ocean. The ships anchored at the wharves were a haphazard mixture of Hythrun square-riggers and Fardohnyan oared traders, and occasionally a garishly painted Karien galleon squatting nervously between her pagan neighbors. Farther around the bay, moored at the dock reserved for visitors to the Royal Enclosure at the foot of the huge white palace, Brak noted the sleek lines of a Fardohnyan oared warship displaying a Royal Standard. He spared the ship barely more than a passing glance. At last count, King Hablet of Fardohnya had enough offspring to populate a fair-sized town. Any one of his children might be here to seek guidance from the Sorcerers, make an offering at the Temple of the Gods, or just cause trouble.

There was no other port quite like Greenharbor and Brak fervently wished that he had not been forced here this time. In his experience, Greenharbor meant the Sorcerer's Collective and that meant they wanted something of him. Something he undoubtedly did not want to give them. But he could hardly blame Captain Soothan for his decision to head for the lucrative Greenharbor markets. Finding a rare school of blue-finned arlen at this time of year was a gift from the gods. Arlen was a prized delicacy in Greenharbor. That one catch alone would see him through the rest of the year.

Brak had been at sea long enough to know that finding a school of blue-finned arlen in such warm waters was not unusual—it was damned near impossible! He kept his suspicions to himself about the source of this unexpected bounty, collected his pay and his bonus, and left the ship as soon as it docked. His prudence was well founded. The ship was in port less than half a day before it was visited by a smartly dressed troop of soldiers from the Sorcerer's Collective. Brak watched them from the safety of a dockside tavern, downed his ale in a gulp, and slipped away while he still had the chance.

Greenharbor had only two seasons—hot and muggy or unbearably hot and muggy. With the northern winter approaching, fortunately it was just hot. It was also the High Prince's birthday and the white, flat-roofed city was crowded to overflowing with visitors from every Province in Hythria. Merchants and slavers, farmers and thieves, prostitutes and gamblers, the jaded and the awestruck—all descended on the Hythrun capital this time every year. All seven Warlords were in the city to make their annual offering at the Temple of the Gods. By law, they were restricted to three hundred Honor Guards each, but that was more than enough to cause trouble. They would need little encouragement to brawl with their enemies, and their enemies were any poor sod wearing the colors of another Province. Brak despaired of Hythria. Two centuries ago, they had been a proud and enlightened nation. Now they were little more than barbaric warmongers.

Zegarnald, the God of War, had much to rejoice in, he thought sourly. But it was not the God of War's fault that Hythria had fallen into a constant state of armed conflict. Like any primal god he merely took advantage of the circumstances. The blame lay squarely with the Harshini, who had withdrawn unexpectedly and left these people without guidance. Neighboring Fardohnya was just as bad. The current Fardohnyan King was a profiteering opportunist whose facility for changing sides left the casual observer's head spinning. Maybe that accounted for the Fardohnyan ship in the harbor, Brak mused. Perhaps Hablet had decided that his antagonistic attitude toward Hythria for the past three decades was no longer profitable and had sent an envoy to make peace. Brak doubted it, but anything was possible.

Brak pushed his way through the streets thinking about the current state of affairs in Hythria and Fardohnya. The Harshini King had thought only to leave Medalon to its own devices, to save lives by vanishing from sight so the Sisterhood would think their Purge successful. When the continued Harshini presence in the southern nations alerted the Sisterhood to their survival, the Purge in Medalon had gained savage momentum. Every Harshini in Hythria and Fardohnya had eventually been called home, leaving the southern courts without the calming influence of Harshini advisers, and the Sorcerer's Collective without teachers and mentors.

Brak nimbly sidestepped a fistfight that spilled out into the street from a tavern across the way. As he did so, he wondered if Lorandranek had ever thought what the Harshini withdrawal would do to the nations of the south . . . Brak was sometimes sorry he had never asked him. Then he remembered that he had not given Lorandranek a chance to say much at all. Brak pushed the thought away. He had been running from that memory for almost two decades. He turned down the next street and walked straight into the High Prince's birthday parade.

Cursing, Brak tried to step backward, but the crowd swept him up and carried him forward along the wide avenue lined with golden palms. Children clung like limpets to their ringed trunks in an effort to see over the heads of the crowd. Brak was taller than most men, and over the spectators' heads, he could see the High Prince's grandiose retinue slowly wending its way toward the Royal Compound overlooking the harbor. With a frustrated sigh, Brak gave up fighting against the crush. He let the throng carry him along and settled for watching the High Prince instead.

The prince was an old man now, a fact that startled Brak. He had not set eyes on him for years; but seeing how the man had aged reminded him sharply how he was different from normal men. Brak looked no older now than he had when he first met the High Prince as a young man, whereas Lernen Wolfblade was in his dotage.

The High Prince rode in an open carriage, a pretty young man by his side—no doubt Lernen's latest plaything. Brak was a little surprised to think the old man still had it in him. Perhaps it was just habit, these days, which substituted for lust. Brak frowned as he watched the carriage roll by, Lernen smiling absently and waving at the masses. The High Prince's predilection for young boys was, indirectly, another reason to fear for Hythria.

This nation had grown used to High Princes who had little but ceremonial value, and in that respect Lernen Wolfblade had fulfilled his duties better than anyone could have hoped. The Warlords valued their independence, and the once-powerful house of Wolfblade had degenerated over the past two centuries. Lernen epitomized the depth of their descent into depravity. The weakness of successive High Princes allowed the Warlords to rule their provinces as they saw fit, without interference. And Lernen was childless. From what rumor and gossip Brak had heard over the years, he had no interest in producing an heir, not even for the sake of his country. Consequently, the heir to the throne was not a simpering, court-raised dandy, as the Hythrun heir had been for a century or more. The current heir was Lernen's nephew. The son of his only sister Marla, he had been raised far from court in Krakandar Province and was already a Warlord in his own right. Brak silently and fervently wished Lernen a long, long life as he disappeared from view.

The Warlords of Hythria did not want a strong High Prince, and by all accounts, Damin Wolfblade was unlikely to be anything else. There were tough times ahead for these people. What was currently a nation of provinces constantly niggling at each other could well explode into a full-blown civil war.

The elaborate open carriage that followed the High Prince answered Brak's earlier question about the identity of the Fardohnyan from the ship bearing the Royal Standard in the bay. It was a young woman in her mid-twenties, undoubtedly one of Hablet's countless daughters. She rode in the carriage and waved to the passing crowd with the experience of one raised to perform such mindless ceremonial duties. Brak wondered which daughter the raven-haired beauty with the bored expression was. A young couple standing in front of him, stretching up on their toes to see over the crowd, answered his unspoken question as they watched her carriage pass by.

"That's Princess Adrina of Fardohnya," the young woman sighed. "Isn't she beautiful?"

Her companion laughed. "I heard she's such a shrew, Hablet can't find a husband brave enough to take her on."

"Maybe that's why she's here," the young woman suggested. "To find a husband?"

"Well, I hope she doesn't have her eye on poor old Lernen," the young man chuckled. "She'd be wasting her charms on him."

Brak listened to the conversation with a faint smile. It seemed the Hythrun were under no illusions about their High Prince.

By the time the parade had passed, the crowd began to thin a little, and Brak was able to push his way through to a tavern a few streets over that he had last visited more than three decades ago. He was relieved to find it still standing and pushed his way inside to the cool interior. The establishment's clientele had moved up a notch or two since his last visit, he noted idly.

The owner was new and eyed his rough sailor's clothing warily as he entered. However, one look at Brak's full purse was enough for the innkeeper to put aside her concerns. Brak took a room, ordered a bath, and settled down to wait.

He knew if his old friend, Wrayan Lightfinger, was aiding their search, it wouldn't take them long to find him.

Brak was sleeping when they burst into his room. He was dreaming of home: of white walls and peace and a forgiveness that he could never accept. It was a pleasant dream, one he rarely allowed himself. It was too easy to slip into, too hard to leave. The pull he felt toward home that filled him like a dull ache every waking moment flared into white-hot desire if he allowed himself to feel too much. Better not to dream of it. Better not to think about it.

The crash of the door being kicked in jerked him awake. Before his eyes were fully open the room was full of soldiers and he was pinned to the bed, the sharp point of a sword at his throat. The soldiers were from the Sorcerer's Collective. They were smartly dressed in their silver tunics, and there were enough of them to take a Harshini by surprise. They asked no questions, certain of his identity, and gave him no chance to deny it. He wondered at the advisability of trying to escape. It would be easy enough. These men were soldiers, not sorcerers. He could cast a glamor over himself that would make him vanish before their eyes and walk out of the room unchallenged. But the sorcerers would feel his magic, and it would lead them to him like bloodhounds on the sent of a fresh kill. He was still debating the matter when a sorcerer entered the room.

"Gently, Sergeant," the young sorcerer warned the soldier holding the blade to his throat. "Lord Brakandaran is an honored guest."

The pressure of the blade eased a little, and Brak found himself able to breathe again. He looked at the young man. He wore a long black robe with the hood pushed back. He was fair-haired and older than he looked, Brak guessed. One did not normally wear the black so young.

"Honored guest?" he asked dubiously.

The sorcerer shrugged apologetically. "Would you have come if we simply sent a message, my Lord?"

"No. And I've no intention of going anywhere with you now."

"My Lord, it grieves me that you feel that way," the Hythrun sighed. "I am under instructions to see you delivered to the High Arrion, and she simply won't take no for an answer."

"She?" Brak asked curiously, despite himself. He had been away longer than he thought.

"Kalan of Elasapine has been High Arrion for the last two years, my Lord," the sorcerer informed him. "I am Rorin, the High Arrion's personal seneschal. She begs me to inform you that while she appreciates your desire for anonymity, she must insist on an audience. And, might I add, on a personal note, I am honored to be in your presence, Divine One."

That did it. Brak pushed the sergeant away angrily. The man raised his sword threateningly but lowered it instantly as Brak's pale blue eyes began to darken to almost black.

"Get rid of them," he snapped.

Rorin ordered the men out with a wave of his hand. They left as quickly as they could without running. Brak could taste their fear like the tang of metal on his tongue. He sat up and swung his legs over the side of the bed as his eyes returned to their normal color. He took a deep, calming breath, a little surprised that even after all this time, his power was still enough to frighten other men.

"Let's get something cleared up right now," he said. "I am not a Divine One."

Rorin's expression did not change. "As you wish."

Brak shook his head with frustration. "Don't give me that look! I'm a half-breed, nothing more. I know you pray for the return of the Harshini, but don't look to me for your salvation. I'm not the one you want."

Rorin listened politely. "My Lord, I know of you, by reputation at least, and if you wish to deny your divinity, that's fine by me. But I must insist that you accompany me back to the Sorcerer's Palace."

"Do you have some sort of hearing problem, young man?" Brak asked irritably. "Have I not explained myself clearly enough for you? Give my compliments to the High Arrion and tell her I declined her invitation."

"I would if the invitation came from her, my Lord."

"If not the High Arrion, then who?" Brak snapped, afraid he already knew the answer. He had suspected it ever since the remarkable arlen catch in waters where they had never been seen before. Such a feat was beyond the simple tricks and spells of the Sorcerer's Collective.

The sorcerer glanced over his shoulder, pushing the door shut to ensure they could not be overheard. That action alone confirmed the worst of Brak's fears.

"The Seeing Stone spoke for the first time in almost two centuries, my Lord," Rorin told him with a hint of awe in his tone. "His Majesty, Korandellen, King of the Harshini, appeared to us."

It was odd hearing Korandellen referred to by his full title. Uncomfortable, too, particularly for the man who had made him king. Brak frowned at the news.

"What does Korandellen want?"

"He wants to speak with you," Rorin told him.

Brak regretted his decision almost as soon as he made it. He had fought for so long to put Sanctuary behind him. He had spent years trying to let his human blood dominate his Harshini heritage. He thought he had succeeded. Sometimes the ache faded so much that he thought it was gone. Sometimes he went days without reminding himself of why he could never return home.

Rorin had a golden sorcerer-bred stallion waiting for him outside the inn. When it gave him a soft nicker of recognition he realized just how much he had deluded himself—and how sure that Rorin had been of his agreement. One did not offer such a priceless animal to an inexperienced rider.

The horse tossed his head as he approached, the touch of his equine mind filled with images of hay and oats and young fillies. Brak smiled at the stallion's thoughts, privately delighted that the Sorcerer's Collective had kept the breed true, even after all this time. The stallion's iridescent coat shone gold in the light of the street lamps. Rorin nodded knowingly as Brak reached up and scratched the stallion's forelock.

"No other could approach Cloud Chaser so fearlessly, my Lord," Rorin told him. "You may not like to think of yourself as a Divine One, but there is no denying the bond."

"Getting along with animals doesn't make me divine," Brak snapped as he swung into the saddle.

"It does with that beast," Rorin chuckled. He turned to the soldiers who had mounted their own, less noble mounts and were waiting patiently, staring at Brak with a mixture of curiosity and awe. "Lead on, Sergeant."

"Don't bother," Brak said, leaning forward to pat Cloud Chaser's neck. "I know the way." He reached for Cloud Chaser's mind and told him where they were headed. With a shake of his magnificent head, the beast galloped off toward the Sorcerer's Palace, leaving Rorin and his escort behind.

Brak's mad ride was halted soon enough as he rode through the streets to the Sorcerer's Palace, picking his way through the nighttime revelers. The palace sat high above the city on a bluff overlooking everything in Greenharbor, even the Royal Compound. Although everyone called it a palace, it was actually a complex of Temples and residences, encircled by a thick white wall constructed of stone quarried from the chalk cliffs west of the city. Their fragile strength was reinforced by age-old Harshini magic. It had stood for over two thousand years, almost as long as the Citadel.

He rode through the palace gates unchallenged. The guards stood back to let him enter, not knowing who he was but certain that anyone riding a sorcerer-bred mount had a right to be there. The night was dark although the buildings were lit in almost every window, crisscrossing the central paved courtyard with a tapestry of shadows and light. Brak paid the imposing buildings no mind at all. He rode straight up to the steps of the Temple of the Gods and dismounted, leaving Cloud Chaser waiting patiently. He took the marble steps two at a time, grimly determined to do this before he changed his mind.

The Temple was almost empty, but for a few sorcerers praying silently or staring in wonder at the large crystal Seeing Stone, which had suddenly spoken after nearly two hundred years of silence. He ignored them, striding down the center aisle of the Temple, his boots clicking loudly on the mosaic tiled floor. They looked up as he passed, muttering to themselves, some even thinking to object to the presence of this stranger. As he approached the front of the Temple, where a solid lump of polished crystal as tall as a man sat on an altar of black marble, a young woman stepped forward, blocking his path. Brak stopped and stared at her, surprised to see the diamond-shaped pendant of the High Arrion resting against her simple black robe.

She bowed elegantly. "My Lord Brakandaran."

Brak studied her for a few moments. "You're very young to be High Arrion."

"And you don't look nearly as old as you should," she replied evenly, with the hint of a smile. "Would you like me to clear the Temple?"

Despite himself, Brak returned her smile. It was good to see a High

Arrion who didn't simper at the sight of a Harshini, even a half-breed with a bad reputation.

"Thank you."

She waved her hand imperiously and within minutes the Temple was empty of everyone but the two of them. Brak was rather impressed by her air of authority. As soon as Kalan was certain they were alone, she turned to him, her expression serious.

"My Lord, the Seeing Stone has been silent for almost two hundred years. The political ramifications of this event are not to be underestimated," she warned. "I have no idea why Korandellen wishes to speak with you, and I suspect I don't want to know . . . But you must understand something: when the Stone came to life, the Warlord of Krakandar was here, making his annual offering to the Temple. If you know anything of Hythrun politics, you can imagine what effect that news will have, and I don't know how much longer I can keep it secret. I beg you, my Lord, speak with your King and leave Greenharbor as soon as you are able."

Your King, she said, not *our* King. The days when the Hythrun paid fealty to the Harshini were long gone.

"I will, my Lady, I can assure you." He stepped up to the altar and studied the Stone for a moment before he turned to her. "What was Lord Wolfblade's reaction?"

"His reaction?" she echoed. "One of great caution, thank the gods. My brother is no fool, my Lord. He plans to leave the city as soon as possible. Being divinely sanctioned might make the people of Hythria happy, but it won't make him popular with the other Warlords. He quite sensibly fears assassination."

Her *brother*? Suddenly many things became clear, while at the same time, the mystery deepened. The heir to the High Prince's throne had already placed his sister in the Sorcerer's Collective as High Arrion. She, in turn, was obviously surrounding herself with her own people. When Lernen died, he would take the throne with the most powerful group of individuals in Hythria supporting him. And now Korandellen, the King of the Harshini, had appeared in the Seeing Stone after two centuries of silence, in the presence of Lernen's heir.

Would they never stop accidentally interfering with these people? If Damin Wolfblade was assassinated because the other Warlords feared his growing power, would Korandellen think himself responsible? He would have had no way of knowing who was in the Temple when he used the

Seeing Stone . . . no way of predicting what effect it might have on this nation. The knowledge that he had been responsible for someone's death might drive him mad, as it had his uncle. Brak could not imagine what was so important that he would break his silence and risk contacting these people after all this time. Another thought sliced through Brak like a sliver of sharpened ice. What would happen when word reached Medalon and the Sisters of the Blade? Brak suddenly wanted to speak with Korandellen very badly, if only to tell him he was a fool.

"I will leave you now, my Lord," the High Arrion said with a small bow. Brak barely paid her any attention. He was focused on the Seeing Stone, almost afraid to touch it, knowing that as soon as he did, he would undo almost two decades of hard work, forgetting who he was. Forgetting what he had done.

With a sigh, Brak closed his eyes. He reached for the river of power nestled within his mind which he had tried so hard not to touch for so long. As he dipped into it, the power leaped at him with frightening intensity, as if it was anxious to escape the bonds he had so carefully placed around it. He opened his eyes, which had changed completely now. No longer were they a faded shade of blue, weathered and disillusioned. They were totally black. The whites of his eyes were consumed by the power that coursed through him. Brak reached forward, placed his hands on the cool crystal surface of the Seeing Stone, and sent his mind out to his king.

Brakandaran.

It seemed hours before the voice filled his mind, although he knew it could only have been minutes since he laid his hand on the magical stone. Korandellen's face appeared in the surface of the Stone—no longer a lump of polished crystal but a milky backdrop for the proud face of the king. He wore his kingship a little uncomfortably. He had not wanted to be king. First Lorandranek's insanity and then Brak's own hand had forced him into it. Until now, Brak had thought he was doing a reasonable job.

"Your Majesty," Brak replied silently. Although the High Arrion had vanished from sight, he did not put it past her to be listening in. She was human, after all. Better this conversation be of the mind. Brak was out of practice, but his telepathic ability was merely rusty, not forgotten. It was frightening how easily it all came back to him.

"I wasn't sure you would answer my call," Korandellen said.

"Your minions left me little choice," Brak retorted. "Have you any idea what you've started by suddenly appearing in the Stone after two centuries of silence?" He realized this was hardly the way to address one's monarch after a twenty-year absence, but he couldn't help himself. His temper got the better of him. It always did.

Korandellen looked unrepentant. "I would not have called on you unless the matter was urgent. I know how you feel."

"You have no idea at all how I feel, Korandellen. You cannot kill. You cannot even contemplate the thought. You cannot know what it is to live with what I've done."

"But you are forgiven," Korandellen assured him generously.

"By you, perhaps," Brak said. "But I'll never forgive myself."

Korandellen shook his head sadly. "You were not to blame, Brak. You took a life to save a life. Lorandranek was insane. What you did could be viewed as a kindness. You put an end to his pain."

"I killed my King. I took his life to save a miserable human." Brak closed his eyes for a moment as the long-buried memories threatened to overwhelm him. He could still recall every detail as if it had happened only yesterday.

Brak had gone looking for Lorandranek té Ortyn at Korandellen's request. The mad King disappeared quite often from Sanctuary, sometimes for months at a time. The Sanctuary Mountains seemed to soothe his tortured mind in a way that not even the magical halls of the Harshini could, and nobody had the heart to deny him that peace. But winter was coming on, and they were worried about him. Lord Dranymire and his demon brethren could feel the King through the bond they shared with the té Ortyn family, but Lorandranek was too close to human settlement for the demons to risk going after him. Brak was half-human. He could move among humans without the need for disguise. He had promised Korandellen he would bring his uncle home.

He had followed the Harshini King for weeks, through mountains painted a riotous blend of autumn colors, although the trail was almost cold by the time Brak was given the task of tracking down the King. He knew Lorandranek had a fascination for humans that bordered on dangerous. It did not surprise Brak to find Lorandranek heading for a human settlement. He sought out humans to reassure himself that they still flourished.

When he finally found Lorandranek one chilly, starlit night, almost a month after he had set out from Sanctuary, the scene that confronted him was too unreal to comprehend. He knew what he had seen but even now found it hard to accept. The King was living in a cave littered with the chattels of long habitation, perched high on the side of a mountain above a small human village. Brak had entered the cave cautiously, softly calling Lorandranek's name.

The cavern was dark, lit only by the glowing coals of a dying fire. Brak saw a shadowed figure with a knife, poised over another prone body. The figure was trembling so hard the assailant could barely grip the blade. Brak reacted without thinking. He had drawn his own blade and hurled it with deadly accuracy at the assailant's chest before he knew who it was.

The assassin cried out as he clutched at the knife. The enormity of his crime hit Brak like an anvil dropped on him by the gods. He vaguely remembered yelling something, barely remembered the screams of the sleeping girl as she awoke to discover Lorandranek dripping blood on her face. He recalled catching the dying King and holding him as the lifeblood pumped from his chest. The Harshini were long-lived, but not immortal. Brak didn't need to look to know the wound was fatal. He knew his own ability too well.

"The gods . . . they ask too much of me, Brakandaran," Lorandranek had breathed softly as he lay dying in Brak's arms. Brak's eyes were blurry. It had taken him a moment to realize he was crying.

"Why?" he had asked desperately. What had the gods asked him to do? "Who were you trying to kill? How could you even think of it? The Harshini cannot kill."

But Lorandranek had never answered the question. Brak had held him until he grew cold in his arms and harsh daylight flooded the cave. When he could finally bring himself to move, the girl, whoever she was, had fled—presumably back to her village—and Brak never spared her another thought. Brak laid out the King and kept vigil over him for two days and nights, not eating, drinking, or sleeping. The following day he reached out through his bond to Lady Elarnymire.

Her demon had appeared soon after in the shape of a swallow, landing with incredible grace on the narrow ledge in front of the cave. To assume a larger shape meant melding with other demons, and Brak had specifically asked her to come alone.

The shock of seeing Lorandranek's cold body startled the demon back into her true form. Elarnymire had stood on the ledge, her black eyes wide, her wrinkled skin a motley shade of gray, as Brak told her what he had done. He asked the demon to tell Korandellen. He could not bring himself to do it. Elarnymire had placed her tiny, cold hand in his and promised him faithfully that she would deliver the message.

Brak had buried his King in a grove of tall pines near the cave and never gone back to Sanctuary; never given in to the pull toward home; ignored the demons' attempts to coax him back. He could never face the Harshini again in that palace of peace and harmony. They had always known his capability for violence and with typical Harshini tolerance, had accepted it as a part of him. But he could not—would not—ask them to accept this. He had turned his back on his people, denying the nagging need to see Sanctuary again, rejecting the magic that only those who cannot kill should be allowed to possess.

"I need you to finish what was started by Lorandranek," Korandellen told him gently as he relived the memory through the mental link he shared with Brak.

"You do not need me at all," Brak replied, shaking his head.

"There is a child. Lorandranek's child."

Brak looked up sharply, the painful memories pushed aside by Korandellen's startling news.

"A child?"

"Lord Dranymire says the demons can feel the bond. It grows stronger every day. Somewhere, there is a child of té Ortyn blood approaching maturity."

Brak's eyes narrowed. The child of the girl in the cave? No. It was too soon. Harshini did not reach maturity until they were well into their third decade. On the other hand, a half-human child might mature earlier than a full-blood. He had come into his own power in his teens.

"If Lord Dranymire can feel the child, why doesn't he seek it out?" It was a bitter irony, Brak thought, that he had killed his King to save a human woman, just so that nearly twenty years later he could hunt her child down.

"The child is living with humans, Brakandaran. Which is why I must call on you."

"I am surprised the gods have let it live this long."

Korandellen shrugged. "The gods have their own agenda. The thought of this child does not seem to concern them, only that it will do what they ask of it."

Brak frowned. "And what is that, exactly?"

"They have not chosen to share that with me. I only know that they want the child found."

Brak sighed. A human child of té Ortyn blood was a very dangerous being. The humans who worshipped the gods called such a being the demon child. And the gods, who had placed the prohibition on such a child ever existing, wanted this child for something. *The gods, they ask too much of me*, the King had said. For the first time in twenty years, Brak thought he understood what Lorandranek meant.

"Where is the child?" he asked, cursing the gods and their interference.

Korandellen hesitated. "The Citadel," he said finally. "The demons say the child is at the Citadel."

chapter 8

"You're awake."

Joyhinia stood over her, her arms crossed, her expression annoyed. It took a moment or two for R'shiel to realize she was in the Infirmary.

"Mother."

"You at least could have had the decency to announce the onset of your womanhood in a less public place," she scolded. "I suppose I should be grateful that it was Tarja who found you, although why he insisted on running through the Citadel, yelling like a fishwife, instead of dealing with the matter discreetly, is beyond me."

"I think I fainted." R'shiel wished she had never left the peaceful serenity of unconsciousness. Any hopeful thought she might have had about sympathy from her mother was dispelled in an instant.

"Sister Gwenell says you lost a great deal of blood," Joyhinia continued impatiently. "I expect you to follow her instructions to the letter and ensure that you recover as soon as possible. It's not as if you're the first woman to hemorrhage on her first bleeding."

"I'll try to do better next time."

"If you eat properly, there won't be a next time," Joyhinia told her, ignoring the edge in her voice. "I don't know what you think you hope to gain by starving yourself, my girl, but I have given orders that you are to be force fed, if you continue to refuse meals."

Who had she been talking to? R'shiel wondered. Junee? Kilene? Some of the other Probates? But thank the Founders, her headache was gone. Even the dull throbbing at the back of her eyes had miraculously vanished. The pain had been such a constant companion lately, she almost felt empty without it.

"I'll do as Sister Gwenell orders."

"Good," Joyhinia announced, as if that was the end of the matter. "Gwenell says you'll need some time to recuperate, once she has discharged you. I suppose you'll have to come back to the apartment until Founders' Day. After that, I expect you to return to your studies, and I'll hear no more about this."

The discussion at an end, Joyhinia turned on her heel and strode out of the Infirmary, past the long lines of perfectly made-up beds, which for the most part were empty. R'shiel watched her go, wondering what it would take to make Joyhinia happy. For five years Joyhinia had been angry with her for not reaching her menses. Now that she finally had, she was angry with her for doing it in public. R'shiel turned over and pulled the covers up over her head, shutting out unexpected tears, and tried to wish herself back into oblivion.

Joyhinia did not visit the Infirmary again. Sister Gwenell kept her bedridden for almost a week, before she relented and let R'shiel out for short walks in the gardens outside the long windows of the Infirmary. R'shiel liked Gwenell, and once she was convinced her charge was not about to keel over if she sat up too fast, she would sit and talk with R'shiel or play a game of two-handed tharabac with her, even though R'shiel always won.

R'shiel suspected her continuing weakness was more from forced idleness than loss of blood. Her aversion to meat seemed to vanish with the headaches and the onset of her menses. She still did not actually crave meat, but it no longer smelled rancid or repulsive to her, which was a good thing, as Gwenell was firmly convinced that red meat was the only cure for loss of blood, and R'shiel was served it for breakfast, lunch, and dinner.

Junee and Kilene were allowed to visit her on the third day of her confinement. Her friends were bubbling with the gossip sweeping the Citadel regarding the fight in the Arena. According to Junee and Kilene, Loclon had been treated for the gash that Tarja had given him, but it would scar him horribly, a fact that seemed to both delight and dismay the Probates all at once. The general opinion around the Citadel was that it was a shame such a handsome officer was going to be marked for the rest of his life, but he probably deserved it. Kilene claimed that Georj was dead before they got him out of the Arena. To die in such an awful way was just the worst luck, she declared, although he only had himself to blame. R'shiel wanted to strangle her.

To Kilene the Defenders were just soldiers, good for entertainment and an occasional roll in the sack. R'shiel chafed at the restrictions placed on her by Sister Gwenell and her own weakness, refusing to believe Kilene's assertion that Loclon would not be tried for murder. Junee promised to see if she could find out something more reliable and the girls left, leaving R'shiel quite depressed by their efforts to cheer her up.

Two days later, sitting on a wrought-iron recliner piled with pillows, on the terrace overlooking the Infirmary gardens, she was still brooding about their visit. She was wrapped in a blanket against the cool autumn breeze, reading some forgettable text that Junee had left her, when Tarja finally paid her a visit.

He took the seat beside her, wearing his high-collared red jacket, his boots polished to a parade-ground gleam. She glared at him, angry that he had taken so long to visit her.

"Go on, tell me how terrible I look," she snapped, before he could say a word.

"Actually, you look like hell, but it's an improvement from the last time I saw you. How are you feeling?"

"Better," she admitted. "Mother has already told me to get well or else, so I don't really have a choice."

"That sounds like Joyhinia," Tarja agreed. "She'll probably disown you, if you don't."

"Sometimes I wish she would," R'shiel muttered, still smarting from Joyhinia's unsympathetic reaction to her plight.

"It does have its advantages you know, being disowned," he assured her.

R'shiel looked at him closely, but there was no bitterness in his tone. "Why does she hate you, Tarja?"

Tarja shrugged. "Who knows? For that matter, who cares?"

"I care."

He took her hand in his. "I know you care, R'shiel. That's because no matter how hard Joyhinia tries to mold you into another version of herself, there is a part of you she can't seem to corrupt. I hope she never succeeds."

Uncomfortable with Tarja's scrutiny, R'shiel forced herself to scowl at him. "You're not suggesting I won't make a good Sister, are you, Captain?"

"From what I hear, you'll be lucky to make the Blue at all, R'shiel."

"That's not my fault."

"Isn't it?" He looked at her skeptically.

"Well, maybe it is," she conceded. "But I don't ever recall being asked if I actually wanted to be a Sister. Joyhinia just assumed that I would."

"And what would you do if you didn't take the Blue?" he asked. "You're singularly unsuited for anything else. Joyhinia has seen to that."

She thought for a moment. *What would I do, if I refused to follow the path Joyhinia has so clearly laid out for me?* The fact that she could not come up with an answer was disturbing. Perhaps that was why she teetered on the brink of outright defiance, instead of taking that last, final step. There was nothing beyond.

"Tell me about the Arena, Tarja," she said. Joyhinia was not a comfortable subject for either of them. Besides, he would know what had really happened in the aftermath of the brutal fight. "Is it true that Georj is dead? Kilene said he was dead before he left the Arena."

Tarja nodded. "I'm sorry, R'shiel."

For a moment, R'shiel saw her own grief reflected in his eyes, but he covered it easily. He had dealt with death too often and was hardened to it.

"What did Lord Jenga do to Loclon?" she asked.

"There's nothing he can do, R'shiel. There is no rank in the Arena and no written rules. Georj went in knowing the risk he took."

R'shiel was appalled. "But he was murdered! Loclon is a monster!"

"Well, Loclon didn't win himself any friends, but that doesn't make him a monster. Men have died in the Arena before," he reminded her. "Loclon might have let his bloodlust get the better of him, but it was Georj who kept fighting."

"I can't believe you're defending him, Tarja! Georj was your best friend!"

"I'm not defending him or what he did. But Georj was a fool for not realizing the sort of man Loclon was. Know your enemy, R'shiel. It's the first rule of combat."

"*You* should have killed Loclon when you had the chance."

"To what purpose?"

"To rid the world of him!" she declared. "He is evil. If I believed in the heathen stories I'd say he was their demon child!"

Tarja looked at her curiously. "Evil? You haven't been sneaking a peek at those pagan murals again, have you?" When she glared at him angrily, he shrugged. "If it's any consolation, Jenga's talking of transferring him to the Grimfield."

R'shiel was only slightly mollified by the news. The Grimfield was

Medalon's prison town, and the Defenders who guarded it, like the prisoners who peopled it, were the dregs of Medalon. A posting to the Grimfield was the end of any promising career.

"That's something, I suppose," she grumbled. "Though it seems too lenient, to my mind."

"I shall inform the Lord Defender of your displeasure," Tarja told her solemnly.

"Don't patronize me, Tarja! I'm not a child."

"Then accept the reality, R'shiel. Georj took a risk and he paid the price. The simple solution would have been to refuse Loclon in the first place."

"Like you did?"

"I've no need to prove myself against the Loclons of this world. I've met much more worthy opponents."

R'shiel sighed. "I will never understand you."

"Good. You're not supposed to."

"Where do you get all this big brother nonsense from?" she demanded. "Every time you want to weasel out of explaining yourself, I get the same excuse."

He smiled but refused to answer. "You take care of yourself, young lady. Big brother will be checking on you when he gets back."

She hurled a pillow at him, wishing it was something more substantial. "Where are you going?" she asked.

"Up north," he said as he ducked. "Garet Warner wants me to check on something."

R'shiel's eyes narrowed. "Why are you working with him? You're a cavalry officer, not intelligence."

"You mean I'm all brawn and no brains?"

She frowned in annoyance. "You know what I mean. Garet Warner is always plotting and planning something. Mother hates him. She says he's the most dangerous man in the Defenders. If she had her way, he'd be removed."

"Then let's hope she never gets her way," Tarja said. "But you needn't fear, R'shiel. All I'm doing is a survey of the northern border villages. There are no deep plots involved."

"Well, be careful, anyway," she ordered.

"As you command, my Lady," he replied with a small bow.

R'shiel frowned, certain he was making fun of her, but she had nothing left to throw. "When will you be back?"

"With luck, by Founders' Day. I shall make a point of being here, just to annoy Joyhinia, if for no other reason."

"Since when have you cared about riding in the Founders' Day Parade?"

Tarja looked entirely too smug. "Mahina is going to announce some changes. I want to be where I can see the look on our beloved mother's face." He leaned forward and kissed her gently on the forehead, something he had not done since she was a small child. "Take care, R'shiel."

"You too," she replied, but when she opened her eyes he was gone.

chapter 9

For three weeks Tarja and his small troop rode north toward the sparsely populated high plains on the border with Karien. As they neared the border the snowcapped Sanctuary Mountains in the distance loomed closer every day on the western horizon and the air grew chill with the onset of the coming winter. Low clouds gathered, blocking out the sun, but did little more than threaten rain, for which they were grateful. In a few weeks, the same clouds would gather over the mountains and bring snow to the high plains. Tarja hoped to be long back at the Citadel before that happened.

Garet had sent Tarja north to survey the villages close to the border for logistical reasons. He wanted a cavalry officer's view of their ability to cope with the influx of Defenders that construction of fortifications on the border would entail. There also were the long-term effects of a permanent garrison to consider. Although horses could be grazed, a cavalry mount ate about twenty pounds of feed a day, which would have to be shipped to the border, along with everything else the garrison needed. Garet speculated that convenience, as much as trust, had kept the treaty with the Kariens alive so long. Having seen how inadequate the villages north of the Glass River were for the task, Tarja was inclined to agree with him.

The most vulnerable point on the border between Medalon and Karien was this high grassy plain, where the mountains ceased abruptly, exposing an open and undefended expanse of knee-high grass, which was rapidly browning as winter approached. Tarja and his small party reached the crumbling border keep, the only sign of human habitation on the plain, on the first day of Brigedda. He remembered the date as he rode at a trot toward the old keep, wondering who Brigedda had been. All the Medalonian months were named for the Founding Sisters, some of whom, like Param, who had wrested control of Medalon from the Harshini and established the Sisterhood's government over Medalon, were quite famous. Others, like Brigedda, were remembered for no other reason than their names now marked the changing of the seasons.

He had not even realized this old keep was out here, until the innkeeper in Lilyvale had mentioned it to him. Curiosity had gotten the better of him, and he judged they had the time for a small detour. One look at the distant ruin was enough to convince him that strategically it was useless.

The keep was still some distance away when Tarja slowed his horse to a walk. Five small mounds of freshly turned dirt, topped with bunches of wilted wildflowers, were spaced at intervals beside the faint track that led to the keep. He stopped and dismounted, followed by Davydd Tailorson, the lieutenant Garet had assigned to him. He was a brown-haired, serious young man. Tarja had come to enjoy his quiet company. On the rare occasion he offered his opinion, it was usually an astute one. Davydd examined the mounds with a slight frown.

"Pagan graves," he remarked, squatting down beside the closest mound.

"And too small to be adults," Tarja agreed, glancing toward the abandoned keep.

"What do you suppose they're doing way out here?"

"Better here than close to a town. Perhaps they thought no one would find them in such an isolated place."

Davydd stood up and followed Tarja's gaze toward the keep. "Or perhaps the keep isn't abandoned?"

"Well, there's one way to establish that for certain, isn't there?"

Davydd nodded and remounted his horse. Tarja followed suit and waved to the four troopers who accompanied them to move out. The two officers rode side by side at a walk, making no gestures that could be construed as threatening—although if there were heathens hiding in the ruin, their uniforms would be threat enough.

"You know, it just occurred to me," Davydd remarked, "that red coats against a background of brown grass make us an excellent target."

Tarja glanced at Davydd and laughed. "I should introduce you to a certain Captain Gawn, currently stationed on our southern border. He has firsthand knowledge of the perils of brandishing one's uniform against a brown background when there are enemy archers in the vicinity. But, I think in this case, we're safe enough."

"Unless the heathens in the keep are followers of Zegarnald."

"If they followed Zegarnald, they'd be heading south. There isn't much point in worshipping the God of War out here in the middle of nowhere, where there's no one to fight."

As they approached the keep, Tarja noted signs of human habitation. A small field had been cleared and planted along the western side of the ruin. Stones from the crumbling wall had been painstakingly dragged to form a rough enclosure that housed a thin milk cow and several unshorn sheep. The faint smell of burning dung reached his nose. On this treeless plain there would be no wood to burn. They rode past the wall and into the rubble-strewn courtyard, where a boiling copper sat unattended over an open fire. There was no sign of the inhabitants.

They stopped and waited for a while, to see if anyone would approach. The air was still. The smoldering dung stung Tarja's nostrils.

He finally turned in his saddle and yelled: "Show yourselves!"

The keep was silent except for a slight breeze that stirred the dusty yard and the creaking of leather as the horses tossed their heads, as curious about this place as their riders.

"We mean you no harm!"

They waited in silence for a long moment until a figure appeared from behind the fallen wall of what had probably been the main hall. She was a thin woman of late middle years, dressed in rough peasant homespun, a toddler clutched at her hip. She eyed the soldiers warily, staying close to the wall.

"If you mean us no harm, then leave now," she said, her cultured accent belying her rough clothing.

Tarja stayed on his horse, making no move toward her. Out of the corner of his eye, he caught sight of a boy, perhaps ten or twelve years old, hiding up on the decaying steps of the old tower to his left.

"It will be night soon, Mistress," Tarja pointed out. "This is the only shelter for miles, and it looks like rain. Would you deny us what little comfort there is to be had on this barren plain?"

The woman took a step closer and glared at him. "You and your kind would deny me, quick enough. Do you really think I care if your men suffer a little, Captain?"

"But Kalianah, the Goddess of Love, says that all bounty should be shared," Davydd answered, before Tarja could reply. He glanced at the younger man in surprise and then followed his gaze to the amulet hanging from a leather thong around the woman's neck. It was an acorn tied together with several soft white feathers. The symbol of Kalianah. Tarja had seen some of Damin Wolfblade's Raiders wearing the same amulet. The woman looked both startled and annoyed to have her own beliefs used against her by a Defender. "You speak the words, young man, but you have no idea of their true meaning. Leave us in peace. We harm nobody here."

By now, Tarja had caught sight of another half dozen or more children hiding in the ruins. Was she alone out here, with all these children?

"We could insist, Mistress," he warned.

The woman snorted at him contemptuously. "Have the Defenders fallen so low that they would attack women and children for the sake of a night out of the rain, Captain?" she asked, bending down to place the child on the ground. It looked up at the soldiers with wide eyes, sucking its thumb nervously. The woman walked across the yard and stood beside Tarja's horse, looking up at him. "I had respect for the Defenders once, Captain, but no longer. Give me one reason why I should share anything with your kind?"

"You have no need to share anything, Mistress," Tarja replied, meeting her accusing gaze. "We will share with you."

The woman looked at him doubtfully. "You're not ordinary Defenders, are you? Intelligence Corps is my guess. Nasty as the rest of them but marginally better educated. Well, we are finished here anyway, now that you've found us. If you mean what you say about sharing, then I'll take whatever you can spare. I've seventeen motherless children to care for, and I'm not too proud to accept charity."

Tarja dismounted carefully, anxious not to threaten the woman and her odd brood anymore than he already had. He was curious about these children. He had seen heathen cults aplenty across the length and breadth of Medalon but never anything that so closely resembled an orphanage. As they dismounted more children appeared, staring at the Defenders silently from the safety of the crumbling walls. To a child they were ragged and thin. None wore shoes, their feet bound with rags against the cold. It was more than likely they would not survive a winter here. Tarja called forward the trooper leading the packhorses and ordered him to leave them enough for their return journey and to give the rest to the woman. The trooper nodded and went about his task without question. That surprised Tarja a little. He was expecting some resistance. After all, feeding a bunch of starving heathens was hardly the patriotic thing to do.

"Where do all these children come from?" he asked as another trooper took his horse and Davydd's to be unsaddled and watered.

The woman looked at him sharply, as if expecting the question to be the beginning of an interrogation. "Why do you want to know that?"

When Tarja did not answer, she shrugged, as if too tired to argue with him.

"They're orphans, mostly. Their parents were accused of being heathens, or worse. Some were sentenced to the Grimfield or killed by Defenders. Not fighting, mind you, simply trying to save their homes from wanton destruction. I would ask that you tread carefully here, Captain. Most of these children associate that uniform with death."

Tarja and Davydd followed the woman into the remains of the great hall, stepping carefully over the crumbling masonry. It had been a large hall once, but the roof had caved in and only the far end offered any shelter. Several children huddled around a small fire in a hearth so grand that he could have almost stood upright inside it. The children looked up at their approach, shying away from the Defenders.

"Don't worry, my dears," the woman assured the children with forced cheerfulness. "I'll not let the red men harm you."

"If it would be easier for you, we can stay outside," Tarja offered, looking at the children with concern. One of them, a small girl of about five, was racked with painful coughs that made Tarja wince just to hear her.

"They'll learn soon enough that there is no avoiding your kind, even in this remote place," the woman replied with a shrug. "Perhaps if you leave without killing anyone or destroying anything, they may learn to hate the Defenders a little less." She met Tarja's gaze defiantly, but he refused to rise to her provocation.

"Why bring them out here?" he asked. "You can't hope to survive the winter in such a place."

"Where else do I take them, Captain . . . what's your name?"

"Tenragan. Tarja Tenragan."

The woman stared at him, her face suddenly pale, then turned on her heel and walked out of the hall. With a curious glance at each other, they hurried after her. She strode purposefully toward the trooper who was dividing the supplies.

"Don't bother with that, soldier. I'll not be needing any help from you, after all." The man glanced at Tarja with a puzzled expression as the woman rounded on the two officers. "Take your provisions and leave, Captain. You are not welcome here."

Understanding suddenly dawned on Tarja. "You know Joyhinia."

The woman planted her hands on her hips. "You're her son, aren't you? I remember seeing you around the Citadel when you were a boy."

Tarja was not surprised to learn that this woman had lived in the Citadel. Her accent betrayed her education. He nodded slowly, curious to learn what had turned her from the Sisterhood and what his mother had done to provoke such a reaction.

"Is my ancestry so abhorrent to you, that you would refuse my help?"

"Ever heard of a village called Haven, Captain?" she retorted bitterly.

"It's a village in the Sanctuary Mountains, southwest of Testra," Davydd said. He had a good grasp of geography as well as heathen customs it seemed.

"It *was* a village, Lieutenant," she snapped. "It no longer exists. Joyhinia Tenragan ordered it burned to the ground and all the adults killed three winters ago. They turned the children out into the snow and left them to perish. There were over thirty children in that village. Nine of these children are the only ones left. The rest I have collected since then, for similar reasons. I was a Sister back then. After that day, I swore an oath to every Primal God that exists that I would never wear the Blue again."

"Why?" Tarja asked in astonishment.

"You don't know?"

"Should I?"

"She burned it to keep a secret, Captain. She burned it to cover her tracks and bury her lies." She gave a short, bitter laugh. "Looks like she succeeded too, by the expression on your face. Have you no inkling?"

Tarja shook his head, glancing at Davydd, but the young man looked as puzzled as he was.

The woman glanced longingly at the supplies and then sighed. "I shouldn't be surprised, I suppose. Nor should I let my anger get in the way of these children having a decent meal. I will take the provisions you offer, Captain. It makes up, in some small measure, for the actions of your mother."

"You're welcome to anything we have," Tarja assured her, "but I want to know why . . . What possible reason could Joyhinia have for burning a village in the Sanctuary Mountains?"

She studied him closely for a moment, as if debating how much she should tell him, then she shrugged. "I suppose you have as much right to know as anyone. Come, let's get out of this wind and I'll tell you the whole story."

They went inside the crumbling great hall and sat on the floor near the hearth. The fire gave little warmth, but Tarja barely noticed.

"Nineteen years ago, your mother was posted to Testra, just as I was, to administer the town and the surrounding villages. It's what they train us for, you know. The Sisters of the Blade are the best-trained bureaucrats in the world."

Bereth, that was the woman's name, had shooed the children out to do their chores and help bring in the supplies that the Defenders had offered to leave them. The only child left was the little girl with the painful cough. She crawled into Bereth's lap and stared at the Defenders with wide, frightened eyes.

Tarja tore his gaze from the child and looked at Bereth. "I remember. She enrolled me in the Cadets and left me at the Citadel. I was only ten."

Bereth nodded. "Joyhinia arrived in Testra with quite a reputation. She'd already had you, and it was rumored that your father was Lord Korgan, although he always denied it. Four or five months after she arrived my mother died, and I was called back to Brodenvale to settle the family's affairs. Joyhinia volunteered to take over from me, doing my rounds of the outlying villages. We all thought it strange at the time. She loathed being away from her creature comforts and despised the cold. Taking over at that time meant wintering in one of the mountain villages until the spring thaw. But she had her eye on a seat on the Quorum, even in those days, and we weren't exactly swamped with volunteers, so she got the job."

The child in her lap began coughing again, and Bereth stopped her narrative to gently rub the child's back. When the coughing fit subsided, Bereth resumed her tale.

"By the time I returned to Testra, it was spring, and Joyhinia was on her way back from the mountains. She had wintered in Haven, which was a remote village populated with loggers and furriers, mostly. Hardworking, decent people, every one of them." Bereth's voice trailed off for a moment, as if she was lost in the past, then she looked at Tarja, her eyes hard and bitter. "Joyhinia returned to Testra with a child. A babe of a few weeks, which she claimed was hers and Jenga's get, although anyone who

knew Jenga doubted her claim. He was never a man for casual relation-
ships, particularly with anyone as ambitious as your mother. And she'd
shown no signs of being pregnant before she left for the mountains. Nor
did she act the part. She had lovers aplenty, rumor had it. She called the
child Rochelle, or something like that."

"R'shiel," Tarja corrected softly, afraid that if he spoke too loudly,
Bereth would not finish her tale.

"R'shiel," Bereth repeated, as if the word carried special meaning.
"That's a mountain name, by the way, not the name given to any child of
the Citadel.

"Anyway, Joyhinia returned, claiming she had been pregnant, and the
child was of the right age, so nobody thought much more about it. Jenga
never formally acknowledged the child, but his silence was confirmation
enough for most, I suppose. To this day, I don't understand why he has
never denied it.

"So, I went back to my duties and thought little more about it. Haven
is very remote, and even I only managed to visit it every couple of years or
so. By the time I returned to the village, it never occurred to me to ask
about Joyhinia's visit or the child."

"You said the village was burned only three years ago," Tarja
reminded her. "What happened?"

"I learned much of the story from a woman in Haven, a furrier named
B'thrim Snowbuilder. She was a widow who had lived alone for years,
ever since her younger sister, J'nel, died the year Joyhinia wintered in
Haven. The rest I learned from the survivors, some of the older children.
B'thrim had an accident about eight months before the village was
destroyed. She got caught in one of her own traps and lost her left foot to
frostbite. It meant she could no longer trap the snow foxes, and the
season before had not been a good one. She was on the verge of destitu-
tion. The last time I saw her, she told me she had sent a message to
Joyhinia at the Citadel, asking for help, in return for the favor she had
done her years before. Joyhinia's response was to send a troop of Defenders to burn the village. B'thrim was one of the first to be killed."

"What favor?" Tarja asked. Bereth had told him much, but in reality
she had told him nothing.

"B'thrim's sister, J'nel, died in childbirth, Captain. She died giving
birth to the girl you know as your sister."

Tarja stared at the woman, stunned.

"Who is she, then?" Davydd asked, giving voice to the question Tarja was unable to ask.

"R'shiel? She's the child of an illiterate mountain girl and an unknown father, I suppose. The story I got was that J'nel had disappeared into the Mountains at the beginning of spring and returned just before winter, heavily pregnant. She was frightened, hysterical, and covered with blood when she returned but refused to name the father. Haven was a superstitious village, and while they profess adherence to the laws of the Sisterhood, there were many who believed the Harshini still inhabited the Sanctuary Mountains. As no man in the village would own the child, they decided the child must be a sorcerer's get and rejected it. Joyhinia didn't care what the villagers thought. The child was the right age for her to invent her deception and an orphan that nobody wanted. All she needed was Jenga to go along with her. She probably thought the villagers would forget all about the child after a while."

"Until B'thrim sent a message asking for help," Tarja said.

"Taking an orphan in is one thing," Bereth continued, "but to claim that child is your own and try to foist paternity onto the Lord Defender goes beyond the pale." She glanced at Tarja thoughtfully. "The child must be almost grown by now."

Tarja nodded. "She's a Probate at the Citadel."

Bereth shook her head. "So Joyhinia has a daughter to follow in her footsteps, and I have a clutch of starving orphans whose parents died to keep her secret. Most of those villagers in Haven would not have even remembered the child. That was her worst crime, Captain. It was so unnecessary." The child in her lap had fallen into an uneasy sleep. She stroked her fine hair absently and looked at Tarja. "I'm sorry to be the one to tell you this. I suppose you have some affection for the girl, although if Joyhinia has succeeded in raising her in her own image, I doubt she is very lovable."

Tarja shook his head. "Joyhinia tries, but she hasn't succeeded yet."

"That's something to be grateful for," Bereth sighed. "But perhaps now, Captain, you can understand my reaction on learning who your mother is."

Tarja climbed the crumbling tower later that evening and looked out over the dark plain. The clouds were breaking up, revealing patches of blue velvet sky sprinkled with pinpoints of light. He leaned on the cold stone, oblivious to the chill wind that cut through him, wondering what he should do with the information Bereth had given him. For that matter, would it even be his decision? Davydd Tailorson had heard the whole story and would report it to Garet Warner, without hesitation. That sort of information about a Quorum member was too important to keep to himself. He should have insisted on hearing the tale in private. He would have, had he any inkling of what he would learn.

The consequences to Joyhinia, when her lies were revealed, bothered Tarja not one whit. Joyhinia deserved whatever punishment the First Sisters deemed fit and the more severe the better. Expulsion from the Quorum, at the very least. She might even be forced into retirement. That prospect filled Tarja with savage delight. To see Joyhinia's plans crumble at her feet like the ruins of this keep was almost worth it.

Almost.

There was R'shiel to consider. Joyhinia's fall would drag R'shiel down with her. She deserved to know the truth, but did she deserve to suffer for it?

Tarja turned at the sound of a boot scraping on the stairs. Davydd took the last two steps in one stride and joined Tarja on the tower, glancing out over the plain, his arms wrapped around his body against the wind.

"Looks like it won't rain, after all," the young man remarked.

"Looks like it." He waited for Davydd to speak again; he had not climbed the tower to talk about the weather.

"I have to tell the Commandant," he said finally, breaking the uncomfortable silence. "It would be treason to withhold what I learned here."

"Treason?" Tarja asked.

"The Commandant might not . . . " he began, but his voice trailed off. Both he and Tarja knew that Garet Warner would use the information against Joyhinia as surely as Davydd would have to report it.

"He will. But he has to know the truth. So does R'shiel, for that matter, although I worry more about her than Joyhinia. My mother deserves whatever is coming to her."

"I've seen your sister at the Citadel. She's very pretty."

"She is," he agreed. "And apparently she's not my sister."

"At the risk of sounding trite, there'll be a lot of officers at the Citadel quite pleased to learn that, sir."

Tarja laughed, despite himself. "Including you, Lieutenant?"

"I . . . er . . . well, it's not that I ever . . . " Davydd stammered, the first time Tarja had seen him lost for words.

"Don't worry, Lieutenant. I'm sure your intentions are entirely honorable. But before you tell Garet Warner what we learned here today, spare a thought for R'shiel. Once this becomes common knowledge, she'll be an outcast."

"It's hardly her fault," Davydd objected. "You don't think people will hold it against her, do you? I mean, she's a Probate. She'll be a Sister within a couple of years."

"You've a lot to learn about the Sisterhood, Davydd," Tarja told him wearily. "They won't care that Joyhinia lied to them. But they'll be very put out that she has played them all for fools."

"It doesn't seem fair, sir."

"That's life, Lieutenant," Tarja replied, more bitterly than he intended. The young man was silent for a moment, surprised at Tarja's tone.

"Will you report this to Lord Jenga?"

"Jenga has a right to know the truth, too. Joyhinia has been trading on her supposed relationship with him for years."

"Assuming he doesn't already know," Davydd remarked.

"What do you mean?"

"Well, someone in the Defenders sent those men to destroy the village. Joyhinia didn't do that alone. Besides, the Lord Defender could have exposed Joyhinia years ago, unless he had a reason not to."

Tarja stared at the young man, appalled by his suggestion. "Jenga would never order such a thing!"

Davydd shrugged. "You know him better than I do, sir. But unless Sister Joyhinia forged the orders and the Defender's seal that authenticates them, there is at least one senior officer involved. And you have to admit, Jenga's refusal to deny he's R'shiel's father does look suspicious."

Was it possible? Tarja shivered in the darkness, but the cold that chilled him came from inside. Ever since he had been old enough to recognize it for what it was, Tarja had watched the Sisters of the Blade grow increasingly tainted by the stench of corruption, like milk slowly souring in the heat on a hot summer's day.

For the first time, Tarja allowed himself to wonder if that corruption had spread to the Corps and reached as high as the Lord Defender.

arja spent a sleepless night in the ruined keep, listening to the heartbreaking coughs of the little girl by the fire and wondering who in the Defenders had followed Joyhinia's orders to destroy Haven. Any Commandant could, in theory, have issued the order. That narrowed the suspects down to about fifteen men, excluding Jenga, whom he was certain would never have countenanced such an act, despite what Davydd thought. Commandant Verkin, Wilem Cortanen, Garet Warner, and about a dozen more senior officers had sufficient authority. It was a depressing train of thought. He resolved to question Bereth again in the morning before they rode out. Perhaps she knew the name of the officer in charge of the raid. If he could discover that, he might be able to track down the culprit.

They stayed in the keep longer than he intended. Tarja had hoped to get away at first light the following day. His mission was to check on the border villages, and he had completed that task before riding out here on impulse to examine the ruined keep. It would be next to useless if Medalon were invaded. It was strategically ill placed in the middle of an open plain and had been built, hastily and poorly, by men with no understanding of war. An invading army would simply swing past it into Medalon, as if it were no more of an obstacle than a rock in the road. In the future, any defenses constructed would be farther north, right on the border itself, where the plain narrowed and the open grassland was flanked by the Sanctuary Mountains on the western side and the Glass River, where it emerged from the Jagged Mountains, on the east.

But his men undermined Tarja's plans for an early departure, subtly and deliberately. First, Sandar, the trooper responsible for the packhorses and the supplies, announced that he thought he could possibly spare even more for the children, given time to sort through their provisions carefully. Then Nork, his corporal, suddenly announced that his horse had bruised his fetlock and would need a poultice to relieve it. One of the children had told him of a herb that grew wild on the plains that was ideal for the poultice, and would it be all right if he took several of the children and went in search of it? It would not take long, and a lame horse would slow their journey, he pointed out reasonably. By the time Ewan asked if the captain would mind if he made some repairs to the roof over the end of the main hall while they were waiting, Tarja threw his hands up in defeat. He climbed the tower again and looked out over the grasslands toward the border, trying to convince himself that he wasn't wasting time. Davydd followed him up the crumbling steps.

"Let me guess. You'd like to build a schoolhouse for them, while we're here."

Davydd smiled. "Actually, I thought perhaps a morning room, facing east, with a vine-covered trellis, and maybe a solarium on the west wing"

Tarja shook his head. "Tell me Lieutenant, just exactly how are we going to explain the presence of these heathens to our superiors? Or the fact that we did nothing to evict them?"

"Heathens, sir? I've seen no altars, or sacrifices, or other signs of pagan worship. They are orphans in the care of a retired Sister, aren't they?" Davydd had conveniently forgotten about the acorn amulet Bereth wore.

"You could be right. Besides, the keep is of no strategic value." He leaned against the crumbling wall and studied the young man curiously. "I'm not sure what surprises me most, Lieutenant, your willingness to overlook this irregularity or the fact that every man here seems bent on aiding these children."

The younger man shrugged. "Garet Warner's first rule is to assess any situation according to the seriousness of the threat. A handful of orphans and a bitter old woman hardly constitute a danger to Medalon's security, sir. As for the men, most of them have children of their own. There's nothing sinister or treasonous in their reaction to the children's plight."

"There's that word 'treason' again. You seem to use it a lot, Lieutenant."

"It's this fort, I think. It has that effect on people."

"I know what you mean. Perhaps we should name this place Treason Keep?"

Davydd smiled. "I imagine you'll have some explaining to do if you put that in your report to Commandant Warner, sir."

Tarja smiled thinly at the thought and looked back toward the border as a flash of sunlight reflecting off metal caught his eye. He scanned the horizon curiously until he saw it again. A cloud of dust hanging in the still air of the cool morning approached the keep, although it was yet several leagues away.

"What do you suppose that is?" he asked, pointing in the direction of the dust cloud.

The lieutenant moved to Tarja's side and studied the plain for a moment. "Horses. Quite a few of them, I'd say. Coming in from the north, which means they're coming from Karien. It could be a trading caravan."

"Wearing armor?" Tarja asked, as the sunlight flashed like an irregular signal in the distance. "Still, it's too small to be an invasion force."

"A delegation, perhaps?"

"Possibly." Tarja rubbed his chin thoughtfully. "Lord Pieter prefers to travel by water. He doesn't like the idea of overland travel."

"But it's also the long way round. Maybe time is more important than impressing a few Medalonian peasants with his big boat. The Fardohnyans might be making things difficult, too. King Hablet enjoys reminding King Jasnoff that Fardohnya controls Karien's access to the only decent port in the north."

"That's assuming it is Lord Pieter."

"It almost has to be," Davydd told him. "No knight is permitted to leave Karien for fear of them being corrupted by the godless mores of the south—unless they're at war or have a special dispensation from the Church of Xaphista. Pieter is the only knight with a standing dispensation, due to his role as King Jasnoff's Envoy to the Citadel."

Tarja looked at Davydd. "You appear remarkably well informed about the Kariens, Lieutenant."

"I'm an intelligence officer, sir. It's my job," the young man shrugged.

He nodded, willing to accept the lieutenant's quiet confidence. "Get the men together, then. Tell Nork to take the second packhorse as a spare mount and head for the Citadel. He's not to stop for anything. He must let them know what's coming."

"Do we know what's coming?" Davydd asked curiously.

"Trouble," Tarja told him with certainty. "Find the banner. It should be packed among the gear somewhere."

"We're going to meet them?"

Tarja nodded, glancing back at the advancing Kariens. "I want to know what they're doing out here. I would also rather they avoided this keep. Besides, if they are trying to surprise us, imagine how annoyed they're going to be to find themselves being met by an official guard of honor."

Davydd saluted sharply and hurried down the perilous steps to carry out his orders. Tarja turned back to watching the Kariens uneasily, wondering what trouble their unexpected appearance heralded.

A single rider cantered forward to meet them as Tarja and his men rode to confront the interlopers. His initial instinct was confirmed as he noticed pennants being hastily unfurled and the party forming into some sort of official order as the Defenders approached. The rider wore a full suit of elaborately gilded armor, his helmet topped by an impressive plume of blue feathers. His breastplate was adorned with a golden star intersected by a silver lightning bolt. The symbol of Xaphista, the Overlord.

"Halt and identify yourselves," the armored knight demanded as he neared them. His lance was topped with a blue pennant that snapped loudly in the cold wind.

"Identify yourself," Tarja called back. "You are on Medalonian soil now."

The knight slowed his horse and raised his faceplate to look at them. "I am Lord Pieter, Envoy of the Karien King, His Majesty Jasnoff the Third."

Tarja bowed in his saddle. "Lord Pieter. I am Captain Tenragan. I believe we met at the Citadel on your last visit."

The knight rode closer and studied Tarja for a moment, before breaking into a relieved smile. "Joyhinia's son! Of course! You gave me quite a start there, young man. For a moment, I thought word of my visit had preceded me. It really wasn't necessary for your mother to send an escort, although I appreciate her gesture. It augurs well for our future negotiations."

"Time and discretion are of the essence, my Lord," he replied, trying to give the impression he knew what Pieter was referring to. "We are here to ensure your safe and timely arrival."

"Excellent!" Lord Pieter declared. "Let's head for that ruin behind you and have some lunch, shall we?"

"That would be inadvisable, my Lord," Tarja advised. "The ruin is in a dangerous state of repair, and I would rather forgo an elaborate meal for the chance to expedite your journey."

Pieter sighed but nodded in agreement. "You are right, of course.

Your prudence does you credit, Captain. We shall place ourselves in your care."

The remainder of Lord Pieter's caravan had now reached them. It consisted of two heavily laden wagons, twenty men-at-arms, and, to Tarja's surprise, a number of veiled women riding side-saddle in front of the lead wagon. But the figure that caught his attention was a small, tonsured man, who glared at the Defenders suspiciously. Pieter turned as his party reached them and waved the priest to him. "Elfron! Come here! Joyhinia has sent her son to guide us to the Citadel."

The priest rode forward and stared at the Defenders for a moment, before raising his staff and laying it expectantly on Tarja's shoulder. When nothing happened, he withdrew the staff.

"He is who he claims to be," the priest announced with satisfaction.

Tarja looked at the priest curiously. "Was there any doubt that I was not?"

Elfron's expression darkened. "Only through eternal vigilance can the light of the Overlord be allowed to shine in its full splendor, Captain. The wicked glamors of the Harshini can be used to disguise one's true nature. Had you been an agent of evil, you would be writhing in unbearable agony by now. Such is the power of the Overlord."

"The Harshini are extinct. How do you know the staff works?" It was a dangerous thing to say. Xaphista's priests were notoriously fanatical, but he couldn't resist baiting him.

"You do not believe in the power of the Overlord?" the priest asked, a dangerous edge to his voice.

"Medalonians believe in no gods," Tarja reminded him. "Not your god, nor the dead Harshini gods, nor anyone else's. Loyalty to the state first is our creed, as well you know. I ask merely out of scientific curiosity."

"Yes, yes," Lord Pieter snapped. "Enough theology for now. You can convert him along the way, Elfron. We must keep moving. Tell me, Captain, how far is it to the nearest village?"

"If we make good time we can be in Lilyvale by this evening, my Lord."

"Does this village have a decent inn? I am heartily sick of roughing it out here in the wilderness."

"It's small but adequate," Tarja assured him. With the prospect of sleeping in a bed tonight, Pieter would lose all interest in stopping at the keep. "I suggest we get moving, if we are to reach it by nightfall."

"Yes, yes," Pieter agreed. "By all means. Will you ride with me, Captain?" Pieter glanced meaningfully at the priest for a moment. "I find myself in need of some secular conversation."

"I would be honored, my Lord."

Elfron wheeled his mount around so hard that Tarja winced in sympathy for the poor beast's mouth. He turned his own mount and fell in beside Pieter as the caravan moved off, leading them on a wide route to avoid Treason Keep. Davydd and the Defenders waited until the wagons had passed and then joined the caravan at the end of the line.

Once Elfron was out of earshot, Pieter leaned across to Tarja. "I would give my life for the Overlord, but I wonder at his choice in ministers, sometimes. I am sure Elfron has been set on me as some sort of test."

"He seems very dedicated," Tarja agreed, forcing himself not to smile. It was a relief that not all Kariens were as dedicated to the Overlord as Elfron. On the other hand, Pieter was Jasnoff's Envoy. He was just as dedicated to the pursuit of power and territory as Elfron was to his god. It made the knight more dangerous than he appeared. At least the priest made no secret of his ambitions.

"Dedicated!" Pieter scoffed. "He's a raving fanatic! It must come from such an unnatural upbringing. They all come from the same island, you know. The Isle of Slarn in the Gulf. It's a godforsaken lump of rock, and I'm sure it does something to their minds. If I hear one more word about sin on this journey, I shall go mad."

"I have no experience with the concept of sin, my Lord, so I promise not to raise the subject," Tarja assured him.

Pieter looked at him thoughtfully. "No experience with sin, eh? In that case," he added, lowering his voice, although none of the party following them would be likely to overhear their conversation. "When we get to this inn, do you think you could arrange some . . . company, for me?"

"Company?" Tarja asked innocently.

"Don't be obtuse man. You know what I mean!"

Tarja glanced over his shoulder. "Isn't the company you have with you sufficiently entertaining?"

"They are nuns, Captain," the Envoy complained. "Dry old virgins, every one of them. Sworn to the Overlord. I'd get more satisfaction out of a knothole in a tree stump! I need something young and plump and alive!"

"Lilyvale is a small village, my Lord," Tarja warned. "There may not be any professional company available."

"Find me an innkeeper's daughter then, man! Somebody like that young Probate at the Citadel who was so willing on my last visit. She was most enthusiastic."

Tarja remembered Pieter cornering one of the Probates at Joyhinia's reception, but he hadn't realized the man had actually bedded the girl. The thought made him cringe. The man was old enough to be her grandfather.

"I'll see what I can do, my Lord," Tarja promised, a little uneasily. He was a captain of the Defenders, not a panderer. He had no wish to find himself procuring women for this man all the way to the Citadel.

"I know you'll do your best, Captain," the Envoy said confidently. "I trust your presence here means that your mother intends to keep her promise."

Tarja glanced at the Envoy, hoping his ignorance didn't show.

"Perhaps Joyhinia has not shared our agreement with you?"

The honor of the Defenders prevented Tarja from lying outright, but there was the truth—and there was the truth.

"I hold a special place in my mother's heart, my Lord," he assured the Envoy with complete honesty. No need to mention that Joyhinia did not actually have a heart. "I would not be here, otherwise."

"Of course," Pieter agreed. "I meant no offense. I'm just a little surprised she so willingly gave me what I asked for. Or that you appear unperturbed by the arrangement. But then, you Medalonians do look at the world differently from the rest of us."

What? Tarja wanted to scream impatiently. *What had Joyhinia offered this man?*

"I mean," the Envoy continued, oblivious to Tarja's frustration, "when the Sisters themselves pop out bastards by the score, one can hardly expect the same sort of familial attachment as we in Karien hold dear. I can recount to you my family's history for the past thirty-five generations. Most of you Medalonians don't even know who your fathers are. You're a bastard, I believe?"

"Legitimacy is determined by one's mother in Medalon," Tarja pointed out. "Her marital status is irrelevant."

"A convenient policy. It accounts for your complacency. Although, there is such a difference in your ages, one could hardly expect you to feel much attachment to the girl."

Tarja's stomach lurched as he thought he understood what Pieter had meant about his complacency, his lack of family ties. He gripped his reins until his knuckles were white, to stop himself from reaching for the

Envoy and pulling him to the ground in a metallic clatter to beat the truth out of him.

"You speak of my sister?" Tarja inquired as calmly as possible. *My sister, who isn't my sister*, he thought. *The child for whom a whole village was destroyed to protect Joyhinia's lies.*

"Delightful girl," Pieter agreed with an enthusiastic nod. "Met her the last time I was at the Citadel. Not my type, of course, much too skinny for my taste, but who am I to question the Overlord? Still, I think your mother should be quite satisfied with her bargain."

"I'm sure she will be," Tarja agreed with an equanimity he did not feel. "Provided you keep your end of the deal."

Pieter was offended by the mere suggestion. "Captain, I can assure you, I will do as I promised. I will stand before the Quorum and denounce Mahina's handling of the heathens. King Jasnoff takes the whole issue of the treaty most seriously, and Mahina's inability to suppress the heathens is of great concern to him. If the Sisterhood does not gain some measure of control over the situation, we will be forced to take the matter into our own hands. Fortunately, your mother seems aware of this, which is why we are prepared to support her as First Sister."

"If you are so firmly behind my mother, I wonder that you need R'shiel to sweeten the deal," he remarked, holding back his rage by sheer force of will. His horse sidestepped nervously, as if he could feel his rider's fury. Why? Why does he want R'shiel? As a hostage to ensure Joyhinia's cooperation?

"I don't want the girl, Captain, the Overlord does. Why do you think I suffer a priest on this journey? Elfron had a vision or something, probably the result of too much self-flagellation, I suspect, but one does not question a priest when he's on a mission from Xaphista. If the Overlord wants your sister, then he shall have her." He looked at Tarja closely. "Perhaps you are not as comfortable with this arrangement as you first appeared, Captain?"

Tarja forced himself to shrug. "As you said, my Lord, we Medalonians have a different view of the world. You might do well to remember that, when dealing with my mother."

The Envoy nodded in agreement, and they rode on in silence for a time. The keep and its desperate occupants slowly disappeared from view. Tarja kept his anger tightly under control. Lord Pieter's agreement with his mother was too awful to comprehend. Joyhinia was planning to impeach Mahina and was prepared to sell R'shiel to the Kariens to do it.

Yesterday, he might have considered such a plan beyond even her, but in light of what Bereth had told him, he did not doubt it at all. R'shiel was not even her child. Which brought to mind another disturbing question. Whose child was she?

Tarja glanced back down the column wondering where Davydd and the others were. When they got to Lilyvale this evening, maybe he could invent an excuse to send the lieutenant on ahead. He had to warn Mahina that the instrument of her downfall was riding toward the Citadel while she unsuspectingly made plans for the future. He had to warn R'shiel that Joyhinia had traded her for the First Sister's mantle.

And he had to find out why the Kariens wanted R'shiel so badly they were prepared to unseat the First Sister just to get their hands on her.

chapter 11

It was another week before Gwenell declared R'shiel was fit enough to return to her mother's apartments. She was discharged with strict instructions regarding her diet, how much weight she was expected to gain, and the herbal infusions she was required to take daily to regain her strength. R'shiel grimaced when she saw the list. Gwenell was one of those physics who thought the worse something tasted, the better it was for you.

It was late in the morning, and Joyhinia was not home when R'shiel knocked on the door of her mother's apartment. Old Hella opened it, pushed back a strand of wiry gray hair, and sighed mournfully when she saw R'shiel.

"Come in, then," she said. "Your mother told me you'd be arrivin' today. It's not as if I don't have enough to do, without nursin' an invalid."

"I don't like this any more than you do, Hella. I won't be in the way."

"Easy for you to say, girl," the old woman grumbled. "I've already wasted a whole mornin' airin' your room out. I've sent the wall hangin's to be cleaned, so you'll have to suffer the heathen creatures on the walls till they get back. I don't know what your mother was thinkin'," lettin' you come here. It's not as if I don't have anythin' to do round here."

Hella enjoyed being a martyr, a handy attribute when one worked for Joyhinia. R'shiel let her grumble on without interruption and carried her bag through to the room she had occupied as a child. She pushed open the door and looked around in astonishment.

The wall on her right glowed softly with the late morning Brightening, filling the room with gentle white light. Her bed, a large, carved four-poster, sat in the same position it always had against the wall. On the far wall, underneath the diamond-paned window beside the hearth, a match-ing dresser, polished to a soft gleam, stood unmoved from where it had always been. As long as she could remember, the wall on her left had been covered by a floor-to-ceiling tapestry depicting the stern countenance of Sister Param holding court with the first Quorum.

But now, the wooden frame where the tapestry had been nailed was empty, revealing the most astonishing scene R'shiel had ever seen.

A huge golden dragon, its wings outstretched, swooped down over a tall mountain range, where a white palace of impossible beauty sat perched high on the central peak. The wall was etched, yet smooth to the touch. The colors had not faded, despite the mural's great age. It was as if the etchings were living images sealed behind glass. As she moved closer, the individual components of the illustration became clearer. What had at first seemed just a large landscape was filled with exquisite detail.

On the slopes of the mountain leading to the many-spired palace were figures of slender, naked, golden-skinned children, gamboling with small, wrinkled gray creatures amidst trees that seemed to have every individual leaf depicted in minute and loving detail. The closer she looked, the more complexity she discovered, the more the mural revealed. R'shiel thought with wonder that she could stand here for hours and still not take it all in. Were these the long dead Harshini? Were the tall graceful men leaning on the balconies and the black-eyed, elegant women the people of the lost race? Were the squat, ugly creatures supposed to be demons? She had expected them to be much more fearsome. She studied the dragon again, wondering how anyone could have conceived of such a creature, even in their imagination. A rider sat on the shoulders of the dragon, dressed in dark, velvety, skin-tight leathers, his dark red hair streaming out behind him, his expression rapturous. R'shiel smiled as she looked at him, think-ing she would be wearing a similar expression if she had been riding such a glorious creature.

"Hope it don't give you nightmares," Hella said, pushing past R'shiel clutching fresh linen for the bed. The old woman looked at the mural for a moment and shuddered. "Damn, if that thing don't give me the creeps."

"It's beautiful."

All the years she had slept in this room she had never suspected the mural was there, although she had seen other etchings and other murals in more public places throughout the Citadel. Usually such artworks were painted over, but some of them had a surface that simply refused to take the whitewash. Those were covered with heavy, concealing tapestries. It was almost mandatory to accept a dare to sneak a look at the images of the forbidden Harshini depicted behind the tapestry in the Lesser Hall, which listed the virtues of the Sisterhood in dry, formal stitches. But she had never before seen a Harshini mural in the full light of day. Guilty glimpses of pale murals by torchlight were nothing compared to this.

"Beautiful?" Hella snorted. "It's wicked! Look at those heathens! Not one of them is doing a lick of work. Just lollin' about naked or fornicatin' like animals."

R'shiel had to study the mural for quite a while before she discovered the couple Hella referred to, through one of the tall windows in the palace, locked in an explicit embrace that made her blush. She wondered how long Hella had studied the mural to find them.

"Well, I'll try not to let it distract me," she promised.

"See that they don't," Hella warned, tugging on the sheets to tuck them in. She finished making up the bed and straightened her back painfully. "There! Now you get yourself unpacked, and then we'll be seein' about lunch. You look thin as a broom handle. I don't know about young girls, these days. In my day, you took what food you was given and gladly. And you didn't starve yourself till you looked like a refugee, neither."

R'shiel wanted to tell Hella that she had done nothing of the kind, but there didn't seem much point. As she left the room, still muttering about what it was like in her day, R'shiel crossed the room to the dresser and picked up the silver-backed hand-mirror that Joyhinia had given her on her twelfth birthday. It had never left this room. Such a gift was too valuable to leave lying around in the Dormitories, where girls of less noble breeding might be tempted. Or so Joyhinia had claimed.

She looked at her reflection, a little surprised at how thin her face was. Gwenell had prescribed a number of infusions to cleanse her liver, claiming her skin was yellowing, a sure sign that her liver was not functioning properly, and no doubt the reason for her inexplicable aversion to meat. R'shiel couldn't see it herself, but one did not argue with Gwenell and hope to win on matters relating to the human body. The black circles under her eyes had faded a little, but her violet eyes seemed darker than normal, almost indigo. It was no doubt a sign of her failing kidneys, she thought grumpily. Or perhaps a sign of irregular bowels. R'shiel was heartily sick of the whole topic of her health. She actually felt better than she had in months. Her headaches had vanished, her appetite had returned, and everything seemed clearer, sharper than it had before. The prospect of spending another four weeks until Founders' Day, recuperating under the watchful eye of her mother and Hella, was extremely depressing.

"R'shiel!"

She sighed at the sound of her mother's voice and placed the mirror carefully on the dresser. No doubt Joyhinia had returned to the apartment for lunch. That she might have come home to check on her daughter, to assure herself she was well, did not occur to R'shiel, anymore that it would have occurred to Joyhinia.

Now that she was home for every meal and her mother was no longer compelled to set aside time for her daughter, dinnertime in Joyhinia's apartment became an informal meeting of her cronies. Hella was given the evenings off, and R'shiel served her mother's guests, as befitted her status as a Probate, albeit a temporarily inactive one. The most frequent guest was Jacomina, who would sit in silence and listen to Joyhinia list her endless complaints regarding Mahina's mismanagement of the Sisterhood and Joyhinia's plans to correct things, once she was First Sister. Much of Joyhinia's rhetoric sounded as if she were rehearsing for a public forum.

One evening, soon after R'shiel arrived, Harith joined the small gathering. She appeared uncomfortable to begin with, gulping down her first glass of wine with indecent haste. Joyhinia wisely kept the conversation on mundane, everyday things all through the main course and dessert. Not until the women took their wine and moved to the armchairs around the fire, did Harith finally seem sufficiently at ease to discuss the reason for her visit.

"As you know, I've little patience with your schemes normally, Joyhinia," she began, staring into the flames to avoid meeting the other woman's eyes. Joyhinia and Jacomina remained silent. R'shiel cleared the table as quietly as possible, afraid that the clattering of dishes would draw attention to her presence. For once, this looked like being interesting, and she did not want to be banished to her room. "But this time, I fear you may be right."

Joyhinia nodded solemnly. "My first care has always been for Medalon, Harith."

"Perhaps," Harith remarked, rather more skeptically than Joyhinia would have liked. "But as you know, Sister Suelen, the First Sister's Secretary, is my niece. She brought something to my attention that I find disturbing."

"Much of Mahina's administration is disturbing," Joyhinia agreed. "Exactly what has she done that causes you concern?"

Harith took another gulp of her wine. "I think Mahina is planning to declare war on Karien."

Joyhinia looked astonished, although R'shiel suspected she was acting for Harith's sake. "I believe Mahina capable of many things, but I doubt she would deliberately provoke an armed conflict with an enemy so much stronger than us."

"Jenga has had several meetings with Mahina in the past few weeks," Harith told them. "One of which included that sly little bastard Garet Warner and your son, who, I might add, has not been seen in the Citadel for weeks. Rumor has it he is in the north already."

Joyhinia leaned back in her chair and rested her chin on steepled fingers.

"R'shiel!"

"Mother?" she replied, startled to be included in the conversation.

"Did Tarja say where he was going when he visited you in the Infirmary?"

The question surprised her. Was Joyhinia keeping tabs on her? "He said he was doing a survey of the northern border villages for Commandant Warner."

Harith nodded with satisfaction. "There! What did I tell you!"

"That hardly proves she's planning to start a war, Harith." Joyhinia was enjoying this rare chance to be the voice of moderation.

"No? Then why has she got detailed plans, costs, even troop numbers and plans for a civilian militia, sitting on her desk?"

From where R'shiel stood, gently stacking the dishes on the small cart, ready for their return to the kitchen, her mother looked to her like a hawk about to swoop down on an unsuspecting rabbit. "Are you certain of this, Harith?"

"I've seen them myself. She plans to create a civil militia to bolster the Defenders and move a good half of the troops to the northern border."

"King Jasnoff will take that as an act of war," Jacomina pointed out with alarm.

"Perhaps Mahina already knows that." Joyhinia looked at the two women closely, gauging their mood. "I have just learned that Lord Pieter is on his way back to the Citadel. King Jasnoff of Karien is unhappy with the upsurge of heathen cults, and these demon-child rumors refuse to go away. Mahina's lenient attitude toward the heathens is just as dangerous as her plans for war."

"Who would have thought a mouse like Mahina would turn out to be a warmonger?" Jacomina smirked. Both Joyhinia and Harith looked at the Mistress of Enlightenment in annoyance.

"She has to be stopped. If she continues on this course, she will destroy Medalon."

"I wholeheartedly agree, Harith, but such a course of action could be considered treason, if not handled correctly."

Harith's eyes narrowed. "What do you mean?"

"Mahina must be impeached. Legally, openly, and without any doubt that the Quorum is in full agreement. If not, the Defenders will refuse to swear allegiance to the new First Sister. Mahina would be quite within her rights to have us hanged as traitors." Joyhinia seemed to be deliberately trying to frighten her cohorts. Maybe she wanted to be sure now, before this moved from discussion to action, that her coconspirators would see this through to the bitter end.

"Then we need Francil," Harith said.

"Francil will never agree," Jacomina scoffed.

"She will if you give her what she wants. Everyone has their price, even Francil."

"So what is her price?" Harith asked.

Joyhinia shrugged, smiling coldly. "I have no idea, Harith, but believe me, I intend to find out."

As Founders' Day drew nearer and with it the start of winter, the frequency of tense and furtive meetings in the apartment increased. Blue-robed sisters came and went, often looking up and down the hall nervously before they entered to ensure they were not observed. Joyhinia displayed a disturbing lack of trust in her daughter, so R'shiel was excluded from the discussions. But she overheard enough to know that her mother was planning to denounce Mahina at the annual Gathering following the Founders' Day Parade, with the aide of the Karien Envoy.

R'shiel wanted no part in the plot. As Mistress of Enlightenment, the First Sister had educated hundreds of Novices, Probates, and Cadets— R'shiel and Tarja included. Mahina was a popular figure, particularly among the Defenders. She had championed the cause for Cadets to receive an education equivalent to that of Probates.

Torn between loyalty to her mother and her affection for Mahina, R'shiel didn't know what to do. Short of going to Mahina and warning her personally, she could think of no way to foil her mother's plans—and even that notion proved a futile hope. Joyhinia was well aware of R'shiel's sympathy for Mahina's policies and had obviously taken precautions. Hella seemed to be under orders to ensure that she remained cut off from the outside world and watched her like a fox sitting outside a chicken coop. Junee and Kilene were turned away when they came to visit. There was no way of getting to the First Sister, no way of warning her. Even a note would be subject to Suelen's scrutiny. R'shiel fretted over her helplessness. It burned in her gut like a bad meal.

In spite of Joyhinia's schemes, R'shiel recovered her strength quickly, gained a little weight, although not nearly as much as Sister Gwenell would have liked, and began to feel almost like her old self again.

Almost. Some things were not quite the same. For one thing, she had grown even taller, as if her menses had triggered one final growth spurt. She had always been tall for her age, but now she could look many of the Defenders in the eye. Joyhinia did not seem to notice, although she only came up to her daughter's chin. R'shiel wondered if her height came from her father. Jenga was a big man, and she guessed she was as tall as he was now. She had not had another bleeding, but Gwenell did not seem concerned about it. These things took time to settle into a cycle, the physic had assured her when she came to visit under Hella's watchful eye. R'shiel fervently hoped her next cycle would not be as spectacular as the first.

Strangely, her skin had retained the golden cast it had acquired during her illness, despite the herbal infusions. Gwenell was far more worried about it than R'shiel was. She felt fine and did not think, as Gwenell grimly forecast, that her liver was in imminent danger of collapse. However, she drank the bitter herbal tea each day to avoid a well-meaning lecture, if nothing else.

As Founders' Day drew nearer, R'shiel became aware of something else that she could not even explain to herself, let alone Sister Gwenell. It happened the first time when she was sitting by the fire, waiting for Joyhinia to come home. She had dozed off in the warmth of the room, which was stuffy and overheated. Hella had come in, fussing about something or other. R'shiel opened her eyes and glanced at the old woman, startled to discover a faint shimmering light surrounding her, fractured with pale red lines and swirling with dark colors. She blinked in surprise and the vision disappeared, but she had seen it again, on odd occasions, about other people. She could not explain it or control it and was quite certain that if she mentioned it, Gwenell would produce another evil-smelling concoction to cure her of the spells.

But even more disturbing was something so intangible that she wondered if, like the auras she imagined around people, she was just inventing it. It had begun as a gentle tugging that caught her unawares as she was about to fall asleep one evening to the muted voices of Joyhinia and Harith plotting the downfall of Mahina in the other room. It was a feeling that someone or something was waiting for her, calling to her. A feeling that there was something just out of her reach and that if only she embraced it, it would make her complete.

The notion had grown steadily stronger in the past few weeks, until R'shiel had to consciously force herself to ignore it. It made no sense. Finally, R'shiel decided that it must be the result of her inability to prevent Joyhinia's coup. Mahina may not be ruling Medalon the way Joyhinia liked, but she did not deserve to be unseated for it. Harith was, perhaps, genuinely concerned, but Joyhinia's power grab was entirely selfish. Jacomina simply followed along in her mother's wake. Francil, whom R'shiel had always considered the least corruptible member of the Quorum, had sold out for the promise of immortality.

Joyhinia had, as she predicted, quickly discovered the old sister's price. Francil wanted to remain Mistress of the Citadel until she died. She wanted to name her own successor, and she wanted her name immortalized, in recognition of her long service to the Sisterhood. R'shiel was appalled when Francil had joined the others for the Restday dinner fully prepared to support them. On Joyhinia's elevation to First Sister, the Great Hall would be renamed Francil's Hall, the conspirators agreed. It was no wonder, R'shiel decided, that she was feeling as if the Citadel was suddenly alien to her. The honor of the Sisterhood had proved to be a commodity that could be bought and sold as easily as fish at the Port Sha'rin markets. She asked herself the same question that Tarja had posed in the Infirmary, over and over again. She was coming to think of it as The Question. *What would you do if you don't become a Blue Sister?* She had no answer, and the nothingness beyond paralyzed her.

Three days before Founders' Day, R'shiel was in her room, lying on her stomach across the bed staring at the Harshini mural. Losing herself in the forbidden mural meant not having to answer The Question. Every day she discovered something new in the picture, whether it was a den of snow foxes filled with playful, black-eyed cubs, or the solitary, golden figure who stood on the peak of a snowcapped mountain, reaching up with hands outstretched, to speak with the thunderstorm that hovered above him. Perhaps the man on the mountain was a sorcerer or a wizard and the clouds his magic? Was the storm meant to represent the Weather God, she wondered?

Did the Harshini have a Weather God? They seemed to have gods for everything else.

"R'shiel!"

She jumped guiltily. Joyhinia glared at the mural before turning to her daughter.

"Where are the wall hangings?" she asked, irritably.

"Hella sent them to be cleaned," R'shiel explained, hurriedly climbing to her feet.

"That was weeks ago. Hella!"

The old maid appeared at the bedroom door wiping her hands on her apron. "My Lady?"

"Find out where the wall hangings for R'shiel's room are," she ordered. "At once! I want them back where they belong by this evening!"

"As you wish, my Lady." Hella turned away muttering to herself.

Joyhinia ignored the maid and turned her attention back to R'shiel. "You're still too thin."

"Oh, so you noticed?"

Joyhinia seemed distracted. So distracted she did not rise to the taunt. "That's what I came to see you about. You appear to be recovered, and I see no reason for you to stay any longer. You may move back to the Dormitories today. I will send for you when I need you."

With a sinking heart, she realized her emancipation meant that Joyhinia's plans were so well advanced that she could do them no harm, even if she marched straight from the apartment to the First Sister's office. "As you wish, Mother."

Joyhinia nodded absently and glanced at the mural again. "Damned heathens. That wall makes my skin crawl."

chapter 12

It took nearly two hours for the Founders' Day Parade to wend its way through the streets of the Citadel to the amphitheater. The weather was perfect for the event: cool but sunny, not a cloud marring the cobalt blue sky. First Sister Mahina, her Quorum and their families, Lord Draco, and the Lord Defender watched the parade from the steps of the Great Hall. The Defender's drum band led the parade; their crisp marching tattoo almost drowned out by the cheering spectators who lined the route five deep on either side of the street. They were followed by every Defender in the Citadel not engaged in controlling the crowd that had flocked to the Citadel for the parade.

Following the infantry, who marched ten abreast in precise unison, the cavalry appeared, their perfectly groomed horses stepping proudly on the cobbled street, bringing an even louder cheer as they rode by. Jenga's stern expression softened a little as he took the salute, his fist over his heart. The Defenders were his life, and the sight of them, in their full dress uniforms, their red jackets pressed, silver buttons glinting in the sunlight, never failed to touch him. Mahina stood beside him and smiled at him as the cavalry passed.

"Your Defenders do us proud, my Lord," she said.

"They are *your* Defenders, your Grace," he replied, with genuine respect for the old woman.

"Then they do us both proud," she agreed graciously.

Jenga bowed to the First Sister and turned back to watch the Parade. Following on the heels of the cavalry were the floats of the Merchant Guilds. The first was a huge wicker pig on a flower-draped wagonbed drawn by ten burly men, all dressed in matching green aprons, their thick

MEDALON ·

leather belts displaying an impressive array of dangerous-looking knives. Behind the Butcher's Guild, the Brewer's Guild and their float appeared. If they could not be first in the parade, then they were determined to be the most popular, Jenga decided. A number of young women, dressed in barely decent white shifts, were dipping into the barrels, passing out free tankards of ale to anyone within reach. The float had collected a tail of enthusiastic youngsters, eager to take advantage of this unexpected bounty.

On the tail of the raucous throng trailing the Brewer's Guild, the float of the Musician's Guild trundled into view, although he heard them well before they rounded the corner. Their wagon was packed with fiddlers, harpists, and flautists, belting out a merry air as their wagon trundled past the Great Hall, the melody interrupted sporadically as tankards of ale were passed along from the Brewer's wagon in front. The parade was entertaining, but after ten or more floats had passed by, Jenga found his mind wandering to other things.

Five days ago Corporal Nork arrived with a message from Tarja warning that the Karien Envoy was probably on his way to the Citadel. There was no good reason why the Envoy would return to the Citadel so soon or why he would discomfort himself by traveling overland to do it. The only thing he could think of was that perhaps the Envoy had a deadline to meet. If Nork's information was correct, and he had no reason to assume that it was not, then they should have arrived days ago. Had something happened to the Envoy? Or Tarja? Had they been delayed by accident? Or by design? The worry niggled at Jenga like a toothache. Even more worrying was that Mahina was not expecting the Kariens. When Jenga had passed on Tarja's message, Mahina had been as surprised as he was.

To further add to his woes, Garet Warner was certain that Joyhinia Tenragan was up to something and had sought permission several weeks ago to investigate the matter.

Jenga's responsibility was the defense of Medalon. He had no charter to investigate the goings on among the Sisters of the Blade. Nor did he wish to become involved in anything that Joyhinia Tenragan was mixed up in. She had been scheming and plotting for as long as he had known her, and even he was not immune to her machinations.

His brother had been gone from the Citadel these past twenty-three years, his crime forgotten. Dayan had hardly distinguished himself on the southern border, but he had kept out of trouble. Joyhinia remembered

Dayan, though. The woman standing on Joyhinia's left, Jacomina Larosse, the Mistress of Enlightenment, had her position because Joyhinia delighted in reminding Jenga that her testimony would see his brother hanged. The fact that Dayan had been little more than a foolish Cadet at the time and Jacomina a frivolous Probate, did not lessen his crime. Rape was a capital offense and Jacomina's silence was the result of Joyhinia's intervention. For that he had turned a blind eye to a great deal, and he did not want a man of Garet Warner's piercing intellect investigating anything about Joyhinia, if he could avoid it.

He had refused Garet permission and been content with his decision, but since Nork had thundered into the Citadel on a horse that was almost foundered, Jenga wondered if he had done the right thing. Was Joyhinia up to something more serious than usual? Did it have anything to do with the sudden return of the Envoy? And where was he? Where was Tarja?

For all that he loathed Joyhinia and despaired of the hold she had over him, her unwanted son held a special place in Jenga's affection. His mother had placed him in the Cadets at the tender age of ten—the youngest boy Jenga had ever accepted as a Cadet—and then only because Trayla had ordered him to take the boy in. Despite his misgivings about the boy's ability to cope, Tarja had thrived away from his mother. If anything, Jenga suspected he had excelled to ensure that he was in no danger of being returned to her care. As an adult, Tarja was one of a handful of men whom Jenga trusted implicitly and among the even smaller number of men whom Jenga counted as a friend. He had missed Tarja sorely, when Trayla banished him to the southern border, although he had considered the young man lucky to escape the First Sister's wrath so lightly. One did not insult the First Sister so publicly and expect to get away with it, no matter how much even Jenga had silently agreed with Tarja's blunt and extremely tactless assessment of her character.

"Shall we join the people for lunch, my Lord?"

Jenga started a little at Mahina's question, rather surprised to see the last float slowly disappearing around the corner of the huge Library building across the street. The crowd flowed into the street in the wake of the wagon, heading for the amphitheater and the banquet laid out for the citizens of the Citadel. For the next few hours the First Sister and the Quorum would mingle with the people as they partook of the bounty of the

Sisterhood, until the amphitheater was cleared at sundown to allow the annual Gathering to take place.

"Of course, your Grace," Jenga replied with a bow. He offered the First Sister his arm, and together they walked down the steps of the Great Hall, followed by the other dignitaries. As he turned, he caught sight of Joyhinia, muttering something to R'shiel. The girl had changed somewhat since her illness, he thought with concern. She seemed even taller than he remembered, her skin touched by an unfashionable golden tan, her once-violet eyes now almost black. The overall effect was one of strangeness, giving her an almost alien mien, and he found himself wondering again at her parentage. Who had really fathered Joyhinia's child? No Medalonian, that was for certain. Had Joyhinia found herself a Fardohnyan paramour? They tended toward the same swarthy complexion. Or perhaps a Hythrun lover, although they were fairer than their Fardohnyan cousins. But the long-standing mystery of R'shiel's paternity seemed unimportant at this moment. Joyhinia looked annoyed. Had R'shiel said something to upset her mother, or was Joyhinia's concern the same as his, but for different reasons?

Jenga escorted the First Sister into the street and the cheerful, happy crowd. He saw Joyhinia glancing back down the street in the direction the parade had come from, toward the main gate, her expression for a moment unguarded. She was expecting something, he knew with certainty, feeling decidedly uneasy.

The sandy floor of the Arena had been set up with trestles laden with food for the celebrations. The people of the Citadel and the outlying villages, from as far away as Brodenvale and Testra, milled about the tables, loading wooden platters with slices of rare beef, minted lamb, fresh corn, potatoes roasted in their jackets, and wedges of fresh bread that had kept the bakers' guild busy since early this morning. Jenga moved among the crowd, nodding to a familiar face here and there, keeping an eye on the men assigned to ensure that the food was distributed as evenly as possible in this chaos. Generally, once the citizens had their food, they moved up into the tiered seating around the amphitheater, more to avoid being trampled than for comfort. Still, it was early afternoon before the crowd in the Arena began to thin noticeably.

Jenga was on the verge of deciding he could risk trying to get a meal without being crushed when he spied Garet Warner striding purposefully toward him. He had not seen the Commandant all day and wondered where he had been. Even command of the Defenders' Intelligence Corps did not exempt one from the Founders' Day Parade, although Garet undoubtedly had a perfectly good excuse. As he did Tarja, Jenga trusted the man implicitly, but although he respected him, he would hesitate to call him a friend.

"Nice of you to join us, Commandant," Jenga remarked dryly as Garet reached him. "Not keeping you from something important, are we?"

Garet did not even smile. "Actually, you are. Can you get away from here without attracting notice?"

"Whose notice in particular?" Jenga asked.

"Joyhinia Tenragan's," Garet replied.

Jenga frowned. "I specifically ordered you not to involve yourself in matters concerning the Sisterhood, Commandant."

Garet did not flinch from Jenga's disapproving gaze.

"Tarja's back."

Jenga had to force himself not to run.

Tarja's disheveled appearance was in stark contrast to the parade-ground smartness of the rest of the Citadel's Defenders. He was waiting in Jenga's office, standing by the window looking out over the deserted parade ground behind the Defenders' Building, with a young, brown-eyed lieutenant in an equally unkempt condition. Both men looked exhausted.

"Is the Envoy with you?" Jenga asked, without preamble.

Tarja nodded. "I had him taken to the guest apartments with his priest."

"His priest?" Jenga asked in surprise. Lord Pieter rarely traveled with a priest. It inhibited his enjoyment of life outside of Karien far too much. "What's he doing here? Why has he come back?"

"The Karien Envoy is here to denounce Mahina. He and Joyhinia have made some sort of pact."

Jenga sank heavily into his leather-bound chair. "What does she hope to gain from such a display?"

"The First Sister's mantle, probably," Tarja said wearily. "But it gets worse. Joyhinia has agreed to let him have R'shiel in return for his support. According to Pieter, the Overlord spoke to the priest and told him to take R'shiel back to Karien."

Jenga made no attempt to hide his shock. "That's absurd! Surely you're mistaken? Not even Joyhinia would stoop so low!"

"How little you know my mother," Tarja muttered. "But it's a little easier to comprehend when you realize that R'shiel is not her daughter. Or yours, for that matter."

"I can assure you, I have always known she was not my child," he said grimly. "Anyway, what do you mean—not *her* daughter?"

Tarja folded his arms across his chest and leaned against the window. "You tell him, Lieutenant."

With remarkable composure, the lieutenant related the tale of their meeting with Bereth and the orphans, although he omitted any reference to Bereth's conversion to heathen worship. Jenga listened with growing concern as the young man told him of the fate of Haven. He spared Garet a glance, but the Commandant had heard the tale already, and his expression betrayed no emotion. Tarja stared out of the window at some indeterminate point, almost as if he wasn't interested. When the lieutenant finished his report, Jenga sagged back in his chair, not sure where to start.

"Why would she pretend the child is hers?" he asked finally, of nobody in particular.

Tarja glanced at him, as if he should already know the answer. "The only child she gave birth to was inconveniently male. Joyhinia wants a dynasty. For that she needs a daughter. Acquiring somebody else's child is a far less troublesome way of ensuring the succession."

Jenga was a little surprised at Tarja's ability to so objectively analyze his mother's motives, particularly as he had been cast aside to make room for them.

"Perhaps her dynastic ambitions explain her willingness to send R'shiel to Karien," Garet suggested. "This Overlord business could be merely a ruse. If Joyhinia gains the First Sister's mantle, R'shiel becomes an eminently suitable consort for Jasnoff's son. Cratyn is the same age as R'shiel and still unmarried. Why stop at the First Sister's mantle when you can have the Karien crown?"

Tarja shook his head. "Pieter spoke of the priest having a vision. He didn't act like a man coming to escort a bride home."

"What do you intend to do, Tarja?"

"R'shiel is not a child any longer, Jenga. She might be relieved to discover she's not related to Joyhinia. Or me. For that matter, I'm not at all certain she won't jump at the chance to leave the Citadel with the Kariens, whatever the reason. But the real issue here is who ordered that village burned."

Jenga had been wondering the same thing. "Did Bereth know the name of the officer who led the raid?"

Davydd shook his head. "We asked her, but she couldn't name him. She wasn't there when the village was raided."

"Would it surprise anyone to learn that Jacomina was the Administrator in Testra three years ago?" Garet asked.

"Our recently elevated Mistress of Enlightenment?" Tarja replied. "Well, that explains a lot. Order a few hapless villagers torched and get a seat on the Quorum in return."

There were other reasons for Jacomina's elevation, but Jenga did not bother to elaborate. He rubbed his chin as he considered the news, not sure what bothered him most. A whole village had been destroyed by his men, without his knowledge. Who had done such a thing? Who among his officers would so readily turn on his own countrymen?

"Garet, what can Joyhinia hope to achieve by this? Realistically?"

The Commandant thought for a moment before he answered. "At best, it would merely embarrass Mahina. It depends on what the Kariens are threatening. It could just be bluff and bluster on their part."

"And at worst?" Jenga asked, almost afraid to hear the answer.

"Well, in theory, if she has the support of the Quorum and enough of the Blue Sisters, Joyhinia could move to have Mahina impeached."

"Can she do that?" Davydd asked.

"It's happened before," Garet shrugged. "Once. Although in that case the First Sister was accused of murder. I guess the question is whether or not Joyhinia has sufficient support to try it."

Jenga shook his head. "Jacomina would support her, but Harith opposes her on principal and Francil has never been one for involving herself in the power games of the Quorum. I find it hard to believe that a majority of the Blue Sisters would support her."

Tarja laughed harshly at Jenga's assessment of the situation. "I admire your optimism, Jenga, but if Joyhinia moves to impeach the First Sister, I promise you, she has the numbers."

"Then we must warn Mahina."

"Tell her about R'shiel, too," Tarja suggested. "It will give her ammunition to use against Joyhinia. If she's exposed as a liar, it may shake the faith of her supporters." Tarja looked him in the eye, his expression a blatant challenge. "Although there will be some who wonder why you've never denied R'shiel, my Lord."

"Aye, there will be," he agreed uncomfortably. "But that is none of their concern. Or yours."

"But with proof of Joyhinia's deliberate lie . . . " Garet began.

"I said the matter is none of your concern. I'll hear no more about it." The distrust in Tarja's eyes pained him, but he was too far down this road to turn back now. "Tell R'shiel if you must, Tarja. She deserves to know. But you will not reveal it publicly. Nor you, Garet, and that's an order."

The Commandant nodded his agreement with some reluctance and more than a little suspicion.

"Maybe you should tell Lord Pieter," Davydd suggested. The other men looked at him in surprise, and the young man found himself having to defend his statement to the senior officers. "I mean, he's expecting to return with the daughter of the First Sister, isn't he? His enthusiasm might wane a little when he learns she's nothing more than an orphan from the mountains."

"He has a point," Garet remarked thoughtfully.

"If Pieter believes Elfron has spoken with Xaphista, I doubt R'shiel's parentage will unduly concern him."

"Aye, and much as I am fond of the girl, I cannot worry about her at the moment," Jenga added. "I'm more concerned with Joyhinia's plans for this evening,"

"We still have several hours before the Gathering," Garet reminded them. "Perhaps we can think of a way to disrupt her plans by then."

"And perhaps not," Tarja predicted. He looked straight at Jenga. "Have you considered, my Lord, that if Joyhinia succeeds, you will be required to swear allegiance to her?"

"I am the Lord Defender, Tarja. If Joyhinia wins the First Sister's mantle by legal means, I will have no choice but to swear the Oath of Allegiance to her, on behalf of the Defenders."

"You may swear the oath on behalf of everyone but me," Tarja told him bleakly. "I'll not serve under Joyhinia's rule."

"You are a captain of the Defenders," Jenga pointed out, surprised that Tarja would even contemplate such a thing. "You are not some common trooper who can run home to his farm when he is tired of playing soldier. Your oath is binding until death."

"Then I'll desert," Tarja replied. "You can hunt me down and hang me for it, Jenga, but not for any price will I serve in the Defenders if Joyhinia is First Sister."

chapter 13

Despite the promise of perfect weather earlier in the day, impatient storm clouds gathered over the Citadel during the afternoon. By the time the amphitheater was due to be cleared for the Gathering, a blustery wind stirred the treetops, and the dull rumble of thunder could be heard in the distance. Mahina ordered the Gathering moved to the Great Hall and sent word that revellers could stay in the amphitheater as long as the weather held.

The announcement was met with a general cheer, and the Guild musicians struck up another lively tune. They had moved their wagon into the Arena as an impromptu stage, pushed tables back to make way for dancing, and a bonfire was started to stave off the chill of the evening. Every Blue Sister in the Citadel would be at the Gathering as soon as the sun set. The Novices and Probates were left with a rare opportunity to enjoy themselves away from the watchful eyes of their superiors. Fully aware that the young women would be unsupervised until well after midnight, the Defenders hovered around the Arena, waiting for that magical moment when the last blue figure disappeared from view.

R'shiel watched the dancing from the side of the Arena, unconsciously tapping her foot in time to the music, as Junee and Kilene filled her in on all the latest gossip from the dormitories.

"By the Founder's!" Kilene suddenly declared dramatically. "It's him!"

A little taken aback by Kilene's sudden change of subject mid-sentence, R'shiel looked at her friend in puzzlement.

"Davydd Tailorson," Junee explained with a world-weary air. "Kilene goes to sleep every night dreaming about him."

"Who is he?" R'shiel knew most of the officers who had graduated with Tarja by name, but as a rule, she did not follow the goings-on in the

Corps with quite the same dedication as her friends. Having spent the last few weeks in virtual imprisonment in Joyhinia's apartments, she was even more out of touch than usual.

"Over there," Kilene said, "In the red jacket."

"In the red jacket? Kilene, every man here is wearing a red jacket, you fool."

"You know what I mean. He's standing next to Luc Janeson. No! Don't look at him!"

R'shiel had no idea who Luc Janeson was either and in the crowd of red jackets in the fading light, was hard pressed to tell one Defender from another. She glanced at Junee who laughed at both of them. "You'd better get a look at him soon, R'shiel. She'll be in love with someone else before dinnertime."

"Don't be so cynical!" Kilene declared with a wounded look. "I will love him until I die."

"Or until someone better comes along."

"So what's so special about . . . what's his name?"

"Lieutenant Davydd Tailorson," Kilene said with a reverent sigh. "He's in Intelligence."

"He's very intelligent, too," Junee agreed with a wink at R'shiel. "He avoids Kilene like the pox."

"He does not! He's been away, that's all."

"With you panting after him like a bitch in heat, it's a wonder he didn't volunteer for the southern border."

Kilene loftily ignored Junee and stared across the Arena at her idol for a moment before clutching R'shiel's arm painfully. "They're coming over!" she gasped with a mixture of terror and delight.

R'shiel finally spotted Kilene's object of adoration walking toward them with two other lieutenants, weaving their way between the dancers and the helpful souls dragging several large logs toward the bonfire. The sun was almost completely set, and shadows concealed the faces of the Defenders as they approached. Kilene's champion, when he finally drew close enough to be seen clearly, was a young man of average height with a pleasant but unremarkable face.

"Would you ladies care to dance?" he asked, with an elegant bow. "It's too cold to stand around gossiping."

Kilene was on the verge of fainting with happiness. "Yes, please!"

She stepped forward eagerly and was immediately whisked away by the officer standing on Davydd's right, her face crestfallen as she looked back over her shoulder toward the object of her affection as her partner pulled her into the crowd. The young man on his left grabbed Junee with equal enthusiasm, and they too rapidly disappeared.

R'shiel realized she had been very effectively cornered. "Nice maneuver, Lieutenant. Do they teach you that in the Cadets?"

"Actually, they do," he replied. "It's called Divide and Conquer. But fear not, my designs on you are completely honorable."

"Is that so?"

"Tarja wants to see you."

"My brother is in the north." She'd heard her share of lines from dozens of Cadets and Officers, but nobody had ever tried using Tarja before.

"He arrived back earlier today. We both did. With the Karien Envoy."

"Where is he, then?"

"In the caverns under the amphitheater. He asked me to take you to him."

R'shiel studied him for a moment before deciding he was telling her the truth. She let him lead the way toward the tunnel, more curious than concerned, wondering why Tarja wanted to see her.

"Keep watch," Tarja ordered. The lieutenant nodded wordlessly and vanished into the shadows. She looked around curiously. The last time she had been in these caverns, Georj had died fighting Loclon, and she had fainted from the onset of her menses.

"You look a lot better than the last time we met," he told her, taking her hand and leading her deeper into the caverns.

"I can't say the same for you," she remarked, pulling away from him to study him more clearly. He looked exhausted. "In fact, you look like you haven't slept in days."

"I haven't," he agreed wearily, "so that probably accounts for it."

"Are you in trouble again?"

"Not yet," he assured her with a faint grin. "But the night is young."

"I'd laugh, except I have a bad feeling you're not joking. Why all the secrecy? If you wanted to see me, you didn't have to send your lackey. You could have just come to the party, you know."

"I'm not in a party mood." He walked further into the dim cavern. In the distance, R'shiel could hear the faint sounds of a couple giggling and urging each other to silence. They were not the only ones seeking privacy down here tonight.

"So you sent for me? I'm not one of your troopers, Tarja. You can't just order me around like a Cadet." R'shiel knew she sounded angry, and it was hardly fair to take it out on Tarja, but the closer the Gathering came, the more she fretted over what would happen when Joyhinia set her plans in motion.

Tarja didn't seem to notice. He studied his boots for a moment, which were scuffed and dusty with wear, then took a deep breath and looked at her. "I have to tell you something, R'shiel. It's going to be difficult for you to hear it, but you have a right to know."

"What are you talking about?" She could not imagine what he could say that warranted such a warning. Tarja was not normally so cryptic.

He took another deep breath before he answered. "Joyhinia is not your mother."

She stared at him. "What?"

"You're not Joyhinia's daughter."

"That's ridiculous! Of course I'm her daughter! Where would you get such an idea?"

He stood leaning against the wall, his arms crossed. "Your mother was a girl named J'nel Snowbuilder. She lived in a village called Haven, up in the Sanctuary Mountains west of Testra. She died giving birth to you."

"That's absurd!" She walked to the back of the cavern. "I know I was born in Haven. Mother never hid that from anyone. She was pregnant when she left Testra."

"No, she wasn't," he said. "Although it's true that she wintered in Haven that year. You were born to a girl in the village. She took you back to Testra in the spring, claiming you were hers. But you are not her daughter, R'shiel."

The whole idea seemed too bizarre to be real. "If that's true, why hasn't Lord Jenga ever denied me?"

"I've no answer to that, I'm afraid," he said. "Perhaps you should ask him."

R'shiel sank down against the wall, until she was sitting on the sandy floor, her chin resting on her knees. Tarja stayed where he was. She could not read his expression in the dull light.

"Then who is my real father?"

"Your mother, your real mother, refused to name him. You had an aunt there, your mother's older sister, but no other family, from what I know."

R'shiel felt numb. "Where is she now, this aunt of mine?"

"The whole village is dead, R'shiel," he told her. "Joyhinia had them killed three years ago, when your aunt threatened to expose her."

R'shiel looked up at him. His voice had the ring of certain truth, but it was too dreadful a truth to acknowledge. She thought it odd that she felt nothing. No anger, or hurt, or even surprise. "How did you find out?"

Tarja kept his distance, leaning against the bare stone wall, studying her with an unreadable expression. "There were a few survivors. Children, mostly. And a Blue Sister. I met her while I was in the north. She spurned the Sisterhood after it happened."

"Why?"

"I suppose she considered the Sisterhood—"

"But why did Joyhinia lie about me?" R'shiel interrupted impatiently.

"She wanted a daughter," Tarja said with a shrug. "I don't think she ever forgave me for being born male."

"Then why not simply have another child?"

"And go through all that pain and discomfort with no guarantee the child would be a girl? Come on, R'shiel, you know Joyhinia well enough. You figure it out."

A heavy silence settled over the cavern as R'shiel digested the news. Suddenly the feeling she did not belong here seemed eminently reasonable.

"Who else knows?" she asked eventually.

"Lord Jenga, obviously. Garet Warner. And Davydd Tailorson."

"You stopped short of announcing it on the parade ground to the entire Defender Corps, then?"

He shook his head at her question. "And you accuse me of not taking things seriously enough."

"Well, what do you expect me to say, Tarja? You drag me in here and calmly announce that I'm not who I think I am. You tell me Joyhinia and the Lord Defender have lied all these years about my birth and that Joyhinia had my real family and an entire village murdered. I don't know what to say, Tarja. I don't even know what to feel!"

"I warned you this wouldn't be easy, R'shiel, but it's not the worst of it, I fear."

"You mean there's more? Founders! If this is the good news, I can't wait to hear the bad!"

Tarja sighed, as if he understood her anger. "She's done a deal with

Lord Pieter. She's sending you back to Karien with the Envoy. She traded you for the First Sister's mantle."

R'shiel could feel the blood drain from her face. *I'll call you when I need you,* Joyhinia had said. She stood up and paced the cavern until her angry steps brought her face to face with him. His expression was bleak.

"You must be mistaken." It was more a hopeful question than a statement of fact. She knew Joyhinia's ambition had no limit. "Why would the Kariens want me? It can't be true!"

Just then, Davydd Tailorson appeared at the cavern entrance with Garet Warner at his side, coughing politely to alert them to his presence.

"I hate to break this up, children," Garet said, his laconic tone easing the tension a little. "But Lord Pieter has just entered the Great Hall to address the Gathering. I suggest we get a move on, or we'll miss all the excitement."

R'shiel looked sharply at Tarja. "You can't attend the Gathering! They won't let you in. You know it's restricted to the Blue Sisters."

"And the Lord Defender," Garet reminded her. "And whatever aides he deems suitable to the occasion. Now, if you will excuse us, R'shiel, we are rather pressed for time."

Garet stood back and waited for Tarja, who spared her nothing more than a sympathetic look. R'shiel watched the three men leave. The torches hissed loudly in the sudden silence, leaving her alone with her anger. Impulsively, she ran after them.

"Wait! I'm coming too!"

"They won't let you in, R'shiel," Tarja warned her.

She looked at him defiantly. "Care to wager on that?"

"Come on, then," Garet ordered, obviously annoyed but knowing there was little he could do to stop her. Davydd hurried after the Commandant, but Tarja caught her arm and held her back. She struggled against his hold but could not break free.

"R'shiel!" he said sharply, surprising her into stillness with his tone. "Look, whatever you may think of Joyhinia, whatever happens after tonight, you still have Lord Pieter to deal with."

"That's simple. If he tries to lay a hand on me I'll slit his lecherous throat!"

"Which won't achieve anything, except you being hanged for murder," he pointed out with infuriating logic. "Anyway, the Envoy isn't your problem. It's his priest, Elfron, you need to watch for. He claims he had a vision or something from his god. He's the one who wants to take you back to Karien."

"Tarja!" Garet and Davydd had reached the end of the tunnel and were waiting impatiently for him.

"I have to go. Be careful, R'shiel." Without another word Tarja strode off toward the entrance.

R'shiel had to run to catch up.

chapter 14

hen R'shiel and the Defenders reached the Great Hall, Tarja and Garet continued up the steps to the massive bronze-sheathed doors. The two Defenders on guard saluted the officers sharply and stood back to let them enter. They were attending the Gathering as the Lord Defender's aides and had a valid reason to gain admittance. R'shiel had no such excuse. She glanced at Davydd Tailorson questioningly.

"Now what?" she whispered, afraid her voice would carry in the deserted street. Everyone was still at the amphitheater. A soft rain had begun to fall, and the cobblestone street was slick and glistening in the moonlight.

"There's no way they'll let you in, R'shiel."

She looked at him, her eyes glinting. "Oh, yes there is."

R'shiel glanced up and down the deserted street then ran across to the alley between the Great Hall and the slightly less impressive Administration Hall next door, from where Francil ruled the Citadel. Davydd followed her down the alley to a shoulder-high brick wall that blocked the end of the lane. She grabbed the top of the wall and pulled herself up, turning to help Davydd. Balanced on the top of the narrow wall, Davydd looked up.

"You've got to be joking!"

"I hope you've a head for heights," she said.

She pointed to the window ledge above them, which was out of reach by a few hand spans. With a shake of his head at his own folly, he cupped his hands and gave her a boost up to the ledge. As soon as she was safely up, she turned carefully, and lying flat on her stomach on the cold, wet ledge, she reached down to him. Davydd grabbed her outstretched arm and used it to anchor himself as he climbed up. Once he was beside her on the narrow ledge he helped her stand, and they carefully edged their way along the building toward the rear. The tall, stained-glass windows shed dull light from the torchlit interior, but it was impossible to see through them. Muted voices drifted up occasionally, as if the Gathering was voting on something. Once, she heard a male voice, accented and clipped, that she was certain must be Lord Pieter, although she could not make out the words. With a shudder, she forced her concentration back to what she was doing. She might not be afraid of heights, but that would not make falling from the slick ledge to the pavement below any less fatal.

They finally reached a small protruding balcony as the rain began to fall a little harder. Distant lightning flickered to the north, illuminating their way sporadically with flashes of whiteness. Davydd hauled himself up over the balustrade and reached down to help R'shiel up. As soon as she had clambered up beside him, shivering in her damp dress, he turned to the lock on the diamond-paned doors that led onto the balcony. The lock snicked open in a surprisingly short time. Hugging herself against the chill, R'shiel looked at the young man curiously.

"How did you do that?"

The lieutenant placed a finger on his lips, warning her to silence, then eased open the door. They slipped inside, and he pulled the door shut behind them, wincing as the wet hinges squealed in protest. Fortunately, a loud shout suddenly rose from the gathered Sisters below, masking the sound. Dropping into a crouch Davydd moved quickly and silently along the gallery. R'shiel picked up her dripping skirts and followed him, bent double to keep her head below the marble balustrade that circled the upper level of the Great Hall. About halfway down the gallery, Davydd stopped and motioned her forward. He dropped onto his belly, wiggling forward until he could see the floor below. R'shiel silently followed suit.

He had chosen an excellent vantage point. From here she could see the raised marble steps where the Quorum stood in their stark white dresses amidst a sea of blue skirts and capes. The only other splash of color was the bright red jackets of the Lord Defender and his two aides, Tarja and Garet, who stood silently behind their commander, and the huge symbol of the Sisterhood on the wall behind the podium. The Great Hall was filled with Blue Sisters who had traveled from all over Medalon for the Gathering.

Wondering how much she had missed, R'shiel looked down curiously at the podium. Mahina stood stiffly in the center, and even from this distance, she appeared angry. Standing in front of her, below the steps, in a small clearing in front of the podium, Lord Pieter and a slender, tonsured man confronted the First Sister. R'shiel looked at the priest who wanted to take her back to Karien in response to a vision. He must be insane, she reasoned. She could not see his face, but he was dressed in a magnificent cape. A five-pointed star intersected by a lightning bolt was embroidered in gold thread across the back. In his right hand he held a tall staff, topped by the same gilded symbol and encrusted with precious stones. It threw back the torchlight into the faces of the gathered women like chips of colored light.

"Your concerns are noted, my Lord," Mahina was saying to the Envoy in a voice that dripped icicles. "But Karien has no leave to dictate internal policy in Medalon. I will deal with the heathens as I see fit."

"Ah now, that is the problem, First Sister," Lord Pieter remarked in an equally cold tone. "Your idea of dealing with the heathens is not to deal with them at all. There are more heathens in Medalon now than there were when the Harshini despoiled this land with their vile customs!"

A general murmur of anxiety rippled through the gathered Sisters. Lord Pieter's statement was a gross exaggeration, everyone knew that, but that he would accuse Medalon of breaking the centuries-old treaty so publicly, was cause for concern.

"You waste the Gathering's time with your wild accusations, my Lord. Return to your King and pass on my best wishes for his continued health and well-being. You might also like to tell him to mind his own business."

R'shiel was surprised at Mahina's undiplomatic rejoinder. She glanced at Joyhinia for a moment and saw the look of satisfaction that flickered across her face. Mahina was playing right into her hands. Even Davydd, lying silently beside her, hissed softly at the First Sister's tactlessness. The sharp smell of wet wool filled her nostrils from her own wet clothes and the lieutenant's damp jacket.

Lord Pieter sputtered in protest. Joyhinia smoothly stepped forward and held up her hand to quiet the startled mutterings that swept through the crowd.

"My Lord, the First Sister is right to be concerned that you accuse us of breaking the terms of the treaty so freely. Substantiate your claims, or leave her to rule Medalon as she sees fit."

Had she not known how cleverly Joyhinia had orchestrated this scene, R'shiel would have been impressed by her mother's—rather, she reminded herself grimly—her *foster* mother's support of the First Sister.

R'shiel could tell that many of the Blue Sisters were impressed. Joyhinia presented a façade of loyalty to the First Sister that was as touching as it was false.

"Elfron!" Expecting this cue, the priest took a step forward.

"There have been one hundred and seventeen heathen cults uncovered in Medalon in the past two years," the priest announced in a voice that was high pitched and rather grating on the ears. Were the Overlord's priests eunuchs, perhaps? She had never heard that they were, but his voice lacked the masculine depth of the men R'shiel knew. Perhaps that accounted for his absurd vision. "Until the ascension of Sister Mahina, these cults were all dealt with in a similar manner. That is, confiscation of property and a prison sentence for the miscreants. Since Sister Mahina, however, there have been only three cases of confiscation and none of prison sentences."

"Perhaps it simply means that the heathens are under control," Joyhinia replied. R'shiel caught a movement out of the corner of her eye and saw Garet whispering to Tarja. He was no doubt concerned where the Kariens had gained their intelligence.

"Far from it, my Lady," the priest replied. "From your southern border to the north, we have identified a growing number of cults and supplied that information to the First Sister. Yet many of these cults continue to flourish unmolested."

Joyhinia glanced at Jenga. She had all but taken over the meeting. "Is this true, Lord Defender? Has the First Sister ordered you not to act on the information supplied by our allies?"

"The matters are under investigation, my Lady," Jenga replied, not happy to be drawn into the discussion. "Prudence should not be confused with inaction. The Defenders will take every action allowed by the law, when the information has been verified."

"There, you see, my Lord? You have it from the Lord Defender himself. Everything is under control."

"I am afraid that is not good enough, my Lady," Pieter warned with a shake of his head. "My King desires more than vague assurances. We were given those the last time we were here, and nothing has come of them. King Jasnoff requires a firm commitment to commence an immediate Purge against all heathens, known or suspected, in Medalon. If not, a force of Church Knights will be dispatched immediately, and we will deal with the problem ourselves."

The Envoy's statement brought a howl of protest from the gathered

Sisters. Mahina stepped forward and held up both hands. The Sisters took noticeably longer to fall silent than when Joyhinia had used the same gesture. R'shiel watched the First Sister with a touch of pity. She was short and dumpy and lacked Joyhinia's cold elegance. There was nothing regal in her bearing. She did not inspire confidence standing on the podium in the shadow of Joyhinia and Harith, both of whom stood a head taller than her. Mahina did not look like a First Sister should.

"Your advice will be taken under consideration, my Lord," Mahina said, almost shouting to be heard over the slowly subsiding din. "I would ask that you leave us now to consider our formal reply to your King."

Pieter bowed and motioned the priest back. "I will await your response, your Grace." The two men turned as the crowd parted before them, to allow them to leave. The Kariens walked the long length of the mosaic-tiled Hall, ignoring the Sisters who watched them depart. As the doors boomed shut behind them the crowd once again broke into an uproar.

Mahina let the noise wash over her for a while, considering her next words carefully, before she held up her hands for silence. Slowly the Sisters quieted. Their mood was hard to fathom, but the idea of Church Knights on Medalon soil was unthinkable. Medalon had fought long and hard to rid itself of all religious ties. To the majority of the Sisters, even the small heathen cults were preferable. At least they, as a rule, were not armed.

"I have long expected such duplicity from the Kariens," Mahina announced to the Gathering. R'shiel watched Joyhinia as the First Sister spoke. "Had I instigated a Purge when I became First Sister, the Envoy would have used the need for one as a weapon against us. I will not bow to blackmail."

A cheer greeted Mahina's statement, albeit a muted one. Rhetoric was a fine thing, but it did not remove the threat of an armed incursion.

"Fine sentiments, First Sister," Harith scoffed. "But I fear the Envoy is not bluffing. What are you going to do? Stand at the border and ask the Church Knights, very nicely, not to move any further?"

"I will not suffer Karien knights on Medalon soil. We will meet their force with equal force," Mahina replied confidently. "The Defenders will turn them back."

"Warmonger!" The cry came from the back of the hall, no doubt a Sister in Joyhinia's camp, primed before the meeting for such an opportunity. Several other Sisters took up the cry, and within moments the hall was filled with the chanting. "Warmonger! Warmonger!"

Joyhinia stepped forward and silenced the crowd. *You have to admire her ability to manipulate people*, R'shiel thought, rather begrudgingly.

"Sisters! Shame on you! I am appalled by this disrespect. If the First Sister says we can defeat a force of Karien knights, then we must believe her! Please, First Sister, explain your position. Have you thought of how we might face such a threat?" Joyhinia smiled so pleasantly, so supportively at Mahina, that the older woman had no idea what was coming next.

"I have, for some months, been examining our options in case such a situation ever arose," Mahina explained. R'shiel glanced at the Defenders and saw Garet Warner shaking his head, as if trying to warn Mahina of the trap she was walking into. "I have detailed plans of how we might defend our northern border and the disposal of our forces. We can face the Karien threat confidently."

"Then you have planned for this war, all along?" Joyhinia asked.

Mahina obviously assumed her colleagues would applaud her forethought. "I have, Sister. I have given the matter a great deal of thought."

"You deliberately planned a war with the Kariens?" Harith asked, right on cue. "You have purposely set us on a course that is likely to destroy us? You *planned* a war with our allies?"

Before Mahina could deny Harith's interpretation of her actions, the crowd once again took up the cry of "Warmonger!" This time many more Sisters joined in, and Joyhinia made no move to stop them. As the chant went on and on, it began to dawn on Mahina how expertly she had been duped. Her expression changed to one of anger as she looked first at Harith and then Joyhinia. Francil and Jacomina stood behind her, but they were yet to play their part. The First Sister tried to defend her position, but the chanting drowned out her voice.

Finally, it was Harith who managed to silence the angry Sisters. She stood at the front of the podium and addressed them loudly. "I am sworn to protect and govern Medalon. To serve the Sisters of the Blade. But I cannot serve under a woman who would so easily send us to war, with no thought to the deprivation such an act would cause. I cannot serve under a woman who shows so little thought to the safety of our people. Karien is a hundred times larger than Medalon. Her soldiers outnumber our Defenders ten to one. I cannot be a party to this!"

The crowd fell expectantly silent at Harith's impassioned speech. They had not expected this.

Mahina looked at the Mistress of the Sisterhood in surprise. "Are you resigning, Harith?"

Harith glanced at Mahina briefly, then turned back to the crowd. "I am not offering my resignation. I am proposing that Sister Mahina Cortanen be removed. I propose that Sister Joyhinia Tenragan, who has already proved, this evening, that she is a match for the Kariens, be appointed the Interim First Sister, until a formal election can be arranged. I propose that we immediately instigate a Purge to rid Medalon of the heathen cults that flourish under Mahina's rule. Do I have a seconder?"

The silence was so loud following Harith's proposal that R'shiel could hear the blood pumping in her ears. She waited, unconsciously holding her breath, even though she knew that Jacomina would step forward. It seemed an eternity before she did. An eternity in which Mahina visibly paled and Lord Jenga's expression grew bleak. Garet and Tarja behind him exchanged a glance but did nothing. There was nothing they could do. This was a matter for the Sisterhood.

"I second the proposal," Jacomina announced loudly as she stepped forward. "I too cannot bear the thought of Medalon being plunged into war."

The crowd muttered softly, oddly subdued in the face of such an extraordinary situation.

"You need the whole Quorum to agree, Harith," Mahina pointed out. "I have no doubt Joyhinia shares your sentiments, but you have not polled Francil yet."

All eyes turned to the oldest member of the Quorum. Francil had managed to stand aloof from the vicious politics of her Sisters for thirty years. She now seemed rather uncomfortable to be the focus of so much attention. She avoided looking at Mahina, instead focusing her eyes on a point somewhere above the heads of the crowd.

"I stand with Harith," she said, her voice only reaching those in the front ranks. The message was passed along with a murmur, like a wave of astonishment washing over the Gathering.

"The Quorum stands united," Harith announced. "Do you have anything to say in your defense, Sister Mahina, before I ask the Blue Sisters for their vote?"

R'shiel had never seen Mahina so angry, but she forcibly pushed away her fury to address the Sisters. If ever her lack of charisma worked against her it was now.

"Think well before you vote on this issue, Sisters. Do not let the clever words of ambition cloud your judgment. Think what is best for Medalon! A Purge will do nothing but make our people suffer for no better reason than to appease the fanatics in the Karien Church. We have freed ourselves from the chains of religion. Don't let them bind us again!"

The Gathering heard her out, but R'shiel could tell they were in no mood to heed her words. Had it just been Harith or Joyhinia who had rebelled against the First Sister, they would have shrugged it off as the political games played among the Quorum members. But Francil's defection carried enormous weight. She had survived three administrations without a whiff of scandal or a moment of disloyalty. Her support of Joyhinia was fatal to Mahina's cause.

"How do you speak, Sisters?" Harith called. "Do you say 'yea' to my proposal?"

The "yea" that thundered through the Great Hall was deafening.

"Those of you who support Mahina?" Harith knew they had won. She did not even bother with the title of Sister. The silence that followed Harith's question was like a death knell. Harith waited, letting the significance of the silence sink in before she continued.

"Then I declare Joyhinia Tenragan the Interim First Sister," Harith announced. "Long Live First Sister Joyhinia Tenragan!"

"Long Live First Sister Joyhinia Tenragan!" the Gathering cheered. "Long Live First Sister Joyhinia Tenragan!"

"Sisters!" Joyhinia held up her hand. "Please! This is no time to rejoice! This is a time of grave peril for Medalon, and I will do my utmost to be worthy of the trust you have placed in me." That brought another cheer from the crowd, as Joyhinia knew it would. "We face a crisis that must be dealt with immediately. My Lord Defender, will you swear the allegiance of the Defenders to me?"

Jenga hesitated for a fraction of a second before he stepped forward, a fact that did not escape the new First Sister. Together, the Lord Defender and his aides stepped forward to stand before the podium. Jenga unsheathed his sword and laid it at Joyhinia's feet and then knelt on one knee. Garet also knelt, as tradition demanded.

Tarja remained standing defiantly.

Joyhinia looked at him, her expression betraying nothing of the anger she must be feeling as her son defied her so openly.

"Did you have something to say, Captain?" she asked, her voice remarkably pleasant under the circumstances.

Tarja's back was turned to R'shiel, so she could not see the expression on his face, but she could tell by the stiff set of his shoulders that he was furious beyond words.

"What did you pay Francil for her support, mother?" he asked, loud enough to be heard throughout the Hall.

"Kneel with your commander and take the oath, Captain." R'shiel was astounded that she was able to keep her temper so well.

"Afraid to answer my question?" he taunted. "Should I tell the good Sisters what you offered in return for Lord Pieter's support? Your own daughter? Ah, but then I forgot. She's not your daughter, is she? You lied about that, too."

"Kneel with your commander and take the oath, Captain!" Joyhinia cried, her anger finally surfacing in the face of his dreadful charges. The Gathering murmured worriedly, wondering if there was any truth to Tarja's accusations.

Tarja met her anger with a rage that matched it, breath for breath. "Never!"

Pale and shaking with fury, Joyhinia suddenly turned to the Lord Defender. "I will take your oath now, my Lord."

Still on one knee before Joyhinia, Jenga turned and glanced over his shoulder at Tarja. "Kneel, Captain," he said, his tone as close to begging as it was ever likely to get. "Take the oath."

"Not if it costs me my life," Tarja said.

"The oath, my Lord," Joyhinia reminded him frostily.

"Why doesn't she order him arrested?" R'shiel whispered to Davydd. "Why is she insisting Jenga take the oath?"

"She can't order Jenga to do anything until he does," he whispered.

"A moment, your Grace," Jenga said, rising to his feet. He turned to Tarja. "You have brought disgrace on the Defenders, Captain. To take this oath with you present, while you defy the First Sister, is unconscionable. You will leave this Gathering and place yourself under house arrest until I can deal with your disobedience."

Tarja stood in front of the Lord Defender for a moment, before saluting sharply. He then turned on his heel and strode toward the doors at the back of the Great Hall, his back stiff and unrelenting. The crowd parted for him and then closed again in his wake. R'shiel watched him leave in a cloud of anger and humiliation. She had not expected Jenga to turn on him so readily. She looked back at Joyhinia and felt such a surge of hatred that she trembled with it. At the front of the Hall, Jenga once more knelt, and his voice rang out clear and strong as he repeated the Oath of Allegiance to the new First Sister. The doors boomed shut, like a gong announcing Tarja's impending doom.

"Tarja's in a lot of trouble, isn't he?" she said, glancing at the young lieutenant.

"He surely is," Davydd agreed. "If they can catch him."

"What do you mean?" she whispered.

"By ordering him out of the Hall before he took the oath, Jenga's given Tarja time to get away." He pushed himself backward and rose to a crouch. "Come on, we'd better get out of here, too."

R'shiel followed Davydd back the way they had come, wondering at his words. Had Jenga really ordered Tarja out, to give him a chance to escape Joyhinia's wrath? And if he had, would Tarja be smart enough to take the opportunity Jenga offered him, or would he stay to face the consequences of his rebellion? Knowing Tarja, it was quite likely he would choose the latter course out of sheer bloody-mindedness.

Then again, maybe he wouldn't.

Maybe he would take the chance for freedom, take the chance to escape the Citadel and be forever free of Joyhinia's manipulation and ambition.

The Question suddenly loomed in her mind, and the nothingness beyond it. *Forever free of Joyhinia's manipulation and ambition . . .*

"We can't go that way, we'll be blown off the ledge." The storm had reached the Citadel, and rain lashed furiously at the windows.

"I have to get out of here!" she hissed.

"We'll have to wait, R'shiel. No one is likely to come up here until the meeting is over."

"No!"

Davydd looked at her determined expression and shook his head. "If I get killed doing this, I'll be very annoyed with you."

"You're a Defender! You're supposed to enjoy this sort of thing," she said, easing open the balcony door. The rain struck her like cold, sharp needles, but she didn't care. *Forever free of Joyhinia's manipulation and ambition.* The phrase repeated itself over and over in her mind. She still had not answered The Question, but for the first time she saw something beyond the emptiness, and no storm, no treacherous ledge, and no amount of common sense was going to stand in her way.

part three

THE PURGE

chapter 15

inter's bite could be felt in the brisk wind that swept across the border from Medalon into Hythria. Although it never snowed this far south, it did not stop the chill wind, which blew off the snowcapped Sanctuary Mountains, cutting through everything with icy fingers. The sky was overcast and leaden and smelled of rain.

Brak sat on his sorcerer-bred horse overlooking a shallow ford that marked the line between Medalon and Hythria. It was a long time since he had been home. If he rode across the border and just kept heading northwest to the mountains, eventually he would reach the peace and tranquillity of Sanctuary. He could feel it calling to him. He could feel the pull, the closer he came to Medalon. The ache niggled at him constantly, tempting him to weaken. He pushed it away and looked north.

"They call it the Border Stream," Damin told him, mistaking the direction of his gaze. "The gods alone know why. You'd think somebody would have given it a grander name, considering its strategic importance."

Brak glanced at the Warlord and nodded politely. The High Arrion had arranged for him to travel with her brother, the Warlord of Krakandar. Damin Wolfblade was anxious to be gone from Greenharbor, and it seemed logical that they should travel together. So Kalan had claimed. Brak had a bad feeling she was using him. Korandellen's appearance in the Seeing Stone might place Damin in immediate danger, but it did no harm at all to his long-term claim on the Hythrun throne. Nor would escorting a Divine One north on a sacred mission. Of course, he had not told the High Arrion what he was doing, just as he continued to deny his right to the title of Divine One, but that didn't stop her using it. Or making the most of his presence. Damin Wolfblade had at least been more amenable in that respect. Brak had asked simply to be called by his name, and the Warlord had agreed, quite unperturbed about the whole issue. He even went so far as to apologize for his sister.

Brak had learned much in the month he had spent in the young Warlord's company on their journey to Krakandar Province and the Medalon border. He had known that Damin's mother was Lernen's younger sister, but he had not realized that she had gone through five husbands and her extended family included three children of her own and another seven stepchildren. Every one of them was carefully placed in a position of power. Kalan was High Arrion. Narvell, Kalan's twin brother and the issue of Marla's second marriage, was the Warlord of Elasapine. Luciena, her stepdaughter from her marriage to a wealthy shipping magnate, owned a third of Hythria's trading ships. Damin's youngest stepbrother, at the tender age of nineteen, was training in the Hythrun Assassins' Guild.

Marla had known her brother would never produce an heir. She had used her considerable wealth and influence to raise her entire brood with one purpose in mind: securing the throne for her eldest son. Considering Damin could not be much past thirty, it was astounding that she had achieved so much, so soon. Brak also found the loyalty among Marla's clan quite remarkable. Damin seemed certain of the support of each and every one of his siblings, a rare thing among humans, he thought cynically. Brak had only met Marla once, when she was but a child of seven and he could remember nothing about her that hinted at her strength of purpose in years to come. Brak's fears for Hythria were allayed a little. Damin seemed an intelligent and astute young man. On the other hand, with the exception of Narvell, the other Warlords in Hythria were not terribly happy about the situation. It would be much better if old Lernen just kept on living.

"Am I boring you, Brak?"

"I'm sorry, did you say something?"

Damin laughed. "I was boasting of my many battles at this very site," he said. "I suppose I shouldn't be surprised that such heroics don't interest you. I do miss Tarja, though."

"Tarja?"

"Captain Tarja Tenragan," Damin explained. "One of the Defender's finest. The son of a bitch could read me like a book. Damned if I know how he did it. He was recalled to the Citadel a few months ago, right after Trayla died." Damin frowned, his expression miserable. "The idiot they sent to replace him hardly makes it worth the effort anymore."

"How disappointing for you," Brak remarked dryly. The news that there was a new First Sister surprised him. It reminded him sharply of how long he had been away.

"No doubt the God of War had him recalled as some sort of punishment," Damin added. "He probably thought I was having too much fun."

"Zegarnald is like that," Brak agreed.

Damin stared at him, awestruck. "You have spoken with the God of War?"

Brak nodded reluctantly, wishing he had kept his mouth shut. Damin Wolfblade was a reasonable fellow, but like all Hythrun and Fardohnyans, he was in awe of the gods. Brak tended to take them much less seriously. Anyone who spent time in the gods' company usually did. They were immortal, it was true, and powerful, but they were fickle and self-absorbed and generally a nuisance, as far as Brak was concerned. His present mission was proof of that. He often thought humans would be much better off without them.

"You said you had contacts in Bordertown," Brak said, deciding a change of subject was in order. Damin would be calling him Divine One soon.

Damin nodded, taking the hint, although he was obviously dying to ask Brak more. "When you get to Bordertown, seek out a Fardohnyan sailor named Drendik. He has a barge that trades between Talabar in the Gulf and the Medalonian ports on the Glass River. At this time of year, he'll be getting ready to sail north to Brodenvale so he can catch the spring floods on his way home. If you mention my name, he'll give you passage. If you mention that you know Maera, the Goddess of the River, he'll probably carry you there on his back."

"How is it you have Fardohnyan allies? I thought Hythria and Fardohnya were enemies."

"We are," Damin agreed. "When it suits us. At least we were when I left Greenharbor. That may have changed by now."

"You mean Princess Adrina was in Greenharbor to broker peace?" Brak asked.

Damin shrugged. "Who knows? With some difficulty, I managed to avoid meeting Her Serene Highness, thank the gods. By all accounts, she's an obnoxious and demanding spoilt brat. I hear that Hablet can't even bribe anyone to marry her."

Brak smiled, thinking that the young woman must be a harridan indeed if everyone, from the citizens in Greenharbor to the Warlord of a distant foreign province, knew her reputation. Damin reached down and patted the neck of his own sorcerer-bred stallion. Lacking any magical ability to communicate with the beast, Damin and his raiders controlled their mounts by nothing more than superb horsemanship. The Warlord glanced at Brak, his smile fading.

"One thing unites Hythria and Fardohnya, Brak: the Sisterhood's persecution of pagans. Drendik has saved many lives in his time. For that, I can forgive him a lot. Even being Fardohnyan."

Brak dismounted, lifting his pack off Cloud Chaser's back. He would miss the stallion but would not risk such a valuable animal in Medalon. It was unlikely anyone in Medalon would recognize the breed, but the horse's unmistakable nobility would cause comment. He preferred to remain anonymous.

"If there is anything else I can do for you," Damin offered as he took Cloud Chaser's reins, "you only have to ask."

"You could try not starting a civil war while I'm away," Brak said.

"Speak to the gods then," Damin suggested. "They have more control over that than I do."

Brak shook Damin's hand. He genuinely liked the young Warlord, but that didn't mean he thought he would listen to him.

"Trust your own judgment, Damin," he advised. "Don't leave it to the gods. They have their own agenda."

Damin's expression grew serious. "As do the Harshini."

Brak did not deny the accusation. For a moment the silence was heavy between them.

"You seek the demon child, don't you?" Damin asked quietly, although there was nobody within earshot who could overhear them. The troops who had escorted them to the border were well back behind the treeline.

"Who told you that?"

"Call it an educated guess," Damin shrugged. "The rumors have been around for as long as I can recall. It is the only thing I can think of that would cause the Harshini to break their silence after all this time. Do you plan to kill him?"

Brak was a little taken aback by the blunt question. "I don't know."

"Well, before you do, answer one question for me," Damin said.

"If I can."

"If this child is truly Lorandranek's child, then it will be like you, won't it? Harshini, but not constrained against violence? If that's the case, then he could kill a god, couldn't he? Is that why Lorandranek withdrew all the Harshini to Sanctuary? To wait until a child was born who could destroy Xaphista?"

Brak wondered how the Warlord had been able to piece together so much from so little. But his sister was the High Arrion. The Sorcerer's Collective knew much to which the general population was not privy. His question made a frightening amount of sense. It would explain why the gods were anxious to ensure that the demon child lived. Was Xaphista becoming so powerful that the Primal Gods would countenance the existence of the demon child? Brak shuddered and turned his attention back to Damin.

"One question, you said," he snapped. "That was five questions."

"So I can't count."

"And I can't answer any of them," Brak admitted.

"You *won't* answer them," the Warlord accused.

"I can't," Brak replied with a shake of his head, "because I simply don't know."

Bordertown had changed a lot since the last time Brak had seen it. It had grown considerably—new redbrick houses bordered the western edge of the town, and there were more taverns than he remembered. There were more soldiers, too. More red coats than he could ever remember seeing. The Defenders had changed since their rather inauspicious beginnings. They were no longer eager young men with more enthusiasm than skill. They were hard, well trained, and deserving of their reputation as the most disciplined warriors in the world. But their presence caused an indefinable tension in the town. People looked over their shoulder before they spoke. Even the talkative market stallholders seemed less garrulous than usual.

It had taken Brak almost two weeks on foot to reach the town. Discretion, rather than time, was of the essence. He had traded his sailor's clothes for leather trousers, a linen shirt, and a nondescript but warm cloak provided by Damin Wolfblade. But for his golden tanned skin and unusual height, he looked as Medalonian as the next man. His father had been a Medalonian human, and besides inheriting his blue eyes, Brak inherited his temper. Although raised among the Harshini, his temper had been his constant enemy. Even the peace that permeated the Harshini settlements had never been able to quell completely his occasional violent outbursts. It was ironic, he sometimes thought, that twenty years of self-imposed exile among humans had taught him more self-control than the centuries he had spent at Sanctuary.

Captain Drendik proved to be a huge blond-bearded Fardohnyan, an unusual feature in a race that tended toward swarthy dark-haired people. There was Hythrun blood in him, Brak guessed, which perhaps explained his willingness to aid the Warlord. His boat was crewed by his two brothers, who were almost as large and blonde as Drendik, although not nearly as broad around the girth. Brak introduced himself as a friend of the Warlord's, and Drendik seemed happy to take him at his word. He was not running a charity, however, he explained. He could work off his passage north or pay the going rate for a berth. Brak chose to work. Drendik was rather impressed with his seafaring experience so it proved to be a satisfactory arrangement on both sides. The Fardohnyan had no inkling of Brak's true heritage or his reason for wanting to travel north, and Brak made no effort to offer one.

They sailed from Bordertown on the twentieth day of Margaran into a blustery breeze that pushed the small barge upstream in fits and starts. Drendik predicted it would take almost until midspring to reach Brodenvale. From there, Brak planned to make his way overland to the Citadel to find Lorandranek's child.

The problem he faced when he reached the Citadel did not bear thinking about. He had no idea if the child, or rather the young adult by now, was male or female. He had no idea what he or she looked like, no idea what his or her name was. He had nothing to go on other than the knowledge the demon child was at the Citadel, a city of thousands of people. It was the very heart of the Sisterhood's power. Presumably, the child favored its human mother in appearance. It was hard to imagine a Harshini child living in the heart of the Citadel going unremarked. It was quite reasonable to assume then, that the child looked as human as any other young man or woman.

Brak figured there was only one way he was likely to find the child: sheer bloody luck.

chapter 16

The day was as bleak as Jenga's mood as he headed across the parade ground toward his office to the tattoo of booted feet as a squad of fourth-year Cadets practiced formation marching. The Citadel looked as unchanged as it had yesterday or the day before. The domes and spires still sparkled in the dull light. The Brightening and Dimming still waxed and waned as it had for two millennia or more. Winter was slowly relinquishing its grip on the highlands and soon the plains would bloom with their carpet of spring flowers. But for now, the day was cold and miserable, and Jenga was looking forward to the warmth his office promised. It seemed to have been such a long winter.

The atmosphere in the Citadel had changed dramatically after the fateful Gathering at the beginning of winter that saw Mahina unseated, the first time in living memory such a startling event had occurred. There was an air of tension now that permeated every part of the Citadel from the taverns to the Dormitories, from the Sisters of the Quorum to the lowliest pig-herder.

The Defenders were on constant alert as Joyhinia kept her promise to the Karien Envoy. Daily, red-coated patrols marched or rode out of the Citadel, returning days or weeks later, grim-faced and silent, with wagonloads of helpless-looking prisoners accused of following the heathen gods. Some of them were little more than children. It was obvious to everyone that the Defenders did not agree with the Purge, but the Lord Defender had sworn an oath. Jenga had been forced to discipline more than one of his officers for voicing opinions at odds with the First Sister's policy of suppression. It was his duty.

To cater for the sudden increase of accused heathens, Joyhinia had set up a special court, chaired by Harith, which dealt with the influx of prisoners requiring trial. From what Jenga had seen, the trials were little more than a formality, the sentences the same, regardless of circumstance. Arrest was proof enough of guilt, and every Fourthday another caravan of tried and convicted heathens was dispatched to the Grimfield mines, where before the prisoners of the Citadel had only needed to be dispatched once a month. Jenga found himself constantly having to remind his men to be certain, beyond doubt, before they arrested anyone, while Joyhinia undermined him by addressing the Defenders personally, telling them that suspicion was enough. Where there is smoke there is fire, the First Sister was fond of saying.

In the aftermath of Mahina's removal, Wilem Cortanen, Mahina's son, was hastily appointed as Commandant of the Grimfield and was gone from the Citadel within days, his mother, now officially retired, and his dreadful wife, Crisabelle, in tow. To Jenga's mind, it was the one bright spot in the whole miserable affair. Many might regret Mahina's banishment, and it was common knowledge that Wilem's posting was not to his liking, although he was well qualified for the post and would undoubtedly prove an effective administrator. But nobody in the Citadel, Jenga thought, was going to miss Crisabelle.

Lord Pieter had stayed at the Citadel until the day before, when he rode out of the gates with a full guard of honor to escort him to Brodenvale. He had stayed through the winter—partly to supervise the implementation of the Purge and partly because he wanted to sail home. He had no choice but to wait while his ship sailed north against the current to the nearest port. The Saran River that flowed past the Citadel was too shallow to be navigable. News had finally come that the ship had docked in Brodenvale and planned to take full advantage of the spring flood to hasten the Envoy's journey home. Lord Pieter had cooled his heels in the Citadel, frustrated and helpless under Elfron's watchful eyes, for long enough.

Lord Pieter had not had a moment's privacy in the three months he spent at the Citadel. The rest of the Envoy's party, including Elfron's nuns, had shared the protection of the Envoy between them, apparently terrified that he might be tempted into sin by some wicked atheist. Jenga wondered if the Karien clergy had any inkling of Pieter's behavior when he came to the Citadel without them. The nuns were dedicated in their duty, and Pieter's frustration was a palpable thing. He waited and fretted, and spent a vexatious winter of abstinence. Elfron had looked thoroughly miserable riding out of the Citadel empty handed. Jenga still had no clue as to why the priest wanted R'shiel, and even Pieter seemed annoyed when the priest suggested they wait at the Citadel until she was found. Whatever the priest had in mind for the girl, Pieter did not share his enthusiasm. He wanted to go home.

Occasionally, Jenga overheard a few of the Defenders muttering something about Joyhinia and whether or not R'shiel was really her daughter, but such conversations usually stopped as soon as he entered the room. Tarja's accusations had spread through the Citadel like a summer cold. R'shiel's disappearance had fueled speculation, but fear of Joyhinia kept the rumors to an occasional furtive whisper. It was not a safe topic. The First Sister had spies everywhere. Jenga was grateful for that. Exposing Joyhinia's lies meant exposing his own, and Dayan could still be tried, even after all this time.

Tarja had wisely fled the Citadel. Jenga assumed R'shiel went with him to avoid being handed over to the Kariens, although he could not say. Even Davydd Tailorson, the last person to have seen her in the Citadel, didn't know where she had gone. Although there were many reported sightings, nothing reliable had been heard of either Tarja or R'shiel for months. A warrant had been issued for Tarja's arrest, listing him as a deserter. If caught, he would be hanged. R'shiel had been branded a thief—she had taken a silver hand mirror or some other trifle from Joyhinia's apartment before she vanished.

Tarja had always been a favorite son of the Defenders, respected by his peers, even when he had run afoul of Trayla. Defying Joyhinia had, if anything, increased the admiration of his fellow officers, who applauded his courage, though they questioned his wisdom. But when he walked away from the Defenders he had broken a sacred oath to the Corps, if not the current First Sister. That was unforgivable. Jenga knew, just from the talk in the taverns, that if found, Tarja would be unlikely to make it back to the Citadel alive. Too many officers felt that Tarja had betrayed them.

As the Purge continued unabated, there was a growing feeling of discontent among his officers. Arresting heathens was one thing, but the evidence required to convict a citizen of pagan worship was becoming less and less substantial. There were cases, Jenga suspected, where neighbors had accused each other to gain land.

It was rumored that the Purge was being used to settle old scores. It was as bad as the old days, some claimed, when two centuries ago the Sisterhood had set out to destroy the Harshini. Jenga found that hard to believe. Even the Sisters of the Blade acknowledged that had been a time of darkness. To think Joyhinia had returned Medalon to that bleak and best forgotten past, while he was in command of the Defenders . . . it was too awful to contemplate. He did not wish to be remembered by history as a butcher or a tyrant.

Jenga opened the door to his office, and the relative warmth of the room brought his thoughts back to the present.

"I was hoping you'd be back soon," Garet Warner said, lifting his feet from Jenga's desk without apology.

"Make yourself at home."

The Commandant removed himself from Jenga's chair to make room for his superior. He took the hard-backed wooden chair on the other side of the desk as Jenga reclaimed his own leather seat.

"How did your meeting with the First Sister go?"

"The same as usual."

"That bad, eh?" Garet Warner had little respect for Joyhinia, but he usually had the sense to keep his opinion to himself. "Well, I hate to be the bearer of bad news, but I think things are about to get worse."

"It must be bad news indeed," Jenga agreed heavily. "Have the Kariens invaded? The Hythrun, perhaps? Or is there a Fardohnyan fleet sailing up the Glass River to attack us?"

"If only we should be so lucky. I'm afraid my news is about Tarja."

Jenga's eyes narrowed. "You've been bringing me reports of Tarja's whereabouts all winter, Garet. None has proved worth a pinch of horse dung."

Garet appeared unconcerned by the criticism. "Tarja's one of the best officers the Defenders have ever produced, my Lord. Does it surprise you that he's been able to give us the slip for so long?"

"No more than it surprises me that you've been unable to locate him. Have you something useful this time?"

"There's been some trouble with a patrol. In a village called Redding-dale."

"What happened?"

"The patrol was attacked. Three men were killed."

"So the villagers fought back? I'm surprised none have tried it sooner."

"I agree, we've been lucky so far. But I think the Purge has finally pushed some of the heathens too far. There are rumors of an organized rebellion. I've nothing definite yet, but not all the pagans worship benign gods. There are quite a few willing to put up a fight."

"And you think this incident in Reddingdale is somehow connected with this organized rebellion?" Jenga asked.

"I'm almost certain of it."

"And what of Tarja? You said you had news of him?"

"He was there," Garet told him. "So was R'shiel, by all accounts. Tarja killed two Defenders. The other, I'm not certain about, although one report I have says it was R'shiel who killed him. The sergeant of the patrol identified them."

Jenga shook his head. Had the world become so skewed that Tarja would turn on the Defenders? Or that R'shiel would kill a man?

"What do you think?" he asked. Perhaps Garet's more objective view would offer some comfort.

"I think we have an organized rebellion on our hands," Garet said. "And that Tarja and R'shiel are involved with them. Tarja's a captain of the Defenders and R'shiel was raised to be a Sister of the Blade with Joyhinia Tenragan as her role model. I don't think we're facing a few fanatical heathens anymore, Jenga. With those two on the loose we could be facing a bloody civil war."

chapter 17

arja left the Citadel in the storm that beat at the city with angry whiplashes of lightning, taking the chance that Jenga had offered him without giving much thought to the consequences. He took only his horse, his sword, and the clothes on his back, with the exception of his distinctive red Defenders jacket, which he left folded on his bunk. He rode out of the Citadel in the rain, dressed much as he had been when he was fighting on the southern border.

R'shiel was waiting for him at the small village of Kordale, cloaked against the rain, riding her long-legged gray mare with a pack thrown over her shoulder. She had fled the Citadel taking with her only a change of clothes, a few personal belongings, and every single coin Joyhinia had in her apartment. Her decision to run away appeared to have been far easier than his. She was bound by no oaths, hampered by no thoughts of treason. But she was nursing a smoldering rage which manifested itself as stubbornness. He had no more hope of convincing her she should turn back than he had of convincing himself.

At first, R'shiel's determination and the coin she had stolen had sustained them. Of course, she did not consider it stolen. If Joyhinia was prepared to sell her to the Kariens, she told him, then she was entitled to a share in the profits. They rode south for want of a better direction. North was Karien. To the south lay Hythria and Fardohnya. Both countries were big enough to lose themselves in. Tarja was, after all, a professional soldier. There were plenty of openings for men with his skills, particularly in Hythria, where the seven Hythrun Warlords constantly waged war on each other. R'shiel was well educated, and there were plenty of noble families in the south who would pay well for a Medalonian governess, or even a bookkeeper. As Bereth had pointed out, the Sisters of the Blade were the best-trained bureaucrats in the world. Without even discussing it, they found themselves heading for Hythria.

They were on the road for a week or more before Tarja realized he had unconsciously decided to seek out Damin Wolfblade and hire himself out as a mercenary. The Defenders thought mercenaries the scum of the earth, but in Hythria, they were a necessary part of life. The southerners considered an army far better manned by career mercenaries, whose survival depended on their battle skills, than resentful slaves, or conscripts whose first concern was their farm or their sweetheart back home. Tarja found himself having to revise his own opinion. He no longer had the luxury of taking the high moral ground. He was a deserter. His life would be forfeit should the Defenders apprehend him, and he did not doubt that Joyhinia had ordered them to hunt him down relentlessly until they did. He had humiliated her in public. That thought almost made defying her worthwhile.

But it was a long way to Hythria, and what coin they did have would not last long if spent on inns. Besides, they were too well known in the lands around the Citadel to risk such creature comforts. So they cut inland, away from the Glass River, across the low Hallowdean Mountains and the Cliffwall, through the isolated farms and villages of central Medalon.

For most of the winter they survived by R'shiel's wits and Tarja's hunting skills or by hiring themselves out for a few days at a time to farmers, who would gladly trade a warm stable and a hot meal for chores around the farm. They dared not stay in one place too long. News of his desertion was only hours behind them. It would not take much for the farmers to recall the tall redhead and the dark-haired stranger who had stopped at their holding at a time when few people chose to travel.

R'shiel's anger abated after a while, although Tarja suspected it would take little to fan it back into life. She began to treat their desperate flight like some grand adventure. She was pleasant company for the most part, provided they stayed off the topic of Joyhinia. R'shiel never complained, never shirked any task he asked of her. She had surprised him at the first farm where they sought shelter, when she had introduced herself as his wife rather than his sister. The Defenders were hunting for them, she explained when they were alone. If they questioned the farmer later, they might not connect the nice young couple on their way to visit their families in the south with the deserter and his runaway sister they were pursuing. Tarja didn't think the Defenders were quite so easily fooled, but it seemed a wise precaution, so he didn't make an issue of it.

Joyhinia's Purge further complicated matters. Defender patrols were everywhere, despite the weather, in places they had not been seen for years. They had a narrow escape in the village of Alton, a small hamlet in central Medalon that consisted of a handful of families, all so interrelated that it was impossible to tell where one family began and another ended. They had just settled down for the evening. R'shiel was huddled close to him for warmth, drifting into a light doze to the pungent smell of the warm stable. He had grown used to her sleeping next to him over the winter.

He was weary and stiff from an afternoon spent swinging an axe when the sound of horses reached him, jerking him awake. He peered through the split wood of the loft and discovered a Defender patrol milling about in the street below. The lieutenant in charge was asking something of one of the villagers. Perhaps they were not looking for them specifically, but that would soon change if they were discovered here. Even his horse, stabled below, would give him away. The distinctive breeding of a Defender cavalry mount was easily recognizable. He shook R'shiel awake, motioned her to silence, and pointed down toward the street. She understood immediately and quickly pulled on her boots then gathered their meager belongings, hastily throwing them into saddlebags. Once down among the horses, Tarja threw their saddles over their mounts, loosely cinched the girths, and quietly led them out of the stable by the back door. They did not stop to saddle the horses properly until they were well into the trees outside of the town. They rode until the sun came up and then only rested for an hour or so, before moving on.

It was a hell of a way to live.

The incident in Alton forced Tarja to reconsider his plans. Although they had avoided pursuit thus far, the very isolation of the villages they rode through made them stand out. Strangers were rare enough to be commented on. Sometimes, it was the only noteworthy event for weeks. They decided it might be safer if they cut across to the Glass River, where the towns were more populous and strangers were the norm rather than the exception. So they had turned southwest and made their way slowly toward the river, avoiding patrols and villages as much as they could. He hoped they had left a clear enough trail that the Defenders would continue to search for them away from the river.

By the time they reached the small village of Reddingdale, the first tentative signs of spring had begun to manifest themselves. The air was warmer, the days a little longer, and the lethargy of winter was slowly being shed by the townsfolk. Tarja and R'shiel had ridden into the village at dusk and had chosen the first inn they came to. They were both tired of sleeping on the ground, and they worked out that they could afford one night in a warm bed with a fire and a belly full of ale and hot stew.

It was well into the night when the Defender patrol burst into the tavern and began rounding up the patrons, demanding names and occupations. They were sitting near the back of the taproom, having chosen the place carefully, both for its view of the front door and its proximity to the kitchen, which would offer a quick exit if they needed one. As the Defenders burst in, Tarja shrank back against the wall, judging the distance to their escape route. The taproom was quite large, and it would take the Defenders several minutes to get around to where they were sitting. R'shiel was edging her way along the bench slowly, to avoid attracting attention, when one of the Defenders hit the tavern keeper across the jaw with the hilt of his sword, presumably for some insult.

The rest of it happened so quickly, Tarja had trouble recalling the details later. A boy of about twelve or thirteen, the innkeeper's son Tarja guessed, ran at the Defenders from the kitchen, yelling something incomprehensible. He clutched a small dagger in a hand still chubby with baby fat. His face was red and tear-streaked. He lunged at the man who had struck the tavern keeper. The Defender reacted instinctively to the threat and thrust his sword out to block the boy's attack. The child ran onto the blade before he knew what had happened to him.

A high-pitched, heart-rending cry of agony rent the air. Screams of the tavern wenches, the tavern keeper and shouts of the Defenders yelling for order filled the smoky taproom. With a shocked expression, the Defender jerked his blade free and the child fell to the floor, blood spurting from the wound. Somebody else, Tarja had no idea who, tried to attack the Defenders and was dealt with as efficiently as the child. Tarja knew these men, if not personally, then at least how well they were trained. A taproom full of villagers stood no chance against them.

He glanced at the kitchen door and then caught the look on R'shiel's face. Before he could stop her, she snatched his dagger from his belt and hurled it with astounding accuracy at the Defender who had killed the child. The blade buried itself in the man's chest with a solid *thunk*. The man cried out, dropping his sword with a clatter as he fell. Tarja barely had time to wonder where she had learned such a deadly skill as the Defenders turned on them. He kicked the table over, ramming it into the oncoming Defenders and unsheathing his own sword all in one movement. R'shiel rolled to the side, pulling a sobbing serving wench with her as she went, to give him room to fight. He was on the attacking Defenders before he had a chance to stop and think about what he was doing. The first man fell with a bone-crunching thump as Tarja smashed his elbow into his face, driving splinters of bone up into the man's brain, killing him instantly. He snatched the sword from the Defender's fist and threw it across the room to a young man who had charged into the fray and was trying to hold off two Defenders with a table dagger and a gutful of courage. The lad caught the sword in mid-air and swung it wildly, his unpredictability making up for his lack of skill. In almost the same movement, Tarja turned on the remaining Defenders.

There was a startled moment of recognition as the lieutenant realized whom he faced. They stood in a tense island of stillness amidst the chaos as it dawned on the officer that he was vastly overmatched. It did not stop him attacking. Neither did it save him. Tarja parried his strike and countered it so effortlessly that he wondered for a moment at the dwindling standards of the Defenders. The man should never have made it to lieutenant. He would never make it to captain.

It had taken only moments, but the sergeant of the troop called the retreat before the carnage got any worse. Tarja recognized him. A battle-hardened man with more skirmishes behind him than his dead lieutenant had years. The Defenders were hampered by the tight quarters, the screaming civilians, and the fact that the men they faced seemed to care little if they lived or died. He ordered his troops back, and they battled their way to the door, fighting off both the men in the tavern who had leaped into the fight and the women who were hurling mugs, plates, and food at them, screaming hysterically. As the last Defender withdrew, Tarja lowered his sword and leaned on it, his chest heaving as he looked at the carnage that surrounded him. There would be no mercy for them now. R'shiel was climbing to her feet near the kitchen door. She looked angry. The rage she nursed against Joyhinia and anything to do with her was back and burning ferociously.

"Did you see them run!" cried the young man who had caught the sword, his eyes glittering. He stood on one of the few tables left standing, brandishing the weapon bravely. The letdown would come later, Tarja knew, when his blood had cooled and he had time to consider his own mortality. "We made them run!"

"They retreated because the fight was pointless," Tarja said, wiping his blade off before he replaced it in its scabbard. "If you've any brains, you'll do the same thing. They'll be back, and next time they'll be prepared for resistance."

"I fought them off once!" the lad boasted. "The next time—"

"The next time they will cut your throat for being a fool, Ghari," the tavern keeper snapped. He was sitting on the floor, cradling the head of the child in his lap, tears streaming down his cheeks. He looked at Tarja, his eyes bitter. "I thank you for your intervention, sir, but I fear you have made things worse. They will be back."

Tarja squatted down beside the older man. "If you've done nothing to be guilty about, then the Defenders will be reasonable."

The man shook his head. "How little you know them, sir. There was a time when that might have been the case, but not now. My son attacked a Defender. That is all the proof of guilt they need. Jelanna cannot protect us now."

Jelanna. The pagan Goddess of Fertility. "Then you really are heathens," he said, with the bitter irony of knowing that he had killed Defenders to protect a heathen. He glanced up and looked at R'shiel, but her expression was unreadable.

"When this is justice according to the Sisters of the Blade," the man retorted, stroking the fair hair of his dead son, "do you blame us?"

Tarja didn't answer. Everything he believed in had taught him that the heathens were a danger to Medalon. He had spent a large part of his adult life stamping out pagan cults. He had never expected to find himself fighting to protect them.

"What will you do?" R'shiel asked, picking her way through the wreckage toward them.

"Flee," the man said with a shrug, looking around at the ruins of his tavern. The cries of the wounded settled over the taproom like a blanket of misery. A woman in the corner was making an attempt to right some of the overturned stools. Others just stared, aghast at what had happened. "What else can we do?"

"Do you have somewhere to go?"

The old man nodded. "Some of us have families in other villages who will take us in. Others, like young Ghari and Mandah there, are far from home. It is the ones like them I fear for. They are the ones the Defenders will hunt down first."

Tarja nodded in agreement. Joyhinia might want every heathen in the country destroyed, but the Defenders would do it their way. They would take out the dangerous ones first. Those who were young and hot-headed enough to resist. The Defenders might be acting under spurious orders, but it had not rendered them stupid.

The man clutched at Tarja's arm suddenly, his grip painfully tight. "You could help them. You could lead them to safety."

"There is no safety for your kind in Medalon," Tarja pointed out, rather more harshly than he had intended. "The Sisterhood will destroy you."

The tavern keeper shook his head. "No, the demon child comes. He will save us. Jelanna has given us a sign."

Tarja stood up and glared at the man. "Jelanna could write it across the sky in blood, old man; that still won't make it true. Forget this nonsense and get away while you can."

"Are you afraid of the demon child?" Ghari challenged.

"No, we just don't believe fairy stories," R'shiel said. "And neither would you if you had any brains."

"If you had any faith, you would know the truth of it," the young heathen retorted. "Jelanna protects us."

"Really?" R'shiel asked cynically. "I didn't see her doing much to aid you this night."

"But she has," a female voice said behind him. Tarja turned to find a young, fair-haired woman standing behind him. She looked enough like Ghari to be his sister, with the same hair and pale green eyes. "The gods do not always work in the way we expect them to. Jelanna brought you here, Captain, to aid us."

Tarja stilled warily as she addressed him by rank. "You mistake me for someone else. I have no rank."

"You are Tarja Tenragan, Captain of the Defenders and the son of the First Sister. You and your sister are on the run, and there is a price on both your heads. Your presence here will distract the Defenders. They will ignore a simple cult of heathens for the chance to capture either of you. By bringing you here, Jelanna has, therefore, protected us."

Tarja turned from her and discovered Ghari and the others staring at him, open-mouthed.

"*You* are Tarja Tenragan?" Ghari asked in a tone that bordered on awe.

"I am nobody," Tarja countered. "Stay and face the Defenders if you must. We're leaving. Unless your goddess has made you impervious to steel, you might think about doing the same."

"We can help you," the young woman said. "If you will help us."

Tarja gripped the hilt of his sword as he glared at her. "Help you? As you so accurately pointed out, our presence will draw the Defenders' attention from your cult. Haven't we done enough?"

She stepped closer and looked up at him. "What you see here is nothing, Captain. This same scene is enacted every night in villages across Medalon. People are dying. *Your* people. Heathen and atheist alike. And what are you two planning to do? Ride south and live the high life in Hythria or Fardohnya, maybe? While your people are slaughtered by a woman who kills to assure nothing more than the consolidation of her own power?"

Tarja studied the young woman for a moment, wondering how a simple villager could glean so much from gossip and rumor.

"I was a Novice," she said, as if she understood his unasked question. "For a while. Until I saw the truth about the Sisterhood. I was a couple of years ahead of you, R'shiel."

He glanced at R'shiel who nodded slightly. "I remember. You were expelled."

"That's when I embraced the old ways."

"Just what is it you expect of us?" he asked her.

"Teach us to fight!" Ghari declared enthusiastically.

The young woman held up her hand to restrain her brother. "Ghari, you talk too much."

"But Mandah!"

Mandah turned back to them. "You could teach us how to resist."

"If I had a hundred years, I could not teach your heathen farmers how to fight like the Defenders."

"Most of our people have no wish to fight, Captain," she said. "But you know the Defenders, and R'shiel knows the Sisterhood. You know how they operate. You know their strategies. Armed with that information, our people would be able to protect themselves."

"You are asking us to betray them," Tarja said.

"You deserted the Defenders and just killed three of them," Ghari pointed out. "I'd say you crossed that stream a long time ago."

Tarja shook his head. "You'll have to fight your own battles."

Mandah nodded understandingly and stood back as he strode through the debris to collect their saddlebags. R'shiel stood looking at the young woman, then followed him to the door. Mandah said nothing. He had jerked the door open, kicking a broken stool out of the way when her voice stopped them.

"Captain. R'shiel."

Tarja glanced over his shoulder at her. The other men and women in the room watched them expectantly.

"What?"

"The Purge that destroyed the Harshini killed a thousand men, women, and children. It lasted a little over ten years. This one has been going on for three months and it has already taken more lives than that. The woman responsible is your mother. I hope you sleep well at night."

"She's not *my* mother," R'shiel retorted.

He slammed the door behind them as they walked away.

etting into Reddingdale had been easy. Getting out was a different matter entirely. They crossed the dark street to the Livery where their horses were stabled to the sounds of shouted orders further down the road. They did not have long, he knew. The sergeant had recognized them, and word of their presence in the town would have already reached the other troops. The men who had raided the inn were only a small part of a much larger force, which was unlikely to be under the command of another raw lieutenant. Telling the drowsy stableboy to go back to sleep, they saddled their horses quickly in the dim light cast by a shielded lantern and led them to the door.

Dousing the lantern, he opened the stable door fractionally, glancing into the street. Although he could not see anything in his limited line of sight, he could hear the Defenders moving toward the inn. The officer in charge called out an order to move up. Tarja cursed silently as he recognized the voice. Nheal Alcarnen was a friend, or had been once. They had served together on the border for a time. Tarja had no wish to confront him, no wish to kill him, and certainly no wish to be killed by him. As he pulled back into the stable, a figure detached itself from the shadows by the inn and ran across the muddy street toward him, slipping past him and into the stable as he pushed the door shut.

"You can't escape that way," Mandah warned as she pushed back the hood of her cape.

"You should be more concerned with yourself, than us," Tarja whispered.

"Our people will be safe."

"Jelanna's looking out for them, I suppose?" R'shiel muttered.

"Jelanna taught us to honor her and the other gods, believe in them faithfully, and to build an escape tunnel through the cellar. My friends are well clear of the inn by now."

"So, you heathens aren't as helpless as you look."

"We are still human, Captain," she replied. "We simply choose to believe in the forces of nature, not man. We believe that humans should embrace the forces of the natural world, rather than—"

"Convince him some other time," R'shiel interrupted as the sound of the advancing troop drew nearer. Doors slammed and angry shouts erupted as the Defenders checked the houses and stores on either side of the street. Nheal was an experienced captain. He was too adept to leave his rear exposed as he moved on the inn, even if his attackers might be little more than angry storekeepers. It was a maxim to the Defenders, drummed into Cadets from their first day: A weapon without a man is not dangerous; any man with a weapon is. They had only minutes before they reached the inn. "Jelanna didn't happen to tell you to build an escape route out of here too, did she?"

"If I show you the way out of here, I place my friends at great risk. I cannot take such a risk unless there is something in it for us."

Tarja frowned. "That's blackmail."

Mandah met his gaze, unconcerned by the sound of the advancing Defenders or by their imminent danger of arrest. "Not at all, Captain. The choice is yours. Escape or capture."

Tarja wavered with indecision for a moment. He looked over her shoulder at R'shiel who shrugged, as if to say they had little choice in the matter and no time to argue about it. "All right, show us the way out."

"And you will help us?" she asked, refusing to act until she had his promise.

"Yes!" he snapped. "Now move it!"

But it was too late. The door rattled as a Defender tried the latch. A fist pounded heavily on the door, waking the stableboy, who staggered toward the door, staring at them owlishly for a moment as he reached for the locking bar. Mandah pushed R'shiel toward the ladder that led to the loft.

"Quickly!" she hissed. "Up there!"

R'shiel kicked their saddlebags under the nearest stall and then scrambled up the ladder as Mandah grabbed Tarja's arm and pulled him toward the first stall, pushing him so hard he landed on his back. She tore open her blouse and literally threw herself on top of him, kissing him furiously. Startled, it took a moment for Tarja to realize what she was doing.

By the time he had the presence of mind to kiss her back, the Defenders were inside.

Mandah screamed piercingly as a red-coated trooper peered into the stable, holding a torch high above his head. She allowed him a good long look at her generous pale breasts before she snatched up her skirts to cover herself, effectively hiding Tarja's face in the process.

"What have we got here, then?" the Defender asked. He sounded like an older man.

"Get out!" Mandah screamed, then she burst into tears. "Oh! Please don't tell my mother, sir! I love Robbie! Really I do! He loves me too! Tell him, Robbie!" She poked him under her skirts and he squawked with the sharp pain.

"I'll not tell your mother, lassie," the Defender said. "We're lookin' for a deserter. Tall chap with dark hair. Dangerous lookin' fella, he is. Got a redhead with him, near tall as him and very pretty. They were around here tonight."

"Tall, you say? With dark hair?" she asked thoughtfully. "And red-head?"

"Aye, that's our pair."

"Then I saw them!" she cried, poking Tarja painfully in the ribs again. "We saw them, didn't we Robbie? Don't you remember? They were here! They ran off when they heard you coming!"

"How long ago?" the trooper demanded.

Mandah thought for a moment, letting the skirt drop a little so that there was more flesh than was decent visible in the flickering torchlight.

"Well, Robbie and I had already . . . you know . . . once . . . and it was a bit before that. Half an hour, maybe? I think they went that way," she added, pointing east, away from the river.

The Defender nodded and turned to the saddled and patiently wait-ing horses with a shout. Defenders swarmed around the entrance to the stables as the beasts were led outside. Nheal's voice rose over the others as he issued his orders, which carried clearly to Tarja, even buried under the weight of Mandah, who still sat astride him, and the smothering skirts that concealed him.

"They're on foot!" Nheal informed his men. "And about half an hour ahead of us! Sergeant Brellon, check what's left of the tavern. The rest of you with me!" The thunder of hooves made the ground tremble, even in the stable, as the Defenders rode off in pursuit of their quarry.

"Sir!" Mandah called as the Defender turned away to join his Company. Tarja bit back an exasperated sigh. *Now what was she doing?* The man was leaving! *Don't call him back*, he pleaded silently. "You won't tell my . . . anyone . . . about us, will you?" she asked sheepishly. "Ma doesn't like Robbie much, you see. But once he's finished his apprenticeship . . . "

"No, lass, your secret's safe with me," the Defender chuckled. "Good luck to you. To you and Robbie."

Tarja raised an arm in salute as Mandah pulled the skirts off his face, threw herself down again, and resumed kissing him fervently. She did not stop until she was certain the Defenders had left the stable.

There were three boats docked at Reddingdale's small wooden jetty that jutted out bravely into the dark waters of the mighty Glass River. The river was broad and deep but riddled with tricky currents that could lure the unwary into disaster. No one sailed the Glass River at night by choice. Lanterns bobbed in the darkness, their reflection poking holes in the black glass of the river's surface. Mandah motioned Tarja and R'shiel to silence as they waited in the alley beside the chandler's store for the Defender on guard to march to the far end of his beat. As soon as his back was turned, they ran in a low crouch toward the boats.

The first two boats were Medalonian barges, with distinctive shallow drafts designed for navigating the tributaries of the Glass River. The third boat, tied up at the far end of the jetty, was Fardohnyan. It was to this boat that Mandah led them. As they jumped aboard, Tarja noted with surprise that the sky was beginning to lighten. They had spent all night working their way toward the docks with the young heathen woman. She had said barely a word in that time, motioning them to follow with hand signals or a look. Since climbing off him in the stable and unselfconsciously lacing her blouse, ignoring R'shiel's speculative gaze, she had been all business. Tarja found himself somewhat bemused by the young woman. And more than a little angry at her. She had extracted a promise from him that he had never wanted to make and showed no remorse at all for the way she had gone about it.

As they landed in a crouch on the boat, a big blond-bearded Fardohnyan appeared. "We almost sailed without you," he told Mandah. "Who are they?"

"Friends," Mandah assured the captain. "Tarja, R'shiel, this is Captain Drendik of the *Maera's Daughter*."

The Fardohnyan offered Tarja his hand and pulled him to his feet. "Maera's blessing on you, friend," he said.

"And you," Tarja replied. It did not surprise him that the Fardohnyan worshipped the River Goddess, but he was a little surprised to find him actively helping the Medalonian heathens.

"It will be light soon," Drendik warned, "and I'd like to be away from here before it occurs to those red-coated fancy boys to search my boat. You three get below and tell Brak and those good-for-nothing brothers of mine to get up here. We'll be out into the current before they realize it."

Mandah stood on her toes and kissed Drendik's cheek. "May Jelanna bless you with many more sons, Drendik."

"Jelanna has been too kind already," he complained. "Now get below."

Mandah led them down a companionway to a narrow passage that Tarja was almost too tall to stand upright in. They followed her through the gloom to a door at the end of the passage, which she opened without knocking. The cabin was full of people, crowded around a small table, many of them from the inn.

Ghari flew off the narrow bunk as they stepped inside and hugged Mandah with relief.

"You made it!" he cried, unnecessarily. "And you brought them!"

"A little unwillingly, perhaps," Mandah said. "But they have agreed to help us. Captain, R'shiel, this is my younger brother Ghari, and this is Padric, Jarn, Aldernon, Meron, and Hari." The young men around the table studied him warily, all except Padric, who looked old enough to be the grandfather of the others. He seemed openly hostile. "And of course, this is Gazil and Aber, the captain's brothers," she said, indicating the two Fardohnyans who stood leaning against the bulkhead. "And you must be Brak," she added to the man who stood next to the door, his faded blue eyes watching them guardedly. "Drendik wants you up top."

The two sailors, both younger and more slender versions of the captain and the tall crewman, pushed past them into the passage.

"How do we know we can trust them?" Hari asked Mandah as soon as the sailors had left.

"I gave my word," Tarja replied.

"Do you think the word of a Defender, especially one who has already betrayed his oath to his own kind, is supposed to reassure us?" Padric asked.

"I don't particularly care what you think, old man. I said I would help you and I will, as much as I'm able. But don't try converting us to your cause or assigning noble motives where there are none. Mandah helped us, and we will help her in return. That is all."

"Spoken like the professional killer he is," Jarn scoffed. "Why do we need him?"

"Because," R'shiel answered, her voice steely with determination, "properly organized, you could bring down Joyhinia Tenragan and the Sisters of the Blade."

Silence descended on the shocked heathens at her words.

It was Ghari who recovered first. "We could even restore Medalon to the old ways."

Tarja stared at R'shiel. He opened his mouth to object, to deny that he had promised to do anything of the kind. He could show them how to defend themselves. Teach them the laws that defined the Defender's actions. Warn them of the tactics the Defenders would use against them. But he had not agreed to topple the Sisterhood. He certainly had not agreed to restore Medalon to heathen worship. The expression on R'shiel's face was savage. She had nursed her anger all through winter, he knew, letting it smolder while she pretended she didn't care. These pagans had offered her a chance to even the score, to hurt Joyhinia on an unprecedented scale. She grabbed it with both hands.

"It's time the First Sister learned a little about suffering."

The heathens glanced at each other, taken back by her ferocity. Tarja looked at her with concern. She had no care for the heathens or their cause. R'shiel just wanted to pay back twenty years of lies and manipulation. She wanted revenge.

chapter 19

After Mandah sent them up to help Drendik cast off, Brak went forward to untie the mooring ropes on the prow. This was not the first time Drendik had helped fugitive heathens since Brak had joined his crew. Between that and the smuggling the Fardohnyan indulged in, it was a miracle he had the time or the space for legitimate trade. Nevertheless, these last two who had come on board worried Brak. They were not the usual dispossessed pagans Drendik aided, frightened and grateful for any assistance. This pair was dangerous—the First Sister's errant offspring with a price on their heads and the entire Defender Corps on their heels. Their mere presence was a threat to them all.

Brak was still hauling in the thick rope, worrying about the new passengers, when the River Goddess suddenly appeared, draped over a bale of Bordertown wool. Her expression, Brak supposed, was meant to be seductive and alluring. Unfortunately, on Maera, it tended to have the opposite effect.

One of the drawbacks of being a god, Brak privately thought, even a Primal God, was that one was inevitably forced to assume the characteristics that one's worshippers attributed to you. Only the very powerful gods, like Kalianah, the Goddess of Love, Zegarnald, the God of War, Dacendaran, the God of Thieves, or the Sea God, Kaelarn, were strong enough to assume any form they chose. Most were doomed to appear in the aspect their believers wanted to see, and Maera was no exception. Consequently, the Goddess of the Glass River was half-woman, half-fish, but not in the elegant manner of a mermaid. Rather, she sprouted a spiny dorsal fin down her back, small unblinking silver eyes, webbed hands and feet, and gills that made her appear to have numerous chins. She smiled her version of a smile at him, rather pleased that she had caught him off guard.

"You were not expecting me, Brakandaran?"

Glancing a little nervously toward the stern, where Drendik and his brothers were working, Brak shook his head. Following the direction of his gaze, she laughed. It was a wet, bubbling, and thoroughly unpleasant sound. "They cannot see me," she assured him.

"What are you doing here?" Brak asked. Drendik would have been appalled by his lack of respect, but Brak knew the gods. They rarely made social calls. She was here for a reason, and if he did not get the reason out of her soon, Maera would probably forget why she came.

"You are not pleased to see me, Brakandaran?"

"I'm beside myself with happiness," he assured her. "What are you doing here?"

"You've been visiting with Kaelarn, haven't you?" The Sea God was almost as powerful as Kalianah or Zegarnald and far above a mere River Goddess in the general scheme of things.

"I never saw him. And anyway, I left the ocean to return to you," he reminded her, which seemed to appease her vanity somewhat. "Why are you here, Maera?"

"What? Oh, that! I came to tell you about the child."

"What child?" Brak made an effort to appear patient. Maera, like the river she held divinity over, was a fickle creature.

"Lorandranek's child," she said, as if Brak was just a little bit dense.

"Maera, I'm half-human. I need details. What do you have to tell me about Lorandranek's child?"

Maera sighed heavily. "I can feel it. I felt it the last time it was on my river, but that was ages ago. Zegarnald told me I had to tell someone if I felt it again. So I'm telling you." She pouted and stroked her scaly skin. "I don't like Zegarnald. The river bleeds when he's around."

Brak's eyes widened at the revelation. "You've felt the child before? Why didn't you tell someone?"

"I did," she objected with a frown that made her gills wobble. "I told Zegarnald."

The War God had kept the information to himself for his own reasons, Brak thought in annoyance. "The demon child is on the boat now?"

"I said that, didn't I?"

Brak ground his teeth with frustration. "Who is it?"

The goddess shrugged. "I don't know. All humans look the same to me. They just arrived, though. I only felt it a moment ago."

A moment to Maera could have been a second or a week, depending on the mood she was in. But if he assumed that she was speaking in human time frames, that narrowed it down to either Mandah, Tarja, or R'shiel. He dismissed the two from the Citadel immediately. Lorandranek had impregnated a mountain girl, not the future First Sister. He thought of Mandah's placid nature and unswerving faith. She had been a Novice for a while. She had been at the Citadel. She was around the right age. It all fitted perfectly.

"How do I tell for certain?"

"By his blood," Maera explained, a little annoyed at his inability to comprehend.

"You said 'his.' Do you mean it's a man?"

"I don't know! I told you, all humans feel the same to me."

He was silent for a moment. "You don't happen to know anything else about this child, do you?" he asked. "Its name, perhaps?"

Maera shrugged. "It is té Ortyn. Even you should be able to feel the bond."

"I can only feel the bond if they draw on their power."

"Stay with the humans, then," Maera advised. "You'll figure it out eventually."

Before Brak could answer, the Defender patrolling the wharf finally noticed the Fardohnyan boat had slipped its moorings. He yelled at them as the boat floated into the current and was picked up by the river, which grabbed hold of the barge greedily and sent it speeding downstream. Drendik stood in the stern yelling back at the Defender.

"What you say? No speak Medalonian!" he was calling. "NO SPEAK MEDALONIAN!"

By the time the other soldiers had joined the guard on the wharf, signaling the boat to return with wild arm gestures, the barge was safely into the current. Drendik, Gazil, and Aber were waving at the Defenders, wearing uncomprehending expressions. Brak followed suit. They kept waving until the boat slipped around the bend of the river and the small Reddingdale dock vanished from sight in the gray dawn. Amused at Drendik's simple but effective subterfuge, Brak turned back to the goddess, not surprised to find that she had vanished.

With a sigh, he secured the ropes and made his way below. If Maera was to be believed, he was going to have to join the rebels.

They sailed downriver to Testra for the next few days, Brak watching Mandah closely for some sign that she really was the one he sought. The young woman had a natural serenity about her that reminded him of the Harshini. A sort of trusting innocence that led one easily into trouble if he or she were not careful. If this was truly Lorandranek's child, and the gods expected her to face down Xaphista, they were going to be sorely disappointed. Mandah worshipped Jelanna and Kalianah and held life sacred. She appeared to have none of the violent human tendencies that characterized Brak and his ilk. In fact, after watching her closely for several days, the only word he could find to describe her was . . . nice.

He did not have the same problem finding words to describe the young woman she had brought with her. R'shiel was trouble. Raised in the Citadel, she was intelligent and articulate and could talk the heathens into just about anything she set her mind to. That in itself did not concern him, however, but her fierce determination to destroy Joyhinia did. Since R'shiel had come on board, even old Padric had begun talking like a revolutionary. The runaway Probate had a gift for stirring the passions of her companions. She spoke of restoring religious freedom. She spoke of ending the Purge. She spoke of freeing those sentenced to the Grimfield. But she did not believe in the gods, and her motives were far from altruistic. She wanted revenge on Joyhinia for crimes Brak could only guess at. He considered her dangerous in the extreme. Tarja was far less complicated. He obviously intended to keep his promise to the rebels, but it irked him. Brak trusted Tarja's reluctant oath over R'shiel's savage enthusiasm for rebellion.

Brak sought out Mandah, the night before they reached Testra, to ask if he could join them. If she truly was the demon child, he did not plan to let her out of his sight. The young woman accepted him gladly, not questioning his decision to follow their cause. R'shiel raised a brow at the suggestion but did not object, and neither did Padric and the others. Brak was a member of Drendik's crew, and that was enough for them. Only Tarja looked at him with a questioning frown. Brak could feel his distrust from across the cabin. He did not let it bother him. Tarja could do what he damned well pleased. He had found the demon child, he hoped.

All he had to do now was protect her from the foolish bravado of her companions, so that she lived long enough to reach Sanctuary. With R'shiel Tenragan inciting her companions to take up arms against the Sisterhood, Brak had a feeling that would not be easy.

chapter 20

As spring blossomed into summer, news of the heathen rebellion was the main topic of conversation in every tavern in Medalon. Even Brak had to admit that, with Tarja's help, the rebels were becoming a real danger. He was a natural leader. People gravitated toward him almost unconsciously. If Tarja issued an order, others obeyed it without thinking. Brak mused that in her worst nightmares, Joyhinia Tenragan could never have imagined that her Purge would prove so costly. She did not expect any sort of organized resistance and certainly not of the caliber Tarja mounted.

No longer did Defenders ride unchallenged into villages to search for evidence of heathen worship. Often, they were turned away with no violence at all. The villagers of Medalon had acquired an astounding knowledge of the law, which they used most effectively in their defense. They began demanding warrants and refusing entry without them. They knew who could sign the warrants and who couldn't. For a mostly illiterate population, they were suddenly and remarkably well informed about the letter of the law.

Of course demanding warrants and quoting the law did not stop the Defenders, it merely slowed them down a little. It was obvious where the information had come from, but while annoying, it was hardly a reason to be concerned. It simply meant the Defenders had to act within the law. Their staunch determination to do so annoyed Joyhinia intensely. Her answer was to present Lord Jenga with a list of officers she wanted transferred and others she wanted promoted. If the officers in the Corps did not suit her, she would fill their ranks with men who did. No First Sister had ever interfered so directly with the Defenders before.

It was common knowledge that Jenga was counseling an end to the Purge. By the end of summer news came that Joyhinia considered the Lord Defender's objections proof of his attempts to undermine her authority. She had dismissed his recommendations out of hand and threatened to have him removed if he continued to defy her.

Not long after that, the desertions started.

Never, in its entire history, had the Defenders suffered more than the odd misfit deserting from his unit. Until Tarja, no *officer* had ever dared such a thing. With the growing strength of the rebellion, a number of troopers simply changed sides mid-battle. The Purge was hurting everyone, and the families that were being dispossessed and arrested were sometimes families with sons in the Defenders. Brak had overheard Tarja telling Ghari that more Defenders had deserted this year than had deserted in the previous two centuries.

Joyhinia's response was as predictable as it was callous. News arrived soon after that she had issued an order decreeing that for every deserter, one of his brothers-in-arms would be hanged in his place. The desertions stopped overnight. Nobody thought Joyhinia was bluffing. The blow to the morale of the Defenders was enormous.

But enough men had joined the rebellion, moving it from an embarrassing nuisance to a real threat. Disorganized heathens brandishing pitchforks was one thing, but when well-trained, battle-hardened former Defenders joined the fray, the conflict became deadly. Every day it dragged on, the rebellion became less and less about the heathens and more about the Sisterhood.

There was one bright spot, Brak thought. A rumor had surfaced recently claiming Tarja was the demon child, sent by the long-dead Harshini to liberate the pagans from the Sisterhood. Tarja had been unimpressed when he heard it, and R'shiel had laughed at the notion, but more than a few rebels had looked at him speculatively. Some even ventured to call him Divine One, which caused Tarja to explode. Brak found the whole idea quite amusing, which for some reason made Tarja distrust him even more. Still, Brak could not help but wonder what Joyhinia Tenragan's reaction would be on hearing the news. Being known as the mother of a Divine One was not a situation a First Sister would welcome.

The rebels had set up their headquarters in a deserted vineyard, abandoned by its owners after one too many spring floods had drowned the struggling vines. They made the farm their headquarters for several reasons. It was close to the Glass River, the lifeblood of Medalon. It was south of Testra, the largest town in central Medalon, but far enough away from it that they were not in danger of accidental discovery, and it was easily defensible against an attack. From here Tarja trained his fledgling army, assisted by the wave of deserters who had joined him in the spring. Of course there were no deserters now—not since Joyhinia had threatened to hang those left behind—but there were enough to make a difference. However, thought Brak, without a lot more resources and men, the best they could hope to do was merely annoy Joyhinia.

R'shiel disagreed. She was the one who constantly urged taking the offensive. And the bellicose young men in their group, like Ghari and his friends, lapped up her rhetoric. There had been several near-disastrous raids, unauthorized by Tarja, that R'shiel had been involved in, either directly or indirectly. When he first met them, Brak had thought Tarja and his sister were close, but they fought more often than not these days. Tarja counseled caution, while R'shiel advocated aggression. Given the chance, Brak thought she might try to tear down the Citadel, stone by stone, with her bare hands. R'shiel's smoldering rage made him wonder what had been done to the girl to cause such resentment. Today's argument had merely reinforced his opinion that she was dangerous.

Several rebels had been captured in a raid on a farm north of Testra and had unaccountably been released within hours. When they returned to the vineyard this morning, they carried a message addressed to Tarja in Joyhinia Tenragan's own hand. The note was short and to the point.

This has gone on long enough, the letter said. *Be at the River's Rest Tavern in Testra at noon on Fourthday next. Draco has full authority to negotiate on my behalf.*

The note reeked of duplicity. Had Joyhinia sent Jenga, Tarja argued, he may have been less concerned, but Draco was the First Sister's tool. He had served three of them and never given one of them a moment's pause.

The rebels were ecstatic at the news. This was the proof they needed that their resistance was having an effect. Tarja argued against believing anything that came from Joyhinia until his throat was raw, and R'shiel agreed with him, for her own reasons. The rebellion had been a coherent force for less than a year. They were not yet strong or numerous enough to make a real impression. A few slogans splashed on walls and a handful of lucky skirmishes did not constitute a significant threat to the Sisterhood, Tarja tried to explain. The rebels argued otherwise. They listed their victories. They insisted that Joyhinia was under pressure from the Quorum to end the Purge.

Tarja had finally won a minor victory by insisting he be allowed to attend the meeting alone, although Ghari and several of his companions planned to enter Testra a day early to ensure the way was clear. Brak had volunteered to accompany him and bear witness to the negotiations, out of curiosity more than anything else. Tarja was not given a choice in the matter.

Since making the decision, the rebels had been in a buoyant mood. Some were talking about going home. Others dreamed of seeing lost family sentenced to the Grimfield. Their confidence was premature, and nothing Tarja said made an impression on them. They were not fighters at heart. They could not see that their optimism was misplaced. All most of them wanted was to be left in peace to worship their gods and reminisce about the old days, when the Harshini roamed the land with their demons and their sorcerer-bred horses. Brak sympathized with the rebels, but he could see Tarja's point.

The meeting was still in progress in the vast cellars beneath the run-down farmhouse. Brak had excused himself, pleading the need for fresh air. In truth, he escaped to avoid listening to R'shiel speak. Tarja advised caution for sound tactical reasons, but R'shiel wanted this conflict to continue. Her anger still had a lot of fuel to burn, and she was not ready to quit the fight. The girl had a gift for saying exactly what the rebels wanted to hear, particularly the young, belligerent ones. Brak wondered if there would ever be an end to it. She seemed to have enough hostility to last a lifetime.

Brak walked away from the darkened farmhouse, between long lines of withered vines, pondering the problem. The note from Joyhinia was a trap, perhaps, but the real danger to these rebels came from within. Tarja was smart enough to see the problem; Brak did not worry about him. In fact, despite Tarja's obvious distrust, he quite liked the man. R'shiel, however, could best help the rebels by getting herself killed in the next available skirmish.

"Why so miserable, Brakandaran?"

He started at the voice and looked around. The night was dark, the air still and cool. He felt the presence of the goddess but could not see her.

"Kalianah?"

"You do remember me!" The figure of a small child appeared between the wilted vines. She had a cloud of fair hair and wore a pale flimsy shift that rippled in the still air with every move she made. Her feet were bare and hovering just above the ground. "I told the others that just because you hadn't spoken to us for so long, it didn't mean you'd forgotten us."

"How could I forget you, Kalianah?" he asked. As the Goddess of Love glided toward him, he could feel her power radiating from her like a cheery fire on a cold night. She was hard to resist in this form.

"That's what I told Zegarnald," she agreed, settling on the ground in front of him. She looked up with wide eyes and frowned. "You are too tall, Brakandaran. Come down here."

"Why don't you just make yourself taller?" he suggested. Kalianah could chose any form she liked, but she often appeared as a child. Everybody loved children.

"Because I'm a god and you're a mortal," she told him. "I get to make the rules."

He squatted down to face her, resisting her efforts to overwhelm him with her essence. "What do you want, Kalianah?"

"I want to know what's taking you so long," she said. "Well, no, that's not true. I just want you to love me. It's Zegarnald who wants to know. You've found the demon child. It's time you took her home."

"Since when have you been Zegarnald's messenger?" he asked. Twice now, a goddess had appeared at the War God's behest. Such cooperation among the immortals was unusual. Zegarnald might be able to order the weaker River Goddess around, but Kalianah did no one's bidding.

"I am *not* his messenger," she protested. "I just happen to agree with him. Besides, I wanted to see you. You've been gone from Sanctuary so long. And you never talk to me anymore."

"I've been gone twenty years, Kalianah. You've probably only just noticed I was missing."

"That's not true! Pick me up!"

Brak did as she bade him, and she wrapped her thin arms around his neck, laying her head on his shoulder. "Do you love me, Brakandaran?"

"Everybody loves you, Kali. They can't help it."

"Does the demon child love me, too?"

"She worships you," Brak assured her.

"I want to see her!" Kalianah announced. She wiggled out of his grasp and landed on the soft earth without making a mark. "Show her to me!"

"You want me to take you into a cellar full of mortals just so I can point her out? You're a god. Can't you find her yourself?"

"Of course I can! But I want you to do it. And because I'm a goddess, you have to do as I say!"

Brak sighed. "Very well. But not until you change into something more grown up. I can't take you in there looking like that."

Instantly the child before him vanished, and a plain young woman, dressed in a simple homespun dress, took her place. "Is that better?"

"I suppose." Somewhat reluctantly, he headed back toward the farmhouse with the goddess at his side. When he glanced down, he discovered her gliding over the ground. "Walk, dammit! Unless you want to cause a riot by announcing who you are!"

"There's no need to be rude, Brakandaran. I forget sometimes, that's all."

As they neared the small stone wall that enclosed the yard, Brak held out his hand to halt her. A spill of yellow light appeared as the door opened and two figures appeared. It was Tarja leading R'shiel by the hand, none too gently. He pulled her around to the side of the house, turning on her as she pulled free of him.

"Just what in the Seven Hells do you think you're doing?" he demanded.

Brak's eyes darkened as he drew on enough power to conceal his presence. He didn't try to include Kalianah. No mortal ever saw her when she did not want them to.

"I'm helping them fight for their beliefs!" R'shiel retorted.

"You don't give a damn about what these people believe in! You're doing this to get revenge on Joyhinia!"

"Now there's a mortal who needs my help," Kalianah sighed. Brak put a finger to his lips, urging her to silence. He wanted to hear the rest of this.

"So what if I do?" R'shiel declared. "What do you care? You just want to pretend you're still in the Defenders by turning this rabble into your own private little army. Next you'll be asking them to swear an oath!"

Ouch! thought Brak. R'shiel knew better than anyone what breaking his oath to the Defenders had cost Tarja.

"That girl needs someone to love her," Kalianah said. "Shall I make them fall in love, do you think?"

"Sshh!"

"At least they'd be swearing to something they believe in, R'shiel,"

Tarja replied, his voice so low, Brak could barely make it out. "You don't believe in anything."

"And you do?" she asked. "You don't hold with these pagan gods any-more than I. Perhaps Mandah's kisses have so addled your brain that you're starting to believe in them?"

"She's jealous, that's a good sign."

"Kali, shut up!"

"Leave Mandah out of this, R'shiel," Tarja warned.

"Oh! Did I say something to offend your insipid little girlfriend? Founders, I am so sick of that girl! She only has to look in your direction and you go running! You accuse me of using these people to get revenge on Joyhinia. Well, Captain, if you want my opinion, you're here because you enjoy being worshipped like one of her damned gods! Have you slept with her yet?"

"He's going to have to kiss her," Kalianah announced with a frown. "We can't have her like this." The goddess waved her hand and Tarja, who Brak had feared was on the brink of slapping R'shiel, suddenly grabbed her by the shoulders, pushed her against the wall and kissed her with bruising force. Although taken by surprise, R'shiel did not appear to mind in the least.

"Kalianah! Stop it! They're brother and sister!"

"Don't be silly, Brakandaran. How could they be brother and sister? Lorandranek only had one child."

"But that's not—"

"The demon child?" the goddess asked, with a puzzled look. "Of course, it is. Who did you think it was?"

Brak glanced at the couple, who appeared so lost in the power of Kalianah's spell that they might see it through to it's inevitable conclu-sion, right there in the yard. "Enough, Kalianah. Let them up for air, at least."

She sighed and waved her arm. The gesture was an affectation. Her will was imposed by thought alone. They broke apart and stared at each other wordlessly for a moment, before R'shiel fled into the darkness. Tarja watched her leave then sagged against the wall, as if he could not under-stand what had come over him. Hardly surprising, under the circum-stances, Brak thought.

"It's done now, you know," Kalianah warned. "He'll only ever be able to love her. Do you think Zegarnald will be mad when I tell him what I did?"

Right then, Brak could not have cared less what the War God thought. He looked at the goddess in despair. "R'shiel is Lorandranek's child?"

"I thought we'd settled that."

"It can't be. Not R'shiel. Anyone but her."

chapter 21

It was just on dawn when Tarja finally admitted to himself that he
would get no more sleep this night. He rose from his makeshift bed
and made his way quietly through the sleeping bodies in the cellar,
climbed the narrow stairs, and let himself outside. The sun was yet
to show itself over the horizon, but it had sent out ribbons of scarlet
light to herald its imminent arrival, making the scattered clouds appear as
if they had been dipped in blood. He glanced around the silent farmyard,
noting almost unconsciously the position of the sentries.

Despite the optimism among the rebels, Tarja was well aware that the
rebellion was nothing more than an irritation to the Sisterhood. They had
no serious chance of overthrowing the Sisters of the Blade. It angered
Tarja when he heard the young, foolish men making plans about what
they would do when they took the Citadel. They had no real concept of
what they faced. They had skirmished with the Defenders and been
lucky, more often than not. They had never been attacked in force, never
faced a cavalry charge, never felt the paralyzing fear of a pitched battle.
They skirmished and retreated and thought they were heroes.

The faint smell of burning incense reached him on the still air, and he
turned curiously in the direction of the aroma. He followed it around the
side of the ramshackle farmhouse to the stables. No doubt hoping his presence heralded breakfast, several of the dozen or so horses stabled there
nickered softly as he looked inside. When he found nobody there, he
walked back around the side of the building, stepping over the low stone
wall that circled the yard. His footfalls made no sound on the soft earth as
he followed the sweet smell to a small clearing amid the wilting vines
some hundred paces from the house.

Mandah was kneeling on the damp ground, her back to him, as she tended a small stone altar. He watched silently as she placed a small bunch of wildflowers on the altar and sat back on her heels, her head bowed in prayer. Tarja studied her curiously for a moment, wondering which of the Primal Gods she was praying to, then deciding against disturbing her, he turned to leave. Without giving any indication that she was aware of his presence, she suddenly spoke to him.

"You're up early this morning, Captain."

"So are you," he replied, as she stood up and dusted off her mud-stained skirt.

"I always get up this early. It's said that the gods listen better in the mornings."

"And do they?"

"I don't really know. But it doesn't hurt to try."

"Which god were you praying to?"

"Patanan, the God of Good Fortune," she said. "I was praying that he would be with you today."

"Do you have a God of Damned Fools?" Tarja asked, a little bitterly. "He's more likely to be with me than Good Fortune."

Mandah smiled. "No, but I'm sure if you believe in one long enough he will come into being."

Tarja frowned, her statement made no sense. "If I believe in him?"

Mandah fell into step beside him as they headed back toward the house.

"There are two sorts of gods, Captain," she explained. "The Primal Gods, who exist because life exists. Love, Hate, War, Fertility, the Oceans, the Mountains—every one of them has a god. The Incidental Gods come into being when enough people believe in them." She smiled at Tarja's blank expression. "Let me explain it another way. You've heard of Kalianah, the Goddess of Love?"

Tarja nodded.

"Well, she is a Primal God," Mandah continued. "Now Xaphista, whom I'm sure you've heard of, is an Incidental God. That's what they call a demon who gathers enough power to become a god. Once they achieve the status of a god, the bulk of their power comes from their believers, so the more they have, the stronger they are. If their believers lose faith, they whither and die. Primal Gods will exist as long as life does."

She laughed at his uncomprehending expression.

"You've heard of the Harshini, I suppose?"

"Of course, I have."

"Well, the Harshini are sort of a bridge between humans and the gods. The Harshini and the demons are bonded."

He nodded thoughtfully. "And you actually believe this?"

"That's the nature of faith, Tarja," she replied.

"So what do these demons do, besides running around all day trying to become . . . what did you call them . . . Incidental Gods?"

"I've no idea. You would have to ask the Harshini."

"I see," Tarja said. "So how did Xaphista get to be a god, if he was just a demon?"

She shrugged. "I'm not sure. Demons acquire learning by shape shifting and merging with other demons. I think that every time they merge, each demon acquires some of the knowledge of every other demon in the link. That's how the Harshini could fly on dragons. Hundreds of demons would merge to create the dragon, and each one learned from the others while they were in that form. I suppose Xaphista eventually acquired enough knowledge and power to gather human worshipers. He left Sanctuary, taking his Harshini clan with him. It's rumored the Karien priests are descended from those Harshini who broke away from Sanctuary."

"And he moved north to Karien," Tarja added. "So he needs all those Karien worshipers to maintain power?"

"That's the nature of an Incidental God," Mandah agreed, looking rather pleased with him. "Without people to believe in them, they are just harmless demons."

Tarja looked down at Mandah. "Then wouldn't you be better off praying to an Incidental God? He'd have more of a vested interest in answering your prayers than a god who doesn't care whether you believe in him or not."

Mandah shook her head. "You have the most infuriating way of twisting everything I say, Captain. Perhaps the gods have sent you here to test my patience."

"They've definitely sent me here to test mine," Tarja added, a smile taking the sting from his words.

She stopped walking and looked up at him. "You're starting to feel sorry you joined us, aren't you?" she asked intuitively.

He shrugged. "This rebellion can't hope to win, Mandah. All we are is a burr in the Sisterhood's saddle blanket. Sooner or later they'll turn on us in full force, and this pitiful attempt at resistance will be annihilated."

"You should have more faith, Captain. You have brought hope to our people. You have saved hundreds of lives, heathen and atheist."

"Much good that will be if those lives I'm supposed to have saved are killed later in retaliation," Tarja pointed out. "Can't you see how useless this is? You have a handful of heathens and even fewer atheists on your side. The vast majority of Medalonians don't want war. They want peace. They want to go about their lives and not be bothered by anything more serious than whether or not their crops will thrive."

"That might have been the case a year ago, Captain," Mandah replied. "But the Purge has changed that. I agree that most Medalonians could not have cared less about what the Sisterhood was doing, but things have changed. Innocent people are being hurt. People who never broke a law in their lives are being thrown off their land. Every time that happens they look at us and wonder if perhaps we're not the threat the Sisterhood claims we are. And now, even the Sisterhood has been forced to recognize us."

"You still can't win. This is a futile fight, Mandah, doomed to failure."

"Then why don't you leave us?"

"I keep asking myself the same question."

"I'll tell you the answer, Captain. It's because you know, deep down, that what you are doing is right," she said with total confidence. "It might be foolish and futile, but it's right. Today will prove that."

They resumed walking, and Tarja wondered if it was that simple. He had a bad feeling his motives were just as ignoble as R'shiel's. By fighting Joyhinia, he was making a stand. He was more than a deserter and an oath breaker; he was a champion of injustice. It would be a bitter irony if his efforts to ease his own conscience ended up costing even more lives.

By the time they reached the small stone wall that enclosed the packed-earth yard, the sky had lost its bloody tinge, and gray light bathed the old farmhouse. Tarja insisted they leave the outside as untouched as possible. Training was held amid the vines, where it was out of sight of the casual observer. The farmhouse itself looked as if nobody had been inside it for years. As much as was practicable, all business was conducted underground, in the vastly extended cellars. That was another advantage of using the old vineyard as headquarters. The cellars here were extensive, despite the relative meanness of the house.

As they drew nearer, a figure appeared in the doorway. It was the sailor from the Fardohnyan boat who had joined them, seemingly on the spur of the moment, nearly a year ago. He gave no reason for his decision. He simply offered his help. Mandah, being Mandah, accepted it gratefully. She had a bad habit of thinking everything was a sign from the gods, and Brak's offer of help was no exception. Tarja didn't trust him, although he could think of no reason why. He had never done anything to make Tarja doubt his loyalty. The man was vague about his past, but that was common among the rebels. Brak caught sight of Tarja and Mandah and crossed the yard toward them.

"I thought perhaps you'd left without me," he said to Tarja as he approached. Brak was even taller than Tarja but of a much more slender build. He moved with an economy of gesture that made Tarja wonder if he had trained as a fighter. He had thick brown hair and weary, faded eyes and the manner of one who had seen just about everything there was to be seen in the world and found it wanting. "Good morning, Mandah."

"Good morning, Brak," she replied. "I've just made an offering to Patanan to aid you on your journey."

"That was very thoughtful of you." Tarja saw the expression that flickered over the older man's face and wondered about him again. He professed to believe in the Primal Gods, but unlike the other heathens, Brak seemed almost skeptical about the value of the prayers and sacrifices of his brethren. "I hope it won't be wasted."

"You're as bad as Tarja," she scolded. "Have a little faith."

"Faith I have in abundance, Mandah," he said. "It's hope I run short of, on occasion." He turned his attention to Tarja and added, "Like hoping we're not walking into a trap this morning."

Tarja found himself once again forced to reassess his opinion of Brak. Nobody else had supported him when he warned that the meeting today in Testra was more likely to be a trap than a true chance at a resolution of the conflict—no one except R'shiel, who cared more about the rebellion continuing than finding a chance to end it. Even the Defenders who had deserted the Corps to join him seemed to think it was a genuine chance to end the conflict. Perhaps they were just beginning to regret their decision. Living with a price on your head was not easy, as Tarja could readily attest to.

"I wish others shared your opinion," Tarja said, with a meaningful glance at Mandah. The young woman looked at them both and frowned.

"We have gone over this again and again," she reminded them. "It might be a trap, but it might be a genuine offer of peace. We cannot ignore it. The Sisterhood recognizes the threat we pose and wants to talk. If we can negotiate an end to the Purge and religious freedom for our people, then the fighting can stop. I thought that's what you wanted, Tarja?"

"Of course it's what I want," he said, exasperated by the argument that had been going on for over a week.

"The gods will be with you both," she assured them with quiet confidence. "It will not be long now, before this is over."

Tarja glanced at Brak, who seemed to share his skepticism. He stood back and let Mandah pass, then turned to Tarja.

"You know this is a trap, don't you?"

Tarja nodded. "I'm almost certain of it."

"Then why are you going?" Brak asked.

Tarja glanced at the retreating figure of the young woman and shrugged. "Because there is a remote chance that it's not," he said. "Joyhinia might genuinely want this to end without costing any more lives."

Brak shook his head doubtfully. "I've been away from Medalon for quite a while, son, but I remember the last Purge. This is no rout of a few heathens. This is systematic extermination."

"All the more reason to end it," Tarja pointed out wearily.

"Well, you know Joyhinia better than anyone, I suppose," he said. "But I suspect you may live to regret this."

"Living through it at all will be a good start."

Brak shook his head at Tarja's flippant reply and turned away, walking back toward the farmhouse with long, graceful strides. He stopped after a few paces and looked back over his shoulder.

"By the way, have you seen R'shiel anywhere?"

"No." He had not seen her for days, not since the night outside the farmhouse when their argument turned into something much too uncomfortable and confusing to dwell on. He assumed she was avoiding him, not a difficult thing to accomplish in the large network of cellars under the house. He wondered what Brak wanted with her. The sailor saw through R'shiel easily and normally paid her little attention. "Why?"

"I was just curious. I'll ask Ghari. He might know where she is."

"Ghari left last night for Testra," Tarja reminded him. "You don't think she went with them, do you?"

"The gods help us if she has," Brak muttered. "Still, it's not that important. No doubt she'll turn up."

"No doubt," he agreed, a little concerned at Brak's sudden interest in

R'shiel, and more than a little concerned that R'shiel might be missing. As he followed him to the house, another uncomfortable thought occurred to Tarja.

Brak claimed to remember the last Purge.

The last Purge the Sisterhood had launched against the heathens was during the reign of First Sister Brettan almost one hundred and twenty years ago.

chapter 22

Tarja and Brak rode in silence toward Testra, timing their arrival for around two hours before noon. Tarja wanted to scout the area before meeting with Draco. He might be walking into a trap, but he wasn't planning to walk in blindly. Brak rode beside him along the sunlight-dappled road with the ease of one raised in the saddle, a fact that merely added to Tarja's concern about him. By all accounts the man was a sailor. Sailors didn't ride so well. Most sailors didn't ride at all, treating horses with a sort of awed animosity. It was another piece of the puzzle that was Brak.

"You ride well for a sailor," he remarked. The wind had picked up, and a chill breeze tugged at Tarja's cloak. The bright sunlight was deceptive, with little warmth in it.

Brak glanced at him and shrugged. "I've not always been a sailor."

Tarja hardly expected anything more enlightening, but the man's answer annoyed him, nonetheless.

"You came from Hythria recently, didn't you?" he asked, deciding he was going to find out something about this man before they got to Testra. His life might depend on him before the day was out. He wanted to know what sort of man was watching his back.

"Yes," was Brak's unhelpful reply.

"What were you doing there?" He hoped he sounded as if he was just making conversation, but he suspected Brak knew what he was after, when the older man suddenly smiled.

"I was advising the Sorcerer's Collective on matters of policy," he said.

Tarja felt a little foolish for being so transparent. "I deserved, that, I suppose. I'm sorry, I didn't mean to pry."

"Yes, you did. You're burning up with curiosity about me. I'll tell you if you like. Which version do you want, the one that sounds plausible or the truth?"

Tarja glanced at the older man, wondering at his question. "Is there a difference?"

"A vast one," Brak told him. "I doubt if you'd believe the truth, though. The plausible explanation is far easier to live with. Particularly for a man with your prejudices."

Thoroughly bewildered now and rather sorry he had ever broached the subject, Tarja frowned. "If you've nothing to hide, what need for anything other than the truth?"

"What need, indeed?" Brak agreed.

Tarja could feel his patience wearing thin. "If you've no wish to tell me about yourself, then don't," he snapped. "I'm only concerned that you are who you claim you are."

"Then I give you my word that I am," Brak replied.

The silence was strained after that. Tarja kicked his horse forward a few paces, angry at himself for losing patience so easily as much as Brak's reticence. He didn't trust the man, and their conversation had done little to ease his mind. Brak had joined them so suddenly, so unexpectedly, that it was hard to credit he had any abiding belief in their cause. He professed to be a pagan, yet his attitude to the gods that the pagans held in such high esteem was almost contempt.

And now he was riding into an almost certain trap with Brak at his side. It was no wonder he was feeling uneasy, he told himself.

After letting Tarja brood for a few moments, Brak caught up with him. "I left Medalon a long time ago, Tarja," he said, as if there had been no break in their conversation. "I did something that meant I couldn't return to my family. Don't ask what it was, because I won't tell you. I've roamed the world ever since. I've spent time in Fardohnya working in the diamond mines, even in Karien as a wagon driver, although no one in his right mind spends long in that country without being seen to convert to the Overlord. For the past few years I've been working a fishing boat in the Dregian Ocean south of Hythria."

"What made you come back?" Tarja asked.

"My family asked me to do something for them. I have to find someone very important to them who is lost," Brak told him carefully.

"Yet you joined us," Tarja pointed out. "Shouldn't you be looking for this lost soul? Or do you expect to find him in our ranks?"

Brak was silent for so long, Tarja thought he was not going to answer the question.

"I . . . believe this person is someone close to you," Brak said finally, as if it had been a major decision to admit such a thing.

Tarja was astonished. "How do you figure that?"

He gave a short, humorless laugh. "Call it the will of the gods. You are the demon child, after all."

Tarja glared at Brak in annoyance. "Surely you don't believe that nonsense?"

"That you are the demon child? Of course not. Although it was a clever tactic," he added. "It must be driving the Sisterhood crazy."

"Don't credit me with any cleverness," Tarja objected. "I've no idea who started that rumor, but I'd like to throttle whoever did."

"Well, anyone who understands the nature of demons won't believe it."

"What do you mean?"

"Demons have a reputation that far outweighs the damage they can actually do," Brak told him. "As a rule, demons only cause trouble when their insatiable curiosity traps them in something they can't figure a way out of."

"You sound quite the expert."

"Hardly that," Brak disagreed. "But I can tell you this much: young demons have limited intelligence and absolutely no sense of direction. If the demon child were truly part-demon, he or she would be a half-witted troublemaker with just enough power to snuff out a candle."

"You believe there is a demon child, then?"

"I know there is," Brak assured him. "And when the demon child is finally revealed, you'll be there at the forefront of the action, I suspect."

"I'm a little surprised to hear you speak so knowledgeably about demons," Tarja remarked suspiciously. "I wonder sometimes that you even believe in the pagan gods."

"Oh, never fear on that score," Brak assured him. "Nobody knows better than I that the gods exist. Whether I believe them worthy of adoration is an entirely different matter." He was silent for a time, then added, "I met someone who knows you in Hythria."

The news startled Tarja. He had no friends in Hythria that he was aware of. "Who?"

"Damin Wolfblade," Brak said. "He misses you, actually. Says life's been pretty dull since you left the border."

"What I wouldn't give for a few Centuries of his Raiders now," Tarja muttered. It suddenly occurred to him that with Hythrun allies he could truly threaten the Sisterhood. A few hundred Krakandar Raiders would tip the scales in their favor. He was flattered that the Warlord remembered him and that he held him in such high regard. It was a sign of how far he had fallen, he decided, that he could wish for aid from a nation that was so recently his enemy. Then another thought occurred to him, and he looked at Brak with narrowed eyes. "How is it that you were speaking with a Hythrun Warlord?"

"I was traveling north and so was his party," he explained. "Nobody in his right mind travels Hythrun roads alone. It's a long trip. We got talking. There's no need to look at me like that. If I was a Hythrun spy, I'd hardly be boasting of having met a Warlord, would I?"

Tarja looked at his companion warily. "I don't know, would you?"

"You know, if you treated this meeting with Lord Draco with half as much suspicion as you treat me, I would not be nearly so concerned about it. Save your doubts for those who deserve them, Tarja."

With that, Brak kicked his horse into a canter and rode on ahead.

The River's Rest Tavern appeared no different from any other dockside tavern along the Glass River. Its painted shutters were thrown wide open, to air out the previous evening's aromas of stale beer. The faint sounds of furniture being dragged across the wooden floor indicated someone was probably laying out fresh rushes. The docks on the other side of the street were as raucous and chaotic as normal. Tarja and Brak watched the tavern for over an hour from the shelter of the wharves and saw nothing that would indicate a trap. There was no sign of Ghari or his companions either. That meant one of two things: either they had already been caught in the trap, or they had finally learned something from all the training and lectures Tarja had been forcing on them. Trying to curb youthful enthusiasm and replace it with discipline and common sense was not easy.

"There's no sign of the lads," Tarja remarked, a little concerned.

"That could just mean they picked the wrong tavern," Brak replied without looking up. "Those boys aren't the most reliable advance guard."

Tarja nodded in agreement. Any number of things could have happened to them that had nothing to do with the present situation. He glanced at Brak who was whittling away at a piece of driftwood with a small knife, looking for all the world like the sailor he professed to be.

"It's almost noon," Tarja said, glancing up at the sun, which had warmed little as it journeyed across the sky.

"Do you want me to go in first?" Brak asked.

"Yes," Tarja agreed, his eyes not leaving the tavern for a moment. "Take a seat near the door. Don't try to be a hero. Just back me up if I need it. If worst comes to worst, just get clear and warn the others."

"I'm not the heroic type," Brak assured him as he stood up, brushing wood slivers from his trousers. "If anything happens to you, I'll be on the next boat to Fardohnya." Tarja glared at him. "I was joking, Tarja."

"I'll see you inside." Tarja said, wondering when he had lost his sense of humor.

Brak crossed the street with a swaggering walk that marked him as a sailor as surely as his tan and his rough linen shirt. He wandered up to the tavern and disappeared inside. Tarja waited expectantly, but nothing happened. For a moment he wondered if he had gotten the day wrong, or if Draco's ship was late and he had yet to arrive in Testra. Or perhaps Joyhinia had changed her mind. As the doubts began to pile up, he fought them back with an effort. He waited another few minutes, until the bell in the distant Town Square tolled midday. Swallowing down a lump of apprehension that had lodged in his throat, he crossed the street to the tavern.

chapter 23

Brak wandered casually across the street, carefully drawing on his power as he neared the tavern, his eyes darkening as the magic filled him. He did not draw much. He only wanted to be inconspicuous, not vanish completely midstride. He drew a simple defensive shield around himself that protected him against being noticed. It made people's eyes slide past him, preventing them from finding purchase on his form.

By the time he reached the swinging tavern door, the only person in Testra who was aware of him was Tarja, who had watched him cross the street. His eyes blazed black as the power consumed him, its sweetness like an intoxicating tonic. Why had he denied himself, he wondered, even as the answer came to him. He pushed his past and the ever-present ache away to focus on the now.

Nobody looked up as he entered, nobody remarked on his presence or even noticed it. He took a seat near the door and sighed as he realized that the illusion would prevent the tavern keeper from seeing him. He was thirsty, too.

They were waiting for Tarja, as Brak had suspected they would be. Not obviously, of course. There were no red uniforms in sight, no conspicuous weapons. Two men sat at tables either side of the door, their stiff posture and nervous expressions giving away more than they imagined. Near the rear of the large, low-ceilinged taproom, two more men waited at a long scrubbed table. One was an older man with an unconscious air of authority. Brak wondered about him for a moment. He thought he might be Lord Draco, but there was something familiar about him that Brak could not quite put his finger on. No doubt the younger man with him was a captain. He wore his civilian clothes uncomfortably. How long had they been here, he wondered, waiting for Tarja to walk into their trap? The men kept looking at the door expectantly. Brak resisted the urge to follow their gaze. Tarja would get here in his own good time.

As he waited, Brak wondered again about the disgraced Defender. Tarja did not trust him, but that was understandable, Brak supposed. He had experienced a few uncomfortable moments when he listened to Tarja instructing the rebels to treat betrayal as a capital crime, the Defender's eyes firmly fixed on the Harshini as he spoke. But, despite Tarja's distrust, he had helped the rebels as much as he could, and that had actually been fun. Or it would have been, had not R'shiel kept urging the rebels to even more aggressive acts of defiance.

Brak tried not to think about the demon child too much. He had not come to terms with Kalianah's distressing revelation and was rather relieved he had not had to confront her yet. There would be time for that later, once this day was past.

Although he would leave the rebels soon to take R'shiel back to Sanctuary, Brak had enjoyed these past few months. Frustrating the Sisterhood was a worthy pastime for any Harshini. His full-blooded cousins would not have agreed with him. Their willingness to sit back and take whatever was thrown at them was one reason he had never really fitted in.

The door to the tavern swung open and Tarja appeared, squinting blindly as he moved from the bright sunlight to the gloom of the tavern. A bubble of tension began to build in the room. Tarja stood on the threshold for a moment, until his eyes adjusted to the dimness, then he walked into the room. He spotted Draco and the captain immediately, but if he noticed the other ill-disguised Defenders around him, he gave no sign.

Brak watched him, as Tarja stepped toward Draco and the captain, seeing immediately what had bothered him about Draco earlier. The resemblance between the two men was unmistakable, and it concerned him that Tarja had made no mention of it. Was Draco an uncle perhaps? Or a cousin? The Spear of the First Sister swore an oath of celibacy, so it was unlikely he was Tarja's father. On the other hand, if he was . . .

Brak pushed the thought away. He would ponder Tarja's parentage some other time. For now, he had to concern himself with the safety of the rebellion and this ill-advised meeting with the First Sister's closest ally in the Defenders.

The human part of Brak was telling him Tarja should have simply ignored the note from Joyhinia. The Harshini part of him was advising patience. Some things were meant to be.

Lord Draco did not rise from his seat as Tarja approached—a deliberate insult—although the captain with him did. Tarja stopped a few paces from the two men and looked at them expectantly. The silence in the tavern was heavy. The tavern keeper and his wenches had made themselves scarce. There was nobody left in the room who was not directly connected with this meeting.

"Tarja," the captain said finally, breaking the thick silence.

"Nheal," Tarja replied with a cautious nod. "Lord Draco."

Draco glared at Tarja.

"Fetch them," Draco ordered.

Nheal disappeared into the kitchen as Tarja and Draco continued to look at each other with open hostility. He returned in a few moments with several other Defenders, dressed in their distinctive red uniforms. Between them, they dragged Ghari, Rodric, Tarl, and Drenin, the four rebels who had ridden into Testra the night before to ensure that Tarja was not walking into a trap.

Brak shook his head. They were all too young, too enthusiastic, and too hotheaded for this sort of work. The young men were bound with heavy ropes, and all bore evidence of beatings. Ghari looked the worst, but he had probably resisted the most, so it was hardly surprising he had fared the poorest in custody.

As the rebels were hustled into the room, a sudden change came over Draco. He stood up and approached Tarja.

"Thank you, Captain," he said, as if the younger man was his best friend, his most trusted ally. "You've been a great help. The First Sister will no doubt give you a hero's welcome when you return to the Citadel. Did they never suspect you?"

Tarja's expression was puzzled for a moment, until he realized what Draco was doing. Ghari, however, understood immediately what Draco was implying and lunged forward in his captor's arms toward Tarja.

"You lying, traitorous, son of a bitch!" he cried. "You're a spy!"

"Draco is lying," Tarja warned Ghari, his tone admirably even under the circumstances. Brak thought he sounded shocked, as if he could not believe a Defender would be capable of such a blatant lie. In his own way, Brak thought, Tarja could be remarkably naive. "He's trying to make you believe I betrayed you. Don't listen to him."

"Come now, Tarja," Draco laughed. "There's no need for pretense any longer. I'll wager you're looking forward to getting home, eh?"

Tarja glared at Draco. "This is your idea of negotiating peace?"

"What peace?" Draco shrugged. "The pagans must be destroyed. And you are sworn to the Defenders until death. Did these fools really believe you would betray your oath so readily?"

Draco turned to Nheal. "Let one of them go. When they hear the news about Tarja, the blow to their morale should be devastating. Take the rest to the boat. We'll hang them when we get to the Citadel."

Nheal saluted, then bustled the prisoners out of the room. As soon as they were gone, Draco stepped closer to Tarja and delivered a stinging blow across the former captain's cheek. "You are a disgrace to the Corps. I would kill you myself, if the choice were mine."

Tarja took a step backward, unsheathing his sword in one fluid movement. As soon as he touched his weapon, the disguised Defenders sitting by the door leaped to their feet, ready to take him from behind. Draco held up his hand, forestalling them. He looked at Tarja contemptuously. The rebel was poised on the balls of his feet, ready and anxious to fight his way clear. There would be no negotiations. Brak wondered if Tarja was regretting his decision to come or simply concentrating on getting out of the tavern in one piece.

"I'll not give you the satisfaction of throwing yourself on a blade," Draco told him. "If you resist, I will slit the throats of the prisoners now. Put down your sword or watch your heathen comrades die. The choice is yours."

Tarja hesitated for a moment, his blue eyes blazing with anger and frustration. Brak felt for him, but made no move to intervene. Thanks to Kalianah's ill-timed intervention, Tarja was linked to R'shiel more closely than he could imagine. Kalianah, having gone to the trouble of making him fall in love with her, would not allow anything as inconvenient as a death sentence ruin her plans. Tarja might suffer a little, but Kalianah would not permit him to die.

Tarja glanced around the taproom quickly, no doubt looking for Brak, but the illusion he had drawn around himself made his eyes pass over Brak without pause. Once Tarja had lost sight of him on entering the Tavern, he would not find him again until Brak willed it. He saw the look of disappointment and betrayal that flickered over Tarja's face and knew that the next time they met, he would have a lot of explaining to do.

"You're going to kill them anyway," Tarja pointed out. "What difference does it make?"

Draco considered the matter for a moment then nodded. "A valid point. Sergeant, fetch the innkeeper."

The man in question must have been listening at the door. Almost before Draco had finished speaking, he appeared, wiping his hands on his apron, anxious to be of service, his balding head sheened with sweat.

"My Lord?" he asked obsequiously.

"Come here," Draco replied evenly. Without warning, he grabbed the innkeeper's arm, and jerked the man off his feet. As the innkeeper hit the rush-covered floor with a startled cry, Draco snatched his own sword from its scabbard and placing a booted foot on the terrified man's chest, held the point just above his throat. He glanced up at Tarja.

"Perhaps a few civilian corpses will change your mind," he remarked callously. "The innkeeper first, then his daughters, perhaps? I'm in no hurry."

Brak could imagine what was going through Tarja's mind. He could almost see him calculating his chances of reaching Draco before he plunged his sword into the innkeeper's throat, judging distances out of the corner of his eye, marking the position of the men behind him. The odds were hopeless. Brak said a silent prayer to Jondalup, the God of Chance, that Tarja would realize it.

Jondalup must have heard him. Tarja hesitated for a moment then threw his sword down. The two men behind him were on him in an instant. Brak winced as he watched Tarja overwhelmed with brutal enthusiasm by the soldiers. Draco stood back and let the innkeeper scramble to his feet and flee the room. He sheathed his sword with an expression of intense satisfaction and ordered Tarja taken out the back way. Brak debated following them, then decided against it. He would be better off helping Ghari and the others escape. It would ease his conscience a little, at any rate. For now, Tarja was on his way back to the Citadel, and that was exactly what Brak wanted.

All he had to do now was find R'shiel.

chapter 24

'shiel had been raised to believe that tears were a sign of weakness. She had not cried as a child. Not when she was whipped for being defiant. She never shed a tear when Joy-hinia had her pony put down after she caught R'shiel trying to run away rather than join the Novices when she was twelve. She did not cry over anything, not even when Georj was killed. But as she fled Tarja in the darkness, tears she had bottled up for years burst forth, determined to undo her.

She ran blindly through the vineyard for a time, until she reached the marshy ground on the edge of the river. Sinking to her knees on the damp ground, she sobbed like a child. The worst of it was that she didn't even know why she was crying. It could not have been the argument—she and Tarja had so many these days. And it wasn't because he kissed her. She had long ago stopped thinking of him as her brother and was envious enough of Mandah to recognize jealousy when she felt it. Perhaps it was because he didn't want to kiss her, that he had done it against his better judgment. His expression when he finally let her go was enough to tell her that he regretted it.

"Why are you crying?"

R'shiel had turned at the voice, startled to find a little girl watching her curiously. The child had bare feet and wore a flimsy shift, yet she appeared unperturbed by the cool night. R'shiel had not seen the girl before. No doubt she belonged to one of the many heathen families who sought refuge at the vineyard. R'shiel's instinctive reaction to snap at the child and send her on her way suddenly dissipated as the child stepped closer.

"I don't know," she admitted, wiping her eyes.

"Is it because you fought with Tarja?" the child asked.

"How do you know I fought with Tarja?"

"You don't have to worry about him," the child assured her. "He loves you. He'll only ever love you. Kalianah has made sure of that."

"Your legendary Goddess of Love? I don't think so. And anyway, how would you know?" R'shiel couldn't understand why she was bothering with this child. She should just order her back to the house. It must be well past her bedtime.

"I am named for the goddess," the child said. "She and I are very . . . close."

"Well, next time you see her, tell her to mind her own damned business," R'shiel said, climbing to her feet and wringing out her sodden skirts. She wiped away the last of her tears and sniffed inelegantly.

"I know why you're crying."

"Really?"

"It's because Tarja's mad at you."

"Mad at me?" she scoffed. "He thinks I'm a monster."

"Why?"

R'shiel looked at the child irritably. "Because he thinks I'm just in this to get back at Joyhinia!"

"Well, aren't you?"

"Who are you?" she demanded.

"I'm your friend," the little girl told her. "And I think you need to get over Joyhinia. You've much more important things to do."

"You don't know anything about me, you impudent little brat! Go back to your family. You shouldn't be out this late anyway!"

The child looked rather put out. "Nobody has ever called me a brat before!"

"Well, it won't be the last time, I'll wager. Now, go away and leave me alone!" R'shiel turned her back on the child and stared out over the black surface of the Glass River.

"You're the spoilt brat," the child retorted loftily. "You've spent your whole life as a privileged member of a ruling class, and now you want to punish them for making you suffer. If you want my opinion, you've got a chip on your shoulder the size of the Seeing Stone, and the sooner you deal with it the better. I thought if somebody loved you, you'd be much more amenable! I don't know why I bothered!"

Startled by the child's very unchildish outburst, R'shiel spun around, but she was alone. There was no sign of the girl. Not even footprints in the soft ground. There was nothing but a small acorn tied with white feathers where the child had been standing. R'shiel picked up the amulet and studied it for a moment before hurling it into the dark waters of the Glass River.

More than six weeks later, as the white spires of the Citadel loomed in the distance, R'shiel was still wondering what the child had meant.

She had been right about one thing, though, and so had Tarja. Her anger was directed at Joyhinia, and until she dealt with it, it would fester like a gangrenous wound, eating away at her until nothing was left but a hard bitter shell. So she had gone back to the cellars, gathered her few meager belongings, and set out on foot for Testra. She had told no one of her intentions. She did not want to explain herself to Tarja, and she doubted if anybody else really cared.

On reaching Testra, R'shiel traded her silver hand mirror for passage on the ferry to Vanahiem on the other side of the river and began heading on foot to the Citadel. During her second day on the road she was fortunate enough to hitch a lift with a stout couple from Vanahiem delivering furniture for their newly married son in Reddingdale. Their names were Holdarn and Preena Carpenter. She told them she was a Probate on her way back to the Citadel after her mother had died in the Mountains. It was barely even a lie. The couple had been so considerate, so solicitous of her comfort, that she almost regretted her deception. When they reached Reddingdale, Holdarn paid for passage on a freight barge to Brodenvale for her, claiming a Probate should not have to walk all that way. R'shiel tried to refuse their generosity, but they would hear nothing of it. So she had reached Brodenvale far sooner than she expected, and from there undertook the relatively short overland trek to the Citadel.

The road was busy, filled with oxen-drawn wagons, Defenders on horseback, farmers pulling handcarts laden with vegetables, and people either heading for, or away from, the Citadel on business R'shiel did not care about. She did worry that somebody might recognize her. Although it was unlikely she was known to any of the enlisted men, there were many officers in the Defenders who knew her by sight. Fortunately, the weather was cool, and her simple homespun cloak had a deep hood that shadowed her face. She stooped a little as she pushed through the gate, but the Defenders ignored her. A lone woman was hardly worthy of notice, amid the traffic heading into the Citadel.

That hurdle successfully negotiated, she breathed a sigh of relief, although she still had no clear idea of what she planned to do. Her impulsive decision to confront the source of her anger and pain had not really manifested itself in a plan of action. There were ten thousand things she wanted to say to Joyhinia, but she could hardly just walk up the steps of the Great Hall and announce herself. Nor was there anybody in the Citadel she really trusted not to betray her presence. Certainly none of her former roommates in the Dormitories. She was sure of only one thing: that she would be arrested on sight if she was recognized. That fact presented a dilemma she had still not resolved, even after six weeks of considering the problem.

R'shiel walked toward the center of the city, head bowed, looking neither right nor left for fear of meeting a familiar eye. Consequently, she did not at first notice the crowd gathering on the roadside. It was hearing Tarja's name that finally alerted her. It rippled through the street like a whisper of excitement. She was caught up in the crowd as she neared the Great Hall and found herself well placed to watch the progress of the small army that escorted Tarja to justice.

And a small army it was. There must have been two hundred Defenders in their smart, silver-buttoned short red jackets, all mounted on sturdy, broad-chested horses. Tarja rode at the center of his escort, his mount on a lead rein, his hands tied behind his back.

Her mouth went dry as she watched him. R'shiel felt no pleasure in discovering that she had been right regarding the meeting with Draco. She had known it would be a trap. Tarja probably knew it, too. He sat tall in the saddle, but his dark hair was unkempt among his closely cropped guard. He had been beaten, that much was obvious, but that he was still alive at all was a feat in itself. He was dressed in leather breeches and a bloodstained white shirt. He was the stuff rebel heroes were made of, she thought with a despairing shake of her head, despite the black eyes and swollen lips. Handsome, strong, and defiant. It was not hard to see why he had so much sympathy among the heathens and a lot of atheists who should know better.

As they reached the Great Hall he looked around him at the thousands of Sisters, Novices, Probates, Defenders, servants, and visitors to the Citadel who were lining every balcony and roadway of the city to watch him brought in. R'shiel thought that Tarja did not look like a defeated man—angry perhaps but not defeated. He rode as if his escort was a guard of honor. He even wore the same slightly mocking, vaguely patronizing expression that he did when he was teasing her.

"The poor man," someone in front of her whispered. "How humiliating for him."

How hard was it to ride back into the heart of the Citadel, having deserted the Corps? she wondered. *Is he dying a little inside?*

"He's so brave," a female voice sighed wistfully.

"He's a traitor," someone else added.

"They said he was going to be the next Lord Defender."

"He's going to be a corpse, now," another wit pointed out, which brought a chuckle from a few and a sorrowful sigh from the others.

The column came to an impressive, synchronized halt in the center of the street. The Lord Defender, with Garet Warner, came down from the shadowed steps of the Great Hall, or rather Francil's Hall, as it was now known, to confront them. R'shiel thought it strange that the Sisterhood was allowing the Defenders to deal with Tarja and not taking a direct hand in his arrest. She half-expected to see the entire Quorum standing there, ready to condemn the traitor. But Tarja had been a Captain of the Defenders and was a deserter, in addition to his other crimes. Maybe Joyhinia thought the Defenders would exact a more fitting punishment. Draco wheeled his horse around to speak to the Lord Defender.

"I wish we could hear what they're saying," someone whispered. The crowd was strangely quiet, straining to catch a few words of the exchange. Anticipation charged the air like a summer storm. It seemed the entire Citadel was holding its breath. R'shiel watched and listened as the voices floated across the street on the preternaturally silent air.

"It is my pleasure to hand over the deserter Tarjanian Tenragan, my Lord," Draco announced, obviously aware of the huge audience he was playing to. It was not often the Spear of the First Sister took a direct hand in any action, and Draco had achieved the impossible. He had done what Jenga had been unable to. He had captured Tarja.

"Has he been any trouble?" the Lord Defender asked, glancing at Tarja.

"Once he realized he was overwhelmed, he came quietly enough."

"And the rest of his rebels?"

"He came alone," Draco said. "Bearing in mind that the First Sister ordered him taken alive, I thought it better to leave his interrogation to you."

"Just as well, I suppose," the Lord Defender grunted. "He probably would have died before he told you anything. Bring him here."

Tarja must have heard the exchange as he swung his leg over the saddle and jumped nimbly to the ground before anyone could reach him. He bounded up the steps and bowed to the Lord Defender, unhampered by the binding that held his hands behind his back.

"Good morning, my Lord, Commandant," Tarja said pleasantly. "Lovely morning for a hanging, don't you think?"

"Tarjanian, don't you think you could act just a little repentant?" Lord Draco asked.

"And disappoint all these lovely ladies?" he asked, glancing up at the crowded balconies. "I think not. How is Mother, by the way? I thought she might be here to welcome her wanton son home."

"The First Sister is probably signing the warrant for your hanging as we speak. Escort the criminal to the cells," the Lord Defender ordered Garet. "And search him."

"I have searched him already, my Lord," Draco said.

"Do it again," Jenga told Garet, making R'shiel wonder at the exchange. Jenga did not look pleased that it was Draco who had brought Tarja home.

"My Lord," the commandant replied with a salute. A brisk wave of his hand brought more guards rushing forward, but Tarja shook them off and marched past the Lords toward the huge bronze doors of Francil's Hall. Just before he disappeared into the shadows, he turned and bowed mockingly to the assembled crowd, then vanished inside.

As R'shiel watched him go, she decided it no longer mattered if she confronted Joyhinia or not. Six weeks of silently rehearsed conversations were suddenly unimportant. Her anger no longer seemed important. The energy it took to sustain it could be better directed elsewhere. That odd child by the river had been right. It was time to get over it. She had much more important things to do.

And the first thing was finding a way to rescue Tarja.

chapter 25

Pain was an interesting area of study, Tarja decided. He was close to becoming an expert in the field. He'd had plenty of opportunity to reflect on the matter over the past few days. To experiment on how much the human body could withstand, how much it could take before blessed unconsciousness pulled him down into the blackness where the pain no longer existed. The annoying part was that he kept waking up again and the pain was always there, waiting for him.

He'd stopped trying to count his injuries. His fingers were broken on both hands and burns scarred his forearms. He had several loose teeth and so many bruises he must look like a chimney sweep. His right shoulder felt as if it had been dislocated, and the soles of his feet were blistered and weeping. There was not a single pore on his skin that did not cry out when he moved, not a hair on his head that did not hurt. The cold cell made him shiver, and even that slight movement was agony.

But despite the pain, Tarja found himself in surprisingly good spirits. Perhaps it was the unimaginative torture of his interrogators that gave him something to focus on. Perhaps it was the fact that he had not uttered a word about the rebellion. He had betrayed nobody, said nothing. Mostly, Tarja suspected, it was because he knew that Joyhinia had ordered this punishment. It made everything he had done seem right, somehow.

He shifted gingerly on the low pallet that served as his bed and listened to the sounds of the night, wondering how long it would be before Joyhinia decided to hang him. There would be a trial of course, a farcical affair to satisfy the forms of law, with a gallows waiting at the end of it. The thought was oddly reassuring. It gave him comfort to know that when news of his hanging reached Mandah, Padric, Ghari, and the others, they would know that Draco had lied. Tarja knew they had escaped in Testra. He had heard it from Nheal during the voyage upriver.

Of course, he did have one regret. He was sorry he would not have the chance to find Brak. Words were insufficient to describe what Tarja would like to have done to the sailor for deserting him in the River's Rest. He had watched him enter the tavern, certain of his support, but when he arrived only moments later, Brak was nowhere to be seen. What had the miserable bastard done? Simply walked out through another door? Tarja cursed himself for not trusting his instincts more. For not insisting on some sort of proof that Brak was truly on their side. That he could think of nothing that would have satisfied him did little to appease his anger. Tarja hoped the pagans were right about reincarnation. Maybe one's spirit did get an opportunity to return to this world again and again. If that was the case, he very much wanted to come back as a flea so that he could find Brak and keep biting him until he went mad with the itching and killed himself.

His images of Brak writhing insanely in agony were disturbed by a noise in the guardroom outside his cell. Tarja wondered vaguely at the noise, but it did not concern him unduly. His world was defined by pain now, and the noises from the other room were not part of that world.

He passed out for a time, though he had no way of determining how long. It was night, he thought. He was unsure of what had woken him, or if it was merely the pain that had dragged him back. He turned his head fractionally and discovered a silhouetted shape moving toward him, small enough to be a child.

"Tarja?" the voice was hesitant, female, and very young.

"Who are you?" It took a moment for him to realize that the rasping voice was his.

"Oh my! What have they done to you?" she asked as she glided to his side. "You don't look very well, at all. Does it hurt?"

"You could say that." His mind was sluggish, but Tarja could not imagine who the child was or how she had found her way into his cell. She moved closer, and he tried to push her away, to warn her not to touch him, but the words would not come. Every movement sent black waves of agony through him.

"Shall I make you better?" the child asked.

"By all means," he gasped.

The little girl studied him thoughtfully. "I'll get in trouble if I do.

Healing people is Cheltaran's job. He gets really annoyed when anybody else does it. I suppose I could ask him, though. I mean, I can't have you dying on me. Not now."

Tarja realized that he must be dreaming. He didn't know who the child was, but the name Cheltaran was familiar. He was the pagans' God of Healing. Mandah had prayed to him often, so often that she placed more faith in his power than in more practical healing methods. Tarja thought it much more useful to actually do something to stop a wounded man bleeding to death than to pray over him and beg divine intervention. His mind wandered for a moment, the blackness beckoning him down with welcoming arms, but he fought to stay conscious, even though he knew he was asleep. Perhaps the pain had unhinged his mind. Why else would he try to remain awake inside a dream filled with pagan gods who were a figment of someone else's imagination?

The child reached out gently and pushed the hair back from his forehead. He wondered how bad he looked. He knew one eye was swollen shut because he could not see out of it, and his lips felt twice their normal size. Every muscle he owned ached, every joint creaked with pain when he moved. The worst of it was that he knew none of his injuries was fatal. His interrogators wanted him alive for the gallows. They were too smart to hurt him seriously. But you could cause an amazing amount of pain without taking a life. Tarja knew that for a fact.

"Who are you?" he groaned as her cool fingers brushed his forehead.

"I'm your friend," she said. "And you have to love me."

"Whatever," he said.

"Say it properly! Say 'I love you, Kalianah,' and you'd better mean it or I won't help you!"

"I love you, Kalianah, and you'd better mean it or I won't help you," he repeated dutifully.

The child slapped him for his temerity, and he cried out with the pain. He could never remember a dream with such clarity, such detail. "You are the most impossible human! I should just leave you there to suffer! I should let you die!"

"The sooner the better. I'll never hold a sword again. If I live, I'll be unemployed."

"You're not taking this seriously!"

"I don't have to take it seriously, I'm only dreaming," he told her.

"Cheltaran!"

Tarja was not certain what happened next. Out of the corner of his eye he thought he saw another figure suddenly appear. A cool hand was laid on his forehead, and pain seared his whole body. A bolt of agony ripped through him, worse than anything he had suffered before. It was as if all his days of torture had been condensed into one moment of blinding torment. He cried out as he lost consciousness, falling into a blackness that seemed deeper and blacker than ever before.

He plunged into it helplessly, wondering if he had finally died.

chapter 26

The Blue Bull Tavern was located near the western side of the amphitheater, along with several other taverns and the licensed brothels where the Citadel's prostitutes plied their trade for an amount set and strictly taxed by the Sisterhood. Although they frequented the Blue Bull often enough, R'shiel had little to do with the prostitutes or, as they preferred to be known, the *court'esa*. The word was a Fardohnyan one—in that country *court'esa* were men and women trained from early youth to provide pleasure for the Fardohnyan nobility. They were educated, elegant, highly sought-after professionals who, R'shiel had heard whispered among the Probates, knew six hundred and forty seven different ways to make love. The idea fascinated R'shiel. She had been raised to believe the Sisterhood's view of prostitution. Men were carnal creatures who had no control over their lust. Better to regulate the industry and make them pay for something they would take by force if it were not readily available. But to choose a life as a *court'esa*, even a pampered, Fardohnyan one, struck R'shiel as being a desperate way to make a living. Particularly in Medalon, where *court'esa* were mostly illiterate young men and women for whom the trade was one of necessity rather than choice.

There was little love lost between the *court'esa* and the Probates. The prostitutes considered Probates annoying amateurs. They robbed them of their hard-earned income every time one had a dalliance with a Defender who, by rights, should be paying a *court'esa* for her services, not getting it free from some uppity tart in a gray tunic.

R'shiel pushed open the door to the tavern and was met by a hot wave of ale-flavored smoke. The tavern was doing a brisk trade, although this late at night the customers were only off-duty Defenders and the working *court'esa*. The Novices and Probates were well abed, or should have been. R'shiel received a curious glance from a number of the painted women as she stood at the door looking around. She spied Davydd Tailorson across the room, drinking with several other officers. A plump *court'esa* with big brown eyes was leaning forward suggestively toward Davydd, her ample bosom threatening to escape her low-cut gown at any moment. Whatever she was saying had all the officers at the table laughing uproariously. R'shiel took a deep breath and crossed the taproom, trying to ignore the curious stares of both the *court'esa* and the Defenders who thought a young female stranger in the tavern this late in the night was bound to be looking for trouble. She was halfway across the room when Davydd glanced up and caught sight of her. He frowned, made some comment to his companions and then left the table. His expression grim, he walked across the taproom, took her arm and steered her back out onto the verandah into the bitter cold.

"What are you doing here?" he hissed, surprising her with his annoyance. "Don't you know how much trouble you could get into?"

"Of course I know," she said, shaking her arm free of his grasp. "But I need your help."

"Can't it wait until morning?" he asked impatiently, glancing back toward the taproom. The *court'esa* who had been thrusting her bosom at him was watching them curiously through the open door. She wiggled her fingers in a small wave and blew Davydd an inviting kiss.

"Well, I'm sorry. Don't let me keep you from your whore," she snapped, annoyed by the *court'esa* and more than a little hurt by his attitude. "You obviously have plans this evening. Your little friend in there seems very accommodating." She turned and ran down the steps into the street.

"R'shiel! Wait!" He ran after her, caught her in a few steps, grabbed her by the arm, and turned her to face him. He glanced around, and, realizing they were standing in the middle of the street, he steered her over to the awning in front of the shuttered bakery. The street was still deserted, and the only noise came from the Blue Bull and the other taverns farther up the cobbled street, the only illumination the spill of yellow light from the taverns' windows.

"Don't you know there's a price on your head? If you're recognized—"

"I don't care," she snapped, regretting her decision to seek him out.

"That's plain enough. What do you want?"

"It doesn't matter."

"It does matter," he disagreed, "or you wouldn't have come looking for me. What is it?"

R'shiel took a deep breath of the cold air. "I want to free Tarja."

Davydd swore under his breath. "Are you crazy?"

"Yes, I am," she said stiffly, "so forget I asked."

"R'shiel, if word got back to Lord Jenga that I'd helped Tarja escape, I'd be in the cell he vacated before morning."

"I said forget it," she assured him, disappointed. This was the young man who had helped her climb the outside of the Great Hall to spy on the Gathering. She had thought him more daring than the average Defender. She had thought him Tarja's friend.

He sighed and shook his head. "Don't you know how dangerous this is?"

"Well, I'm certainly not going to just stand around and watch Joyhinia hang him!" she declared.

Davydd glanced up the deserted street for a moment before looking at her closely. "R'shiel, don't you think you should stay out of this? Your mother would kill you if you're caught. She'd kill me too."

"She's not my mother."

"Maybe not," Davydd said, lowering his voice, "but she's bound to react like one."

"I have to free him, Davydd," she pleaded. "I need your help."

"R'shiel, Tarja has more friends in the Citadel than you realize," he told her cautiously. "Take my advice and leave well enough alone."

"Please, Davydd?"

Davydd studied her in the darkness for a moment, weighing his decision. Then he sighed again. "I just know I'm going to regret this."

R'shiel leaned forward, meaning to kiss his cheek to thank him, but he moved at the last minute and she found herself meeting his lips. He pulled her closer and let the kiss linger far longer then she ever intended it to. With some reluctance, he let her go and shook his head.

"Now she gets romantic," he joked as he let her go. "Come on, then. I know someone who might agree to this insanity. I never did plan to live long at any rate."

The stables that housed the Defenders cavalry mounts were vast, stretching from the eastern side of the amphitheater to the outer wall of the Citadel. They were warm and pungent with so many animals stabled in such close confines, but their soft snores comforted R'shiel. Davydd had left her here and told her to wait. He had been gone more than an hour, plenty of time for R'shiel to imagine any number of unfortunate fates had befallen him. It was also more than sufficient time for R'shiel to wonder if she had misjudged him. He could be reporting her presence at this very moment; gathering a squad to arrest her while she waited here like a trusting fool . . .

"R'shiel!"

She spun toward the whispered call. "Davydd?"

A uniformed figure appeared in the gloom.

"R'shiel." Nheal Alcarnen moved toward her, his expression unreadable in the dim light of the stable. She did not know him well, but he was an old friend of Tarja's. He was also the captain who had been hunting them in Reddingdale. She glanced over his shoulder, but he was alone. "Davydd says you need my help."

"I . . . I want to free Tarja."

Nheal looked at her for a long moment. "Why?"

"Why? Why do you think! They're torturing him, and in a few days they're going to hang him! Founders, Nheal! What a stupid question!"

He nodded, as if her answer had satisfied some other, unvoiced doubt. "Aye, it was a stupid question. I don't agree with what he's done, mind you, and I don't hold with any of that pagan nonsense, but this has gone beyond the simple punishment of an oathbreaker." Nheal took a deep breath before he continued. "I was there when Draco arrested him. The Spear of the First Sister held a blade to an innocent man's throat and threatened to kill him and his entire family. If Lord Draco can betray his Defender's oath so readily and be honored for it, I see no reason why Tarja should be hanged for the same offense."

The news did not surprise R'shiel. She had suspected something of the kind. Tarja would never have surrendered willingly.

"You'll help me then?"

He nodded. "The guard changes at dawn. If I call a snap inspection I can delay them for a time. We don't waste good men on cell duty. The night watch will be half asleep, or drunk if they've managed to smuggle in a jug when their officer wasn't looking."

"I don't know how to thank you, Nheal."

"Don't kill anyone," he told her. "And if you're caught, keep my name out of it. I'm doing this because Tarja was my friend. But he's not so good a friend that I want to be hanged alongside him."

She nodded. "I understand."

"I doubt it," he said, then he turned on his heel and walked away. Within a few steps the darkness had swallowed him completely and she was alone.

chapter 27

Tarja woke at first light. Gray tentacles of light felt their way into his cell from the small barred window as he swam toward consciousness. He opened his eyes and lay there for a while, trying to work out what was wrong, what was different. The smell of his own body disgusted him. It stank of sweat and blood and stale urine.

It took him a while, but eventually he worked out that both his eyes were open. It took him even longer to realize he could move. He sat up gingerly, waiting for the pain to return, but it was gone. Completely gone.

Tarja flexed his fingers, his unbroken, unmarked fingers, with increasing wonder. He pushed his tongue against teeth that were firm in their sockets, ran it over lips that were smooth and supple. Pulling back the torn sleeve of his filthy, bloodstained shirt, he picked at a scab on his arm. The crust lifted with a flick to reveal pink, healed, and unscarred flesh beneath. He rotated his shoulder, and it moved freely and smoothly. Swinging his feet onto the floor, he discovered the soles of his feet were whole and undamaged, only the stains of blood and loose flakes of skin giving any indication of their condition the night before.

Tarja wondered if he was still dreaming. The last thing he remembered was the little girl who had featured so prominently in his dream, and another shadowy, undefined figure. The details were hazy. He'd lost consciousness; he remembered falling into the blackness but nothing after that. For a moment he wondered if perhaps his pagan friends had petitioned the gods on his behalf. There seemed no other explanation for his sudden recovery. It was an uncomfortable thought for someone who did not actually believe that the gods existed.

A noise in the guardroom outside diverted him from taking an inventory of his vanished injuries. They had come for him already. Oddly, pain heaped upon pain was easier to bear than pain inflicted where there was none. Tarja wondered what the reaction would be to his miraculous recovery. Joyhinia would probably have him drowned as a sorcerer.

The door flew open, and the guard stumbled drunkenly into the cell. Close on his heels was Davydd Tailorson. Tarja stared at the guard uncomprehendingly as he fell to the floor.

"He's drugged," Davydd explained. "Don't worry, all he'll have is a hangover."

Tarja looked at the young man blankly.

"Hey! Snap out of it, Captain! This is a gaol break, in case you haven't noticed. Get a move on!"

Tarja jumped to his feet, leaped over the body of the guard, and ran down the hallway after Davydd. "Do you have horses?" he asked, as he skidded to a halt near the door. It seemed such a banal question. What he really wanted to ask was: *How can I be running? Last night I couldn't walk! What has happened to me?*

"Out the front," Davydd assured him.

Another man was waiting for them, this one a man who had still been a Cadet before Tarja had left for the southern border. He could not even recall the man's name.

"You'd best get changed," the young man advised urgently, handing him a clean uniform. "We're going out the main gate as soon as it's opened. You'll never pass as a Defender looking like that."

Tarja took the uniform and changed into it, delighted to be rid of his soiled clothes. As he was pulling on the boots, he glanced up at the men.

"You'll hang if they catch us," he warned.

The lieutenant shrugged. "Can't be any worse than being a Defender these days."

Both saddened and heartened by the man's reply, Tarja stood up and accepted the sword Davydd handed him.

"Thanks." *How can I hold a sword? They broke my fingers! I must be dreaming.*

"All clear," the lieutenant announced, looking out into the yard.

Tarja followed him into the yard and stopped dead as he realized who was holding the waiting horses. R'shiel turned as she heard them. She studied him for a moment, surprised perhaps that he could even stand, then did no more than acknowledge him with a nod.

"They'll be opening the gate soon," she said. "We'd better hurry."

"R'shiel—"

"You take the bay," she said, handing him the reins. Her expression was unreadable. "I heard they were torturing you. I'm glad to see you've not suffered too much."

Tarja stared at her in astonishment. She was angry with him because he was whole! How could he explain to her what had happened, when he couldn't even explain it to himself?

"Come on!" Davydd urged.

Tarja took the reins and leaped into the saddle, following the others out of the yard and into the streets of the Citadel. He rode with R'shiel on his left and the other two close behind. She did not look at him. He could not understand her anger or how she had come to be involved in his escape. *I don't understand how I could go to sleep a broken man and wake whole, either*, he thought.

As they neared the main gate, Tarja pushed aside the question of his astounding recovery. He had to live through the next few hours before he could indulge in trying to solve such an inexplicable riddle. The buildings closest to the main gate were clustered close together, built by human hands, not Harshini. Three stories tall and roofed with gray slate tiles, many were boarding houses, offering accommodation to officers who preferred not to live in the Officers' Quarters near the center of the city. They were popular because they were away from the watchful eye of the Lord Defender. There were no snap inspections here. Tarja rode past them with his head down and shoulders hunched. Chances were good that if they got to the gate, they would be allowed to leave unchallenged. The guards held the gate against *incoming* traffic. They would not bother with officers heading *out*.

They rode at a walk past the last house before the open plaza in front of the gate. A door opened on Tarja's left and a captain stepped out into the street. The movement caught his eye. The shock of seeing such a livid scar momentarily distracted him, and he stared openly at the man. The young captain gasped as he recognized Tarja.

"Guards!" Loclon yelled toward the gate.

"Damn!" R'shiel muttered, kicking her horse into a canter. They followed her lead without hesitation. Loclon ran after them, calling to the guards on the gate who were embroiled in an argument with a burly wagon driver. A large oxen-drawn wagon was blocking the way, as the driver disputed his right to enter. Tarja glanced over his shoulder at Loclon, who had almost caught up to them, even though he was on foot.

The distance between the boarding house and the blocked gate allowed little room for speed. Loclon's cries finally caught the attention of the officer in charge, who glanced at Tarja, shock replacing confusion as he recognized him. Davydd drew alongside him, unsheathing his sword.

"There's only one way out of this now!"

Tarja nodded and drew his own weapon. He looked for R'shiel who had ridden ahead and seemed determined to ride down anyone foolish enough to stand in her way. He didn't know if she was armed, but she could not hope to fight off the Defenders, even on horseback. The wagon driver was ignored as red coats streamed toward them, and he lost sight of her as his attention was drawn to his own survival. He swung his sword in a wide arc as he pushed forward, and the Defenders drew back from the deadly blade. He heard a cry and looked up as Davydd toppled from his horse, a red-fletched arrow protruding from his chest. Tarja looked up with despair at the archers lining the wall walk, their arrows aimed directly at him and his companions. He looked for R'shiel and was relieved to discover she had also seen the archers. She held up her hands in surrender as she was pulled from her mount. The young lieutenant was slumped in his saddle, arrow-pierced through the neck.

"Drop your weapon!" a voice called from the wall walk. Tarja looked up at the bows aimed squarely at his heart and knew refusal would result in death. For a fleeting moment, the idea seemed attractive. But they would kill R'shiel, too. He hurled the blade to the ground and did not resist as the Defenders overwhelmed him.

chapter 28

oyhinia was waiting in the First Sister's office, along with Jacomina, Lord Draco, Louhina Farcron, the Mistress of the Interior who had replaced Joyhinia, Francil, Lord Jenga, and two Defenders she did not know, flanking a young woman. R'shiel was surprised to discover it was the *court'esa* from the Blue Bull who had been flirting with Davydd. Harith escorted her into the office, ordering the two Defenders to remain outside.

The First Sister barely glanced at her as R'shiel stopped in front of the heavily carved desk. Joyhinia's hands were laid flat on the desk before her, her expression bleak as she turned to the *court'esa*.

"Is this the girl you saw in the Blue Bull last night?"

On closer inspection, R'shiel was a little surprised to discover the *court'esa* was not much older than herself. The young woman nodded, sparing R'shiel an apologetic look. "Yes, your Grace."

Joyhinia showed no obvious reaction to the news. "Have the *court'esa* taken to the cells, Jenga," she ordered. It was a sign of her fury that she did not bother with his title. "I trust you can root out the rest of your traitors without my assistance?"

The insult was clear. Joyhinia was blaming the Defenders, and therefore Jenga, for the escape attempt. R'shiel waited in silence as Jenga, Lord Draco, the *court'esa*, and the Defenders left the office.

As the door closed behind the men, Joyhinia rose from behind her desk and walked around to face R'shiel. She studied her for a moment, then turned to face the Sisters of the Quorum.

"I have a confession to make, Sisters," she began, with a sigh that was filled with remorse. "I have made a dreadful mistake. I fear I did something that seemed right at the time but that I now regret."

"Surely if your actions seemed right at the time," the ever faithful Jacomina said comfortingly, "you cannot blame yourself."

Harith was less than sympathetic. "Just exactly what have you done, Joyhinia?"

"I gave birth to a child," she said, taking a seat beside Jacomina, who placed a comforting hand over Joyhinia's clasped fingers, "who should have been an icon. His upbringing was exemplary, his pedigree faultless, yet I suspected the bad blood in him. I had him placed in the Defenders at the youngest age they would take him, in the hope that the discipline of the Corps would somehow triumph over his character. We all know now how idle that hope was."

"You mustn't blame yourself, Joyhinia," Louhina added, right on cue. The Mistress of the Interior was her mother's creature to the core, just like Jacomina.

"And the mistake?" Harith asked. "Get to the point, Sister."

"My mistake was wanting a child of whom I could be proud. When I left for Testra nearly twenty-one years ago, I volunteered to visit the outlying settlements in the mountains. I wintered in a village called Haven," Joyhinia said, her eyes downcast. "It was a small, backward hamlet. While I was there, a young woman gave birth to a child, but refused to name the father. The poor girl died within hours of giving birth, leaving a child that nobody would claim. I took pity on the babe and offered to take it, to raise it as my own, to give it every chance to have a decent life. The villagers were glad to be rid of it. They must have known something about the mother that I did not."

Joyhinia glanced at her Quorum, judging their reactions. Joyhinia's story fascinated R'shiel. This was finally the truth—finally she would have the answers she had come here to seek.

"I took the child back to Testra with me and claimed the child as my own. I was wrong to let people think that, I know. But once again, I must plead youth and pride as my excuses. My mistake was thinking that my love and guidance could overcome her bad blood. This young woman you see before you now, is the result of my foolishness, my weakness." Joyhinia looked up at R'shiel. She actually had tears in her eyes. "This girl who has betrayed us all so badly is the result of my folly. Perhaps I loved her too much. Perhaps I was too lenient with her. My son had been such a disappointment to me that I put all my hopes in a foundling. And now she repays my kindness by turning on us in our most desperate hour."

Harith frowned as she looked at R'shiel. "I always wondered what

Tarja was talking about when he faced you down at the Gathering. How did you get Jenga to play along with you all these years?"

"Jenga and I had—an understanding. He owed me a favor."

"Some favor! Whatever you have on him, Joyhinia, it must be something dreadful. I never thought Jenga capable of a deliberate lie. You have actually managed to surprise me."

Which was exactly what Joyhinia had intended, R'shiel realized. This confession was nothing to do with her. This was Joyhinia in damage control. Joyhinia was distancing herself from R'shiel as fast as she could.

"You should be ashamed of yourself," Jacomina snarled at R'shiel as she put a comforting arm around Joyhinia's shoulders. "After all Joyhinia has done for you. To betray her so foully."

R'shiel could hold her tongue no longer. "*Betray* her! What did she ever do for me? I didn't ask her to be my mother!"

"I tried to protect her," Joyhinia told them, ignoring her outburst. "All I got for my trouble was a thief and a traitor. Where did I go wrong?"

Francil had listened to the entire discussion without uttering a word, and when she spoke, her question caught R'shiel completely off guard. "You've just heard the most startling news about your parentage, R'shiel, yet you don't seem surprised. Did Joyhinia tell you of this before today?"

"Tarja learned the truth months ago. It was the happiest day of my life when he told me!"

"One wonders how he learned of it," Francil said. "I recall him making that wild statement at the Gathering when he refused to take the oath. I hope you can keep the rest of the Sisterhood's secrets better than you've kept this one, Joyhinia."

The First Sister nodded meekly at the rebuke. "All I can promise is that I will do my utmost to see that this evil is cut out of both the Sisterhood and the Defenders." She squared her shoulders determinedly. "I will begin by facing up to the fantasy I held dear for twenty years. This child is not mine—now or in the future. I will leave you to deal with her, Harith, and the other traitors who have defied us this day. Never let it be said that I tried to use my influence to secure leniency."

R'shiel's head pounded, the blood that rushed through her ears almost drowning out Joyhinia's voice. It was as if a great weight had suddenly been lifted from her.

"Take her away," Joyhinia ordered, with a touching and entirely false catch in her voice. "I cannot bear to look at her any longer."

R'shiel was not certain what would happen now. A trial, perhaps? Maybe they would hang her alongside Tarja. At that moment, she didn't care.

She cared only that she was finally free of Joyhinia.

chapter 29

'shiel was marched, none too gently, through the corridors of the Administration Building. The walls were brightening rapidly and people stared as she was marched out into the streets toward the Defenders' Headquarters. Eventually they reached the narrow hall that led into the cells where only last night, she had come to rescue Tarja. The corridor was lit with smoky torches. The Citadel had been built by the Harshini, and they had no need for prisons. The cell block was an addition erected later by the Sisterhood. R'shiel tripped on uneven flagstones in the seemingly endless corridor, until finally, in a spill of yellow lamplight, she found herself in a large open area filled with scattered tables and shadows.

"What's this?"

"This is the Probate who helped them last night," one of her escort explained. "The First Sister wants her locked up."

"Bring her here," the Defender said. R'shiel could detect the sneer in the man's voice. She looked up, focusing her eyes on the captain and was rewarded with a startled laugh. "Well, well, well! If it isn't Lady High 'n' Mighty herself!"

The sergeant who held her frowned as he looked at the young captain. "Don't get too excited, Loclon. She's still a Probate."

"Go to hell, Oron," Loclon snapped.

"Not at your invitation, thanks," he retorted. The sergeant thrust R'shiel at Loclon and marched off.

Loclon stood back and let her fall. "Get up," he ordered.

R'shiel stood slowly, aware that she was in some kind of danger. She grimaced at the ugly scar marring his once-handsome face. Loclon took exception to her gaze. He backhanded her soundly across the face. Without thinking, she lashed out with her foot in retaliation. Loclon dropped like a sack of wheat, screaming in pain, clutching his groin with both hands.

"You bitch!"

"What's the matter?" R'shiel shot back. "Haven't felt the touch of a woman there for a while?"

She regretted it almost as soon as she said it. Loclon was livid, and she had little chance to enjoy her victory. She was overwhelmed by the other guards who held her tightly as Loclon pulled himself up, using the corner of the table for support. This time he punched her solidly in the abdomen, making her retch as she doubled over in agony. He drew back his fist for another blow but was stopped by his corporal.

"Don't be a fool, sir," he urged. "She's a Probate."

Loclon heeded the man's advice reluctantly. "Get her out of my sight."

R'shiel was dragged across the hall into a waiting cell. The door clanged shut with a depressing thud. Holding her bruised abdomen, she felt her way along the wall, using it for support. Barking her shin on the uneven wood of the pallet, she collapsed onto it. Shaking with pain, R'shiel curled into a tight ball on the narrow pallet and wondered what they had done with Tarja.

Time lost all meaning for R'shiel in the days that followed her arrest. Only sparse daylight found its way into the cells. Only the begrudging delivery of meals and the changing of the guard regulated her days.

R'shiel soon learned there were two shifts guarding the cells. Following the abortive escape attempt, the guard had been trebled. The prisoners were no longer in the care of an easily distracted corporal. The first detail left her to herself, ignoring her and the other prisoners in favor of their gaming. The second shift was a different matter. It took R'shiel very little time to discover Loclon was nursing a grudge against the world in general and the Tenragan family in particular.

She knew Tarja was incarcerated in the next cell but never saw him, although she heard him sometimes, talking with the guards on the first shift. When Loclon was on duty though, he remained silent. R'shiel very quickly followed suit. A wrong word, a misdirected glance, would earn a slap at the very least, and on at least one occasion she heard Loclon deliver a savage beating to her unseen cellmate. R'shiel turned her face to the wall and tried to ignore the sounds coming from the next cell, hoping she would escape Loclon's notice.

It was a futile hope. Loclon searched for excuses to punish her. After one meal, when she had refused to eat the slops she was served, he belted her across the cheek with his open hand which sent her flying, her head cracking painfully on the stone wall. She lay where she fell, forcing down the blackness, and made no move to fight back. If she did, he would call the other guards and use it as an excuse to beat her senseless while they held her down.

"Get up."

R'shiel obeyed him slowly. His face was flushed with excitement rather than anger, his scar a fervid, pulsing gauge of his mood. She noticed the bulge in the front of his tight leather trousers and realized with disgust that her pain was arousing him. She backed away from him, inching her way along the wall.

"The only job you'll be allowed is a *court'esa*, once they've finished with you," he sneered in a low voice that wouldn't carry to the guards outside. "I bet you'll enjoy it, too."

"You'd *have* to pay me, before I'd touch anything as pathetic as you," she retorted. It was dangerous in the extreme to bait him like this.

"You smart-mouthed little bitch," he snarled. "You'll get what's coming—"

"Captain!"

"What?"

"The clerk is here with the court list. He says you have to sign for it."

Loclon looked at her and rubbed his groin. "Later, my Lady."

R'shiel sank down on the pallet and let out her breath in a rush. She crossed her arms and laid her head on them. That way she couldn't feel them shaking.

The fifth day of her confinement was Judgment Day. All the cases to be tried and judged were brought before the Sisters of the Blade. Rumor had it that Tarja was to be tried before the full court. Her own case would receive the attention of Sister Harith.

She was awakened at first light and marched from her cell to a tub of cold water on the table in the center of the guardroom. One of the guards handed her a rough towel and ordered her to clean up. Glancing around at the men, she began to wash her face as the other prisoners were assembled with the same instructions. Seven other prisoners were brought out. All men but for a small, chubby woman with a painted face which was tear-streaked and dirty. R'shiel glanced at her, recognizing the *court'esa* from the Blue Bull Tavern. For a moment, R'shiel thought she saw an aura flickering around her, an odd combination of light and shadows. She blinked the sight away impatiently.

"Sorry I dobbed you in," the *court'esa* whispered as she leaned forward to splash her face. "They didn't leave me any choice."

"It wasn't your fault," R'shiel shrugged. She of all people knew how overwhelming Joyhinia could be.

"No talking," Loclon ordered, grabbing the *court'esa* by her hair and pulling her head back painfully.

Suddenly another voice intruded. "Leave her alone."

R'shiel glanced up and discovered Tarja standing behind Loclon, loosely flanked by two guards. He was unshaven and bruised, with one eye so puffy and purple it was almost shut.

"Friend of yours, is she, Tarja?" he asked, then plunged the *court'esa* face first into the tub of water. Tarja lunged forward but the guards held him back. The *court'esa* thrashed wildly in the water. Tarja leaned back into his captors and using them as support brought both legs up and kicked Loclon squarely in the lower back. The captain grunted with pain and released his victim, who fell coughing and choking to the floor. R'shiel grabbed her blouse and dragged her clear as Loclon turned on Tarja. Loclon clenched his hands together and drove them solidly into Tarja's solar plexus. With a grunt, he collapsed in the arms of the guards who held him, as Loclon drew his fist back for another blow.

"That will be enough I think, Captain."

Loclon stayed his hand at the sound of the new voice and turned to discover Garet Warner watching him with barely concealed contempt.

"The prisoner was attempting to escape, sir."

"I'm sure he was," Garet agreed unconvincingly.

R'shiel helped the *court'esa* to her feet, the movement catching the eye of the commandant. He turned to one of the Defenders who had accompanied him into the cells. "Take the women to the bathhouse and let them clean up, then escort them to the court."

The Defender beckoned the women, neither of whom needed to be asked twice. As they followed him up the long, narrow corridor R'shiel glanced back at Tarja. His gaze met hers for an instant, and she saw the despair in his eyes, then she was out of sight of him.

· · ·

The court to which R'shiel was arrayed was crowded with a long list of pagan cases in addition to the two women and four men brought up from the cells behind the Defenders' Headquarters. The *court'esa*, whose unlikely name turned out to be Sunflower Hopechild, was called up first. She was accused of aiding the Defenders who had helped Tarja escape. Apparently, merely being in the Blue Bull with Davydd Tailorson the night before the escape was enough to convict her. Sister Harith gave the woman barely a glance before sentencing her to three years at the Grimfield. The *court'esa* seemed unconcerned as she was led back to her place next to R'shiel.

"The Grimfield. That's supposed to be pretty bad isn't it?" whispered one of the prisoners, a red-haired bondsman.

Sunny looked annoyed rather than distressed. "I'll still be doing the same thing at the Grimfield as I'm doing here, friend. Just irks me to think they'd reckon I'd help any damned heathen escape."

"R'shiel of Haven."

As her name was called a Defender stepped up and beckoned her forward. She shrugged off his arm as she walked to the dock. *R'shiel of Haven*, Harith had called her. She no longer had the right to use the name Tenragan. *I am truly free of Joyhinia.*

"R'shiel of Haven is charged with theft of a silver mirror and two hundred rivets from the First Sister's apartments and aiding the escape attempt by the deserter Tarjanian Tenragan," the orderly announced. R'shiel was surprised, and a little relieved, that the charges had not included the Defender in Reddingdale she had killed.

"Do you stand ready for judgment?" Harith asked, not looking up from the sheaf of parchment in which she was engrossed.

Would it make a difference? R'shiel was tempted to ask. But she held her tongue. Harith was never a friend to Joyhinia. She might be lenient, simply to annoy the First Sister.

"Do you stand ready for judgment or do you call for trial?" Harith asked again.

"I stand ready," R'shiel replied. Calling for trial would just mean weeks, maybe even months in the cells, waiting for her case to come up. Better to plead guilty. It was the faster road to an end to this nightmare.

"Then the court finds you, by your own admission, ready to stand judgment for your crimes. You stole from the First Sister. You aided a known traitor in an attempt to flee justice, and by doing so broke the laws of the Sisterhood. Your actions prove you unworthy. You were offered a place in the Sisterhood as a Probate, which is now withdrawn. You were offered sanctuary in the Citadel, which is now withdrawn. You were offered the comfort and fellowship of the Sisterhood, which is now withdrawn . . . ”

R'shiel listened to the ritual words of banishment, with growing relief. She was being expelled. Thrown out completely.

“You defied the laws of the Sisterhood, and therefore the only fit punishment is the Grimfield. I sentence you to ten years.” Harith finally met her gaze. The Sister was savagely pleased at the effect of her decision.

“Next!” Sister Harith ordered.

Ten years in the Grimfield. Hanging would have been kinder.

The holding pens for the prisoners were outside the Citadel proper, located near the stockyards and smelling just as bad. Sunny latched onto R'shiel as they were herded like cattle, guiding the stunned girl through the pens to a place in what little patch of warmth there was in the cold afternoon sun. She made R'shiel sit down on the dusty ground and patted her hand comfortingly.

“You'll be fine,” the *court'esa* promised her. “With that clear skin and nice long hair, you'll be grabbed by one of the officers, first thing. Ten years will seem like nothing.”

R'shiel didn't answer her. Ten years at the Grimfield. Ten years as a *court'esa*. R'shiel had no illusions about what the Grimfield was like. She had heard of the women there. She had seen the look in the eyes of the Defenders who had been posted to the Grimfield. Not the proud, disciplined soldiers of the Citadel, the Defenders of the Grimfield were the dregs of the Corps. Even one year would be intolerable.

She was shaken out of her misery by a commotion at the entrance to the holding pen. The gate flew open and a body was hurled through, landing face down in the dusty compound. The man struggled groggily to his feet as the guards stood back to allow their officer through. With a sick certainty, R'shiel knew who he was.

Loclon surveyed the twenty or so prisoners. “Listen and listen well! The wagons will be loaded in an orderly fashion. Women in the first wagon. Men in the second. Anyone who even thinks about giving me trouble will walk behind the wagons, barefoot.” He swept his gaze over them in the silence that followed. No prisoner was foolish enough to do anything to be singled out—with the possible exception of the man who had been thrown in prior to Loclon's arrival. As he finally gained his feet unsteadily, Loclon laughed harshly. "At least we'll be entertained along the way, lads," he told his men. "I hear the great rebel has a great deal to say when his neck is on the line." With that the captain turned on his heel and the rough, barred wagons rolled up to the gate.

A circle opened around the staggering figure, and R'shiel realized it was Tarja. He wore a dazed expression and a nasty bruise on his jaw that was new since this morning. Much as she wanted to run to him and find out how he had escaped the noose, she had her own concerns. Loclon stood near the gate, arms crossed. He had a sour expression on his disfigured face and a savagely, black-streaked aura. R'shiel lowered her eyes, as the black lights around him flickered on the edge of her vision, wondering what they meant, not wishing to attract his attention. But he saw her. At a wave a guard grabbed her arm and pulled her across to face him.

"So you'll be joining us, will you, Probate?" he asked curiously in a low voice. R'shiel realized he had been drinking. Was he being sent to the Grimfield as a punishment as well? Garet Warner didn't seem particularly pleased with him this morning. "I could make this trip a lot easier for you."

R'shiel raised her eyes to meet his, full of contempt, but he was drunk enough for her scorn to have no effect. "How?" she asked, knowing the answer, but wondering if he was foolish enough to spell it out, here in the Citadel. With a bit of luck, Lord Jenga might happen by. But even if he did, she thought, would he care? *I'm not his daughter, either.*

Loclon reached for her and pulled her close, feeling her body roughly through the folds of her linen shift. She glanced around her, thinking someone would object, but the prisoners didn't care, and the guards simply looked the other way. "You look after me, and I might forgive you," he said huskily.

"I'd rather rut a snake."

Loclon raised his hand to strike her, but the arrival of the court clerk checking forestalled him. "All present and accounted for, Captain. Except this one, of course." He placed the parchment in Loclon's raised hand. "You can leave anytime you're ready." The man walked off, leaving Loclon standing there, glaring at R'shiel.

"Get her on the wagon."

R'shiel was hustled forward and thrown up on the dirty straw bed. The barred gate was slammed and locked behind her, and the wagon lurched forward. Sunny scrambled back and helped R'shiel to her feet. "You've got it made," the *court'esa* assured her. "That one likes you."

R'shiel didn't bother to reply. Instead she looked up as they trundled out of the Citadel. Loclon and his men rode in front, followed by a full company of Defenders in the rear, leading the packhorses. The Sisterhood was taking no chances with Tarja.

The Citadel's bulk loomed behind them as they moved off. She felt no sorrow at leaving, only an emptiness where once there had been a feeling of belonging. She remembered the strange feeling of belonging in another place that had almost overwhelmed her the year her menses arrived. Perhaps her body had known then what her mind had only just begun to accept. The idea no longer bothered her; the senseless anger that had burned within her for so long had begun to wane.

She looked along the line of wagons, considering her future. Loclon was going to be a problem, although R'shiel felt reasonably safe until they reached Brodenvale. With over sixty Defenders in tow, he was unlikely to try to make good his threats. But after the Defenders left the prison party at Brodenvale, anything could happen. She glanced at the following wagon. There were twelve men crowded into it, but they managed to leave a clear space around Tarja. He looked back at the retreating bulk of the Citadel with an incomprehensible expression. As if feeling her gaze on him, he turned and met her eyes. For the first time in his life, she thought, he looked defeated.

part four

—⁓—

THE GRIMFIELD

chapter 30

A full squad of Defenders had escorted Tarja down to the holding pens. Scorn, and even a little disappointment, replaced the easygoing manner of his guards. For many Defenders, even the loyal ones, Tarja's refusal to betray his rebel comrades, even under torture, had earned him a degree of grudging respect. But then word had spread like a brush fire of his supposed capitulation, and he had lost even that small measure of esteem. Even those who didn't think him capable of such a heinous act wondered at his sentence. By every law the Sisterhood held dear, Tarja should have been hanged for his crimes. Tarja wondered if people would think his mother had spared him out of maternal feeling. The idea was ridiculous. Anyone who knew his mother even moderately well would find it easier to believe that he had turned betrayer.

As the wagons trundled forward, he glanced up at the Citadel. He should have died there. He should have demanded the sentence he deserved. He would have been honored for generations as a martyr. Now he would be scorned and reviled. He would carry the taint of the coward who had betrayed his friends to save his own skin. As the Citadel slowly grew smaller in the distance, his thoughts returned to the events of the morning. He cursed himself for a fool, even as he relived his trial and the farce his mother had made of it.

"We have decided that in the interests of security your trial shall be a closed court," Joyhinia had declared. She sat with the full court in attendance at the bench, the Lord Defender, Lord Draco, the four sisters of the Quorum and the First Sister. The ranks of spectators' seats were empty. Even the guards had been dismissed. Tarja was chained to the dock in the center of the court. On the wall behind them hung a huge tapestry depicting a woman with a child in one arm and sword in the other. It hung there as a reminder to the court of the nobility of the Sisterhood. Its other purpose was less obvious. Etched into the wall behind the tapestry was a Harshini mural that no amount of scrubbing or painting had been able to remove. Tarja had seen it once as a child, on an exploratory mission through the Citadel with Georj.

"You didn't really think we'd let you have your say in an open court, did you?" Harith asked. She had already sat in judgment in the Lesser Court this morning. She was having a busy day.

"Then you really do fear me. I can die content."

"You won't be dying at all, I'm afraid," Joyhinia announced, taking malicious pleasure from his shocked expression. "A martyr is just what your pitiful cause is looking for. Well, they will have to look further afield than you. Hanging you will do nothing but cause trouble. We have decided to accept your apology, along with a list of your heathen compatriots, and in return you will be sentenced to five years in the Grimfield. After which, we shall consider your application to rejoin the Defenders, if we decide you have repented sufficiently."

Tarja was dumbfounded. "There is no list. I do not repent."

"But that is the delightful thing about all this, Tarja," Jacomina pointed out. "There doesn't have to be. As long as there is a suspicion that you have turned against them, the rebels will go to ground. Everyone knows you should be hanged for what you've done. By not hanging you, we have destroyed your credibility. I think it's rather clever, actually. Don't you?"

"Draco promised me a hero's welcome to undermine my standing in the rebellion," Tarja pointed out. "A prison sentence is hardly a reward for outstanding service."

"You've killed in the name of the heathens, Tarja," Harith shrugged. "You must pay for that. Even the rebels would understand our position."

"It won't work," he argued. "No one will believe that I turned."

"No one believed that a captain of the Defenders could break his oath and turn against the Sisterhood, either," the Lord Defender said.

Tarja met the eyes of his former commander without flinching. "It is the Sisterhood who has turned against her people."

"Oh, leave off with all that heathen nonsense," Harith snapped. "No one here cares, Tarjanian. You defied us, and now you will pay the price. I personally think we should hang you, but your mother has managed to convince us that humiliating you would be more effective."

"How thoughtful of you, Mother."

"Have your men escort him to my office, my Lord," Joyhinia said, turning to the Lord Defender. "I would like a word in private with the prisoner before he leaves. The wagons should be able to get away by mid-afternoon."

"As you wish, your Grace."

"Ever the obedient servant," Tarja muttered.

The Lord Defender stopped mid-stride and turned back to Joyhinia. "Your permission, your Grace, to correct this miscreant?"

"By all means," Joyhinia agreed, her expression stony. "I'd be interested to see what you call 'correction.' He seems in remarkably good shape for someone allegedly tortured for a week or more."

Jenga faced Tarja with an unreadable expression. Did he wonder why Tarja was not more battered and broken? Taking advantage of the fact that he was unable to retaliate, Loclon had beaten Tarja savagely several times. He plainly bore the evidence of those beatings, but of the torture he had suffered, there was no trace. Did Jenga suspect something was amiss? He had not visited Tarja during his incarceration. Perhaps he had not wanted to see the results of his orders. Tarja was glad he had not.

"I am disappointed in you, Tarjanian," he said. "You had such promise."

"At least I won't end up like you. Licking the boots of the Sisterhood."

Jenga hit him squarely on the jaw with his gauntleted fist. Tarja slumped, semiconscious, to the floor of the dock. The Lord Defender stared at the inert body and flexed his fist absently.

"That is because you are not fit to lick their boots." He turned to Joyhinia, his expression doubtful. "Your Grace, I do hope you know what you're doing. This is a very dangerous course you have embarked upon."

"When I want your opinion, Lord Jenga," the First Sister said frostily, "I'll ask for it."

Tarja was still rubbing his jaw gingerly as he slumped into one of the chairs normally occupied by the Sisters of the Quorum in the First Sister's office. They were alone. This was the first time he had been alone with his mother in years. He was still chained, however. Joyhinia wasn't that sure of herself.

"That was quite a performance in court this morning," he remarked as Joyhinia went to stand by the window, her back turned to him.

"That was no performance, Tarja. I have the names here of two hundred and twenty-eight known pagan rebels. It has taken us a year to compile the list, and while far from complete, it will do."

Tarja felt his palms beginning to sweat. "Do for what?"

She turned to look at him. "According to the court records, your life was spared because you betrayed the rebellion. As soon as I am certain the last of your cohorts are rooted out of the Defenders, I will begin executing the men on this list. You are already under suspicion. The assumption will be that you really did betray the heathens. I won't even have to kill you. Your friends in the rebellion will do that for me, I imagine."

Tarja stared at his mother, not sure what frightened him most: her ruthlessness or the fact that he could almost admire the web she had woven around him.

"Why are you telling me this?" he asked.

"Because I want you to understand how completely I have defeated you," she hissed. "I want you to die at the hands of your treasonous friends knowing it was me who brought you down! How dare you defy me! How dare you humiliate me!"

"And R'shiel?" he asked, suddenly seeing Joyhinia as nothing more than a bitter old woman, terrified of losing her authority. It somehow lessened her power over him. "What has she done to incur your wrath? All she ever wanted was to be loved by you."

"That ungrateful little cow! Like you, she is paying the price for betraying me!"

"You ruthless, unfeeling bitch." Tarja stood up, towering over his mother, his chains rattling metallically as he trembled with rage. "I'll destroy you. If it's the last thing I do."

"You'll not have the chance, Tarja," she replied. "Your death sentence has already been passed. It merely amuses me to let your friends be the ones who carry it out."

The jolting of the wagon dragged his attention back to the present. Unable to bear the sight of the fortress any longer, he turned around. R'shiel was watching him from the wagon in front. He met her gaze for a moment then looked away.

chapter 31

They passed through Kordale an hour or so later, then began to descend out of the highlands toward the river valley and Brodenvale. At dusk Loclon called a halt, and they made camp in a copse of native poplars. The prisoners were allowed out of the wagons to eat and then loaded back in for the night. As there wasn't room to stretch out, R'shiel made herself as comfortable as possible in the corner of the wagon with the other women. The Defenders were posted around the camp and nervously alert. A rescue attempt was almost a certainty. Even the rumor that Tarja had finally betrayed the rebellion wasn't expected to reduce the risk. On the contrary, the rebels would probably want him even more.

Despite the Defenders' fears, the night passed uneventfully, if uncomfortably, for the prisoners. The expected attack never eventuated. R'shiel thought that some of the Defenders looked a little disappointed. By first light they were back on the road, jolting miserably in the bitter chill. The day passed in a blur of misery as the countryside began to alter subtly. Brown began to turn to green, and herds of red spotted cows grazed in the cold fields, their breath hanging in the still air like milky clouds as they watched apathetically as the human caravan passed by.

Brodenvale came into view near dusk. They were driven straight to the Town Garrison, where the prisoners were given a cold meal and the relative luxury of a straw-covered cell. The Defenders were quartered in the Garrison and on full alert, but there was no sign of the expected rebel attack. The general feeling among the prisoners was that either the heathens knew the route they were taking and would attack later, or they had finally given up on Tarja. R'shiel suspected the former was the case. She knew the rebels.

The next morning, the prisoners were marched through the town to the river docks. Crowds lined the street to catch a glimpse of the famed rebel, but the Defenders kept them pressed close between the horses, so most of the townsfolk were disappointed. The mood of the crowd was strangely subdued. Every one of the prisoners heaved a sigh of relief when they reached the docks.

The Defenders halted the prisoners and arrayed themselves across the entrance to the dock. The boat was a freight barge, its name *Melissa* in faded whitewash on the prow. They were herded forward by the soldiers and pushed up the narrow gangplank. As R'shiel stepped onto the deck a hand reached for her and she was pushed into a group with the other prisoners. The horses belonging to the ten Defenders who were to accompany them to the Grimfield were brought on board, although it took some time. Finally Loclon strode up the gangway, and the captain gave the order to cast off.

Had it been left to Loclon, the prisoners would not have emerged at all from the hold. Loclon was all for locking the door and forgetting about his charges until they docked. The boat's captain exploded when he heard the suggestion, his voice carrying easily to the prisoners locked in the freezing hold.

"Leave them there?" his deep voice boomed. "Be damned if you will!"

The prisoners gathered near the flimsy wooden door to listen to the exchange. Loclon's reply was inaudible, but the riverboat captain could probably be heard back in the Citadel.

"I don't care if they're a bunch of bloodthirsty mass murders! Do you know what that hold will smell like after a few days? I want them out! Every day! And not just for an hour or so! I have to carry other cargo, you know! It's bad enough your horses are stinking up my deck without making the rest of my boat uninhabitable as well!"

A few moments of silence ensued, as Loclon presumably pleaded his case, but the captain was adamant. "I want them out, do you hear? If you don't like it, I will put into the bank, offload the whole troublesome lot of you, and you can wave down the next passing boat!"

A door slammed angrily, followed by silence. Guessing that the entertainment was over, the prisoners wandered back to their hammocks.

The convicts had unconsciously sorted themselves into three distinct groups. The men had gathered themselves nearest the entrance. The women had taken possession of the opposite side of the hold in a cluster of hammocks. Stuck somewhere in the middle was Tarja—a group of one that nobody wanted to associate with, either through fear of him or disgust that he had betrayed his compatriots.

Sunny had taken R'shiel under her wing and had introduced her around to the other women. The tall, dark-haired one was called Marielle. She was on her way to the Grimfield for assaulting a Sister. Marielle's husband was serving time in the Grimfield for theft. She had walked from Brodenvale over the Cliffwall to the Grimfield, only to be turned back when she reached the prison town. Furious, she had walked all the way back to Caldow, where she had hurled a fresh cowpat at the first Sister she saw. She was now quite contentedly on her way to where she wanted to be in the first place.

Danka was only a year or so older than R'shiel. A slender blonde with a lazy eye that had a disconcerting habit of looking in a different direction from the other, her crime was selling her favors in an unlicensed brothel.

Tella and Warril were sisters; both convicted of murdering a man they had been arguing over. The sisters were sentenced to five years, although Harith had informed them sternly that it was more for their irresponsible behavior than the fact they had actually killed the poor man. The sisters were now the best of friends, having decided that no man would ever drive them apart again.

The sixth female prisoner was an older woman named Bek, sour-faced and wrinkled, who offered no information regarding herself or her crime. Sunny had whispered to R'shiel that she was an arsonist who had set so many fires in the Citadel, it was a wonder it wasn't black with soot, instead of the pristine white it usually was. R'shiel wasn't sure if she believed Sunny, but she noticed the old woman staring at the shielded lantern-flame for hours at a time, as if it held some secret fascination for her.

As for Sunny, she was, she explained soberly to R'shiel, a businesswoman. Her unfortunate involvement in Tarja's escape attempt was purely accidental. She was a patriotic citizen of Medalon. This whole thing was simply a mistake, which would be cleared up as soon as she reached the Grimfield and found an officer who would listen to her.

Not long after the argument between the riverboat captain and Loclon, a rattle at the lock in the door had all the prisoners jumping to their feet with anticipation. A sailor pushed the door open and stood back to let two red-coated Defenders step through. They were carrying a number of leg irons in each hand.

"Cap'n says you're to go up on deck where we can keep an eye on you," the corporal announced. "I want you lined up, one at a time."

The sailor remained in the doorway. "And just how do you suppose they're going to get up top with those things on?"

The corporal frowned. "The Cap'n ordered it."

"And I'm sure the Cap'n is quite a wonderful chap, but they'll never get up those companionways wearing leg irons."

"But what if they try to escape?"

"Then you can club them into submission with the chains." The sailor was teasing him, but the soldier did not seem to realize it.

The corporal considered his advice for a moment, before nodding. "All right. But they go on as soon as we get on deck."

"A wise move, Corporal. You'll go far in the Corps, I'm sure."

The corporal stood back and ordered the prisoners out of the hold. They shuffled into a line, and R'shiel found herself standing next to Tarja. She glanced at him for a moment, but they had no chance to speak. He looked a little better today. The bruise over his eye was fading although the one on his jaw looked the color of rotting fruit. As she bent to walk through the doorway, the sailor winked at her, and she silently thanked him and his captain for sparing them from both the confines of the hold and the leg irons.

The sunlight stung R'shiel's eyes as she emerged onto the deck. Although cold, the wind was a refreshing change. Once they were assembled, the corporal didn't seem to know what to do with them, and Loclon was nowhere to be found. With a shrug, he dumped the leg irons at the top of the steps and turned to face his charges.

"A bit of exercise will tire them out," the sailor suggested helpfully as he followed the Defenders up onto the main deck. "Make them much easier to handle."

The corporal nodded. "All right you lot! Move about! You're up here for exercise!"

The prisoners dutifully began moving about. Expecting to be called back, R'shiel headed forward. In the bow, heading swiftly south with the current, a chill breeze swept over her. She sank down behind the temporary corral where the horses were tethered and began to run her fingers through her hair in a futile attempt to tidy it. She had not had a proper bath since the day she had been arrested. She tugged at the tangles as best she could and slowly rebraided her long hair, wondering if she smelled as bad as everyone else did.

"What are you doing?" Sunny asked, lowering her voluptuous frame down beside R'shiel.

R'shiel shrugged. "Nothing."

"That sailor surely has Hurly's mark," she chuckled. For a moment, R'shiel wasn't sure what the *court'esa* meant, then realized she must be speaking of the easily outwitted corporal. She agreed with a noncommittal shrug. Sunny waited for her to contribute something more substantial to the conversation. When R'shiel showed no inclination to add anything further, she took up the challenge herself. "So, where d'you think we'll dock?"

"I don't know."

"You reckon the rebels will try to free Tarja?"

"I don't know."

The *court'esa* seemed to mistake her reticence for interest. "I reckon they will. I reckon they're just waiting for a chance at a clear run. Bet they hang him soon as look at him, too."

"Why would they do that?"

"Because he squealed on them."

"No, he didn't."

"'Course he did," Sunny assured her confidently. "The Sisterhood would've have hung him, otherwise. Anyway, the rebels won't try anything while we're on the river."

"Hurly!" Loclon's angry yell cut through the still morning like a scythe. "What the hell are these prisoners doing roaming around the deck like this? It's not a bloody pleasure cruise!"

Sunny sighed loudly. "Well, there goes our few moments of glorious freedom. Ol' Wick-'em-an'-Whack-'em Loclon is on the warpath again."

R'shiel glanced at Sunny as the Defenders began rounding everyone up to clamp on the leg irons. Hidden in the bow, she figured they had a moment or two yet before they were discovered.

"Why do you call him that?" she asked.

"Our Loclon likes a bit of fisticuffs," Sunny told her knowingly. "You ask any of the girls in the Houses back at the Citadel. He pays good, but he likes to feel like a big man. Know what I mean?"

"He likes to hit people?" R'shiel suggested, not entirely sure she understood Sunny's odd turn of phrase.

"He likes to hit women," Sunny corrected. "Give's him a real hard-on. I bet he isn't near as brave fighting men."

Hurly found them before R'shiel could answer.

It was late that night before R'shiel finally got a chance to speak to Tarja. After a meal of thin gruel she lay awake in the darkness, listening to the creaking of the boat, the soft rasping of swinging hammocks, and the nasal snores of her fellow prisoners. She waited for a long time, until she was certain they were all asleep, before slipping out of her hammock. Feeling her way in the absolute darkness, she relied only on her memory of where she thought Tarja might be sleeping to find him, trying not to bump into the others as she felt her way through the hold. The boat had anchored for the night, and the sound of the river gently slapping against the wooden hull seemed unnaturally loud.

"Tarja?" she whispered, reaching out to touch his face. A vicelike grip snatched at her wrist, and she had to force herself not to cry out with the sudden pain. "It's me!" she hissed.

The pain eased as he released her. "What's wrong?" he said, so softly she had to lean forward until she could feel his breath on her face.

"Can we talk?"

She felt rather than saw him nod in the darkness and stood back as he swung out of the hammock. He took her hand and led her toward the aft end of the hold. A glimmer of light trickled in from a loose board high on the bulkhead. Tarja sank down onto the hard deck and pulled R'shiel, shivering in her thin shift, down beside him. He put his arm around her, and she leaned into the solid warmth of his chest.

"What happened? Why didn't they hang you?" she whispered. Although the sleeping prisoners were on the other side of the hold, it was not a large boat and even normal voices would probably wake them. "Everyone says you betrayed the rebels."

"This is Joyhinia's idea of revenge. She's hoping the rebels will kill me for her."

"But if you explained to them—"

She could feel him shaking his head in the darkness. "You know them as well as I, R'shiel. I doubt I'll be given the chance. But we're still alive, that's something. Maybe I can find a way out of this yet."

"You can rescue me any time you want, Tarja. Anywhere between here and the Grimfield will do just nicely. I'll die if I have to spend an hour as a *court'esa*, let alone ten years."

"Is that what Harith sentenced you to?"

She nodded. A part of her wanted him to explode with fury and kick a hole in the bulkhead so that they could swim to freedom. Another part of her knew that he was as helpless as she was.

"Well," she sighed. "Whatever happens, I'm glad Joyhinia didn't hang you."

"Does this mean I'm forgiven?"

"For what?"

"You tell me."

"Oh! At the Citadel, you mean? I was just surprised, that's all. Everyone was saying you'd been tortured." He did not confirm or deny the rumor. He just held her close. She could hear the steady beat of his heart against her ear. "You should have listened to me, you know. I warned you the meeting in Testra was a trap."

"You also suggested we ambush Draco and kill every Defender in the town," he reminded her.

"We wouldn't be here now, if we had," she retorted, but her rhetoric had lost the passion that once consumed her.

"We'll survive."

"Is that your idea of encouragement? I wish I could die!"

Tarja reached down and lifted her chin with his finger. His eyes glittered in the thin light from the cracked board.

"Don't say that!" he hissed. "Don't even think it! Founders! I think I preferred you when you wanted to take on the whole world! If you want to get even with Joyhinia, then survive this. No. Not just survive. Damned well flourish. Don't let them defeat you, R'shiel. Don't let anybody, ever, defeat you!"

R'shiel was startled by his vehemence. "But I'm scared, Tarja."

"You're not afraid of anything, R'shiel."

She looked up at him. He might think her fearless, but there was one thing she was afraid of. She was terrified he would look at her again, the way he had the night she left the vineyard.

chapter 32

They reached the Cliffwall four days later. Over the eons, the wide, meandering Glass River had worn a deep ravine through the rift between the high and central plateaus, and it was here that the Defenders were ordered on full alert. Loclon was convinced that the cliffs hemming in the river were an ideal place for an ambush. The riverboat captain obviously considered that a very optimistic opinion. Even at its narrowest, the river was still half a league wide, but he obediently kept to the center. They were traveling with the current, and their progress was swift. The day had begun cloudy, but the unseasonal warmth had burned off the last remaining clouds by midmorning, which not even the vast expanse of the river seemed to affect. It was odd, this sudden warm spell, but then R'shiel was further south now than she had been since arriving at the Citadel as a babe in arms.

"How long before we reach Juliern?"

Loclon was standing behind the captain, his tunic unbuttoned and rumpled. His scar was pale against his windburned face. The sun was beginning to set, and the cool of the evening was settling with alarming speed. Cooling sweat turned chill in seconds. The prisoners were just below them on the main deck. The riverboat captain insisted that they clean up after the horses, and the men were on their hands and knees, swabbing the boards. The women were spared the task and for the most part were laying about, too lethargic to do anything else, particularly wearing leg irons. R'shiel cautiously moved a little closer, to better concentrate on the discussion.

"Tomorrow morning sometime, I suppose," the riverboat captain replied. "Is that where you want to land?"

"Why do you want to know?"

"Are you planning to dock the boat yourself?"

"Of course not! But I don't want your men to know. Or the prisoners."

"As you wish."

"And once we've offloaded, you're to head straight back to Brodenvale."

The captain frowned. "That wasn't part of the deal. I'm heading downriver."

"That's too bad, because if you don't dock in Brodenvale two weeks from tomorrow, the Brodenvale Garrison Commander has orders to declare you and your whole damned crew outlaws."

R'shiel heard the sailor curse softly as Loclon walked away.

Juliern was a small village slumped between the Glass River and the barren central plateau. It had little to offer in trade and was not a regular port of call. It consisted of little more than a rickety wooden dock, a tavern, a blacksmith, and a few mean houses.

The village appeared almost deserted when the *Melissa* bumped gently against the dock. A boat with her rails lined by Defenders was enough to send most of the residents scurrying behind closed doors. Two sailors jumped onto the dock, secured the boat, then climbed back on board and pushed the gangplank out. It landed with an alarming thump which shook the whole dangerous-looking structure.

Loclon watched as the horses were led off the boat. Then the prisoners were marched off, stumbling awkwardly in their leg irons. Loclon mounted his horse and cantered to the head of their small column, yelling an order for them to move out.

They were on the road for three days before Loclon sent for R'shiel. Three miserable, foot-sore days that saw the Glass River fade from sight behind the rift of the Cliffwall. As they stumbled along, the countryside slowly changed from the lush pastures of the river plains to the semiarid grasslands of the Central Plateau. The road tasted dusty to the weary prisoners, and the sparse shelter from the blue-oaks lining the road became almost nonexistent. The wind scraped across the plains, scouring the land. Despite the cold, all but a few were windburned. R'shiel escaped the worst of it, her skin somehow not reacting to the relentless wind. A couple of the men who had spent their life outdoors merely tanned a darker shade, and Tarja, who had a naturally olive skin, fared better than most. The others were red, blistered, and miserable. If Loclon noticed or cared about their suffering, he gave no indication.

They spent their nights in the open. After being allowed a short time to relieve themselves and stretch out, they were again fed a thin gruel, while the Defenders ate at another fire dining on the results of the day's hunt. Once they were well into the plains, even that fizzled out, and the Defenders were forced to partake of the same slops as their prisoners. They were shackled at night, although Loclon had ordered the chains removed while they traveled. They hampered movement, and he grew impatient with their shuffling pace.

Of the six women in the party R'shiel was both the youngest and the only one not resigned to being a *court'esa* once they reached the Grimfield. She would have been content to spend the whole journey in solitude, trying to figure out how to escape, had it not been for Sunny's persistent attempts to include her. The men seemed to sort themselves out in a similar fashion. She glanced at them now and then, noticing they gave Tarja a wide berth.

But the third night out things changed. They were well out of sight of Juliern now and still a good week or more from the Grimfield. They ate their meager meal in silence and were being herded into the shackles when R'shiel was singled out by a guard and told to stay put while he locked in the other women. She glanced around hopefully, but there were too many alert guards to try to make a break for it, and nowhere to go if she did. Sunny sneaked up behind her as the guard ordered the women into line and tapped her shoulder urgently.

"Now you listen to me and listen good," Sunny said. "Don't you go doing anything stupid. You give him what he wants, you hear. If you don't, the only one who'll get hurt is you, and it's not that big a prize. Do you understand?"

R'shiel looked at her blankly. Sunny dug her plump fingers painfully into the younger girl's shoulder.

"You be smart, hear?" she insisted. "It's about power. It's the only power he's got over you, see? The harder you fight, the more he has to prove himself."

"I ordered you to get into line," the guard said.

"Just giving the girl a few pointers," she told him, as he led her away.

"I'll bet," the guard said as he locked Sunny into her leg irons.

Taking R'shiel by the arm he led her toward Loclon's tent. R'shiel glanced back at the women, hoping for—what? Rescue? Help? But the women simply watched her go. Tella and Warril looked unconcerned. Danka even looked a little envious that R'shiel had been singled out and not her. The men simply stared at her, or ignored her completely. No one was planning to get involved. All but Tarja. As he saw the direction she was being led, he suddenly lunged toward the guard who was shackling him. The guard cried out, and Tarja was clubbed down by two other Defenders. R'shiel turned away, not able to bear the sight of him being beaten. *Don't let anybody, ever, defeat you*, he had told her. She tried to keep that thought in her mind as the guard thrust her inside Loclon's tent with a shove, then disappeared into the night.

He was waiting for her, sitting on a fold-down campstool with a mug of ale in his hand.

"Enjoying the trip?"

She lifted her chin defiantly and refused to meet his gaze.

"You know, I've been trying to figure out what makes you such an uppity little bitch. Is it because you're the First Sister's daughter? Is that why you're so high and bloody mighty? Except it turns out you're just a common bastard." He rose to his feet in a surprisingly fluid movement and began circling her like a predatory bird.

With a conscious effort she focused her gaze on him. "Class only matters to those who don't have any."

Loclon slapped her for her impudence, making her eyes water. "You arrogant little bitch!" R'shiel glared at him and tried not to imagine what was coming next. Imagination could be a worse tormentor than actual abuse. She had heard someone say that once. "I'll bet you're just like the rest of those Probate sluts, aren't you? I've seen them at the Citadel. How many lovers have you had, I wonder, you and your uppity friends?"

R'shiel refused to dignify his question with a reply.

"ANSWER ME!"

She jumped at the sudden shout. She could feel his anger, his lust for pain—her pain—radiating from him like a heat shimmer off the horizon in summer. Rebellion warred with fear inside her, but Sunny's advice was fresh in her mind. This was a power game, and by defying him she was just asking for trouble. Loclon needed to be in control.

"I don't think I'm better than you," she said, as meekly as she could manage.

Loclon grabbed a handful of her long hair and jerked her head back viciously. "Don't patronize me, you conceited little whore."

She stayed silent, sorry now that she had only kicked him in the balls. Had she known the consequences, she would have made an effort to really hurt him. He twisted her head around to face him. "What would it take to make you beg for mercy, I wonder?"

Held in his painful grip, there was little R'shiel could do but stare him in the face. The puckered flesh of his scar both repulsed and comforted her. Tarja had given him that scar.

"I would rather turn heathen and be burned alive on a Karien altar as a witch, than beg you for anything."

Her answer enraged him, as she knew it would. He raised his arm to strike her again, but she hit out first, raking her nails down his face, leaving a trail of bloody scratches on his right cheek. He yelped and grabbed her wrist, twisting it savagely behind her back. R'shiel struggled wildly, but he forced her arm so far up her back she feared he would break it. He threw her down onto the sleeping pallet, breathing hard, rage boiling over in him. She kicked at him but her aim was wild and she merely connected with his thigh. He slapped her leg away and was on her, his lithe frame hiding surprising strength, pinning her to the pallet. He suddenly laughed at her, coldly, viciously.

"Go on, scream! Scream as loud as you can. I want your bastard brother to hear. I want him to know what I'm doing to you. I want him to go to sleep every night hearing you scream, just as I have to wake up every morning and look at what he did to me!"

R'shiel bit her lip and refused to cry out, her eyes wide and staring. She stopped struggling, lay still and unmoving, refusing to give him the satisfaction of seeing her pain or her fear as he pushed up the rough linen shift. His desire to make her scream only strengthened her will. *Don't let anybody, ever, defeat you.* Her composure infuriated him. He punched her face, making her head swim.

R'shiel closed her eyes. She swallowed the screams he so desperately wanted to tear from her and for a fleeting, glorious moment an intoxicating sweetness swept over her, reaching for her, calling for her. She clung to it, trying to touch the source, but Loclon hit her again and the feeling vanished, leaving behind nothing but cruel reality.

Morning was a long time coming.

.   .   .

Sunny was waiting for R'shiel when she was returned to the women at first light, taking in her bruised face without comment. She pushed the others away and for once did not attempt to fill the silence with chatter. R'shiel sat unmoving as they were served a thin porridge for breakfast.

They got underway a short time later with Loclon bawling orders at his men, obviously in a foul mood. If the Defenders cast her surreptitious glances as they rode by, wondering at the scratches on the captain's face, they said nothing. But they watched and wondered just the same. Tarja was kept well away from her, but she could tell his mood was murderous. If Loclon was fool enough to get within reach of him, Tarja would kill him.

The scene was repeated each night for the next three nights, and each morning when R'shiel was returned to the other prisoners, Loclon emerged from his tent in an increasingly vile temper.

On the fourth night he sent for Sunny, who trotted off happily to ply her trade. Sunny knew the reality of life outside the Citadel. She knew that pleasing Loclon now would ease her lot once they arrived at the Grimfield. R'shiel watched her go and turned back to huddle on the ground. She had won. He had given up in the end. Not a cry, not a whimper, no reaction at all, had Loclon been able to force from her. She bit her lip as hysterical laughter bubbled up inside her, threatening to escape and betray her silent, private victory.

The Grimfield came into sight on the tenth day after they left the riverboat. The town squatted like a mangy dog at the foot of the Hallowdean Mountains. R'shiel watched it grow larger in the distance, half-fearful and half-relieved that her journey was coming to an end. The buildings were dirty and squat, built from the local gray stone with little or no thought for style. Most were single story, thatched affairs with wide verandahs to keep out the intense summer heat. Only the inn, the Defenders' Headquarters and a few other buildings had more than one story. Even the low wall that surrounded the town, glittering in the sunlight with its wicked capping of broken glass, looked as if it was trying to crouch.

The women had assured her that the *court'esa* of the Grimfield were only lightly guarded and the higher the ranked officer one managed to latch onto, the less onerous one's incarceration was. A part of R'shiel rebelled at the idea of deliberately seeking out an officer. She liked the idea of being a barracks *court'esa* even less, so she made an attempt, along with the other women, to make herself presentable. Loclon had done that for her. He had driven home the reality of her situation. Being assigned to the laundry or the kitchen would not save her, and her one ambition now was to avoid any further contact with him until she could take her revenge. If that meant attracting the eye of another officer for protection, then she was willing to do whatever she had to. *Don't let anybody, ever, defeat you*, she reminded herself. It was becoming the rule by which she lived. The men cheered them on good-naturedly, offering hints as to what might attract the eye of this officer or that, until Loclon bellowed at them to shut up. R'shiel caught Tarja's speculative look as she combed her hair with her fingers and turned away from him.

The prisoners were met in the town square by the Commandant. R'shiel had forgotten that Mahina's son was now Commandant of the Grimfield, and she prayed he would not notice her. He watched impassively as the prisoners were lined up, and a small crowd gathered to examine the new arrivals. At his side stood a bearded man who appeared to be his adjutant. Wilem examined the list that Loclon handed him and read through it carelessly until he came to a name that caught his eye. Looking up, he searched the line of prisoners until he spied Tarja.

He ordered Tarja forward. "You are a disgrace to the Defenders and a traitor even to your heathen friends."

Tarja offered no reply.

"It is my duty to see you remain alive," he continued, as if the very thought disgusted him. "That is not likely to happen if I let you loose among the other prisoners. They take a dim view of traitors, and you have managed to betray both sides. But I've no wish to see you enjoy your time here, either. I will be assigning you to the nightcart. Maybe a few years of hauling shit will teach you some humility, at least." He turned away and beckoned his aide forward. "Mysekis, see that the others are taken to the mine. Have Tarja sent to Sergeant Lycren and make sure he's guarded. I don't want any accidents."

"Sir," Mysekis said with a salute and hurried off. The Commandant then turned his attention to the women. He looked them over disinterestedly. "Loclon, take them to Sister Prozlan in the Women's Hall, then report to my office."

Loclon saluted smartly and turned to carry out his orders. As the Commandant turned away, a youth of about fifteen with sandy hair and cast-off clothes slipped out of the crowd and approached him. He said something that made the Commandant look back at the line of women.

"Oh, Loclon," the Commandant called as he strode back toward his barracks, "take the redhead to my wife. She said something about want-ing a maid."

Loclon's scar darkened with annoyance as he herded them away. R'shiel kept her relief well hidden. The welcome news that she had escaped life as a *court'esa* was only slightly overshadowed by the awful prospect of being placed in the custody of the notoriously difficult Crisabelle.

chapter 33

The Commandant's wife was a short, obese blonde with ambitions far outstripping her station as the wife of the prison commandant. She examined R'shiel critically with a frown, plumping her hair nervously.

"Don't I know you?"

"You might have seen me at the Citadel, my Lady."

"What were you sent here for?"

"I was . . . in a tavern. After curfew," she answered, deciding that it was enough of the truth that she could not be accused of lying. "I . . . got involved with the wrong people. They committed a crime, and I got caught up in it . . . accidentally."

Crisabelle nodded, not familiar enough with the prisoners in her husband's charge to realize that they all considered themselves innocent. She thought on it for a moment, then her brown eyes narrowed. "What did you do at the Citadel? Were you a servant?"

"I was a Probate." Then she added another "my Lady" for good measure. R'shiel was determined to make Crisabelle like her. Her safety in this dreadful place depended on it.

"A Probate! How marvelous! Finally! Wilem has found me someone decent! The last two maids he sent me were thieving whores. But a Probate!" Crisabelle frowned at the brown linen shift that R'shiel had been given at the Women's Hall after her own travel-stained clothes had been taken from her. "Well, we shall have to see about more suitable clothing! I will not have my personal maid dressing like those other women. Pity you're so tall . . . never mind, I'm sure we can manage. Go and report to Cook and tell him I said to feed you. You look thin enough to faint. Then you can draw my bath and help me dress for dinner."

R'shiel dropped into a small curtsy, which had Crisabelle beaming with delight, before hurrying off to do as she was ordered.

Crisabelle's cook proved to be a small man named Teggert, with bulging brown eyes, thin gray hair, and a passion for gossip. The large kitchen was warm and inviting, with softly glowing copper pots and a long, scrubbed wooden table. It was Teggert's personal kingdom. He eyed R'shiel up and down when she informed him of Crisabelle's instructions, then ordered her to sit as he fetched her a meal of yesterday's stew, fresh bread, and watered ale. He began to talk to her as he bustled around his tiny realm, and she nodded as she listened to him rattle on. Mistaking her politeness for interest, he launched into a detailed explanation of the household politics. Before she had finished her dinner—the best meal she had eaten in weeks—he was telling her about Wilem and Crisabelle and Mahina and anybody else he thought worthy of notice in the small town.

"Of course, I don't doubt that the Commandant loved her once," he added, after he finished his long-winded explanation, "but what is delightful in a girl is just embarrassing in a woman over forty."

"I see what you mean," R'shiel agreed, not wishing to offend the man who would be responsible for seeing her fed in the months to come.

"The poor Commandant knows she expected more," Teggert continued. "I mean, for a woman not of the Sisterhood or with independent holdings of her own, marriage to an officer of the Defenders is an eminently acceptable course to follow. The trouble is that Crisabelle only ever saw the shiny buttons, the parades, and the pennons. Spending years in a place like the Grimfield is not what she had in mind, let me tell you! Even L'rin, the local tavern owner, has more social standing in the general scheme of things."

Teggert took the evening's roast out of the oven as he talked, the smell making R'shiel's mouth water. As he basted the roast he kept up his tale, delighted to have a new audience. "Sister Mahina only makes things worse," he lamented. "Retirement doesn't suit her at all, and the fact that she simply loathes her daughter-in-law is apparent to everyone. Poor Wilem. Just between you and me, I think he resents her mightily. Had it not been for her disgrace, he would have been able to fulfil all of Crisabelle's fantasies. But he can hardly turn his own mother out now, can he? I mean everyone knows he'll be here forever. The trouble is, Crisabelle knows it, too." Teggert returned the roast to the oven and sat down opposite R'shiel, pouring himself a cup of tea as he continued his litany.

"Status is everything to Crisabelle," Teggert explained. "When she married Wilem, his mother was the Mistress of Enlightenment, a member of the Quorum, and a candidate for First Sister. Being kin to the First Sister was something." R'shiel nodded. Teggert had no idea how well R'shiel could attest to that fact. "It's no help, either, that more than one of the officers stationed here at the Grimfield have married their *court'esa* when they were released from their sentence. And Mahina seems to find their company delightful. She even invites them for tea! Some days, I think Wilem actually envies the prisoners."

"It sounds very . . . awkward," R'shiel agreed, not sure if her opinion was even called for or if Teggert merely liked the sound of his own voice.

"Aye, it is, lassie. But you just keep your nose clean and stay out of trouble, and you'll be fine. How long did you get?"

"Ten years."

"Ooh! You must have been a bad girl. You're going to be here a good long while then."

Not if I have any say in the matter, R'shiel added silently.

Wilem called for R'shiel later that evening. She had not seen Mahina, but Teggert had taken her a tray before he served Wilem and Crisabelle their dinner, so she knew the old woman was here. She entered Wilem's study with her head lowered, hoping he would not remember her. After all, she had been a mere Probate and he was a high-ranking Defender. Their paths had rarely crossed in the Citadel.

She was wearing an old red skirt, which had once belonged to Crisabelle, although even with the waist pulled in and the hem obviously let down it still barely reached her ankles. Her blouse was also one of Crisabelle's castoffs, and it sat far more loosely on her slender frame than it had on Crisabelle's ample bosom. Her long auburn hair was braided down her back, and her slender arms bore several quite nasty, days-old bruises.

Wilem stood before the crackling fireplace, hands clasped behind him, unconsciously "at ease."

"What is your name, girl?"

"R'shiel of Haven, sir," she said with a small curtsy. *Not R'shiel Tenragan. R'shiel of Haven.*

"R'shiel!" he gasped. It was obvious he recognized her. In his shock, he barely even noticed that her face bore the fading remnants of even more bruises. "Why have you been sent here?"

"I ran away from the Citadel. And I was involved with Tarja's escape, sir," R'shiel answered honestly. There was no point in trying to lie to Wilem.

"But your mother . . . "

"Joyhinia is not my mother. I'm a foundling."

The Commandant studied her curiously. "So you're not Jenga's child, either?"

"I'm nobody's child, apparently."

"I didn't realize who you were this morning when I singled you out. When young Dace reminded me that Crisabelle was looking for a servant, I picked you because you were the youngest. You were the least likely to be a hardened criminal. I hope you appreciate your good fortune."

Good fortune was definitely a relative term, R'shiel thought. "I'll try not to let you down, sir."

"You were always reputed to be a bright girl. Prove it and stay clear of Tarja. Perhaps, if you conduct yourself well here, you may be able to return to the Citadel one day."

"Not while Joyhinia is First Sister, Commandant."

"You are not the only one who shares that fate, child," he said, then shook his head as if pushing away his own disappointment. The subject obviously closed, he studied her for a moment, then frowned. "Where did you get those bruises? On the trip here? Or at the Citadel?"

Wilem waited for her answer. Had he guessed what had happened to her? R'shiel did not take the chance he offered her. She would settle her score with Loclon in her own way.

"I tripped over, sir," she said.

Wilem sighed. "Then you will need to be more careful in the future, won't you?" He appeared uncomfortable for being too craven to force the issue and find out what had really happened. "If you continue to please my wife, then I will see that your sentence here is as comfortable as I can make it."

"Thank you, sir. May I go now?"

"You may, but let me offer you some advice. As my wife's servant you will have more freedom than most, but stay clear of the Women's Hall and the Barracks. I will do my best to see that you remain unmolested, but I would prefer not to do it after the fact. Do you understand?"

"Yes, sir."

"As I'm sure you know, my mother lives with us," he added. "She is now simply a retired Sister and you will treat her with the respect you would treat any Sister, do you understand?"

"Yes, sir."

"You may go."

R'shiel returned to the kitchen to ask Teggert where she would be sleeping. Although unsophisticated, the residence was large, and she was foolish enough to hope that her accommodation would be a bedroom, not a cell. As she opened the door that led from the hall into the kitchen, she heard voices. Teggert was gossiping again, this time about L'rin and from the little R'shiel overheard, her tragic but well-publicized love life.

As she stepped into the warmth of the kitchen, Teggert's companion leaped to his feet.

"There! You see! Aren't I clever?" he announced with a beaming smile. He looked to be about fourteen or fifteen, with a shock of sandy hair, clear blue eyes, and a wardrobe that could only be described as motley. "I told them I could help."

Teggert nodded patiently. "Yes, you're very clever. R'shiel, this is Dace. He is the one you have to blame for your appointment here. You may want to wait a few days before you decide whether to thank him or throttle him, though."

"Hello, Dace," she said and then added curiously, "Who did you tell you could help me?"

The boy's eyes reflected a fleeting moment of panic before he recovered himself and shrugged. "Oh, nobody. Just some friends. You know . . ."

"Pay no attention to him, R'shiel," Teggert warned. "Dace is an inveterate liar and an accomplished thief. He's probably committed more crimes than half the prisoners in the Grimfield put together."

The boy seemed to swell with pride. "Teggert, you say the nicest things."

She smiled at Dace before turning to Teggert. "Do you know where I'll be sleeping?"

"In there," Teggert said, pointing to a door leading off the kitchen. "It's not much, but it's warm in winter. Come summer, it's unbearable, I'm afraid."

Come summer, I'll be long gone, R'shiel promised herself.

chapter 34

"Mistress Khira?"

Brak glanced up at the bearded man who had called Khira's name, noticing with relief that he was a captain. They were waiting among the other petitioners—free and prisoner alike—in the cold anteroom of the Commandant's office for the fifth morning in a row to see Wilem for permission to practice as a physic in the prison town. Brak was dressed as a servant, his eyes suitably downcast. His companion wore an expression of annoyance. A middle-aged woman with a sensible head on her shoulders, she had been a surprising choice to accompany him to the Grimfield. Padric's good sense triumphing over Ghari's hot-blooded need for vengeance, he had decided.

"Yes?"

"I'm Captain Mysekis," the Defender told her. "I must apologize for the delay, my Lady. It has only just come to our attention that you are a physic."

"I have been trying to see the Commandant for almost a week. If I don't see him soon, I shall take my services elsewhere!"

"That really won't be necessary, Mistress," Mysekis said. "I shall take you to see him immediately."

Khira nodded and rose to her feet. "I should think so!"

She beckoned Brak to follow as she walked with Mysekis down a narrow polished corridor until the captain knocked on a closed door and opened it without waiting for an answer. Khira swept into the room with a commanding stride and glared at Wilem.

"You are the Commandant of this place?" she asked.

"I am, Mistress," Wilem replied, rising to his feet. "And you are?"

"Mistress Khira Castel," she replied, taking a seat uninvited and indi-

cating with an imperious wave of her hand that Wilem and Mysekis could
sit. "This is my manservant, Brak. I am a physic and an herbalist, and I
wish to establish a practice in this town. I have been informed by the tavern owner that I need your permission to do so. Is that correct?"

"It is, my Lady," Wilem told her, a bit puzzled. He obviously didn't
have too many petitioners actually wanting to stay in the Grimfield.

"Isn't there a woman in charge?" Khira asked. "A Sister I could speak
with?"

Brak cringed a little at the question. Khira was pushing her luck.

"In the Grimfield, I am responsible," Wilem explained. "By order of
the First Sister and the Quorum of the Sisterhood."

"I see. Then may I assume I have your . . . *permission* . . . " the physic
almost choked on the word, "to open a practice in this town?"

"May I inquire why you would choose such a place, my Lady?"

"The people here need me. A simple walk down the main street
could tell you that. And—"

"And?" Wilem prompted, casting a glance at Mysekis who had
remained standing at the back of the room. He responded with a confused shrug.

"Can I rely upon your discretion, Commandant?"

"Of course, my Lady. Nothing said in this office will go any further."

Khira took a deep breath. "I had a small problem. In Testra. I chose to
help a number of young women dispose of unwanted pregnancies. Unfortunately, the Physics' Guild in that city is sadly lacking in compassion or
common sense." Khira waited for her announcement to have its full
impact before she continued. "As you can imagine, such a situation
makes it difficult for one of my profession."

"I can see that."

"Obviously, I am unable to establish myself in any town of note. Here,
in the Grimfield, I thought that such a . . . history might not present a
problem." She lifted her chin proudly. "I am a skilled physic, Commandant, and I do not see that my past actions should affect my ability to min-
ister to those in need."

"I agree, my Lady." The Commandant couldn't believe his luck. No
physic wanted to come to the Grimfield. To have one actually volunteer
was an unheard-of gift. "In fact, I welcome you. We have been sorely in
need of someone of your skills for some time."

"Then I assume I may set up my practice as soon as I find suitable
premises?"

"Of course! If you want for anything, please ask the captain here. He will ensure that you have everything you need."

"Thank you, Commandant," Khira said, rising from her chair. Then she cocked her head curiously. "What is that racket?"

They all stopped and listened for a moment as the sound of raised voices grew louder. Brak thought Wilem must know the rhythm of the town like his own heartbeat. The commotion seemed to be coming from the rear of the building. With a concerned glance at each other, the Commandant and Mysekis excused themselves and rushed from the office.

Khira looked at Brak. "What's going on?"

"Let's find out, shall we?"

They followed the Defenders to the rear of the building and out into the chilly winter sunlight. Thirty or more men, Defenders and prisoners together, stood in a circle, shouting encouragement to a pair of brawlers who were rolling in the dusty yard, bloodied and bruised. Brak had no idea who the smaller man was, but he appeared to have gotten the worst of the fight. The other combatant was Tarja. Brak stepped back into the shadows gently drawing a glamor around himself to avoid recognition and watched as Wilem and Mysekis pushed through the crowd.

Brak winced as Tarja leaped to his feet and delivered a massive, two-handed blow to the side of the other man's head as he struggled to rise, sending the man flying unconscious into the arms of several spectators. From the mood of the crowd, it was obvious they had been on the loser's side. Tarja stood warily in the middle of the circle, his eyes blazing, waiting for someone else to take him on. He had a cut over one eye and his chest was heaving, but he looked fit enough to defeat anyone foolish enough to get within reach.

"Enough!" Wilem bawled, as much to the spectators as to Tarja. "Get him out of here," he ordered Mysekis, pointing at the unconscious man. "See what our new physic can do for him. As for the rest of you, get back to work this instant, or you'll all be facing punishment."

The crowd disbanded with remarkable speed, leaving only Tarja, a sergeant, and another prisoner. Khira hurried to the unconscious prisoner and began checking his wounds. The sergeant had the decency to look contrite.

"What happened here, Lycren?"

"We was havin' a break when Grafe's work detail came back from the stables, sir. He started mouthin' off 'bout Tarja bein' a traitor. Tarja just flew at him! I couldn't stop him!"

Brak was quite sure Lycren was telling the truth. Tarja was a big man and a better-trained fighter than most other men he knew. Had he taken it into his head to defend his honor, the sergeant would have had little hope of holding him back. Wilem turned to the rebel, and Brak was relieved to see the bloodlust fading from his eyes.

"Defending their honor is a privilege reserved for men who have some."

Tarja's eyes narrowed at the insult, but he made no move toward the Commandant. Brak could see the defiance there, lurking just below the surface. Tarja was likely to be a major problem for Wilem if that raw spirit wasn't broken soon, something of an inconvenience for Brak if it was.

"I will not tolerate brawling among the prisoners. The standard punishment is five lashes. See to it, Lycren."

"You think five lashes is going to keep me happily hauling shit?" Tarja's fists were clenched at his sides, his knuckles white.

"Ten lashes," Wilem replied. "Care to try for twenty?"

Tarja stared at the Commandant for a few moments, before he consciously relaxed his stance. "Ten lashes will be fine," he said.

Brak had no doubt that Tarja had chosen not to force the issue. There was no fear in his eyes. He had not backed down because he was afraid of the lash. Brak strengthened the glamor as Tarja moved away, not wanting to provoke another outburst. Tarja would not be pleased to see him, he knew, and the time was not yet right for him to make his presence known.

News that Tarja had been spared the noose reached the rebels in Testra while the disgraced Defender was still in transit for the prison town. The seeds of doubt planted by Lord Draco had done their work on the rebels. Even worse, the Defenders began rounding up rebels whose sympathy for the cause was a well-kept secret. Only one man could have known the identity of so many of their number. By the time news reached them that Tarja still lived and had been sentenced to a mere five years at the Grimfield, the rebels were certain he had betrayed them. The sentence was a joke. Tarja had committed high treason. He should have been tortured and then publicly hanged, his head left to rot over the gates of the Citadel as a warning to others who thought to follow the same course. The rebels were too familiar with the Defenders' methods to believe that he had suffered at their hands. It was further proof of his treachery.

The rebels called a meeting and passed their own sentence. Tarja would die, they declared. The more slowly and painfully the better, Ghari amended. Brak heard the news with mixed feelings. He did not want the man to die, but he suspected the first thing Tarja would do the next time they met was try to kill him.

It was with some relief that Brak learned R'shiel had also been sentenced to the Grimfield. She was long gone from the vineyard by the time he realized she had run away and even the gods had ignored his pleas for help in locating her. Kalianah did not visit him again, and Maera was too vague to be of any use. He cursed Kalianah's interference and his own ineptitude. He had been so certain Mandah was the one he sought, he refused to see the truth about R'shiel. Even if her unusual height or her dark red, té Ortyn hair had not alerted him, her anger should have. He knew what it was to burn with a rage that sought any outlet it could find. If he had not been so blind, he could have picked it a league away. He had made the mistake of thinking the demon child would be Harshini, when in fact, the one she resembled most was himself—a half-breed hungering for a balance between two irreconcilable natures.

The only way to find R'shiel and ensure Tarja's sentence wasn't carried out was to volunteer for the job of assassin himself, hence his arrival in the Grimfield with Khira. Padric did not entirely trust him, although rescuing Ghari and his friends from the Defenders in Testra had gone a long way to easing the old man's mind. He had argued that he couldn't just ride into the Grimfield and run a sword through Tarja, who would be guarded for fear of that very thing. Mandah had agreed that the only way to be certain was to send someone to the Grimfield to investigate. Besides, she thought Tarja should be given a chance to explain, but then Mandah was like that. She tended to think the best of everyone.

The physic Khira had volunteered her services, and their mission had been set. Khira had not lied to Wilem about the reason she left Testra. She really had been expelled from the Physics' Guild for performing illegal abortions. Unfortunately for Khira, her customers had mostly been poor young women from provincial towns. The Sisterhood professed an extreme abhorrence to the practice, but any Probate or Novice who found herself in the same situation was dealt with quietly and efficiently by the physics at the Citadel.

Grafe had regained consciousness by the time Lycren led Tarja and his fellow prisoner away. Khira fished out a small packet of herbs for the man's concussion and ordered bed rest and a poultice for his bruises. Mysekis had the man taken away and smiled at Khira before returning inside. Brak recognized the look he gave her and rolled his eyes. Khira was a handsome woman, with thick, dark hair and a comely figure. Brak

released the glamor and walked over to Khira wondering if she recipro-
cated the captain's obvious admiration. One look at her expression and he
doubted it. Khira hated the Defenders. If Mysekis made a move on her he
was likely to get much more than he bargained for.

"So that was Tarja," Khira remarked as she closed her bag and dusted
off her skirt.

"In the flesh," Brak agreed.

"He's in pretty good shape for a man supposedly tortured in the
Citadel," Khira noted sourly. "I've treated men the Defenders have questioned, and I can promise you, he shows no sign of it."

"Well, never fear, Mistress Physic. Ten lashes should take the fight
out of him."

"He'll probably be sent to me afterward. You could . . . you know, do
it then." For a woman sworn to protect life, she was pretty anxious to see
Tarja's snuffed out.

"Let's not be hasty," Brak advised. "I would rather see him taken
back to the others for a trial, wouldn't you? That way everyone would see
what happens to traitors."

"I suppose you're right," she agreed.

"Of course I am."

Khira nodded, albeit reluctantly. She was as bent on seeing Tarja
brought to justice as Ghari, in her own way. Brak sighed with relief as they
left the yard and headed back to the inn, reflecting on the irony of Tarja's
assassin going to so much trouble to keep him alive. But he wasn't ready
for Tarja to die.

Somewhere in this godforsaken place was R'shiel, and he had not
found her yet.

chapter 35

ews that Tarja was to receive the lash spread through the Grimfield faster than a summer squall. By the following morning, any number of the Grimfield citizens had found a reason to be in the Town Square, where such punishments were normally carried out. Tarja had been in the Grimfield for less than a month, but there was not a man or woman who did not know about him.

The news about Tarja reached Crisabelle just after lunch on the day of the brawl. She spent the rest of the day deciding what to wear to a public lashing. Mahina made a few caustic comments about her daughter-in-law's predilection for enjoying men in pain and announced that she did not intend to watch anybody being lashed. R'shiel thought the old woman sounded upset at the idea.

Mahina had changed since her impeachment, R'shiel decided. Although she still looked like a cuddly grandmother, these days there was a bitter edge to her voice more often than not. Her temper was short and her mood swings pronounced. The entire household tiptoed around her, except Crisabelle, who seemed oblivious to anything but herself.

Mahina's reaction to R'shiel's sentence had been shock, sympathy, and perhaps a little irony. Mahina had known of her true parentage, she told R'shiel. Jenga had given her the information the very day that Joyhinia had moved against her at the Gathering. But she had said nothing. Mahina had decided against using it to spare R'shiel the pain such a revelation would cause.

Whatever the reason for Mahina's reticence in seeing Tarja punished, Crisabelle was delighted by the prospect of seeing the famous rebel publicly whipped. R'shiel was ordered to attend her, carrying a basket of smelling salts and other useful items, such as a perfumed handkerchief in case the smell of the prisoners overwhelmed her. Several pieces of fruit and a slice of jam roll were also included, in case watching a man screaming in agony stimulated one's appetite. The vial of smelling salts was insurance against the sight of all that torn flesh making her feel faint. R'shiel was quite sure that anybody who packed a snack for a public whipping was highly unlikely to swoon at the sight of blood. Crisabelle hurried her out of the house the next morning dressed in a buttercup-yellow dress with a wide skirt and a large frill forming a V down the front of the bodice. R'shiel thought the dress was ghastly, but Crisabelle had decided it was just the thing for this sort of occasion.

The square was almost half-full when they arrived, but the crowd parted to allow Crisabelle through. She strutted up to the verandah of the Headquarters Building, where Wilem was going over a list with Mysekis. He glanced up at their approach, and his expression grew thunderous, before he composed his features into a neutral mien.

"What are you doing here?"

R'shiel hung back. She had no wish to see Tarja whipped and hoped that Wilem would send them home. But Crisabelle was determined to get full value from the morning's entertainment. She ignored her husband and found herself a vantage point near the verandah railing. Wilem shook his head and turned his attention back to Mysekis.

It was not long before the four men who were to receive a lashing were brought out from the cells behind the Headquarters Building. All were bare-chested and shivering in the chill morning. With little ceremony, the first man was dragged to the whipping post, which was a tall log buried deep in the ground and braced at the base. A solid iron ring was set near the top of the post and the man's hands were lashed to it with a stout hemp rope. Once his hands were tied, the guards kicked the prisoner's feet apart and lashed each ankle to the bracing struts. As soon as the criminal was secure, Mysekis unrolled the parchment and read from it.

"Jiven Wainwright. Five Lashes. Stealing from the kitchens."

Once the charge was read, the officer who was to deliver the lashing stepped forward. R'shiel was not surprised to find it was Loclon. He was clutching the vicious-looking short-handled whip with numerous plaited strands of leather, finished with small barbed knots. The infamous Tail of the Tiger, it was called. The whip was supposed to deliver an excruciatingly painful blow in the hands of an expert. Simply by the way he was standing, R'shiel could tell that Loclon not only knew how to handle the whip, but would probably enjoy it.

The man at the post screamed even before the first blow fell and howled afresh with every crack of the whip. By the last blow he was sobbing uncontrollably. As the guards untied him he collapsed, then screamed as a bucket of saltwater was thrown over his bloody back. Two guards dragged him away, and the next victim was brought forward. Again, Mysekis consulted his list.

"Virnin Chandler. Five lashes. Brewing illegal spirits."

The scene was repeated again, making R'shiel sick to her stomach. The crowd watched silently, an audible hiss accompanying every cracking blow. This one didn't scream until the second blow, but he was almost as broken as the first man by the time the guards had untied him. They administered the same rough first aid to the second man, who bellowed as the saltwater hit his torn flesh, but he walked away without any assistance from the guards.

By the time the third man had been similarly dealt with, R'shiel was certain she was going to be sick. She had seen men whipped before. It was a common enough practice in the Citadel for minor crimes. But in the Citadel men were whipped with a single plaited lash and care was taken to cause pain rather than lasting damage. Loclon's purpose seemed to be to inflict as much damage as possible.

As they brought Tarja forward, R'shiel glanced at Loclon and shuddered. His eyes were alight with pleasure, as he watched Tarja walk calmly toward the post. Rather than waiting to have his hands tied, Tarja reached up, gripped the ring with both hands, and braced his feet wide apart. Unused to such cooperation from their charges, the guards hesitated a moment before securing him with the hemp ropes.

"Tarjanian Tenragan. Ten lashes. Public brawling."

A murmur ran through the crowd at the number of lashes to be administered. Ten was a rare punishment. Wilem was known as a fair man who doled out punishment for discipline, not entertainment. R'shiel glanced at Wilem and suddenly understood why Tarja was last. Loclon had already delivered fifteen blows with the deadly Tiger's Tail. Wilem had put Tarja last to spare him a little, but while she appreciated Wilem's gesture, she doubted it would do much good. For a moment, she let her eyes lose focus on the scene and she studied the auras around both men. Her strange and inexplicable gift was becoming increasingly easy to control. Tarja's was clear but tinged with red, the only sign of the fear that he refused to display publicly. Loclon's was fractured with black lines and dark swirling colors. The sight evoked unwanted memories in R'shiel as

she recognized the pattern from her own torment at his hands. She wondered why nobody else could see this man for what he truly was. To her, it
was so obvious, it was almost like a warning beacon shining over his head.

Silence descended on the crowd as Loclon stepped up and swung his
arm back, expertly flicking the tails of the whip. The lash landed with an
audible crack across Tarja's back, and he flinched with the pain but gave
no other sign of the agony he must be feeling. The next blow landed with
similar force, raising a bloody welt across the first cut. Tarja remained
silent, flinching with the pain but refusing to utter a sound. The silence
continued as Loclon laid blow after blow across the rebel's back, which
soon became a bloody canvas of torn flesh and raw muscle. The crowd
shared Tarja's silence; it was as if they were collectively holding their
breath, waiting for him to break. Loclon grew increasingly agitated.
R'shiel recognized Loclon's frustration. He had worn the same look when
she had refused to scream for him.

The only noise that echoed through the Square was the sound of
Loclon grunting with the effort of laying open Tarja's back and the monotone voice of the sergeant who was counting off the blows. When he
reached ten, Loclon raised his arm for another strike, but the sudden
cheer from the crowd distracted him. They might despise him for a traitor, but they were willing to acknowledge Tarja's courage. Loclon looked
disappointed as the guards hurried forward to untie him and douse his
bleeding back with the saltwater. Tarja finally allowed himself a loud yelp
when the water hit him.

R'shiel was thoroughly sickened by the whole affair, but Crisabelle
seemed quite exhilarated by it. She turned to the woman standing on the
other side of her, a blue-robed Sister from one of the workhouses. She
chattered on about what a lovely day it was for this sort of thing, although
the wind was a bit nippy, and shouldn't they put in some sort of seating
for the spectators? R'shiel watched them lead Tarja away and wondered
just how much willpower it was taking for him to stay on his feet.

"Get the physic to take a look at him," Wilem told Mysekis as they
led the rebel away.

"If your intention was to break him, then I doubt you succeeded."

"We'll not have any further trouble," Wilem predicted. "Tarja has
proved his point. He won back a measure of respect today."

"Traitor or not, he certainly has mine," Mysekis agreed. "I've never
seen anyone take ten lashes without a whimper."

"That's the tragedy. He could have been a great man. Now he's nothing more than a common criminal."

R'shiel listened to the private conversation thoughtfully as she waited for Crisabelle to finish her discussion with the Sister, watching the crowd disperse. They were hugely impressed by Tarja's courage, and, as Wilem had predicted, much less ambivalent toward him. She glanced across the square and spied Dace with L'rin, the tall blonde tavern owner, watching the proceedings. The man standing with them gave R'shiel pause.

It was Brak. He was the last person she expected to find in the Grimfield. He refused to meet her eye, but R'shiel was suddenly certain that he had not been watching the lashing. He had been watching her.

chapter 36

The first few weeks of R'shiel's sentence passed so quickly she could barely credit it. Life settled down in a surprisingly short time, disturbed only by Crisabelle's idiotic demands and occasional but disturbing brushes with Loclon. Each incident served only to strengthen her resolve to escape, preferably leaving Loclon dead in her wake.

She would sometimes watch the work gangs being marched out to the mines, which were located in the foothills about a league from the town. The men appeared universally miserable. They worked long shifts, breaking down the rock face with heavy sledge hammers, while others, bent almost double with the weight of the load, carried the ore back to the huge, bullock-drawn wagons for the journey to the foundry at Vanahiem. The female convicts of the Grimfield fared marginally better. They were split into three basic groups: the laundry, the kitchens, and the *court'esa*. The laundry was back-breaking work; the kitchen, although cozy enough now, was unbearably hot in the long central plateau summers. And the *court'esa*—well, that didn't even bear thinking about. R'shiel could still hardly believe her escape from such a fate. Dace's timely reminder to Wilem that Crisabelle wanted another maid had, quite possibly, saved her life.

R'shiel quickly made herself indispensable to Crisabelle. She had taken to constantly reminding people that her maid was the First Sister's daughter, ignoring the fact that R'shiel was not even permitted to use the name Tenragan anymore or claim any familial links with Joyhinia. R'shiel found the constant reminders irritating, but they reinforced Crisabelle's belief that she had some link with the life she felt she should be leading rather than the one she was. Crisabelle blamed Mahina, not Joyhinia, for her current circumstances and rather than take her frustration out on R'shiel, she heaped all of her woes at her mother-in-law's door.

Mahina was a different story, entirely. She was brusque on a good day, unbearable on others, but R'shiel liked the old woman almost as much as she secretly despised Crisabelle. They had developed a private bond, brought about by the shared burden of Crisabelle's constant and frequently idiotic demands.

Mahina treated Crisabelle's pretensions of grandeur with utter contempt and made a point of deflating her daughter-in-law at every opportunity. Nobody else in the Grimfield dared to challenge Crisabelle; most simply went out of their way to avoid her. Mahina had a wicked sense of humor and a keen eye for the absurdities of life. She even joked about her own fall from grace once in a while. R'shiel wished she had found a way to warn Mahina of Joyhinia's plans to bring her down. Had Mahina never been impeached, her life would have taken a very different course.

With a sigh, R'shiel crossed the small village square and shifted the basket of laundry on her hip to a more comfortable position. Crisabelle invited selected officers and their wives to monthly formal dinner parties, which she loved, but everyone else, from the Commandant down, abhorred. No one in the Grimfield dared refuse an invitation. Wilem tolerated them for the sake of peace. Sitting down in his uncomfortable dress uniform once a month was vastly preferable to Crisabelle whining at him daily, and if he had to suffer it, so did his men.

Crisabelle was agonizing over the guest list, wondering who warranted a second invitation, who warranted a first, and who she could leave off without causing offense in the tight-knit community. Mahina helpfully offered her caustic advice for no other reason than to annoy her daughter-in-law. Crisabelle's attire for the party was almost as big a decision as the guest list, hence her hurried order to R'shiel this morning to have all her good dresses cleaned so that she could choose at the last moment.

"One never knows how one is going to feel on the night, and one must be prepared for all eventualities," Crisabelle had instructed her gravely this morning.

"Knowing implies a certain need for a brain," Mahina had muttered, a comment which Crisabelle had loftily ignored.

R'shiel had orders to wait for the garments and to not let them out of her sight. Crisabelle didn't trust those "thieving whores" in the laundry. She was then required to pick up a packet of herbs from the physic so that Crisabelle's evening would not be ruined by one of her "heads." Mahina had suggested loudly that with a head like that, it was no wonder it ached, at which point R'shiel had managed to escape the house. Mahina was in rare form today.

"Move along!"

R'shiel turned at the voice, stepped back against the wall of the tannery, and watched as another wagon load of prisoners trundled into the town square, as it had every week since she had been in the Grimfield. The wind was chill this morning, with winter almost over and spring doggedly trying to gain a foothold on the barren plains. They all looked desperate, she thought. Desperate and hopeless. She stopped and watched as Wilem emerged from the verandah of his office and the prisoners were lined up before him. As he had when she arrived, he glanced down the manifest, glanced at the prisoners, and gave the same orders. Send the men to the mine. Send the women to the Women's Hall. Sometimes, when he had requests from various workhouses for personnel, he selected one or other of the convicts to be assigned elsewhere. The ritual varied little.

As the prisoners were dispatched, the small crowd of onlookers wandered away, and Wilem caught sight of her. He beckoned her to him. She crossed the square and bobbed a small curtsy.

"What are you doing out and about, young lady?" he asked.

"My Lady's washing, sir. She wasn't sure what to wear for the dinner party on Fourthday."

Wilem rolled his eyes. "Well, you'd best be on your way then girl, not hanging about the square."

"Yes, sir," she agreed and hurried off in the direction of the Women's Hall.

The Women's Hall was actually a complex of low, gray, single-story buildings that housed the female convicts and their industries, including the laundry. R'shiel hurried through the main gate unchallenged by the guards, who knew her by sight at least, and wisely left Crisabelle's maid strictly alone. R'shiel passed between the sleeping blocks, shivering as the shadows cut off the struggling winter sunshine. The distinct odor of lye soap hung in the still air as she crossed the small cobbled yard to the laundry to report to Sister Belda.

"My Lady wants these washed and pressed today and told me to wait for them," R'shiel explained. The Sister was stick-thin and old. Belda was so unlike the elegant Sisters at the Citadel, it was hard to credit she was one of them at all. She glared with pale, worn-out eyes at R'shiel before ordering a girl in prison gray forward to take the basket from her.

"Well, you're not waiting in here," Belda snapped. "Come back after the noon break."

R'shiel backed away from the old Sister and glanced around. Despite Crisabelle's order not to let her dresses out of her sight, R'shiel knew whose orders carried the most weight in the laundry. Belda ruled the laundry like a Defender battalion. As there was no one else about— everyone had their assigned work to do—R.'shiel slipped between the buildings to the *court'esa* quarters to see if she could find Sunny.

The *court'esa* normally slept during the day, but they frequently lazed around in the mornings and took their rest in the afternoons. Sunny could usually be found soaking up the meager sunlight after her evening's labors, comparing notes with her cohorts. As she entered the small enclosure at the front of the sleeping quarters she found no sign of the plump little whore.

"Well if it ain't the Probate," Marielle called out, as R'shiel came into sight. "You here to invite us to the Ball, no doubt?"

Marielle, like most of the *court'esa*, envied R'shiel not at all. They considered a position under the constant scrutiny of the Commandant and his monstrous wife to be a dubious honor. Few of them would have traded places with her, even if offered the chance.

"I was looking for Sunny."

Marielle jerked her head in the direction of the sleeping dorms. "She's in there," she said, her expression suddenly grim. "She'll be glad to see you."

The sleeping quarters were long, narrow buildings, with bunks three tiers high running down each side, leaving a narrow corridor in the center. Each bunk had a straw-filled mattress rolled up on the end, with the few possessions of their absent occupants stuffed inside. Light filtered in from an occasional barred window and a number of cracks in the walls where the weathered wood had split and never been repaired. R'shiel gagged momentarily on the smell as she hurried inside. Marielle's tone only partly prepared her for what she found. Sunny was lying on her narrow wooden bunk, her face turned to the wall. R'shiel gently laid her hand on the *court'esa*'s shoulder and gasped as Sunny rolled over to face her. Her face was a battered mess and she flinched as R'shiel touched her, indicating many more bruises under her thin shift.

"What happened?" she asked.

"Unsatisfied customer."

"Did you report him?"

Sunny struggled up onto her elbow and shook her head. "Girl, how long have you been here?"

"Sunny, the Commandant would see that he was punished. He would."

"Now, you listen to me. You might be living the high life, but down here in the real world it doesn't work like that."

"Sunny, this is the third time this has happened to you. Why?" R'shiel had a bad feeling she already knew the answer.

The plump *court'esa* grinned, making her battered face even more distorted. "Maybe I'm losing my touch."

"I could get you out of here. I could talk to Crisabelle or Mahina."

Sunny flopped back onto the bed with a groan. "Forget it, R'shiel. I'm not working for those silly old cows. Drive me loony in a week."

"Better loony than beaten up."

"Maybe." Sunny closed her eyes. "Look, I know you mean well, but I'm not like you. You got yourself fixed up real good here, so don't go spoiling it on my account."

"Do you want me to fetch Sister Prozlan?"

"Founders, no!" Sunny groaned. "Her cures are worse than the beatings. Besides, she'd probably throw me into the box just for being trouble."

"Khira might come if I asked her. You need a physic."

"Khira'd have to report it. You know the rules."

"Can I get you anything?"

"No. You just get along and stay out of trouble."

R'shiel left her alone in the long cold building. When she emerged into the sunlight she sought out Marielle.

"Who did it?" she asked.

Marielle grimaced. "Who do you think?"

R'shiel nodded and walked slowly back toward the laundry. She knew who Marielle was talking about. Three times now, in as many weeks, Loclon had beaten Sunny. Three times, had Sunny reported him, Wilem could have had him charged, maybe even whipped. Each time Sunny bore the brunt of Loclon's temper, it was on a day when R'shiel had thwarted his attempts to intimidate her.

The first time had been only days after her arrival in the Grimfield.

Loclon had been called to the house to meet with Wilem on some matter, and he had caught her coming down the stairs to the kitchen as he waited in the hall. The second time had been last week while on an errand for Crisabelle. Only the fortuitous appearance of Dace in the alley behind the physic's shop had saved her then. R'shiel was certain that Sunny's injuries this time were a direct result of her accidental meeting with Loclon yesterday. Crisabelle had sent her to the inn to collect a bottle of mead from L'rin that the tavern keeper had ordered for her from Port Sha'rin. Loclon had been in the taproom, drinking with several other officers when she arrived. He had called her over to his table, and she had ignored him. No, she hadn't ignored him. She had deliberately snubbed him, which had brought howls of laughter from the other officers at his table. She did not know what Loclon had said to his companions before he hailed her, but her disdain had made him look a fool.

The guilt ate away at her like Malik's Curse, the wasting disease that slowly consumed its victims by eating away at their internal organs. But just as there was no cure for the Curse, there was no easy way of sparing Sunny, or any other woman on whom Loclon chose to vent his frustration. Not if the alternative was to give in to him.

R'shiel collected Crisabelle's laundry from Sister Belda just after noon and headed for the physic's shop that was several streets away, still brooding over Sunny. Khira was a frequent visitor to the Commandant's house. Crisabelle had been delighted to discover a physic in town and quickly added hypochondria to her list of annoying hobbies.

"Why so glum?"

The voice startled her. "Brak!"

"Ah, you remember me then. I thought perhaps you'd forgotten all about us."

"What are you doing here?"

"I am Khira's loyal manservant." He fell in beside her and took the other handle of the wicker basket, sharing the weight between them.

R'shiel cast a wary eye over her companion. "You change occupations fairly often, don't you? A sailor, a rebel, and now a manservant, all in the space of a year."

"I get bored easily."

"Don't treat me like a fool, Brak."

"I would never dream of it," he promised. "So, how are you adjusting to life as a convict?"

"I don't plan to be here long enough to adjust."

He looked at her. "Just say the word, R'shiel. We can be gone from here anytime you want."

"Gone?" she scoffed. "To where, Brak? Back to the vineyard so the rebels can put my eyes out for helping Tarja? Or was your next suggestion going to be that we help him escape, too?"

Brak did not answer. Instead, he helped her carry the basket to the verandah and called out for Khira. The physic emerged from the dim depths of the small shop, wiping her hands on her snowy apron and smiled when she saw R'shiel.

"Hello, R'shiel. What brings you here? Not sickening for something, are you?"

"Mistress Crisabelle wants some of that stuff you gave her last time for her headache."

Khira exchanged a glance with Brak before she answered. "Time for the dinner party, is it? Well, you come inside and have a warm drink while I make it up."

R'shiel followed Khira inside and sat down on a small stool near the cluttered counter while Khira fussed with jars and powders and a small set of scales, carefully measuring out the ingredients for the potion that cured her mistress' "heads." Brak disappeared into the back room and emerged a few moments later with a steaming cup of tea. R'shiel sipped it, looking about the small shop with interest. It was full of jars and dried plants and reminded her of Gwenell's apothecary at the Citadel. She loved visiting Khira, just to sit in the shop and take in the smell. She wondered if the woman was a pagan, like Brak.

Brak placed another steaming cup near Khira. "I hear Loclon beat up a *court'esa* again," he told the physic as she worked.

Khira looked up and frowned. "Someone should do something about that man."

"It was Sunny, but she won't report him," R'shiel explained as she sipped her tea. "She's afraid if she gets him into trouble, he'll just get worse." Footsteps sounded on the verandah outside, and she tensed at the sound. Strictly speaking, she was not allowed to stop and chat while on her errands. A figure appeared in the doorway, and she breathed a sigh of relief.

"Thought I saw you heading this way. Hiding from the dragon lady?" Dace asked. R'shiel wasn't even sure where Dace lived, but he was always around, tolerated by everyone with the same kind of affection one might show to a lovable stray puppy. R'shiel was well aware of the debt she owed the boy. If not for him her sentence would have been intolerable. However, Dace's greatest talent was not his easygoing nature or his natural charm; it was the fact that he seemed to know everyone in the Grimfield and everything that happened, frequently before it actually did.

"Heard the news?"

"What news?" Brak asked.

"There's gonna be trouble."

"How do you know?" Khira asked, looking up from her scales.

Dace tapped the side of his nose with his finger. "I have my ways."

"What sort of trouble?"

"Same sort of trouble you always get when you lock people up," Dace assured Brak. "We're about due for another one."

"What do you mean?" R'shiel asked.

"A riot, of course. The miners are getting restless again. They never actually achieve anything useful, but it's sort of a moral imperative to try it at least once during your sentence. I guess some men think the chance at freedom is worth the risk of a whipping."

"Doesn't that make it harder on everybody else?" Khira asked as she tapped the herbal mixture carefully onto the scales.

"It does for a while," Dace shrugged, leaning over the counter to see what Khira was doing. She slapped at his hand in annoyance, but he snatched it out of reach. "But life settles down again pretty quickly. You humans are funny like that." The boy had the oddest turn of phrase sometimes.

"It's none of our concern," Brak said, giving Dace the strangest look.

"Well, you never know," he said. "Maybe this time the wrong Defender will get in the way, and they'll do some good before they're caught."

"Exactly who did you have in mind?" Brak asked. R'shiel was puzzled by his tone. What could Dace do, she wondered, that would worry the older man so?

"Loclon would be a good start," R'shiel muttered darkly.

"Has he been bothering you, too?"

R'shiel laughed bitterly. "I suppose you could call it that."

"Then why don't you report him?" Khira asked with a frown.

"Yeah, why don't you?" Dace asked.

"R'shiel, Loclon is an animal," Khira said seriously. "I saw the way he wielded that lash. He was enjoying himself. If you've got something on him, then do everyone a favor and tell the Commandant."

"No."

"What about Sunny?" Dace persisted. "Don't you want him to pay for what he's done to her? And what about what he did to you?"

R'shiel looked at Dace sharply. "I never said he did anything to me."

"You don't have to. I can tell just by the way you stiffen every time someone mentions his name."

"I do not!" she protested.

"You do, too, but that's beside the point. Why don't you turn him in?"

R'shiel sighed. "You know what happens to prisoners who betray anyone, even a bent Defender like Loclon. My life wouldn't be worth living. Look at Tarja. He's guarded night and day just to keep him alive, and they only think he betrayed the rebellion."

"You mean he didn't?" Brak asked. Khira looked suddenly alert, too.

"Don't be absurd, Brak," she snapped. "He never said a word, even when they tortured him in the Citadel. He would never betray his friends."

Annoyed, R'shiel tried to stand up, but Dace pushed her down. "Look, no one in this place is going to lose any sleep if Loclon swings."

"That's the problem, Dace," R'shiel said. "Hanging is far too quick for Loclon. He needs to suffer. Suffer a lot."

Khira seemed a little taken aback by the savagery of R'shiel's reply.

"Fine, let Wilem make him suffer."

"Wilem wouldn't know how to. Look, I have to get back. Crisabelle will be having a fit by now." Dace stood back and let her go. Khira handed her the packet of herbs with an odd expression. Tucking the packet in her shirt, she turned back as she reached the entrance to the shop. "Thanks anyway, Dace, but I'll deal with Loclon. In my own way."

chapter 37

Dismal gray clouds were building up over the back of the Hallowdeans in the distance as Brak made his way to the Inn of the Hopeless after R'shiel's visit to the shop. Going the long way around the square to avoid passing the Defenders' Headquarters, he glanced skyward and decided it would probably rain again tonight.

Mysekis had been after him for several days now. Mysekis wanted to know if there was anything between Brak and Khira. The captain often found a reason to drop into the shop, but Brak had neither the time nor the inclination to play matchmaker. Besides, Khira had an abiding dislike for the Defenders. Her façade would crumble in a moment if Mysekis started making serious eyes at her. It was a complication he did not need. Only the ambiguity of his relationship with the physic had kept the captain at bay thus far. The simple solution would have been to admit that there was a relationship, but Brak had his own reasons for not wishing to confirm or deny the rumor, not the least of which was the buxom innkeeper L'rin. He was, after all, half-human.

Brak suspected Mysekis would be at home for lunch, but he didn't want to run the risk of bumping into someone who would make him wait at the Headquarters Building for the captain's return. He skirted the square and slipped down a narrow alley into a muddy lane where the garbage wagon stood forlornly as two prisoners emptied the rotting garbage from the rear yards of the shops into the wagon. A miserable-looking mule was hitched to the wagon, held by Sergeant Lycren, in the unlikely event that the mule had either the energy or inclination to bolt.

"Ho, friend!" Lycren called with a lazy wave. "And just what are you up to? Sneakin' around the back alleys like a convict."

Lycren scratched idly at his unshaven chin as he watched his prisoners working further up the alley. Both men were stripped to the waist and sweating, even in the feeble sunshine that straggled into the lane. The larger of the two men was a double-murderer named Zac, and the other was Tarja. Brak took a step backward into the shadows. To his knowledge, Tarja was not aware he was in the Grimfield, and he planned to keep it that way as long as possible.

He made an excuse for his haste to Lycren before hurrying down the lane in the opposite direction and slipping through the wooden gate at the back of the inn. He let himself in through the kitchen, snatching a freshly baked bun as he strolled through, waving to the angry cook who yelled at him. Tossing the hot bread from hand to hand he entered the dim tap-room. Several Defenders, their uniforms crumpled and unbuttoned, sat near the window in the weak sunlight, hunched over their ale, waiting for lunch to settle. Brak ignored them and walked up the stairs, biting into the bun and burning his tongue in the process.

At the end of the long hall Brak stopped and knocked on the solid wooden door. The hall was gloomy and quiet at this time of day. Most of the inn's guests would be out and about their business. The lunch crowd had departed, so this was about as quiet a time as any there was in the Inn of the Hopeless.

The door opened a crack. "It's me," he said softly. L'rin opened the door with an inviting smile, stepped backed as he slipped in, locking the door behind him.

L'rin's room was the largest in the Tavern besides the taproom. Huge, multipaned windows let in filtered sunlight through the layer of dust and grime that coated everything in the Grimfield. The room was both L'rin's office and bedroom. A large cluttered desk stood under one window, and beside it stood a huge locked chest where she kept the takings from the inn. The bed was a heavy four-poster with rich blue velvet drapes and snowy white rumpled sheets over a thick down mattress. Brak reclined on the bed, the sheets pulled up to his waist, his naked chest as sculpted as a marble statue.

A knock at the door sent L'rin scurrying around the room to get dressed. Although Brak was certain she had locked it, the door opened a fraction, and a blonde head appeared in the crack. Dace glanced at L'rin, who looked rumpled and more than a little guilty, her thick honey-colored hair in total disarray and her gown slipping down over one broad shoulder.

"Did I interrupt something?"

"You're late," Brak snapped, although he was neither surprised nor entirely displeased by the fact.

"Good thing, by the look of you two," Dace remarked with a grin. "You are looking particularly lovely today, L'rin."

"Thank you, Dace," L'rin said, actually blushing from the compliment, as she turned to her dresser and began to straighten her hair. It took her only a moment to arrange it to her satisfaction, and she turned to Brak. "I have to be getting back downstairs. Don't come down straight away. People might talk."

Brak nodded and waited until she had left the room before turning on Dace, who was smiling angelically.

"You have been blessed by Kalianah, the Goddess of Love," Dace remarked.

"And cursed by Dacendaran, the God of Thieves," Brak added sourly. "What are you doing here?"

The God of Thieves shrugged. "Helping."

"How exactly are you helping?"

Dace sat himself down on the stool in front of L'rin's dressing table. "You know, you really should be a bit more respectful, Brakandaran. I am a god, after all."

"You're a Primal God. You don't need respect. A bit of common sense, maybe, but not respect."

Brak had received quite a start when he realized Dacendaran had taken up residence in the Grimfield. It made sense, when he thought about it. The Grimfield probably had the highest concentration of thieves anywhere on the continent, and Dacendaran needed no temples or priests to worship him. He just needed thieves. The Sisterhood would have been mortified to think that a god resided among them.

True to his nature, Dacendaran was a slippery character, and this meeting had taken some time to arrange. This was Brak's first chance to speak with him alone since Dace had appeared on the verandah of the tavern to watch Tarja being whipped, and Brak was a little surprised he had shown up at all.

"According to R'shiel, Tarja didn't betray the rebellion at all," Dace said, swinging his legs under the stool and looking for all the world like an innocent child. "Are you still going to kill him?"

Brak folded his arms above his head against the headboard. "Who said I was going to kill him?"

"I'm a god, Brak, not an idiot. Why else would you be here with another rebel? To save him? You forget that I'm something of an expert on the baser side of human nature. And you are rather unique, you know."

Brak frowned. He didn't need to be reminded of what set him apart from the rest of the Harshini.

"Of course, you should be thinking about the demon child," Dace continued, ignoring the look Brak gave him. "Not dillydallying about pretending to be a rebel assassin. Why do you suppose they call her the demon child? It's not as if the demons actually had anything to do—"

"Don't get sidetracked," Brak cut in. "You know who it is, don't you?"

Dace looked a little annoyed. "Well, of course I do! You don't think I couldn't tell a té Ortyn Harshini from a human, do you? And there's only one outside of Sanctuary. I'm not supposed to get involved though. Zeggie would be really mad at me."

"Zegarnald?" Brak asked with a frown. "Why does the God of War care so much about the demon child?"

Dace bit at his bottom lip. He looked more like a child accused of mischief than a god. "You wouldn't understand. It's a god thing."

"A god thing?" Brak repeated incredulously.

"You know what I mean."

"I have no idea," Brak replied. "Enlighten me, Oh Divine One."

Dace sighed. "Xaphista has to be destroyed. The demon child is the only one who can do that."

"You could just dispose of him yourselves, you know."

"Of course we couldn't! What would happen if the gods started killing each other? Honestly, Brak, you are *so* human sometimes!"

"Honestly? Now there's a word I don't often associate with you."

Dace pouted. "You're really not making this easy for us."

"What's the problem?"

"Well, you are," Dace explained. "Sort of. Well . . . maybe not you personally, but it's what you represent."

"You are not making any sense, Dacendaran," Brak said impatiently.

"Well, you know that when we created the Harshini we gave the té Ortyn line the ability to channel our combined power, just in case we ever needed it? Then we made the Harshini afraid of killing so that they couldn't turn on us. But where we really mucked up was by giving them a conscience. Not you, of course, but the rest of them. It's really proving to be rather awkward."

"How is that awkward?" Brak asked, ignoring the god's assertion that he was not burdened with a conscience. This was the God of Thieves. He probably meant it as a compliment.

"It makes them worry, don't you see? Korandellen is going gray worrying if the demon child is a force for good or evil. We don't care. We just want Xaphista gone. Zeggie thinks that Korandellen sent you to find her, hoping that if you don't like what you find, you'll destroy her."

Brak didn't answer immediately, aware that there was more than a grain of truth in Dacendaran's concern.

"So you decided to help?"

Dace nodded, brightening a little. "I'm looking out for her. I don't think she's evil. Actually, she's kind of sweet. She's not a thief, of course, but no human is perfect."

"I'm not going to kill her, Dace. Korandellen asked me to take her to Sanctuary, that's all."

"But you can't!" Dace pleaded. "Suppose he doesn't like her?"

"Korandellen is Harshini. He likes everyone. He can't help it. That's why they hired me, remember? And I don't have a conscience, according to you."

The God of Thieves thought that over for a moment before nodding brightly. "Well, that's all right then. When do we leave?"

Brak was not entirely pleased with the idea that Dace had invited himself along. "Were you serious about the trouble brewing among the miners?"

"I'm the God of Thieves, not Liars. Of course it's true."

"Then we'll use that for our cover. When they make their move, we'll make ours."

"What about Tarja?"

"What about him? I'm only concerned about R'shiel. Right now, she's the most important person in the whole world."

"Kalianah will be mad at you if you don't bring him along."

"I can deal with Kalianah."

Dace looked skeptical. "Well, I still wouldn't risk it, if I were you."

"Your concern is touching, Divine One."

The god scowled at him. "You know, Brak, sometimes I think you don't hold the gods in very high esteem."

"Whatever gave you that idea?" he asked.

chapter 38

arja dumped the load of vegetable scraps and other unidentifiable matter into the back of the mule-drawn wagon, forcing himself not to gag. They collected the garbage from the Inn of the Hopeless and the other stores in Grimfield whenever the mood took Lycren rather than on any set schedule. Since it was nearly a month since the last time Lycren had felt in the mood, the leavings had had plenty of time to ferment into an odoriferous, cockroach-infested sludge. Tarja swung the heavy barrel down to the ground and glanced up, feeling himself being watched. A young, fair-haired lad stood near the cellar doors watching him with interest. Tarja wondered about the boy. He seemed to turn up in the most unusual places.

"Get a move on, Tarja!" Lycren called.

Tarja glared at the boy as he straightened up. He hated being stared at. Anger, buried deep inside for survival, threatened to surface again. Only once had he made the mistake of letting it show. The lashing he had received as a consequence had done little to humble him, but it had taught him to control his temper. The pain had not bothered him nearly so much as the knowledge that he had let a fool provoke him.

As they moved out of the tavern yard and headed for the smithy farther down the lane, Tarja wondered about the boy. It was not inconceivable that he had contacts in the rebellion. The Grimfield was full of convicted heathens, both real and imagined. Had they sent the boy to spy on him? To confirm that he was still alive? He wondered sometimes how well his fellow rebels had listened to what he had tried to teach them, the foremost of which was never, ever, let a traitor go unpunished. Tarja had spent the winter half-expecting a knife in the back, every time he found himself in a crowd of prisoners. Lycren saw to it that he was segregated for the most part, but at meal times in particular he knew how much danger he was in. It was with mild surprise that Tarja realized how long he had survived in this place. He had not expected to live through the journey here.

Tarja's thoughts turned to the rebels he had left behind. Old Padric, worn out and weary from years of fighting against impossible odds. Mandah, with her ardent faith in the gods. Ghari, so young and passionate. Where was he now? Still fighting? Killed in a skirmish with the Defenders? Or maybe he had given up and returned to his mother's farm in the Lowlands. Was he one of the names on Joyhinia's infamous list? Tarja seethed with frustration as he thought of the rebels. He was doing nothing here. He was not likely to either, collecting the garbage and emptying the privies of the garrison town. Each day he spent here in the Grimfield ate a little more out of his store of hope. Tarja knew he would have to do something before it was all gone.

One of the few advantages—possibly the only one—of being assigned to the garbage patrol was that Tarja was allowed to bathe daily, unlike the miners, who were only allowed the privilege once a week. Being allowed to wash away the stink of rotting food and other despicable decaying matter was the only thing that made his work detail tolerable. Many a time he had wished Wilem had sent him to the mines, where he could have taken out his anger with a sledgehammer on the rock face. He shivered in the chill of the dusk, his skin covered in goose pimples from the icy water, as he rubbed himself briskly with the scrap of rough cloth he used as a towel and glanced up at the sky. Angry gray clouds stained red and bloody flocked around the sun as it cowered behind the foothills until it could finally escape into the night. As he dressed in his rough prison uniform, Tarja glanced at Zac, who was attempting to dry his shaggy head with a saturated towel.

"It'll rain again tonight," he remarked.

"S'pose," Zac agreed.

In almost two months, he could not recall Zac putting more than two words together at a time. The big, taciturn murderer was a good companion for a man who wished to answer no questions. Together they walked to the gate where Fohli, Lycren's corporal, waited for them. He locked the gate behind them and escorted the prisoners across the compound to the kitchens. The garbage detail was always fed last, and out of habit,

Tarja and Zac sank down onto the ground to wait their turn at a meal. The compound was busy in the dusk as the prisoners from the mines and the various workhouses were fed in shuffling lines. Tarja watched them idly, not paying attention to anyone in particular, until he spied R'shiel walking purposefully across the compound toward the kitchens, her gray shawl clutched tight around her shoulders against the cold.

The sight of R'shiel reminded Tarja even more painfully of the mess they had made of their lives. She did not belong here in the Grimfield among the dregs of Medalon, spared a life as a barracks *court'esa* only by sheer good fortune. He had spoken to her only a handful of times since they had arrived and always in the company of Zac or a guard. Unless she happened to be in the yard when they came round to collect the garbage, he never even saw her from one week to the next. He wanted to know how she was doing. He needed to assure himself that the journey here had not destroyed her. His frustration was almost a palpable thing, bitter enough to taste.

He watched R'shiel as she walked toward him, wondering if she knew how beautiful she was. She carried herself in the manner of one unaware of her effect on others. Tarja had expected himself to be immune to her allure, but every time he caught sight of R'shiel, even from a distance, he was startled by the effect she had on him. It was an odd feeling he could not define. It wasn't desire, or even simple lust. It was just the strangest feeling that to be near her, to be noticed by her, would be a very pleasant thing indeed. It had been creeping up on him ever since that night in the vineyard. Despite everything that had happened since, she was always somewhere in his thoughts.

R'shiel was looking around as she approached them. Not finding the object of her search, she turned to Fohli.

"Have you seen Sunny Hopechild?" she asked.

"Lost her, have you?" Fohli replied, with vast disinterest.

"She was supposed to report to the Commandant's house an hour ago. She's been reassigned."

"She'll turn up. Them *court'esa* are too smart to duck an order like that. You'll be in trouble yourself if you don't get back before dark."

"Will you send her along if you see her?" she asked, looking around in the rapidly fading light. "She's about this tall, with blonde hair."

"Sure," Fohli promised. The corporal would promise anything provided he didn't actually have to put himself out to keep his word.

In a slash of yellow light, Sister Unwin, her round face flushed from the heat of the stoves, emerged from the kitchen to survey the lines of prisoners waiting for their dinner. She glared at R'shiel and marched across the compound, planting herself in front of the girl with her hands on her wide hips. Her blue skirt was dusted with a faint sheen of flour, and there was a smudge of something on her chin.

"And just what do you think you're doing here, girl? Does Mistress Crisabelle know you're gallivanting about town at this hour of the day, flirting with the guards?"

"Mistress Crisabelle sent me to look for her new seamstress."

"Well, she's not here. You get along back where you belong and don't let me catch you hanging around my kitchen." Unwin turned her wrath on Fohli. "You take her back to the Commandant and see that he knows what she's been up to." With that, she stormed off back to her kitchen.

Fohli was left in something of a quandary. He could not leave his two charges unattended, nor could he ignore a direct order from a Sister. With a shrug, he glanced at Zac and Tarja.

"C'mon lads, looks like we've a bit of a walk before dinner."

They climbed wearily to their feet and followed Fohli to the gate. The guards let them pass, and the four of them headed across the Square toward the Commandant's residence on the other side of town. Fohli was not the least bit interested in the additional duty Unwin had thrust upon him and dawdled along with Zac at his side. R'shiel was angry, and her step carried her ahead of the others. Trying not to look too obvious about it, Tarja caught up with her. By the time they had crossed the Square, it was almost completely dark.

The threatening clouds rumbled ominously as they turned down the main road, which led to the married quarters. R'shiel glanced at Tarja as he drew level with her but said nothing.

"What does Crisabelle want Sunny for?" he asked. Zac and Fohli had fallen back far enough so that their conversation was unlikely to be overheard.

"Crisabelle wants a new wardrobe before she visits the Citadel in the spring. Sunny is supposed to help with the sewing."

"Can she sew?" Tarja asked curiously. From what he had observed of Sunny, she appeared to excel in only one thing, and it certainly wasn't sewing.

"I truly don't know. But Loclon beat her up again, and I thought she could do with a break. It's sort of my fault she got hurt. I'm sure he only does it because of me," she added with a heavy sigh.

So he's found another outlet for his anger, Tarja thought sourly. The thought relieved him a little. R'shiel was safe from him, for the moment. Tarja had made a silent vow to himself to kill Loclon. All he lacked was the opportunity. He didn't need a weapon. Killing him with his bare hands would be half the pleasure.

"She'll turn up. Fohli's right, you know. Sunny isn't stupid. She won't defy a direct order from the Commandant."

"I suppose so."

"Anyway, what do you mean, it's your fault?"

"He . . . well, he's still mad at me. And you. I guess I'm just the easiest target."

R'shiel was silent for a moment before she continued, as if weighing up whether or not to confide in him. "It seems that every time I turn around he's standing there, just watching me. The way he looks at me makes my skin crawl. A couple of times he . . . well, it doesn't matter. He never gets an opportunity to do anything about it. But each time he misses a chance to get at me, someone else seems to get hurt."

Tarja shook his head, appalled that she would blame herself for Loclon's insanity. "It's not your fault, R'shiel. Anymore than it's my fault—"

"That we're here?" R'shiel finished for him. They walked on in silence. Within a few minutes, they had reached the low stone fence surrounding the Commandant's residence so they stopped at the small gate to wait for Fohli and Zac to catch up. In the lamplight blazing from the windows, Tarja could make out the Commandant and Loclon discussing something in silhouette. R'shiel tensed as she saw them.

"He's here."

Tarja looked at her, not truly surprised by the vehemence in her tone. She still had not forgiven or forgotten the journey to the Grimfield.

"Maybe he's in trouble."

"I wish! More likely here to get tomorrow's orders."

She turned from him, but he caught her arm and turned her back to face him, studying her intently in the gloom. "Are you all right, R'shiel? Really?"

"I'm fine, Tarja," she told him, a little bitterly. "I'm in prison for the next ten years. I've been beaten and raped, and now I'm serving a woman who takes a picnic basket to a public lashing. What more could I ask?"

Tarja had to resist the urge to take her in his arms. To hold her as he had when she was a little girl, following him and Georj around, skinning her knees as she ran to catch up with two boys who thought their red Cadet jackets made them too important to associate with obnoxious little girls.

"I'm sorry, R'shiel," he said, helpless to offer her anything more. "I'll find a way out of this. Soon."

"I can take care of myself."

Before he could add anything further, Fohli and Zac caught up to them. R'shiel shook her arm free of Tarja and faced Fohli defiantly.

"Well, are you going to report me to the Commandant?" she asked.

"Not bloody likely," Fohli muttered. "Less the Commandant notices me, the better. You get along and stay outta Unwin's way." Without bothering to thank him, R'shiel lifted her skirts and stepped over the low gate. She ran around the house and disappeared into the darkness. "She's odd, that one."

"Harshini," Zac said sagely. Both Tarja and Fohli stared at him in astonishment. "She's got the look," he added knowingly. The big man hitched his trousers into a more comfortable position and headed back down the road toward the prisoners' kitchen.

Fohli caught at Tarja's sleeve and pulled him along in Zac's wake. "Here, you was a rebel, Tarja, mixin' with all them heathens. Is it true what they say about the Harshini? Are they really gods?"

"I doubt it," Tarja said, as he watched Zac's retreating back. "How do you suppose Zac knows about them?"

"Zac's from near the border. That's what they sent him here for. He's a pagan. Killed a couple of Defenders they sent to arrest him. I heard the Hythrun reckon the Harshini are still out there somewhere. In hiding. Not that I ever seen no sign of it. You think that girl is one of them?"

"Are you kidding me?" Actually, he thought it was the most absurd idea he had ever heard.

"Aye, you're right at that," Fohli agreed. "Here! Isn't she your sister or something?"

"No, she's not my sister."

"Well, she's foreign, that's for certain," Fohli said.

chapter 39

ews of the riot at the mines reached the Commandant's house early on the morning of Fourthday. R'shiel was woken by the sound of raised voices and the pounding of hooves in the street. Teggert pushed open the door to their tiny room off the kitchen and ordered R'shiel and Sunny to get up and come help in the kitchens while Wilem and his officers held their council of war over breakfast in the dining room. Still rubbing the sleep from their eyes, the two young women hurried into the kitchen. As Teggert issued orders like a little general, he told them of the riot—how the miners had barricaded themselves in the main pit—and the rumor that Captain Mysekis and several other Defenders were dead. Dace had been right, she realized as she lugged the heavy iron kettle to the fire. It was a pity Loclon was assigned to the town and not the mines. Getting up this early would have been worth it to hear that he had been killed.

The racket woke the whole house, and once news of the riot reached Crisabelle, she went into a spin, declaring that she was about to be murdered in her bed. In a rare display of temper, Wilem turned on her and told her that he was too busy to concern himself with her right now and that if she didn't like it, she could visit her sister in Brodenvale and stay there until the damned summer, for all he cared. Wailing like a banshee, Crisabelle fled to her room, screaming for R'shiel to help her pack, making sure that everyone within earshot knew that she was leaving and Wilem would be lucky if she ever came back. The Commandant ignored her and turned back to the business at hand. It was dawn when Wilem thundered out of the town. Fetching and carrying for Crisabelle, R'shiel barely even noticed he had left but for the unusual silence that descended on the house. Of Mahina there was no sign. She had either slept through the entire ruckus, which was unlikely, or chose to remain uninvolved.

The confusion of Crisabelle's departure, hard on the heels of the Commandant leaving for the mines, made the morning fly. Once she had made up her mind to be gone from the Grimfield there was no stopping her, and R'shiel was quite astounded to see how determined the normally absentminded woman could be. The free servants of the Commandant's household were hastily given a holiday, and only R'shiel and Sunny were to remain in the house while Crisabelle was away. As Crisabelle clambered aboard the carriage she was still yelling instructions at R'shiel and Teggert. The cook and the convict girl nodded continuously. Yes, Teggert would empty out the pantry before he left. No, R'shiel wouldn't let any thieving whore from the Women's Hall into the house. Yes, the stove and the chimneys would be cleaned before the summer. No, Teggert wouldn't forget to be back in time for her return. Assuming she did return. Wilem had some apologizing to do before that would happen! The orders went on and on, until the driver climbed into his seat and Crisabelle finally gave the order to move out. R'shiel watched the carriage disappear from sight with a sigh of relief.

Teggert went back inside as soon as the carriage moved off. R'shiel waited a moment, just in case Crisabelle thought of something else and ordered the driver to turn around.

"Prisoner!"

R'shiel turned slowly toward the voice, schooling her features into a neutral expression. She had hoped that Loclon would accompany Wilem to the mines, but one of the captains had to stay in the town until he returned. With a sinking heart, R'shiel realized it might be days before the Commandant returned, depending on how well organized the prisoners were.

"Yes, Captain?"

Loclon dismissed the corporal he was addressing and walked toward her, blocking her way back into the house. He must have been here since early this morning, waiting.

"You are to report to Sister Prozlan for reassignment."

"Mistress Crisabelle said I was to remain here." Wilem was barely gone. Crisabelle's carriage had probably not even left the walls of the prison town yet.

"The Commandant isn't here, and Crisabelle's orders aren't worth a pinch of horseshit," Loclon reminded her. "I am in charge at the moment, and I'm ordering you to report to Sister Prozlan for reassignment."

"Crisabelle said I was to remain here," she repeated. Reassignment meant more than losing the protection of the Commandant's house.

"Are you defying a direct order, prisoner?" Loclon asked. He took a step closer, and she couldn't help but take a backward step. The low fence surrounding the Commandant's house pressed into the back of her knees. "Do you know what the punishment—"

"R'shiel! Get in here at once! I want my tea!" Mahina was leaning out of the upstairs window, her expression thunderous. "Captain! Haven't you got something better to do than annoy my servant? Off with you!"

Without another word to Loclon, she fled inside to safety, aware that this time she had been very, very lucky.

R'shiel spent the remainder of the morning tidying up after Crisabelle. Mahina made no further comment about Loclon. She promised R'shiel she would see her at dinner, but in the meantime, she was off to have lunch with Khira the physic, who was, according to Mahina, the only woman in the Grimfield capable of holding an intelligent conversation.

Sunny announced that she was going back to bed, once they finished. The *court'esa* was not used to getting up in the early hours of the morning. She was not particularly pleased with her new position. R'shiel was a little hurt that Sunny had not been more appreciative of her efforts to free her from the Women's Hall. Sunny's face was still bruised, but the swelling had gone down. Maybe, in time, Sunny would learn that there was more to life than being a *court'esa*, although R'shiel was not hopeful. Sunny simply believed that you should just go with whatever life threw at you and if there was a profit in it, so much the better. But she didn't argue the point. Sunny was already asleep by the time R'shiel finished clearing away the table from lunch.

R'shiel knew that with a skeleton force left to guard the town there would never be a better chance for escape. The sky was dark with thunderheads, and another storm was threatening as R'shiel let herself into the yard to collect more wood for the stove. She glanced up at the sky with satisfaction. A few more hours and she would be free of this place. In the meantime, she decided to follow Sunny's example and get some rest.

It was going to be a long night.

.   .   .

When R'shiel woke it was dark outside. Cautiously, she went to the door and opened it a little. The kitchen was dim and deserted. Gathering up her few belongings, she slipped out of the room softly, so as not to disturb Sunny. She stopped in the kitchen long enough to gather up a loaf of bread, half a wheel of cheese, and a thin paring knife, which she secreted into the side of her boot. She let herself out of the kitchen and ran down the muddy lane, away from the Commandant's house.

The ominous sky rumbled as she ran, jagged lightning illuminating her path. R'shiel reached the end of the lane, crossed the street and then stopped, glancing around the square. Announcing itself with a fanfare of thunder the storm unleashed itself over the Grimfield, the rain lashing the shuttered windows in its fury, bouncing off the cobbled square like muddy glass marbles. She had only taken two or three steps when she froze at the sound of horses. Quickly jumping back into her place of concealment, she held her breath as two Defenders trotted by, hunched over their saddles in the downpour.

"No one would be out in this!" the nearer one said. He was yelling at his companion to be heard over the storm.

She stayed hidden until they had crossed the square, trying to decide which was the safest route to the South Gate. Should she risk the square, and being seen, which was by far the shorter route? Or stick to the back alleys and take even longer, further increasing the risk of being discovered? R'shiel wavered with indecision for a moment before deciding on a simple mathematical fact. The shortest distance between two points was a straight line. The square was completely deserted now, the shops shuttered against the storm. Even the Defenders' Headquarters building on the opposite side looked dark and abandoned for the night. The less time she spent getting to the gate, the better. Besides, the majority of the Defenders were at the mines with Wilem. There were not the men to spare to guard the town effectively.

R'shiel turned out of the lane and headed across the square at a dead run. Drenched to the skin in seconds, her feet slipped on the slick cobbles as she ran, but she righted herself without too much effort and maintained her pace. The thunder crashed overhead as the lightning showed her the way. As she passed the tannery, which marked the halfway point, she smiled grimly to herself. She would make it, she was certain now. However, her certainty lasted only a few seconds. Too late, she heard the pounding of hooves on the wet cobbles behind her, their sound muffled by the thunder. She began to run harder.

R'shiel screamed as she was scooped up from behind. Struggling wildly she fought off a strong arm that encircled her waist as her captor turned his horse toward the Headquarters Building. When they arrived, he hauled savagely on the reins, and she was a thrown heavily down to the cobbles. The second rider was only a split second behind her as he jumped down from his horse and hauled her to her feet. R'shiel wriggled out of his grasp desperately. The other trooper grabbed at her wet hair as she tried to run and pulled her up the short steps to the verandah. She tried to pull away from him, screaming as he gave her hair a vicious twist. The other man opened the door and thrust her inside, stopping long enough to lock it behind him, then pushed her through to Wilem's office.

With a shove, he let her go. A single candle burned on the mantle. The vicious Tail of the Tiger lay on the desk.

Loclon sat behind Wilem's heavily carved desk, as if trying it on for size.

chapter 40

The whole town seemed to relax a little once Wilem departed the Grimfield. It was nothing obvious—a loose collar here, an undone button there. The Defenders of the Grimfield were like any other soldiers the world over. When the Commanding Officer was away, everything slacked off, just a little. The general feeling among the Defenders left to guard the Grimfield was that all the troublemakers were at the mine. They were not expecting trouble. Tarja was an experienced soldier and knew it would happen. He was relying on it. He also knew it wouldn't last. Wilem would return soon enough, and his window of opportunity would be gone.

Since learning of the impending riot, Tarja had been honing his plans. Having had over two months to think things through, Tarja was certain he could escape with relative ease. His first step he had taken by becoming, if not a model prisoner, then at least a tractable one. He had done nothing to give Wilem reason to suspect that he was not accepting his punishment with silent fortitude. The second step he had taken when collecting the garbage from the back of the physic's shop. A small stoppered tube had fallen from a shovel load of garbage. Retrieving it carefully, Tarja had unstoppered the tube and caught a faint whiff of sickly sweet jarabane. The poison was used for trapping animals, and the tube was all but empty. Tarja had pocketed the small vial and hidden it in his small cell under a loose stone. With a small amount of water added, he had a potion that would make the recipient violently ill.

He carried the tube with him now and could feel it pressing against his hip as he sat on the cold ground with Zac, waiting for their dinner. The sky rumbled disturbingly, and Tarja silently hoped that it would rain and rain hard. He had a much better chance of escaping if the Defenders were huddled under shelter, trying to escape the inclement weather. An escape in the middle of a storm was just as likely to be, if not ignored, then overlooked as long as possible. Who wanted to hunt down a miserable escapee in the rain?

"Gonna be a good one tonight," Fohli remarked as another loud rumble rolled across the compound.

"Sure is," Tarja agreed. He felt somewhat ambivalent about Corporal Fohli and Sergeant Lycren. The part of him that still felt pride in the Defenders was appalled by the men. They were unshaven, slovenly, lazy—everything Tarja despised in a soldier. Had either been in Tarja's Company, they would have been straightened out very smartly indeed. On the other hand, were it not for their slackness, Tarja would have little hope of escaping.

It was almost completely dark by the time Tarja and Zac were handed their meals. Tarja offered to collect Fohli's meal, too, and carried it back to the feeble shelter of the cookhouse eaves. It was a simple matter to tip the watery contents of the tube into Fohli's stew. Tarja handed him the bowl, and the corporal wolfed down the contents hungrily. Large raindrops splattered intermittently across the compound. Fohli urged his prisoners to eat faster and had them handing in their bowls and heading back to the relative warmth of the cell block almost before they had swallowed their last mouthful.

They were back in the cell block when the corporal doubled over with pain as a stomach cramp clutched at his guts.

"Mother of the Founders!" he swore, clutching at the back of a roughly carved chair for support. Like model prisoners, Tarja and Zac waited patiently for the corporal to recover. When Fohli showed no inclination to move them anywhere, Tarja stepped closer.

"Are you all right?" he asked. "You don't look at all well, Corporal."

Fohli yelped as another spasm took him. His skin was ashen, and Tarja worried for a moment that there had been more jarabane than he suspected in the tube. He didn't want to kill Fohli, just disable him. Zac thoughtfully lit the lantern on the guard table and waited for Fohli to recuperate enough to lock them up.

"It must have been the stew," Fohli gasped, as another cramp seized him.

"Should we get someone?" Tarja offered.

Fohli shook his head. "In there." He waved vaguely in the direction of their cells. "Have to lock you up first. OW!"

"Not tonight," Tarja said, mostly to himself as Fohli collapsed semi-conscious against the scrubbed wooden table. With a sigh, Zac stepped forward and scooped the Corporal into his arms. He turned his dull eyes on Tarja.

"You go now."

Tarja looked at him in surprise. "Go?"

"Escape. You go. I take care of Fohli."

Tarja was astounded that Zac had read his intentions so easily. "Come with me."

Zac shook his shaggy head. "Got food. Got bed. Zac stay here."

"Good luck, Zac."

"You need luck. Not Zac," the big man pointed out simply.

Thunder continued to roll through the small walled township like an invisible avalanche as Tarja quickly wended his way through the back alleys of the Grimfield. Months of hauling garbage had taught him where every lane and alley led, and he made good time through the backstreets. The uniform he planned to steal was right where he had hoped it would be, although it was damp and proved to be a tight fit. He shrugged on the jacket as he ran.

The storm broke as he neared the quarters of the married Defenders. Within seconds he was soaked as the rain pelted down in sheets. He kept moving, using the storm for cover. As he neared the street where Wilem's house was located, he slowed. The street was deserted but for a couple of miserable-looking horses tied up outside the house. Tarja cursed silently, wondering to whom they belonged. If there were Defenders visiting Mahina, extracting R'shiel from the house would be next to impossible. He moved stealthily up the street until he reached the small fence surrounding Wilem's house. He stepped over it and slipped around to the back. The owners of the horses were a corporal and a trooper, standing on the verandah talking to Mahina. The old woman was holding a lantern, but he could not make out what was being said over the roar of the thunderstorm.

The rear yard was deserted as Tarja made his way to the back door. He eased it open gently and was relieved to discover the kitchen was empty. Leaving an unavoidable trail of wet footprints next to the scrubbed wooden table, Tarja crossed to the door that led into the hall. Voices reached him as he opened the door a fraction. He stopped to listen, hoping that whatever business the troopers had with Mahina, it would not take long.

"I'll do no such thing!" Mahina was declaring in a tone that made Tarja smile in fond remembrance. "You go back and tell Loclon that if he ever sends me an order like that again, I'll personally see that *he* is whipped! Now get out of here! Find Prozlan. That's her job!"

Mahina slammed the door on the hapless message bearers. Tarja wondered for a moment what Loclon had asked of Mahina that had her in such high dudgeon. He moved back quickly as Mahina turned and headed straight toward him. Glancing quickly around the kitchen, he realized there was nowhere to hide. Even had he found a place of concealment, his muddy footprints left a telltale trail straight across the floor. Tarja sighed and stepped back against the wall as Mahina stomped into the kitchen. If he could not hide, then there was no point in trying to.

"Hello, Mahina," he said as she stormed into the room.

She squawked with surprise at the unexpected voice and spun around to face him. "By the Founders, what are you doing here?"

"Escaping."

"Escaping?" she scoffed. "What took you so damned long? You've been here two months or more. Like the food, do you?"

"I've had my reasons."

"Fine. Escape then. Why are you hanging around here?"

"I came for R'shiel. She's in danger."

"Well you're too damned late," Mahina snapped in annoyance.

A door opened off the side of the kitchen, and Sunny stepped into the room, rubbing her eyes sleepily. They widened at the sight of Tarja, and she glanced at Mahina.

"I heard voices." Sunny appeared uncertain as to how she should react to finding Tarja in the kitchen admitting to an escape.

"You heard nothing," Mahina snapped at the young woman. "Where is R'shiel?"

"I don't know. I haven't seen her since lunch."

"We have to find her," Tarja said, as it occurred to him that if Loclon was still in the town, he might well be the ranking officer at present. That gave him almost unlimited power until Wilem returned.

"Why?" Mahina asked. "So you can get her into even more trouble?"

"Loclon raped her on the journey here." Sunny nodded in agreement as Mahina glared at both of them. "You know the penalty for rape, Mahina. If she ever reports it, he's as good as dead. He has to silence her."

Mahina's faded eyes grew cold. "I've had just about enough of Loclon," she snarled. "That arrogant little upstart just sent an order for me to attend to him. Can you believe that? He demanded that I come to him to deliver a whipping to . . . Oh! By the Founders . . . " Mahina's face paled in the lamplight.

"What?" Tarja asked impatiently.

"Tarja, I think he's already found her." She sank down into a chair, looking every one of her sixty-seven years. "He ordered me to deliver a whipping to a female convict who was attempting to escape. Do you suppose it's R'shiel? He wouldn't ask me to do that, would he?"

"Oh, yes he would."

Mahina stood up purposefully. "I think perhaps it's time I had a little chat with Captain Loclon."

"I'll come with you."

"Don't be stupid, Tarja. Escape while you can." She reached up and touched his cheek fondly. "Don't let what has happened sway your resolve, Tarja. Medalon needs you. Go back to the rebellion, get it moving again and unseat your damned mother. I'll take care of Loclon."

"I plan to," he promised her. "But I'm not letting you confront Loclon alone."

Mahina grabbed her cloak off the hook on the back of the door and slipped it over her shoulders. Sunny stared at them blankly, as if she didn't understand what was happening.

"Come if you must, Tarja," Mahina said, "Just don't get in my way. I have a few things I want to say to young Mister Loclon."

Tarja opened the door for her. Together they ran toward the stables. The rain was still pelting down to the accompaniment of a thunderous orchestra. They shook off the raindrops as they entered the relatively dry stables. Mahina reached up and hooked the lantern she had brought from the kitchen on a nail driven into the doorframe.

"You haven't changed a bit, you know," Tarja told her as he led the first horse out of the stall.

"We'll need a horse for R'shiel, too. And yes, I have changed," she corrected. "Now I'm meaner."

He had finished saddling the horses when Sunny suddenly appeared at the entrance to the stable, clutching one of Crisabelle's impractical velvet cloaks around her, not caring that the rain was ruining the garment.

"Can I come, too?" she begged. "If they know I saw you and didn't raise the alarm, I'll be whipped."

Tarja had no particular feelings for Sunny, one way or the other, but having been on the receiving end of the lash, it was not a punishment he would wish on anyone. And she spoke the truth. Annoyed by the added burden but unable to see any other course open to him, he nodded.

"Can you ride?"

"I'll learn as I go," the *court'esa* assured him. Then she reached into the folds of the dripping cloak and handed him a sheathed sword. It belonged to Wilem. He recognized the distinctive workmanship of the Citadel smiths in its wire-wrapped hilt. "I thought you might need this."

Tarja accepted the gift and helped her up into the saddle of the mount he had picked out for R'shiel. "Come on then. And you'd better keep up. We won't wait for you."

Sunny wiggled uncomfortably in the saddle. "I'll be just fine, Captain."

Tarja swung up into the saddle of his own mount and led the old woman and the *court'esa* out into the rain, full of doubts and afraid of what he would find if Loclon really did have R'shiel.

chapter 41

rying to escape, eh?" Loclon asked. R'shiel backed away from him, bumping into the wet bulk of the trooper behind her. "That's what she was doing, wasn't it, Corporal Lenk?"

"Runnin' flat out across the Square, sir," Lenk agreed.

"Where were you running to?"

R'shiel did not bother to answer. There seemed little point.

"What's the punishment for attempting to escape, Corporal?"

"Five lashes I believe, sir," Lenk replied helpfully.

"Five lashes? Delivered publicly?"

"No, sir. The Commandant don't allow women to be lashed in public. It's done by one of the Sisters, out of sight."

"Then be so good as to deliver a message to Sister Mahina, Corporal," Loclon said, leaning back in Wilem's chair with a proprietary air. "Tell her that I have a prisoner in custody who requires a lashing, and I would be most grateful, if the good Sister would attend to it for me."

"Sir . . . well, it's usually Sister Prozlan who does it, sir. Sister Mahina, well . . . she's retired."

"You have your orders, Corporal. The prisoner will be fine with me."

Lenk glanced at his companion for a moment before he saluted and left the office, his partner in tow. R'shiel glanced at the door, wondering if she could get through it before Loclon reached her.

"By all means, try to escape," he suggested, turning the whip over and over in his hands, almost lovingly. "That would be two attempted escapes in the one day. Ten lashes. Maybe you could get through them without a whimper like your brother did, but I doubt it. Ah, but then he's not your brother anymore, is he? You're nothing but a nameless bastard, these days. My, how the mighty have fallen."

"Why did you send for Mahina?" she asked.

Loclon stood up, walking slowly around the desk, stroking the plaited leather tails.

"Well, you see, Mahina will either send Lenk off to see Prozlan, or she'll come here herself. Either way, I don't care. Watching you lashed by that old hag you call a friend would almost be as much fun as doing it myself."

She backed away from him as he approached her, afraid to turn her back on him, moving deeper into the room, until eventually she met the solid resistance of Wilem's desk. Loclon took another step toward her. Trapped by the bulk of the desk she looked around, realizing her mistake. Loclon stood between her and the door. She was trembling, soaked to the skin. He moved closer.

"Don't touch me," she warned.

"Or what?" He brought the handle of the whip up under her chin, not hard enough to hurt, but enough to force her head back. With his other hand he reached out and touched her face with surprising gentleness, running his thumb lightly over her lips. His scar was dark against his skin.

R'shiel bit him with all the force she could muster.

"Bitch!" he yelled, snatching his hand away. He backhanded her across the face, throwing her back onto the desk. Too stunned to move out of the way, her mouth filled with the salty warm taste of her own blood mingled with his, she struggled to a half-sit. With a wordless cry he punched her again. She toppled off the desk to the floor, taking several stacks of parchment and an inkwell with her. The cut-crystal well shattered as it hit the floor, the ink pooling darkly beside her. Shards of broken glass glittered in the dim light of the single candle.

As he came at her again, something inside of R'shiel snapped. Her fear and pain vanished, replaced by an unfamiliar feeling of invincibility. She climbed to her feet as the strange feeling engulfed her. Unaware of the change in his quarry, Loclon grabbed her arm and pulled her to him. An inexplicable wellspring of power surged through her.

Instead of fighting him, R'shiel slid her arms around Loclon's neck and kissed him deeply, open mouthed, making him gasp. Stunned by her sudden capitulation, he fumbled at her clothes, tearing the wet shirt easily from her shoulders. She threw her head back as he buried his face between her breasts. Lightning and thunder crashed in unison with her sudden power surge. She could feel Loclon trembling, shaking from the need to possess and humiliate her. She wanted to cry out as the strength welled up in her. She wanted to feel him trembling, needed to see him quivering at her feet. She ran her hands through his hair as he fell to his knees. She grabbed a handful, jerking his head back savagely. In her right hand the thin paring knife flashed in the jagged glare of the lightning.

Loclon came to his senses with astounding speed. She stood over him, her long hair hung damply over her breasts. Her eyes blazed with power, burning black, even the whites of her eyes consumed by the unfamiliar power. She did not understand the feeling or try to. The paring knife she held to his throat was rock steady. He had the sense to remain absolutely still. It was possible that he had never been so afraid in his life.

"Don't be . . . s . . . stupid," he gasped. "P . . . put it down."

In reply she pressed the point into his neck and a warm trickle of blood slid down the blade.

"No!" Loclon sobbed.

She slid the knife sideways. Not enough to kill him, but enough to make him think she was cutting his throat. She drew the thin blade across his exposed neck, the terror in his eyes thoroughly intoxicating her. The blood oozed out of the thin cut, running down his neck and over her hand. The sharp smell of urine suddenly mingled with the sweet-smelling blood, and R'shiel smirked at the dark spreading stain on the front of Loclon's trousers.

He thought he was dying. Before she was through with him, he would beg for death. Lifting the blade to his face, she pressed it into his cheek with the intention of carving a matching scar along the right side of his face. Tarja had given him that scar. For killing Georj. It was time to give him another one. For killing a part of her.

Loclon suddenly threw himself backward, jerking her off her feet as they tumbled to the floor. The blade was slick with blood, and it slipped from her grasp. With strength born of desperation and fear, he pushed her off him and lunged for the knife. She landed against the desk and cracked her head against the solid carved wood. The power surged again. Without warning, a faggot detached itself from the fire and hurled itself at Loclon. It caught him a glancing blow on the shoulder, but it was enough to deflect him from the blade. He spun around, looking for his new, invisible assailant as another log hurtled across the room toward him. He ducked it as R'shiel dragged herself into the corner. He looked at her in horror, truly seeing her eyes for the first time. He moved toward her, barely avoiding the small three-legged stool that barreled toward him. Her head throbbed with pain from the blow against the desk. She felt the potent strength fading. Whatever strange power had filled her it was losing its strength.

Loclon saw her eyes change. On his hands and knees he scooped up the paring knife and threw it out of reach, never taking his eyes off her. Struggling upright he retrieved the Tiger's Tail from near the hearth. R'shiel lay unmoving, as weak as a newborn, lacking the strength to defend herself. As if time had slowed almost to a standstill, she watched him raise the barbed whip above his shoulder. Still on his knees he moved toward her.

Suddenly a booted foot kicked the Tiger's Tail from his hand. The boot swung up again and caught the captain squarely in the face, throwing him backward in an unconscious heap against the hearth. R'shiel's eyes rolled back as a wave of blackness engulfed her and she fainted.

"R'shiel!" She opened her eyes slowly and looked up, surprised to find Mahina bending over her. Next to the old woman was a man who looked like Tarja, only it couldn't be Tarja because this man was wearing a uniform and Tarja wasn't a Defender anymore. She felt as feeble as an old woman.

"Bloody hell," Tarja muttered. Mahina studied the somnambulant girl for a moment before slapping her face. R'shiel jerked back at the pain and her vision began to clear, but she still felt as though she was swimming through molasses. She looked at Loclon and began to tremble violently.

"R'shiel! We have to get out of here! Now!"

Loclon lay unmoving beside her. His face was a bloodied pulp where the boot had landed. Blood streamed from his mouth and broken nose, mingling with the blood that still dripped from his slashed throat. He looked dead.

"R'shiel, we have to get out of here," Mahina told her again, more urgently. "Do you understand me?" The old woman looked at Tarja. "She's in some sort of shock. Can you carry her?"

Tarja nodded and scooped her easily into his arms. With Mahina leading the way, they headed for the door. R'shiel glanced up and noticed that his hair was damp.

"It's raining," she told him.

"I know it's raining," he said. They had only taken a few steps when he stopped. Then she realized that Sunny was there, too.

"What happened?"

"I don't know, and we're not hanging around to find out."

"You can't take her outside like that. Let me get something to cover her."

Sunny disappeared into the hall, while R'shiel was still trying to wade through the molasses of her mind. Sunny came back with a warm Defender's cloak. R'shiel hadn't realized how cold she was until the warm wool of the cloak touched her clammy skin.

"How are we going to get through the gates?" Sunny asked as she tucked the cloak around R'shiel.

"I'll take care of it," Mahina announced.

Tarja looked as if he might argue the point, but Sunny laid a hand on his arm. "You can't do this alone. Not with her like this."

"All right, but only because we don't have time to argue about it. Check the yard is clear."

Tarja carried her at a run out of the office and down the long hall to the back of the building. When they emerged into the yard the rain pelted down on them, and R'shiel's trembling grew worse. Tarja held her close as Sunny led three horses toward them. Lightning crashed overhead as Tarja lifted her onto the horse and then swung up easily behind her. She snuggled into him trustingly as he urged the horse into a canter.

R'shiel had her eyes closed, so she didn't see the reason that Tarja suddenly hauled on the reins and dragged their mount to a halt. She opened her eyes and squirmed a little in her seat to see what the problem was. Dace was standing beside the horse, holding the bridle.

"Hello, Dace,"

Dace didn't answer her but looked up at Tarja. "Did she kill him?"

"Let me past, boy."

Another flash of lightning lit the rain-drenched road, and R'shiel caught sight of Brak. She pressed back into Tarja's solid and reassuring chest. *He has come for me*, she suddenly knew.

R'shiel tried to pull away as Brak reached up and gently touched her face. A wave of calm swept through her; a gentle peace seemed to flow through her body and she relaxed. Her mind was still foggy but her trembling stopped. She could hear everything that was going on, but it no longer seemed to matter.

"Come with me. I can help you," Brak said.

"Like the last time I needed your help?" Tarja asked.

"You're in no danger from me. But you will never get out of the Grim-field without me. I can help you in ways you cannot possibly imagine."

"Let's go with him, Tarja," she heard Mahina urge. "Any minute now the whole damn Garrison is going to be after her. And you."

"The old lady's right. We don't have time to discuss it here."

"Let's move it then," Tarja snapped. He didn't sound very happy. Dace let go of the bridle and ran to his own mount.

"Is she all right with you? I can take her if you can't manage."

"I can manage, Brak."

R'shiel was having a great deal of trouble staying awake, even though the thunder still crashed and boomed overhead. The lightning hurt her eyes, and a headache of mammoth proportions was beginning to make its presence felt. The rain was cold, but Tarja's chest was warm and solid so she cuddled up to him as they moved off, and somehow, in the middle of their escape, she managed to fall asleep.

chapter 42

The storm blew itself out close to dawn. Brak glanced up at the slowly brightening sky and cursed. The horses were nearly finished. Tarja's was carrying a double load, and although they had swapped mounts at frequent intervals during the long night, there wasn't much more they could do but rest them. He would have traded every horse in Medalon for a Hythrun sorcerer-bred mount right now. A mount like Cloud Chaser who, when linked with his rider, had the stamina of three normal horses. In battle, their intelligence made them almost invincible, although the Harshini had never bred them for war. The horses had been slaughtered in the thousands by Param and the Sisterhood. It was an unfortunate human trait, this desire to destroy things they did not understand.

He looked around at the others and decided it wasn't just the horses that were almost at their limit. They were all cold and wet, their clothes plastered to them by the insistent downpour. Dace, riding in the lead, appeared to be holding up, but then he was immortal. The plump *court'esa* and the old woman looked about ready to drop. Tarja's back was straight, and he hugged the still unconscious R'shiel to him. Brak knew grim determination kept the rebel in his saddle.

With another muttered curse, he decided that this wasn't going well at all. All he wanted was get R'shiel back to Sanctuary in one piece and discharge his debt to the Harshini. Once there, she was Korandellen's problem. When he learned what the gods wanted of the demon child, he decided to let the Harshini King decide if she was up to the task or too dangerous to be allowed to live. It was a decision he did not want to make. Brak had seen R'shiel with the rebels, seen what she had done to Loclon, perhaps even worse, what she had wanted to do to him. There was a streak of ruthlessness buried deep within the half-human girl. He was certain there was a rough road ahead for all of them. Just accepting that she was only half-human might prove an insurmountable hurdle for her.

Dace's addition to the party was more than an inconvenience. He was a Primal God and sufficiently powerful to assume whatever aspect he chose, but he was still bound by the nature of his divinity. He was the God of Thieves and as such was basically dishonest, unreliable, and opportunistic. Dace would only stay with them as long as it suited him and would probably leave them at the most inconvenient time imaginable. He would only be of real assistance if they were trying to steal something. Brak wasn't sure if that was because he couldn't help or wouldn't. Perhaps it was better not to ask. A demarcation dispute between the gods was something to be avoided.

Brak had no idea who the chubby woman was—a friend of R'shiel's he guessed. That could prove awkward. As for the other woman, the thought of her made him pale. Brak tried to imagine the look on Korandellen's face when he appeared at the gates of Sanctuary with a former First Sister in tow. How in the Seven Hells had she become mixed up in an escape attempt?

And then there was Tarja.

Brak just knew there was going to be trouble with him. Tarja thought he had betrayed him at the inn at Testra. He doubted Tarja would be interested in explanations regarding the nature of the glamor Brak had used to conceal himself, or his reasons for it. Tarja was a soldier, and soldiers tended to see the world in black and white. There were no shades of gray that would allow him to consider Brak's actions as anything other than treachery. At the very least, Tarja probably thought Brak was working for the rebellion and his task was to kill him as a traitor. Not an unreasonable assumption, under the circumstances, but one that would take some explaining. The trouble was, the explanation was likely to be unbelievable. Sometimes the truth was just plain awkward.

They had begun with about a three-hour lead over the Defenders sent to hunt them down. Dace assured him that Loclon wasn't dead, not yet at least, and had been discovered by Corporal Lenk, who had raised the alarm. Only the fact that the majority of the Defenders were at the mine dealing with the riot prevented a full Company from riding after them. As it was, there were ten of them, closing the gap fast, unhampered by a horse carrying a double burden. Brak figured they couldn't be more than half an hour behind them now, and they would soon forfeit whatever small advantage the rain and darkness had given them.

"Hold up," he called to the others, dismounting stiffly. Dace wheeled his horse around and trotted back to Tarja. He slipped off his own mount and reached up for R'shiel. Tarja lowered her down and then slowly dismounted himself.

"What's the matter?"

Brak glanced up at the sky again. "It's almost dawn, and we're still too close to the Grimfield. They'll be on us in less than an hour."

"How do you know?"

"I know," Brak told him, then turned to Dace. "Can you keep going on your own for a while?"

The boy pushed back his damp hair. "I live to serve, Lord Brakandaran."

Brak frowned. Dace did not appear to be taking this very seriously. "Keep going with the women. Tarja and I will take care of the pursuit."

"I'm not going with him!" Sunny objected, still mounted.

"You'll go with Dace and do what he says, or I'll kill you now and have one less human to worry about." The woman must have decided he was serious, which was a good thing. Brak had little stomach for killing these days, but she didn't know that. She sniffed at him and looked away without any further sign of rebellion.

"Can you guarantee that we will be safe if we follow this boy?" Mahina asked.

"No harm will come to any of you while you're with Dace," he promised. "You could say the gods will be watching over you."

She studied him for a moment longer with an unreadable expression. She nodded slightly and wheeled her horse around.

Brak turned back to Tarja. "You got enough strength left in you to fight?"

"I can keep going as long as you can."

"I seriously doubt that, my friend," he muttered to himself. "Dace, come here."

The god was bending over the unconscious girl. He led Dace a little way off, out of the hearing of the humans, ignoring their suspicious stares.

"Keep heading southwest, toward the river. We'll catch up as soon as we can. And try not to get distracted."

"You show a disturbing lack of faith in me, Brakandaran."

"I prefer to think of it as a firm grasp of reality. If you start getting ideas about wandering off, just try to imagine what Zegarnald will do when I tell him it was your fault we lost the demon child."

"That's not fair." The boy-god frowned for a moment then shrugged.

That was one good thing about the gods. They didn't agonize over any-thing for very long. "Will R'shiel be all right? I'm not sure what I should do with her. I don't know much about humans. What happens if she dies?"

"She's not going to die. All you have to do is keep her safe. You can do that much, can't you?"

"I suppose," Dace sighed. "Are you sure you wouldn't rather I helped you and Tarja? Looking after the women is sort of . . . well . . . boring."

"We're going to kill them, Dace, not steal their horses." Then he decided to try a different tack. This was a god he was talking to, after all. Their egos tended toward the majestic. He lowered his voice and added in a conspiratorial whisper, "You have to stop R'shiel from being stolen away from us. Who better to do that than the God of Thieves?"

Dace brightened considerably at the idea. "Do you think someone might try to steal her?"

"Definitely. They're probably combing the hills as we speak, just waiting for a chance at her. Of course, if you don't think you're up to the task . . . "

"Don't be ridiculous! If I can't thwart a miserable bunch of humans, I'll give up my believers and become a demon. You take care of the pur-suit, Lord Brakandaran, and I will ensure that the demon child is safe."

"I knew I could count on you," Brak replied gravely.

They walked back to Tarja, who was bent over R'shiel. The girl's face was peaceful and serene. The magic that had possessed her earlier van-ished as if it had never been. The humans eyed him dubiously but stood back to let him check on her. Her pulse was steady and even. He picked her up off the muddy ground and handed her up to Dace, who had mounted again.

"Vigilance," he reminded the god.

Dace nodded and clucked at his horse. They moved off into the dim morning, Sunny trailing with slumped shoulders, although Mahina's back was ramrod straight. Brak turned to his black gelding, whose head hung miserably, his breath steaming.

"There's a gully about a league back," he explained as he tied the gelding to the branch of a twisted white-gum. "We'll wait for them there."

Tarja tied up his own mount and followed Brak back onto the narrow track. They made good time, but the sky was considerably lighter by the time they reached the gully. The track cut through a long-extinct water-course, although the night's rain had caused a trickle to gather in the cen-ter of the path in an echo of its former glory. The cutting was about the height of a man on horseback and near thirty strides long, wider at the far end than the end from which the two men approached. Brak could hear the soldiers faintly in the distance.

"They're coming."

The rebel glanced at him skeptically.

"Trust me, they'll be here soon."

"So what's your plan? You do have a plan, don't you Brak?"

"When they ride into the gully we'll bring down the trees at either end of the cutting. With a bit of luck, a few of them will fall and break their necks in the confusion."

"Bring down the trees? How?" Tarja was looking at him like he was a simple-minded fool.

"Magic," he said. "We will call on the gods for help."

"Who are you?"

"I doubt you'd believe me if I told you, Tarja. Just accept the fact that I'm on your side, for the time being. Explanations can wait."

Tarja did not look happy with his answer, but the rattle of tack and pounding of hooves, loud enough for even the human to hear, distracted him.

Brak turned his attention to the cutting and wriggled forward on the muddy ground toward the edge. He picked out the two trees he had in mind and reached inside himself, his eyes blackening as the sweet Harshini power filled him. He reached out for the slow, lumbering touch of Voden, the God of Green Life. Voden was a Primal God in the truest sense of the word. He rarely concerned himself with human affairs. Voden would listen to the smallest blade of grass or the most ancient, massive tree, but he generally ignored the Harshini. As for humans, Voden considered them a kind of annoying blight that destroyed his trees for shelter and firewood. Fortunately, they occasionally redeemed themselves by planting things, which placated the god enough to leave humanity alone.

Brak felt incredibly puny under the weight of the god's notice, but he concentrated on a mental image of what he needed, hoping Voden would understand. He let his mind fill with thoughts of Xaphista, the demon child, and finally the present moment when the Defenders were hunting them down. One could not use words with a god like Voden. One could only hope that he gleaned enough from Brak's mind to understand that Xaphista could only be destroyed if the demon child lived and that the men who followed them threatened her. It seemed to take forever before he felt Voden's somewhat reluctant agreement.

"Get around to the other side," Brak ordered. He half-expected Tarja to argue with him, but the rebel merely slipped away silently. Within a couple of minutes he was in position.

The first Defender came into view not long after. The hollow was lit in the eerie predawn light, a mass of shadows and darkness. The Defenders rode at a trot, two abreast, following the muddy tracks cut into the ancient watercourse. Brak reached out to Voden, felt the power surge through him, and was gratified to hear the crack of splintered timber, startlingly loud in the gully. The lead horse reared in fright as a white trunk crashed down in front of him, throwing his rider. The other horses reacted to the fright of the first as the base of another tree exploded behind the last rider. It crashed down, cutting off their retreat. He then began, somewhat reluctantly, picking off the riders one by one.

Voden's power was the power of growing things. Long-dormant roots broke through the ground and reached for the soldiers hungrily, strangling them with living tentacles that tightened inexorably around limbs and throats, cutting off terrified screams. The soldiers hacked wildly at a threat they could not comprehend, as the very ground they stood on suddenly became their enemy.

Tarja leaped into the melee and took on the remaining Defenders single-handed. The roots had killed three, and there were two others down, injured in falls from their terrified mounts and unable to get clear of the stamping hooves as the horses dodged and squealed in fright. Brak stayed his power and watched the rebel. He moved like a dancer, one movement flowing into the next with no effort, to the accompaniment of the ring of metal on metal, echoing through the cutting like discordant music. Brak was fascinated. Despite his own low opinion of sword fighting, he had to admit that Tarja was very good. He caught sight of a Defender coming up behind Tarja, his blade raised and ready to plunge between the rebel's shoulders. The man dropped like a sack of wheat, screaming in agony as the ground beneath him erupted in a mass of deadly, writhing roots. Tarja had cut down two Defenders and was tiring, but Brak still stayed his hand, morbidly curious as to how long Tarja could keep up his violent dance of death. The third man fell, impaled on Tarja's blade. The rebel jerked it free and turned to the last survivor. He abandoned all pretense of style and swung the blade in a wide arc, decapitating the shocked Defender where he stood. Exhausted, Tarja slumped to his knees amid the carnage.

Brak slithered down the loose slope and surveyed the damage. The horses were milling, but they were Defenders' mounts and not distressed by the sweet stench of blood. Tarja was literally drenched in gore, and already the buzz of flies attracted to the feast was filling the air.

"Messy thing, sword fighting," Brak remarked as he looked around.

"At least it's more honorable than what you did to these men," Tarja panted. His chest was heaving with the effort of his exertion.

"Honorable? You just decapitated a man. Where's the honor in that?"

"Who are you?" Tarja demanded. "Or perhaps I should ask, *what* are you?"

Brak knew he could no longer put off the answer to Tarja's question. Not after what he had just seen. "My name is Brakandaran té Carn. I am Harshini."

Tarja accepted the information with an unreadable expression. He struggled to his feet, using the sword like a crutch. "I always thought the Harshini didn't believe in killing."

"It's amazing what a little human blood can do."

Tarja apparently didn't have an answer to that. "Do we just leave them here?"

"No, I thought we'd bury them over there in a little grove and plant rosebushes over their graves," Brak snapped. "Of course we'll just leave them here! What did you expect, a full military funeral, perhaps?"

"As you wish. I don't care what they'll think when they find all these men strangled by tree roots."

"Point taken. What do you suggest?"

"Burn them."

Brak frowned. He was Harshini enough that the idea of burning a body, even one belonging to an enemy, was the worst form of desecration.

Tarja noticed his sick expression. "You're quick enough to kill with magic. Yet you balk at destroying the evidence?" He wiped the sword clean on the shirt of one of the corpses before replacing it in the battered leather scabbard.

Brak agreed to Tarja's suggestion reluctantly. Together they pushed the fallen tree out of the way. Brak found himself lending their effort a bit of magical help to move the massive trunk. There was no point in letting the horses wander back to the Grimfield to raise the alarm, and the extra mounts would be useful. Tarja found a length of rope in one of the saddlebags and tied the reins to it, then turned to the grisly task of creating a funeral pyre.

A chill wind picked up as they gathered the bodies and covered them

JENNIFER FALLON

with a layer of dead wood. Brak let Tarja arrange the pyre. He had no experience in this sort of thing and no wish to gain any. It took longer than Brak expected, but once the rebel was satisfied with his handiwork he turned to Brak questioningly.

"The wood is too wet to burn," he told him. "You'll have to use your . . . magic, I suppose."

"It's not that easy," Brak told him with a frown. "Voden doesn't like fire."

"Voden?"

"The God of Green Life. That's what killed those men." Brak looked at the unlit pyre for a moment. "Actually, I think I have a better idea."

Ignoring Tarja's puzzled and somewhat suspicious expression, Brak reached out once more to Voden. He drew a picture in his mind that the god understood instantly. Brak had no wish to antagonize the god by lighting a fire, but what he asked of him this time was well within his power to grant.

Brak opened his eyes and glanced at Tarja. "It'll be all right now."

"What do you mean?"

"Just stand back and watch."

For a wonder, Tarja did as Brak asked. The unlit pyre stood forlornly in the dawn. Brak waited for a moment, feeling Voden's touch on the edge of his awareness as the dead wood they had laid over the slain Defenders began to sprout. Slowly at first, then ever more rapidly, the branches came to life, new leaves and branches growing over the pyre, almost too rapidly for the eye to see. Within a few minutes, the funeral pyre looked like nothing more than a large hedge growing in the middle of the old watercourse.

Brak smiled at Tarja's expression. "It's not exactly rosebushes, but it'll do."

The rebel stared at him. "How did you do that?"

"I didn't do anything; Voden did. He's a bit hard to communicate with sometimes, but he's cooperative enough if you ask him nicely."

"I don't believe any of this," Tarja said, shaking his head. "There are no gods, and the Harshini are dead."

Brak smiled wearily. "I know quite a few Harshini who might disagree with you, Tarja."

chapter 43

"You're disappointed in me, aren't you?" Mahina asked.

"Disappointed might be a little strong," Tarja said. "Surprised would be more accurate, I think."

They were riding at a good pace across the central plateau, following a faint game trail toward the silver ribbon of the Glass River, which was still an hour or more ahead of them. Brak rode in the lead with R'shiel at his side, talking to her earnestly. R'shiel had been strangely subdued since she had regained consciousness. She spoke little, and her eyes seemed focused elsewhere, as if she had seen something that she couldn't tear her gaze from, something that nobody else could see. Tarja could not understand Brak's interest in her. He seemed to be more concerned with R'shiel than any of them. He thought Brak had been sent to either kill him or return him to the rebels for justice. Brak hadn't even mentioned the rebellion, and he certainly had not tried to kill him, although there had been no lack of opportunity in the last few days. In fact he had said little, other than announcing he was Harshini, a statement that Tarja would have rejected out of hand, had he not seen the astounding transformation of the funeral pyre. He had always believed the Harshini to be extinct—and Brak looked as human as any man. But the evidence was hard to deny. Tarja heard Mahina say something and turned his attention to the old woman.

"I said, I'm more surprised that I put up with the Grimfield for as long as I did. As the Kariens would say, Crisabelle was more than sufficient penance for my sins."

Behind them, Dace rode with Sunny, and the boy chattered away to her cheerfully, regaling her with tales of his exploits, none of which, it seemed, Sunny believed. The day was clear but blustery, as spring attempted to blow winter out of the way, although farther north the land would still be firmly in the grip of winter. The sun was shining brightly, but the wind cut through them. Mahina pulled her cloak more tightly around her as she rode.

"What made you do it, Mahina?" he asked.

"Do what? Not challenge Joyhinia when she threw me out? Not call the Defenders when you broke into my house the other night? Help you escape the Grimfield? Be specific, lad."

"You have been rather busy lately, haven't you?"

Mahina smiled, and they rode on in silence for a while.

"So how did you wind up as First Sister?" Tarja asked. The question had always puzzled him.

The old woman shrugged. "There were no clear candidates when Trayla died so suddenly. I'd kept my head down and I suppose I appeared harmless to the rest of the Quorum. Your mother had her eye on the job even then. I guess I played right into her hands. Couldn't believe my luck, actually. I wanted to change the whole world overnight. It doesn't happen that way, though." She leaned over and patted his hand. "I taught you, Tarja, remember that. And remember that evil should not be tolerated, no matter the guise it comes in. I was so proud of you when you defied Joyhinia at the Gathering."

"I'm glad somebody was."

They rode on in silence after that, only the sound of the wind sighing through the trees and Dace's perpetually cheerful chatter filling the morning. With some concern Tarja watched R'shiel's back as she rode. Her shoulders were slumped, and she showed little interest in her surroundings. He wondered what Brak was saying to her.

Brak timed their arrival in Vanahiem to coincide almost exactly with the departure of the ferry, which connected the river town to Testra on the other side. They rode openly past the noisy foundry and through the town, barely noticed by the industrious townsfolk, who had far better things to do than worry about a few more strangers in a town that was frequently full of them.

Tarja expected someone to recognize them. Surely the word had been spread by now of the escapees from the Grimfield? However, they rode on unmolested, maybe because it was market day, or maybe because anyone looking for prison escapees would not consider their well-mounted and well-dressed group to be fugitives. Of course, they would not have fitted any description of them that the Grimfield might have circulated he realized as they neared the ferry. Dace had disappeared last night and this morning had proudly presented them with the results of his night's labors. Mahina, R'shiel, and Sunny were fashionably dressed as successful merchants, and Brak, Dace, and Tarja wore Defender's uniforms. Although he had stolen a uniform the night of their escape, the one he wore now was well-made and a much better fit. It even had the rank insignia of a captain.

They loaded the horses onto the ferry with little fuss and almost immediately the flat-bottomed barge set out across the river. Mahina appeared to be having the time of her life and stood at the bow, watching the opposite shore. Brak settled their passage with the ferryman and then came to stand beside Tarja. Dace was nowhere to be seen. R'shiel stood on the other side of the ferry, staring at the broad expanse of the Glass River. Sunny was chatting to her, but she did not appear to be listening. Tarja was worried about her. It was unlike R'shiel to be so withdrawn.

"Well, so far so good," Brak announced.

"What happens when we get to Testra?"

"There's an inn there owned by a friend of mine," Brak explained in a low voice, although their group were the only passengers on the ferry. "We'll wait there until help arrives."

"Help?"

"Trust me," Brak said with a faint smile.

"You know, there's a saying on the border that 'trust me' is Fardohnyan for 'screw you,'" Tarja replied.

"Ah, but I'm Harshini, not Fardohnyan. 'Trust me' means exactly what it says. In Harshini."

"Look at that!"

Sunny's exclamation drew their attention. They crossed to the other side of the ferry and followed the direction of her pointing finger. A huge, garishly painted blue barquentine was carefully edging her way downstream toward the Testra docks. Her sails were furled, and her smartly dressed crew was scurrying over the decks, pointing and shouting at the oared tugs that were leading the ship in.

"The Karien Envoy," Tarja said. The Envoy's ship was returning from his annual visit to the Citadel. Elfron stood on the poop deck, wearing his ceremonial cape beside Pieter, who watched the docking procedure in full armor. He wondered who they were trying to impress, then glanced at R'shiel. Her expression was blank. She didn't seem to care.

"He has a priest with him," Brak remarked beside him in a tone that made Tarja look at him curiously. "There aren't many things in this world I fear, Tarja, but a priest carrying the Staff of Xaphista is one of them."

Tarja filed that information away thoughtfully, remembering his own meeting with Elfron. The priest had laid his staff on Tarja's shoulder to absolutely no effect.

"Pieter knows me," he warned Brak. "And R'shiel."

"Then pray he doesn't see you. I'd help if I could, but the priest would feel any glamor I wove."

"What's a glamor?" Sunny asked curiously.

"Nothing but wishful thinking in this case."

"It doesn't matter," R'shiel said softly, so softly that Tarja barely heard her. "He's seen us already. He knows we're here."

When the ferry reached Testra the Karien ship had already docked. Pieter and Elfron were nowhere to be seen, and Tarja decided R'shiel's dire prediction was nothing more than her fear talking. Pieter was aware of the situation in Medalon, and Tarja was quite certain that if he had identified the small figures on the ferry, there would have been a full squad of Defenders waiting to arrest them when they docked.

The fugitives remounted for their ride to the inn. It was located on the other side of the neat town, and just as their appearance in Vanahiem had been unremarkable, so their ride through Testra was equally incident free. Tarja was both surprised and relieved. He was not so concerned about the possibility that Lord Pieter had identified him or R'shiel. Testra was a rebel stronghold, as evidenced by several defiant slogans splashed on the walls of the warehouses near the docks, and if he were ever going to be recognized, it would be here. Their horses' hooves clattered loudly on the cobblestones as they rode down the paved street.

Brak read the slogans and glanced at Tarja. "Can I ask you a question?"

"I suppose."

"It's something that's bothered me ever since I joined the rebels. Most Medalonians aren't usually taught to read, are they?"

"Novices and Cadets are," Tarja told him. "Children of merchants usually attend private schools or have tutors, and servants who need it for their jobs are educated a little. Lack of education is the prime tool of the Sisterhood in keeping the population in their place. Why?"

"Well, if the people can't read, why go to the bother of splashing slogans on every flat surface you can find?"

"The Sisters can read. The slogans are put up to make them think."

"Does it work?"

"Well, it makes them nervous. The Sisters see the slogans and begin to wonder the same thing you are—why write them if the people can't read? Then they start to worry that the people might be able to read them, after all. That starts them worrying about all sorts of other things."

"You're very easy to underestimate, Tarja."

"Just you remember that."

They reached the inn without mishap. Red brick and shingled like the rest of the town, it was neat and well kept. They were greeted cheerfully by the innkeeper in the yard as they dismounted.

Her name was Affiana. The woman could have been Brak's sister, Tarja realized with a start. She was statuesque and dark-haired and welcomed them as if she had known they were coming. She greeted Brak first with a relieved smile, before turning to the others. Her next target was Mahina.

"My Lady, it is an honor to have you in my house."

"The pleasure is all mine," Mahina assured her politely.

Affiana then turned to Dace and bowed. "Divine One. I am honored that you should visit my house, but I beg you not to bestow your blessing on it. I have enough trouble with your followers as it is."

Dace grinned broadly at the odd welcome. "For you, Affiana, I will restrain myself."

Affiana nodded with genuine relief at the boy's answer. Tarja glanced at the boy curiously. Was he Harshini, too? It would explain his presence but not the tone Affiana had used or the appellation "Divine One." There seemed nothing special about the boy, and Brak certainly treated him with anything but respect.

The innkeeper turned to Tarja then, her expression curious. "Ah . . . the elusive Tarja, himself. I suggest you keep your head down while in Testra. You have not been forgotten here."

Tarja had no chance to answer her as Affiana had turned her attention to Sunny and R'shiel. "And the last of our little gathering. You are welcome also, my dears. Come. I have rooms where you can freshen up before lunch is laid out."

Sunny looked rather taken aback by the warmth of her welcome, but R'shiel remained as coldly distant as she had since leaving the Grimfield.

chapter 44

Lunch was sumptuous as was dinner later that evening and made a welcome change from the dry trail rations they had survived on for the past week or so. Affiana made a private dining room available to them and kept them well supplied with food and wine. Of Dace there had been no sign since they arrived, but Brak appeared unconcerned about the missing boy. Their rooms were quite grand with soft, down-filled beds and clean linen. The inn was built on a far grander scale than the Inn of the Hopeless in the Grimfield. It had three stories and several suites in addition to the normal rooms, and the taproom attracted an affluent class of customer. Tarja found the whole place both comfortable and stifling.

After dinner, he escaped to the stables on the pretext of checking the horses. They didn't need his attention—Affiana had stableboys in abundance—but Tarja needed to be free of his companions. He needed a chance to think. But more importantly, he needed a chance to get a message to the Citadel. He had to let Jenga know that the Harshini were still among them.

Tarja could not pinpoint the exact moment that the idea had come to him. Perhaps it was in that gully near the Grimfield where he had seen the effect of the Harshini magic on the unsuspecting Defenders. It might have been this morning when he saw the Karien Envoy's ship docking in Testra. Whatever the reason, he felt compelled to warn Jenga. Once word reached Karien that the Harshini still lived, Tarja doubted any treaty would be enough to hold them on their side of the border. Perhaps even worse was the effect such news would have on Medalon's southern neighbors. Hythria and Fardohnya worshipped the Harshini with almost as much dedication as they worshipped their gods. News of their survival would be cause for celebration. Suspicion that the surviving Harshini were under threat by either the Kariens or the Sisterhood would bring an army over the southern border that outnumbered the entire population of Medalon. Tarja had broken his sworn oath to the Defenders, but he did not consider he had turned his back on Medalon. They had to be warned, and Jenga was the only one in a position to do anything about it.

He did check the horses, however, enjoying their simple demands for attention as they heard him approaching, pushing velvety muzzles through the rails in the hope of a treat of some sort. He sat down on a hay bale and pulled out a stick of writing charcoal, sharpened to a point, that he had purloined from the small library of the inn. In the dim light, he began to scratch out a succinct report to Garet Warner on a scrap of parchment. It would be pointless addressing it directly to Jenga. The Lord Defender would more than likely tear up the message unread if he thought it came from him. Garet was the safer bet. Garet would use the information. He did not have to tell Jenga its source. That way Jenga would be free to act, without being hampered by his scruples. Tarja knew from experience that Garet Warner's scruples were a fluid commodity, to be applied or not as he saw fit.

He had barely written the first few lines when a noise behind him startled him, and he leaped to his feet guiltily.

"It's only me." R'shiel stood in the entrance to the stables, her shawl pulled tight around her. He shoved the note into his pocket hastily.

"What's the matter?"

"It's just a bit stuffy inside." She walked over and sat beside him. She seemed so distant. As if the shell of the old R'shiel remained, but the spark of life was gone. "What are you doing?"

"Nothing important," he replied. "Are you all right, R'shiel?"

"Something has happened to me, Tarja, and I don't know what it is. I can't even describe it." She pulled idly at the fringe on her shawl for a moment and then looked at him. "I didn't kill Loclon, did I?"

"No."

"Did you? I can't remember."

"I kicked him in the face. But I doubt it was enough to kill him. I'm sorry."

"Not half as sorry as I am."

They sat in silence for a moment, each lost in his own thoughts. Eventually she looked at him, her expression curious. "Who is Brak?"

"I'm not sure."

"He's been telling me about the Harshini. I think he's worried about me, so he's telling me fairy stories as if I were a little child, to take my mind off things. It's a nice thing to do, I suppose."

"Well, Brak can be very nice when he wants to," he agreed, faintly amused to find himself complimenting a man he was still debating whether or not he should kill.

"I'm sorry, Tarja."

"For what?"

"It's my fault you got mixed up with the heathens. Maybe it's even my fault you deserted. You only did after you learned the truth about me."

"It's not your fault, R'shiel." For some reason he was intensely aware of her, sitting so close, almost but not quite touching.

"I still want to apologize, though." She reached out and placed her hand on his arm. He could feel her warmth and had to consciously fight the desire to take it in his hand.

"If it makes you feel better."

She was so close that he stood up abruptly and walked to the door. He leaned against the frame and studied her from a safer distance.

"What are we waiting for, Tarja?" she asked, a little hurt at his sudden withdrawal. She cocked her head, as if she couldn't figure him out. "Do you think Brak is still with the rebels?"

"If he is, then I suspect Brak was sent to kill me, not rescue me."

"I'm glad he didn't kill you." She stood up and came to stand before him. "If he had, you wouldn't have been there when I needed you."

She leaned forward to kiss his cheek thankfully, lingered for a moment, her cheek touching his. He hesitated for a fraction of a second before he turned his mouth to find hers. For a timeless moment she did not react, then she pulled away from him.

"I'm sorry," he said automatically. But as he looked at her, with her dark red hair, indigo eyes, and her golden skin, he suddenly saw what had been in front of him all along. Saw what Zac had seen in her. R'shiel looked at him uncertainly in the moonlight, unaware of the direction of his thoughts. Totally ignorant of who or what she was. Fairy tales, she had called Brak's stories. How could she even suspect the truth? That was why Brak wanted her. *She was Harshini.*

"Tarja?"

He pulled her to him. Kissed her as he had the night in the vineyard, except this time there was no regret, no surprise. Only the certain knowledge that this was meant to be.

"Well now, isn't this just cozy?" a voice said from the darkness, accompanied by a hiss of unsheathing steel.

Several figures detached themselves silently from the shadows, all carrying naked blades that menacingly caught the moonlight. R'shiel pulled away from him as the rebels surrounded them. The owner of the voice moved into the faint light thrown into the stables by the inn. Tarja recognized the wild-eyed, fair-haired young man, with a rush of despair.

"Ghari!"

"See, lads, he hasn't forgotten us," Ghari told them, as he moved closer to Tarja. As soon as he was within reach, he shoved him against the wall roughly and raised his blade to Tarja's throat. "You lying, treacherous, son of a bitch. I can't believe you had the gall to show up here. Back in uniform, too, I see."

"Ghari, I can explain—" Tarja began, trying to sound reasonable.

"Explain what, exactly, Tarja?" Ghari hissed. "Why you betrayed us? Why you left us to fend off a whole freaking company of Defenders while you were living it up with your mother in the Citadel?"

"They tortured him in the Citadel!" R'shiel cried as Ghari's blade pressed deeper into Tarja's neck, drawing blood. Her cry brought two of the rebels rushing to her side. They pulled her back roughly. "He never betrayed you!"

Ghari turned to look at her as he eased the blade from Tarja's throat. Tarja took an involuntary gasp of air.

"You think I'd believe anything that came from you? Though I must admit, I've not seen such devotion between siblings before. I knew the Sisterhood cared little for morals, but I hadn't realized incest was so popular."

"I'm not his sister!" R'shiel snapped, shaking free of her captors. "And Tarja never betrayed you! Even when they tortured him."

"R'shiel, don't—" Tarja began. Ghari had been one of their most ardent supporters. It seemed that he was now one of their most bitter enemies, his disappointment turned to rage.

"Someone's coming!" a voice hissed from the darkness. Ghari began issuing orders via hand signals to his men. His anger was a palpable thing.

"Let's go somewhere we can discuss this privately," he told Tarja, then turned and ordered the men to grab R'shiel. She had no chance to cry out as a hand clamped firmly over her mouth.

"Don't you—" he warned, but he never had a chance to complete his threat. The last thing Tarja saw was R'shiel struggling against her captors as Ghari brought the hilt of his sword down hard against his head and he swam into a black pool of unconsciousness.

When he came to, he was lying in a wagon, tied hand and foot, and loosely covered with straw. R'shiel was beside him, similarly bound. She had been gagged, but had worked the gag loose and it now hung uselessly around her neck.

"Tarja?" she whispered, as soon as his eyes opened. The wagon hit a bump in the road and his head slammed against the wagon bed, but he fought off the black wave that engulfed him and managed to remain conscious. "Are you all right?"

"Any idea where we are?"

"I think we're headed for the vineyard. What will they do to us?"

"I really don't know, R'shiel," he lied, and then he gave in to the blackness and lost consciousness again.

part five

THE RECKONING

chapter 45

R'shiel suffered through the uncomfortable wagon ride, wondering what was going to happen to them. The savageness of Ghari's hatred surprised her. Tarja had passed out again. A trickle of blood from the wound on the back of his head had dried on his cheek. If her hands were not tied, she would have wiped it away. As it was, all she could do was look at him and hope that the others would be more reasonable than Ghari.

After a time, the wagon was hauled to a stop, and rough hands reached for her in the darkness, pulling her from the wagon bed and bustling her inside the darkened farmhouse. She was pushed down a flight of stone stairs. A dim light beckoned and then brightened as a door opened. R'shiel was shoved through, followed by two men who carried Tarja. They dumped him unceremoniously on the straw-covered floor. Large barrels stood against the far wall. Padric was there, seated on a small keg. In the lantern light, the cellar appeared full of threatening shadows. Ghari and his companions arranged themselves around the walls, watching both R'shiel and Tarja's unconscious form warily.

"Welcome back." Padric looked old and tired rather than threatening. The old man spared the unconscious rebel a glance. "You didn't kill him, did you?"

"No. He'll come around."

The old man stood up and walked to where Tarja lay sprawled on the floor. He looked down at him for a moment, shook his head sadly, then turned to R'shiel.

"Why?"

R'shiel did not answer him, not at all certain that she could.

Before Padric could ask anything else, the door flew open and a fair-haired young man burst in. He stopped dead at the sight of Tarja's prone form and glanced at Padric, his brown eyes widening even further at the sight of R'shiel.

"What is it, Tampa?" Padric asked.

"The Kariens! They're here!"

"Don't exaggerate, boy. Tell me exactly what Filip told you."

"Filip said," Tampa began, catching his breath, "that the Envoy's boat docked in Testra just before midday and the Karien Envoy would pay a hundred gold rivets for the red-headed girl who is traveling with Tarja, no questions asked. He said the news is all over the docks in town."

Tampa had obviously been coached in the message he was to deliver, and he sighed with satisfaction when he finally got it out. R'shiel went cold all over.

"The Karien Envoy is just a lecherous old man," Tarja remarked, from the floor. R'shiel wondered how long he had been conscious. He had pushed himself up on one elbow and met Padric's gaze. "But it's not him who wants R'shiel. It's his priest."

"Who asked you?" Ghari growled, sinking his booted foot hard into Tarja's back. The rebel collapsed with a pain-filled grunt and rolled over, away from Ghari's next kick.

"Enough! You can get your revenge later, Ghari. Get him up."

Two of the rebels hauled Tarja to his feet. The wound on his head had reopened and blood trickled down his neck.

Padric turned his gaze on Tarja. "Let's forget that you're a treacherous liar for a minute and tell me why you say that."

Tarja shook off the men who were holding him and stood a little straighter. "Joyhinia promised R'shiel to the Karien Envoy in return for his help in deposing Mahina. If he wants R'shiel now, it's only to get what he feels he's been cheated of. The Kariens are playing their own games, Padric. Don't get involved."

"At least the Kariens believe in the gods."

"Have you ever been to Karien, Padric?" Tarja asked. "They don't believe in the gods. They only believe in one god. They're zealots. They plan to convert the whole world to the Overlord, even if it means slaughtering every nonbeliever to do it. Dealing with them would be worse than dealing with the Sisterhood."

Padric looked at R'shiel curiously. "A hundred gold rivets is a lot money. Why does he want you so badly?"

R'shiel looked at Tarja for help. She didn't know the answer.

"The priest who travels with Pieter claims he had a vision."

"That's a good enough reason to get rid of her, right there." Padric rubbed his chin. "Although, if you are right about this, we could use it to our advantage. I've no wish to see the Kariens triumph in anything. As you say, they are no friend to our kind. But it would weaken the Sisterhood considerably if the Karien alliance were destroyed."

"That treaty is the only thing keeping the Kariens on the other side of the border. Destroy it and you are asking for even worse trouble than you have now."

"*Worse* trouble?" Padric scoffed. "I don't see how things could be much worse than they are now, Tarja."

Tarja took a deep breath before he answered. "Padric, think about this. Handing R'shiel over to the Kariens won't wreck the alliance; if anything, it will strengthen it. She's already been promised to them. You would simply be carrying out Joyhinia's wishes."

"Maybe. But the Envoy wasn't expecting to have to pay for her. And a hundred gold rivets is a fortune. Given the trouble you two have caused, it seems small compensation."

"You'd sell me to the Kariens!"

Padric turned on R'shiel impatiently. "Give me a reason why I shouldn't! You never believed in our cause. All you did was stir the passions of our young men and abandon us at the first sign of trouble. We owe you nothing. I don't know what the Envoy wants with you, and I don't really care."

"Given a choice between feeding starving pagan families for a year or saving R'shiel's precious neck, I know which one I'd choose," Ghari added.

"They want her because she's Harshini," Tarja said tonelessly.

"What?" R'shiel stared at him, shocked. "That's ludicrous! If that's your idea of helping, Tarja, I'd rather you didn't!"

"She's your sister!"

"She's a foundling. R'shiel was born in the Mountains, not at the Citadel. If you don't believe me, ask Brak. He's Harshini, too."

"You can do better than that, Tarja. We checked the inn where Ghari found you. There is no sign of Brak. Only the former First Sister and a *court'esa* and a few merchants that we already know of. You're lying."

The news that Brak was gone did not surprise him. He had a habit of deserting when Tarja needed him the most. "I'm not lying, Padric."

"Oh? It seems even R'shiel thinks you are. What say you, R'shiel? Are you a Divine One come among us mere mortals?"

She looked at him, puzzled and angry. "Of course not!"

"Well, that settles it then. Take her up to the stables."

"Padric! Don't do this! Even if you have no care for R'shiel, think of the consequences! If the Kariens learn the Harshini still live, they'll be over the border in a matter of weeks, and the Purge will seem like a picnic by comparison!"

The old man turned back to him. "I don't believe the Harshini exist anymore."

R'shiel looked at Tarja, willing him to say something, anything, that would change Padric's mind.

"You can't just hand her over to him like she's a piece of meat!"

"I can," Padric said. "That's one thing I learned from you, Tarja. How to be ruthless. The Karien Envoy wants the girl, we will get a hundred gold rivets to continue the fight, and best of all, you will suffer for it. That's plenty of incentive, don't you think?"

Tarja was taken from the main cellar to a room upstairs. He lay on the stone floor next to the cold hearth, surrounded by his former comrades. R'shiel was nowhere in sight. He struggled to sit up as Ghari entered the room with a shielded lantern. His face looked sinister in the shadows.

"Ghari . . . "

"I don't want to hear it, Tarja."

"The only reason you're still alive is because he's waiting for Padric to get back," Balfor added. "He should be here soon, so if you have any prayers to say to the gods, now would be a good time."

"I never betrayed you."

"I'm not interested." Ghari turned his back on Tarja to stare out into the darkness.

"What happened to Mandah?" He was certain Mandah would not have condoned handing R'shiel over to the Kariens. Had something happened to her, or had she been deliberately excluded from this?

"She'll be here later."

With a sigh, Tarja closed his eyes and leaned his head against the cool hearthstones to wait. What was Padric doing? Where had he gone?

About an hour later, the sound of hooves in the yard brought Tarja out of a light doze. He was stiff and cramped from his unnatural position, but when he attempted to move, a sword jabbed him warningly in the ribs. The sound of voices reached him. Finally, the door opened and Padric came in, looking even older and more tired than he had earlier. Close on his heels was Mandah. Tarja breathed a sigh of relief at the sight of her. Perhaps now someone would listen to him. Padric ordered everyone out. Once they were alone, Padric crossed the room and untied him.

Tarja rubbed the circulation back into his hands and feet. "Thanks."

"Don't be too free with your thanks," Mandah said. "We are only here to supervise your hanging." The woman before him showed little sign of the understanding, placid young woman he remembered.

"I never betrayed you, Mandah."

"Aye, and I'm the First Sister." She threw a scrap of parchment at Tarja. A single more damning piece of evidence could not have been planted on him by the First Sister herself. Ghari must have found it when they were taken from the stables. As the younger man could not read, its importance would not have been immediately apparent. Had Ghari been able to read, it was likely Tarja would already be dead.

"I can explain, Mandah, if you'd give me a chance."

"Explain it to us then," she said. "I'd be interested in hearing what fiction you and that damned mother of yours cooked up between you."

"The Harshini are still alive," Tarja told her. "If the Kariens learn of it, they will cross the border to destroy them. Medalon's only hope is to warn the Defenders."

Mandah did not react immediately. She sat down on a three-legged stool and looked at him, weighing her judgment.

"The Harshini are dead."

"They're not dead. I would have thought the news would please you. You worship their gods, don't you?"

"Can you prove this?"

Tarja nodded. "R'shiel is one of them. So is Brak."

"Padric told me of your wild tale. And you expect us to believe that you were planning to warn the Defenders that the Harshini still live? To what purpose? So that they might protect them from the Kariens? The same Defenders who have spent the last two centuries trying to exterminate them? For pity's sake, Tarja, you rode into Testra in a Defender's uniform with Mahina Cortanen!"

"Mahina was impeached. They threw her out!"

"Once a Sister, always a Sister," Mandah said. "Your story's certainly entertaining, but I'm surprised you couldn't come up with something more believable."

"Mandah, if I was lying, don't you think I *would* have come up with something more believable?"

"Who knows?" she shrugged. "I thought I knew you well, once. But now . . . ? You've had your chance. Padric will take R'shiel to the Karien Envoy and then let the others have you."

She turned toward the door and opened it. As soon as she did, Ghari was inside, looking at them expectantly.

"Make your vengeance swift, Ghari," Padric said as he and Mandah disappeared into the darkness.

chapter 46

R'shiel was thrown into the stable and a guard posted outside. Padric, with several other rebels, galloped off into the darkness. She sank down onto a pile of smelly straw, her mind racing. It was obvious that the rebels intended to kill them. Their only hope was Brak. How long would it take him to discover they were missing? And when he did, would he realize they had been dragged away and had not simply run off of their own accord?

Refusing to let despair take hold, she glanced around. Her hands and feet were tied and she could see the silhouette of the guard posted at the entrance to the stable, although his back was turned from her. She tentatively tugged on her bonds, but they were secure. There was nothing in the old stable she could see that would help her cut through them, even if the guard didn't notice what she was up to.

Padric's intentions regarding the Karien Envoy were clear enough. Pieter wanted her for one reason, she was sure—because he had been thwarted in his deal with Joyhinia. She wondered if he knew she had been disowned, or even cared. Probably not. The reward he had offered for her would have been motivated by spite as much as anything. She cared little about the priest's vision—and did not believe it in any case. If only Tarja had been able to think of something reasonable to say. She had been shocked to hear him claim she was Harshini. Surely he could have come up with something more believable than that!

R'shiel recognized that there was nothing left to her but to wait and hope that Brak would find her and Tarja before their captors acted on their obvious desire to see Tarja swing. As that thought was even more horrible to contemplate than most, R'shiel closed her eyes and tried to doze.

Sometime later she heard horses in the yard, and soon after the figure

of the old rebel appeared in the doorway. He walked over to where she
was sitting on the ground and looked at her closely for a moment. R'shiel
stared back, hoping that he might be having second thoughts.

"I've nothing personal against you, understand," Padric said, as if trying to justify himself. "But you can see our problem. If we give you to the
Karien Envoy, the money will help our cause a great deal."

"If you give me to the Karien Envoy, Lord Pieter will rape me then
kill me," she said. "Why don't you kill me yourself, Padric? Spare me the
rape at least."

"I'm sorry, R'shiel." He stood up and walked back to the guard on the
door, issuing orders to see her mounted and ready to leave as soon as he
had dealt with Tarja. The guard came forward, untied the ropes that held
her and pulled her to her feet. She tried to follow Padric's slight form as
he disappeared into the house, but the guard drew her away, bringing up
a small dun mare.

"What did he mean about dealing with Tarja?" she asked. The rebel
was a balding middle-aged man with an air of weary resignation.

"They're going to hang him," he told her, as he lifted her into the saddle. R'shiel looked around and discovered a number of men standing
under a large tree on the other side of the yard. One of them was swinging
a rope gently, aiming it for the large branch that spread out over the yard.
He threw the rope, and on his second attempt, it looped over the branch.
Another man reached for the loose end and pulled it down. R'shiel turned
to her guard.

"But he never betrayed you!"

"Aye, it's hard to credit," the rebel agreed. "But he convicted himself
with his own hand. Had a letter in his pocket to the Defenders, he did."
He frowned at the shock on R'shiel's face at the news. "He betrayed us,
right enough, lass. You, as much as the rest of us. Don't waste your sympathy on him. He's nothing but a bastard." R'shiel realized this man was
not a hothead like Ghari. This man was truly saddened by the thought
that Tarja might have betrayed him, prepared to believe otherwise until
he had been confronted by incontrovertible proof of Tarja's treachery.

"I don't believe you," R'shiel insisted stubbornly.

"Then more fool you, girl."

Padric emerged from the house in the company of Mandah, who
avoided meeting R'shiel's eye. He remounted, followed by two other
rebels, then walked his horse forward and took the lead rein from the
rebel holding her horse. His eyes were sad as he looked at her.

"It'll be best if we leave now, lass," he said. "You'll not want to see what's coming next."

R'shiel glared at him. "You're murderers! That's all you are! Miserable, cold-blooded murderers. You're going to murder Tarja, and you're going to murder me!"

Padric pulled her horse closer to his. "Tarja has betrayed us both, R'shiel. His death is deserved. Yours will be unfortunate, but I've fought too long to stop now." He kicked his horse forward, jerking her mare with him, and they galloped out of the yard. R'shiel looked back over her shoulder, but there was no sign of Tarja. Within moments, they were out of sight of the old vineyard.

They galloped at a nightmare pace along a track that was barely visible in the darkness. R'shiel was an experienced horsewoman, but her horse was being led, so she could do little but cling grimly with aching thighs and hope that she didn't fall off. A fall at this breakneck pace would kill her. Of course, she was riding helter-skelter to a fate worse than death in any case, so it really did not matter if she broke her neck in a fall. It was almost enticing.

They rode along the edge of the river as the sky lightened into morning, and R'shiel could make out a small jetty where the elaborately decorated ship was moored. It was three times the size of the *Maera's Daughter* or the *Melissa* and looked cumbersome and top-heavy, even to her inexperienced eye. Padric brought his small party to a halt and walked his horse forward onto the jetty.

Lord Pieter, dressed in decorative Karien armor, stepped onto the gangway and walked down the jetty to greet Padric. Following him was Elfron, wearing a simple brown cassock. He carried his glorious golden staff, which glittered in the dawn light. R'shiel dared hope a little at the sight of the priest. Pieter would not be able to indulge in anything remotely sinful with him on board.

"You have her?" the knight asked Padric, looking past the old rebel and straight at R'shiel.

"Aye."

"Bring her here," the knight ordered. "Elfron? What do you think?"

The priest walked down the jetty until he reached R'shiel's horse. He studied her intently for a moment before laying the staff gently on her shoulder.

R'shiel screamed as intense pain shot through her like a white-hot lance. In agony, she fell from the horse and landed heavily on the ground.

Excitedly, Elfron touched the staff to her shoulder again and R'shiel screamed anew, certain her body would explode under the torment. He withdrew the staff and turned back to the knight.

"This is magic!" he declared in astonishment, as if he had never truly expected to see the effect of his staff on another living being. "The heathen magicians cannot fight the Staff of Xaphista. My vision was true! She is one of them!" He reached down and jerked R'shiel to her feet. She was sobbing uncontrollably, pain radiating from her shoulder. As she looked up, the Karien knight took a step backward.

"You have done well," the Envoy told Padric, then he turned to Elfron and added, "Get her on the boat, quickly!"

Padric looked stunned and more than a little guilty as the priest dragged R'shiel away.

"What will you do with the girl?" Padric asked.

"The Staff of Xaphista is infallible! You have brought us proof that the Sisterhood harbors the Harshini. You can be assured that we will be forever grateful for your assistance. As for the girl, she will be burned on the altar of Xaphista in the Temple at Yarnarrow, as the Overlord showed us in Elfron's vision."

"Just you be sure to keep your side of the bargain."

Pieter handed a heavy purse to the rebel, somewhat disdainfully. "I have given you my pledge, sir!"

The Envoy followed the priest onto the boat and gave the order to push off. R'shiel collapsed to her knees and knelt on the deck, watching the old rebel through tear-filled eyes as the boat moved out into the swift current. The old man stared at her, his expression distraught. A fine time to have an attack of guilt, R'shiel thought.

The agony subsided a little as the figures of the rebels on the wharf grew smaller and smaller in the distance. R'shiel cursed them all, fervently hoping that Padric lived a long, long time and suffered the guilt of his betrayal for the rest of his miserable life.

chapter 47

Jenga delivered the news of the escape from the Grimfield personally. Hearing Tarja had escaped with R'shiel was bad enough, but the news that Mahina was with them was of far greater concern. Reports from the Grimfield suggested that Mahina was a hostage, but Joyhinia did not believe that for a moment. She ordered him to face the Quorum and explain how such a thing could have occurred.

The rebellion had hurt Joyhinia more than she cared to admit, both personally and politically. Lord Pieter had been back on his annual visit, insisting that she allow the Kariens to deal with the ongoing problem of the heathen rebels. Her Purge, which had sounded so reasonable when she had removed Mahina, had brought nothing but scorn from the Envoy. He had all but accused Joyhinia of being in league with the heathens.

"How in the Founders' name did Mahina get mixed up in this?" Harith demanded, almost before the Quorum had taken their seats. It was rare that Jenga was invited to the meetings these days. Usually, he must rely on Draco's terse reports. The Spear of the First Sister stood behind the First Sister's desk by the wall, his expression implacable. It was impossible to tell what he was thinking.

"Tarja's friendship with Mahina was no secret. He may have called on that friendship to aid in his escape," Francil suggested. "Did it occur to anyone, when we decided to send him there, that Mahina was also at the Grimfield?"

The women all looked at Joyhinia accusingly.

"Do you have any idea of the damage she could do if she decides to throw her lot in with the rebels?" Louhina added.

"Mahina won't betray us. She may have been misguided, but she would not turn on her own kind."

"That's not what you said when we threw her out," Harith pointed out. "In fact, the word 'betrayal' featured rather prominently in your impassioned campaign to have her removed. Could it be that you might have made an error in judgment, First Sister?"

"I think you are overreacting, Harith. You forget that Mahina is an old woman. Tarja and R'shiel are heading for the Sanctuary Mountains. I suspect they will dump her somewhere along the way so she doesn't slow them down. They may even kill her, which would be convenient."

Jenga was appalled by her remark. None of the Quorum blinked.

"We need to take decisive action," Joyhinia continued. "We must have troops in place to recapture the fugitives as soon as they are located."

Joyhinia's political survival depended on giving the impression that victory was certain. Troop movements would go a long way to convincing the Kariens that she was firm in her resolve to destroy the heathens, and if that meant mobilizing the entire Corps, she didn't seem to care. And it would keep everyone's thoughts occupied, Jenga thought, resenting her use of the Defenders in such a manner.

"Of course, I will announce publicly that we will spare no effort in rescuing Mahina from the rebels." She turned to Jenga, acknowledging his presence for the first time. "I want the Defenders sent downriver to Testra immediately, as many as you can muster. It's the most logical place to stage any offensive on the Sanctuary Mountains and that appears to be where they're headed." She glanced at the Sisters, before adding, "I need not add, my Lord Defender, that Mahina's rescue is not the overriding concern in this campaign."

"Your Grace?" Jenga asked, not at all certain he believed what she had just ordered him to do.

"Is there a problem, my Lord?"

"Such an order might be misinterpreted, your Grace. In my opinion—"

"Your opinion is not required, my Lord. Merely that you do as you are ordered."

"Mahina was very popular among the Defenders, even before she became First Sister," Jenga persisted. He could not take this order without objecting. Joyhinia was very close to pushing him too far. "Such an order will be . . . difficult to enforce."

"He has a point," Harith agreed. "Can you claim to own the same level of respect, Joyhinia?"

The First Sister glared at the Mistress of the Sisterhood. "The Defenders will honor their oath to the Sisters of the Blade. Of that I am sure. Is that not so, my Lord?"

Jenga hesitated for a moment before nodding. "Yes, your Grace. That is so."

Later that evening, Lord Jenga carefully folded the letter he was reading and rose from his chair as his visitor entered his office.

"You've heard the news?" he asked Garet.

The commandant nodded. "I warned you something like this would happen. You have always underestimated Tarja."

"Now is not the time to apportion blame. I doubt we could have prevented this, no matter what we did. Any news on how that officer . . . what's his name?"

"Loclon."

"Any news on how he is faring?"

"He'll live."

"Has he been able to tell what happened?"

"Cortanen says he was muttering some gibberish about R'shiel and Harshini magic."

"Harshini magic? Founders! That's all I need! I want you to question him personally when he gets back to the Citadel."

"I'll see to it, sir. He should be fit to travel in a week or so. Was that all?"

The Lord Defender studied the commandant for a moment, then with a wave of his hand, indicated that he should sit. He remained standing.

"What I am about to reveal to you is highly confidential," Jenga warned. *Highly confidential and possibly treasonous,* he added to himself. But he no longer felt able to bear the burden alone.

"I understand," Garet said, although it was patently obvious that he didn't. He might have even been a little offended that Jenga felt the need to warn him to secrecy.

"I have been ordered to ensure that if we find Mahina Cortanen alive, to see she doesn't stay that way."

"I don't believe that even Joyhinia would go that far."

"Believe it or not, it's the truth."

"But Mahina is no threat to the First Sister. What possible reason could she have for demanding such a thing?"

"Because Mahina *is* still dangerous. Mahina commanded more respect from the Defenders than any other First Sister before or since. Her involvement in this escape has taken the Sisterhood by surprise. Before the Karien Envoy left he was threatening invasion, if the First Sister does not gain a measure of control over the situation."

"And what of the heathens?"

Jenga shrugged. "Numerically, I doubt they're a genuine threat, but we can't afford to have troops tied up routing out heathens if the Kariens appear on our northern border."

"What are you going to do?"

"Follow my orders," Jenga told him. "Most of them, anyway. But I promise you this: No Defender will take any action to harm Mahina, even if it means defying the current First Sister."

Garet flicked an imaginary speck of dust from his jacket before he looked up, his expression grim. "You're talking treason."

"Am I?" Jenga sat down heavily. "Is it treason to refuse to carry out an order that you find morally reprehensible? If the First Sister ordered you to kill every prisoner in the Grimfield, would you do it?"

"Of course not, but—"

"Then you, sir," Jenga said, "would be committing treason."

Garet nodded. "Are you sure you understood your orders? Is it not possible that you misread her intentions?"

"No, I understood the First Sister well enough." He leaned back in his chair and sighed. "It is quite disturbing, after all this time to think that Tarja may have been right."

"What do you want me to do?"

"Find Tarja," Jenga said. "Before Joyhinia does."

"It will cost money," Garet warned. "Informants put a high price on their loyalty."

"Do whatever you have to," Jenga agreed.

Garet nodded. "And in the meantime?"

"In the meantime, we uphold our oath."

"To defend and serve the Sisters of the Blade for the protection of Medalon," Garet quoted, an edge to his voice.

"Mahina is a Sister of the Blade, and the Defenders will defend her with the same vigor as any other Sister."

"Even if it means defying Joyhinia?"

Jenga nodded slowly. "Aye. Even if it means that."

Jenga took a walk among his troops later that evening. The barracks were alive with the sounds of men preparing to move out. They would leave at first light. The jingle of tack and the whine of swords being sharpened on oilstone overlaid the sound of voices talking excitedly at the prospect of action. He moved quietly between the buildings, not wishing to give his men the idea he was checking on them. A good commander always knew what his troops were feeling. A good officer could gauge the mood of his men and know whether they needed bullying or mothering. If these men were going into action, he needed to know, before they left the Citadel, if he had a fighting force or a liability at his back.

"Are you sure it's Tarja we're going after?"

Jenga stopped in the shadow of the Officer's Barracks. He recognized the voice. It was Osbon, newly promoted to captain and itching for excitement.

"I heard a rumor it was the Harshini," another voice added. Jenga thought it sounded like Nheal. He had been in Tarja's class as a Cadet. He had failed to apprehend Tarja at Reddingdale and was the officer who took it into his head to conduct a snap inspection of the cell guards the morning of Tarja's abortive escape attempt. Jenga was still not convinced it was a coincidence.

"The Harshini are a fairy tale," a third voice scoffed. "It's the Kariens we're after. Their Envoy left recently, and he didn't look happy." Jenga wasn't sure who the third man was, but he sounded older than the other two.

"Tarja said the Kariens were the real danger to Medalon," Nheal said.

"And what good did it do him?" the third man asked.

"He's escaped from the Grimfield. It's bound to be him we're after. Do you think they'll hang him this time?"

"They should have hanged him the last time," the other man pointed out. "I heard a rumor that he didn't really desert, you know. That the whole thing was just a cover that he and Garet Warner worked out so that he could join the rebels and expose them."

"Makes sense," Osbon replied thoughtfully. "That would explain a lot of things. He's got more guts than I have, let me tell you. I wouldn't throw everything away . . . "

Jenga moved off, frowning in the darkness. Even publicly condemned, Tarja's influence was still felt in the Defenders. He wished, not for the first time, that he had found the chance to speak with him alone. Not in the interrogation cells or in the company of the guards, but man to man.

Jenga was an honorable man, and his pride in the Defenders had sustained him for most of his life. He truly believed that they had a solemn duty to protect Medalon and the Sisters of the Blade. But he was finding it hard to reconcile his duty with his oath. For a while, when Mahina had been First Sister, he had positively relished his position, as he watched her trying to bring about some genuine change. Her reign had been all too brief.

Satisfied that the Defenders would be ready to move out in the morning, Jenga made his way back to his quarters. He picked up the letter on his desk and read it again. It was from Verkin on the southern border. Jenga had read it so often in the past few days, he knew its contents by heart.

> My Lord Defender
>
> It is with great sorrow that I must inform you of the death of your brother, Captain Dayan Jenga. Although his death was from a fever, brought on by contact with an unclean *court'esa*, he nonetheless served this garrison with dedication for more than twenty years.
>
> Faithfully
> Kraith Verkin

So Dayan was dead. The manner did not surprise him, only that it had not happened sooner. He grieved for his brother, but his death finally freed him from his debt to Joyhinia. He read the letter again, then threw it on the fire and watched the flames consume it. When it was nothing more than white ash he dug out a bottle of illegally distilled potato spirit and for the first time in twenty years, drank himself into insensibility.

chapter 48

arja climbed to his feet warily as Ghari approached, pushing aside his despair in the face of a more immediate threat. They both knew that in a fight, Tarja would be the victor. He was bigger, stronger, and far better trained—a professional soldier—where Ghari was a farm-boy-turned-freedom-fighter. But the younger man wanted him to fight. Tarja could see it in his eyes. He wanted Tarja to resist so that he could take out some of his frustration and anger on the man who had once been his hero. Tarja was in no mood to accommodate him. Neither was he particularly enamored of being hanged.

"I didn't betray you, Ghari," Tarja repeated, partly as a plea and partly to distract the younger man long enough to get his bearings. Out in the yard, he heard voices again followed by horses leaving at a gallop. Padric leaving with R'shiel. How long would it take the old rebel to reach the Kariens? The faint beginnings of dawn lightened the sky through the dusty window.

"I don't listen to traitors." Ghari carried a sword but made no attempt to draw it. "Are you going to come peacefully, or kicking and screaming like the miserable coward you are?"

"I wouldn't give you the satisfaction."

Ghari glared at him for a moment then motioned toward the door. "After you, Captain."

Tarja walked toward the door, Ghari watching him warily. He was level with the young rebel before he brought his elbow up sharply into Ghari's face. The young man barely had time to call out before he dropped to the floor, his hands clutched to his broken nose. Tears of pain filled his eyes as he opened his mouth to call out again, but Tarja silenced him with a second blow to the side of his head. He checked the pulse in Ghari's neck to assure himself the lad was still alive. The young man had been about to escort him to his hanging. He had nothing about which to feel guilty. He quickly relieved the unconscious rebel of his sword and turned to face the door. Either Ghari's cry had not been heard, or the rebels outside had not recognized the sound for what it was.

Tarja moved to the window and glanced out into the rapidly lightening yard. A dozen or more rebels were still out there, most of them concentrating on putting together a workable noose and pushing an unhitched wagon underneath the tree limb where the noose had been thrown. Mandah stood watching them, but her back was to him. Knowing he had only seconds, Tarja ran toward the back of the house and the cellars. He had supervised the construction of this stronghold and knew its every secret. He barreled down the stone steps into the wine cellar and ran through the gloom toward the last huge barrel. As raised voices reached him from above, he knew Ghari had been discovered. Tarja forced himself not to rush as he felt along the wall in the darkness for the concealed latch. Pushing down on it, he waited as the barrel swung slowly outward. He squeezed into the narrow opening and pulled it shut behind him, dropping the locking bar into place.

Muffled voices reached him in the darkness as the rebels searched the cellar. Tarja ignored them, and, stooping painfully, he felt his way along the tunnel. The darkness was complete. He could not even see his hand in front of his face. Forcing himself to stop for a moment, Tarja tried to remember all he could about where the tunnel led. It opened out in the vineyard, he knew that much, but how far from the house he could not recall. It was pointless worrying about it any case. He would just have to rely on the fact that if he had had enough brains to create an escape route, he also had the sense to make the exit a safe distance from the house.

Several nasty bumps on his forehead convinced Tarja that crawling on his hands and knees was the safest way to negotiate the suffocatingly dark tunnel. Scuttling insects scurried beneath his fingers as he crawled along the dank floor. More than once something dropped on him, and he brushed the unseen creature away with a shudder.

Time lost all meaning as he cautiously made his way through the tunnel, and he began to understand what it was to be blind by the time he discovered the exit by crawling headfirst into it. He let out a yelp of pain as he cracked his forehead on the rough wooden barricade. He touched his forehead and felt the wet, sticky blood with a sigh. Sitting back on his heels, he felt along the rough planking that was sealed with turf on the other side. The roots grew through the gaps in the planking and brushed his seeking hands like ghostly tentacles. He found the latch and forced it down, not really surprised when nothing happened. Pushing on the trap-door proved fruitless. With a curse, he maneuvered himself around until he was lying on his back, then brought up both feet and kicked the door solidly. He winced at the sound in the close confines of the tunnel, praying there was nobody outside to hear it. A second kick brought a spear of light from a small crack in the opening. Several more kicks forced the trapdoor clear. Light pierced his eyes painfully as he turned his head away, giving himself a few moments to adjust. It would be pointless to get this far, just to stumble blindly out of the tunnel into the arms of his former comrades.

When he could finally face the light without squinting, he crawled clear of the tunnel into the open air. Tarja threw himself on the ground and took several deep breaths, the air clear and pure after the musty tunnel. His face pressed into the turf, he smelled the fresh dampness with unabashed delight. Nothing had ever smelled better.

Finally, he pushed himself up onto his hands and knees and looked back toward the farmhouse, astounded at the distance the tunnel had covered. It must have taken him hours to crawl through it. Glancing up at the sky, Tarja discovered the sun was quite high overhead. His elation vanished as he realized how great a start Padric had on him. He pushed himself up to his knees and looked around, suddenly aware of a deep rumbling that seemed to be coming from everywhere and nowhere. For a moment he stopped to listen, unable to place the sound, sure that it sounded like nothing so much as someone breathing. Someone very large, admittedly, but breathing, nonetheless. As he identified the sound, he glanced at the tree trunks that grew in front of the tunnel. Their roots spread out evenly like claws gripping the fresh turf. Two coppery-scaled trunks, glinting in the sunlight, grew from the clawlike roots. About the same time it occurred to Tarja that he wasn't looking at tree trunks, he thought to look up.

The massive dragon's head lowered itself slowly until its plate-sized eyes were almost level with his head.

"Are you human or worm?" the dragon asked curiously.

chapter 49

"Y ou found him," a musical voice said behind him as Tarja tore his eyes away from the curious gaze of the dragon.

"Of course," the beast replied, as if there had never been any doubt regarding the outcome. Tarja looked over his shoulder. The woman who walked toward him was of the same tall and slender proportions as R'shiel, dressed in dark, close-fitting riding leathers that covered her like a second skin. The dragon moved his massive head forward to greet her, and she gently reached up and scratched the bony ridge over his huge eye. Her eyes were as black as midnight.

"You must be Tarja. My name is Shananara," she said by way of introduction. "This is Lord Dranymire and his brethren."

"His brethren?" He had not yet recovered from the shock of being confronted by a dragon, but he was certain there was only one creature standing before him.

"Dragons don't really exist, Tarja. This beast is simply a demon meld." She turned to the dragon. "You frightened him. I asked you to be careful."

"He's human. They jump at their own shadows."

Shananara shrugged apologetically. "He's not been around humans much lately. You'll have to excuse him. Where is the child R'shiel?"

"R'shiel?" Tarja asked. "I don't know. They rode off with her in the middle of the night. I think they plan to hand her over to the Kariens."

Shananara's expression clouded. She turned to the dragon. "Can you feel her at all?"

"We have felt little since early this morning when we felt her pain."

"What does he mean?" Tarja asked, forgetting for a moment that he was talking to a dragon and a Harshini magician, two things that only a few days ago he thought were long extinct from his world. "What pain?"

"She might have done something. She's already proved she has considerable power, particularly for a wildling; she just doesn't know how to control it. Or . . ."

"Or what?" The Harshini was not telling him everything. For that matter, she was not telling him anything. What had happened to the rebels?

"If you say she has been given to the Kariens, then the pain may have been caused by a Karien priest," the dragon informed him. "Unfortunately, we can only tell that she suffers. Not how."

Tarja needed no further prompting. He turned for the farmhouse at run, his only thought to find a way to follow R'shiel. Shananara called after him. He ignored her. A thunderous rush of wind almost flattened him as he neared the farmhouse. The dragon landed, blocking his path. Tarja skidded to a halt. The beast was taller than a two-story building, and the span of his coppery wings was almost too wide for Tarja to comprehend. The dragon stared at him disdainfully.

"Human manners have not improved in the last few hundred years."

Shananara caught up to them and grabbed Tarja's arm, pulling him around to face her. "What are you doing?"

"I'm going to find R'shiel. The Kariens have her."

"You don't know that for certain. And even if they do have her, you have no idea where she is or how to find her."

"Then what do you suggest I do?" he snapped, intensely annoyed as he realized that she was right. He had no idea where Padric had taken R'shiel. All Tarja knew at that moment was that he had to find her and that he would happily murder Padric himself, if any harm had come to her.

The Harshini studied him. "Is she a particular friend of yours?"

"What do you mean?" he asked.

Shananara frowned, as if she knew something Tarja was not privy to. "Oh, nothing. Let's wake up one of your rebel friends and ask him where they took her, shall we?"

Shananara led him back to the yard of the farmhouse. The dragon followed, his huge tail leaving a trail as wide as a narrow road in the dirt behind him. The dozen or so rebels who had been planning to hang him lay still on the ground, the noose waving gently in the breeze like a child's swing. Tarja looked away from the uncomfortable reminder of his close brush with death and glanced about him with growing dread.

"Did you kill them?"

The Harshini rolled her eyes with exasperation. "No! Of course I didn't kill them! What do you take me for? They're asleep. Which one should we wake?"

Tarja looked around, but he could not see Ghari among the unconscious rebels. He led Shananara into the farmhouse and found the young man lying in the doorway, his face still bloodied and bruised from Tarja's attack.

"What happened to him?" she asked.

"I hit him. I was trying to escape."

She knelt down beside the unconscious rebel. "And these people were friends of yours? I wonder what you do to people you don't like?"

"Just wake him up. Ghari will know where Padric took R'shiel."

Shananara gently placed her hand on Ghari's forehead, closing her eyes. Tarja watched expectantly, but he felt nothing. Ghari's eyes fluttered open. He looked at them blankly for a moment before jerking backward in fear at the sight of the black-eyed Harshini woman leaning over him.

"Don't be afraid," Shananara said.

Tarja didn't know if there was any magic in her musical voice, but the young rebel visibly relaxed as she spoke. He turned his gaze on Tarja before cautiously climbing to his feet. They stood back to give him room.

"What happened?" he asked, gingerly touching his broken nose.

"I escaped," Tarja told him. "And the Harshini came looking for R'shiel."

Ghari stared at the woman. "They really do exist?"

"Yes, they really do," Tarja agreed. Every moment they wasted R'shiel was getting further away. "And the Karien Envoy will kill R'shiel as soon as he learns what she is. Where did Padric take her?"

Ghari's eyes narrowed. "Why should I tell you anything?"

Tarja's first impatient reaction was to beat the truth out of Ghari, but, as if she knew what he was planning, Shananara stepped between the two humans.

"Now, now, children. There is no need for any unpleasantness. Where did they take her, Ghari?"

The young rebel found his gaze locked with the Harshini's. "To a jetty about eight leagues south of here. The Karien Envoy was to meet them there."

She released the thrall on Ghari and turned to Tarja. "There! That was painless, wasn't it?"

Tarja did a few rapid calculations in his head. The results were not encouraging. "She's long gone, then. They would have handed her over just after dawn."

"About the same time the demons felt her pain," Shananara agreed. "I'm sorry, Tarja."

"What do you mean, you're sorry? Aren't you going after her?"

"Tarja, we risked much coming this far. The demons can only assume a shape as complex as a dragon for a limited time, even with hundreds in the meld. I can't risk taking them so far from Sanctuary. If the meld weakened and we were airborne at the time . . . " Her voice trailed off helplessly.

Tarja was sure that he would have been quite sympathetic to her plight had he the faintest idea what she was talking about.

"Can't you do something?" he asked.

"I can," she conceded, "but a Karien priest would see right through it. And not for you or R'shiel or the King of the Harshini, will I risk my demons being seen by a Karien priest. I'm sorry."

"Then what do we do?" Tarja refused to give in so easily. He could not, would not, leave R'shiel in the hands of the Kariens. Not if there was the slightest chance he could save her. He owed her that much at least.

"Find a boat, I suppose," she suggested. "I don't know much about them, but I imagine there are faster boats on the river than the Karien Envoy's. Shipbuilding was never a strength of the Kariens. Maybe you can catch up with them."

"And then what? Suppose I get her back? Will you help then?"

"Do you know what you're doing, Tarja?" she asked. "Do you know the pain that comes from loving a Harshini?"

"What?"

"We call it Kalianah's Curse," she told him. "You will grow old and die, Tarja, while she is in the prime of her life. Just because we look human, don't mistake us for your kind. You do not understand the differences between our races. They are differences that can only cause you pain."

Tarja opened his mouth to object again and then wondered why he should bother. He did not have the time to argue with her.

"Will you help her or not?"

"You've been warned," she said shaking her head. She slipped a small pendant over her head and handed it to Tarja. He examined it carefully. It was a cube of transparent material with the faint image of a dragon clutching the world in its claws etched in the center. "If you find her. If you are certain you're unobserved and *only* if the Karien priest is dead, you may call us."

"Only if the Karien priest is dead?" Tarja asked. "I thought you people abhorred killing?"

"We do. And I am not asking you to kill the priest. I couldn't do that, even if I wanted to. I am simply telling you that you must not call us unless the priest is dead."

Tarja slipped the fine gold chain over his own head and hid the pendant under his shirt, wondering at the fine distinction she made between not asking him to kill the priest and asking him to ensure he was dead. He glanced at Ghari, who stood staring wonderingly through the open doorway at Dranymire, who had settled himself down in the center of the yard, his huge tail wrapped elegantly around him like a contented cat.

"I'll take Ghari with me," Tarja told her. "What about the others?"

"They'll wake up eventually. They will remember nothing."

"What about Mahina?"

"She is safe with Affiana and the other human. Never fear, Tarja, they will not be harmed."

"Is Affiana one of you?"

The Harshini shook her head. "She is the descendant of Brak's human half-sister. Brak's niece, I suppose you could call her." She laughed at his expression. "Brak is somewhat . . . older than he appears. He was born in a time when human and Harshini were less at odds with each other. Don't let it bother you, Tarja."

With a frown, Tarja pushed Ghari ahead of him into the yard. Dranymire turned a curious eye on the two humans. "Are we taking them, too? You should have told us if you wanted a public transport conveyance. Then we could have assumed the form of a drafthorse."

"No, my Lord," Shananara assured him. "They have other tasks to take care of."

The demons in dragon form stared directly at Tarja. "You seek the wildling?" Tarja nodded, assuming he—they—meant R'shiel. "Then we wish you luck, little human," the dragon said gravely.

Tarja and Ghari rode into Testra midafternoon on the wagon that had taken them to the farmhouse the night before. Tarja's eyes were gritty with lack of sleep, and the wound on the back of his head throbbed at every bump in the road. Ghari looked in even worse shape, his nose swollen and bent, but at least he had the benefit of a few hours' sleep— albeit magically induced. The young heathen had been strangely quiet ever since meeting the Harshini and her demons, for which Tarja was extremely grateful. It was hard enough for him to cope with all he had seen and heard this day, and Tarja at least had some inkling that the Harshini still flourished. Ghari, on the other hand, had confidently considered them long extinct, despite his belief in their gods. Since seeing the mighty Lord Dranymire and his brethren in dragon form, Ghari had been in shock, answering only in monosyllables. Occasionally he reached across to grip Tarja's forearm painfully to demand: "It was a dragon, wasn't it?"

By the time they rode into the town, Ghari had recovered his wits somewhat. Although hardly talkative, he had lost the wide-eyed look of startled terror that he had worn for most of the day. They drove their wagon slowly through the town, heads lowered. Tarja had discarded his Defender's uniform gladly, and they were dressed as farmhands. He turned the wagon for the docks and looked at Ghari.

"Do you have many riverboat captains among your sympathizers?"

"A few. But we'll be lucky if they're here. Do you have any money?"

"Not a rivet."

"Then we'll have trouble. Even our sympathizers won't take us for love. They must have coin to show their owners at the end of their journey."

"We'll think of something," Tarja assured his companion, although how, he had no idea. As they drove along the waterfront, he glanced at the dozen or more riverboats tied up at the docks. Which of them, he wondered, could he convince to risk everything in pursuit of a vessel belonging to a foreign envoy, to save a girl who was one of a race that supposedly no longer existed?

"Here," Ghari told him, pointing at a swinging tavern sign. The Chain and Anchor was the largest tavern along the wharf, and even from this distance, Tarja could hear the rowdy singing coming from the taproom. He pulled the wagon to a stop and climbed down.

Ghari followed him, catching his arm. "I have to ask you, Tarja. Was Padric right about the letter? Were you really writing to the Defenders?"

"We're not ready for a war, Ghari. I wasn't trying to betray you, I was trying to protect you."

"But what of our people who died after you were captured? How did the Sisterhood learn of them?"

"You underestimate the depth of Garet Warner's intelligence network. Joyhinia had those names long before I was captured. She simply held off using them until it would have the most effect."

The young man nodded. He jerked his head in the direction of the tavern, the matter apparently now put to rest. "They know me here," he warned. "And your name isn't very popular. Keep your head down. I'll do the talking." Tarja stood back and let Ghari lead the way.

The taproom was crowded with sailors. The singing was coming from half a dozen men standing on a table near the door, their arms linked, belting out a chorus about a handsome sailor and a very accommodating mistress. Another sailor accompanied them on a squeezebox. He seemed to know only about three notes, but he played each one with great enthusiasm, making up in volume what he lacked in talent. Tarja lowered his head as he followed Ghari through the crush of bodies, trying not to draw any attention to himself. Ghari pushed his way through to the bar, leaning forward to catch the eye of the overworked but extremely prosperous tavern keeper. Tarja glanced around the room, hoping he would recognize someone, praying no one would recognize him. In the far corner of the room, a figure was hunched miserably over his tankard, his back to the revelers, totally uninvolved in the celebrations. Startled, Tarja tapped Ghari on the arm and pointed. Ghari's eyes widened in surprise and he abandoned his attempt to catch the tavern keeper's attention. They pushed their way back through the crowd.

Ghari sat down opposite the old man and placed a hand on his shoulder. Tarja stood behind him, partly to stop him escaping and partly because he needed time to dampen the anger he felt at the sight of the old man. This man, this former friend, had handed R'shiel over to the Kariens.

"Padric?" Ghari said. "Where are the others?"

Padric raised his head slowly. He was as drunk as a bird that had spent the day feasting on rotten jarafruit. "Murderers," he mumbled, miserably. "She called us murderers."

"Padric!"

"We shouldn't have killed him, lad," Padric continued woefully. "I knew him. He wasn't a traitor. He explained about the letter. He was trying to save lives, not destroy them. I should have trusted him. And R'shiel. She really was—"

Ghari looked at Tarja in exasperation. Tarja leaned over the old man and grabbed his collar, pulling him up. "Then it's a damn good thing I'm still alive, isn't it?" he said in a low voice.

Padric turned his red rimmed eyes to Tarja. "Tarja!"

"Shut up!" Ghari hissed, with a nervous glance around the rowdy taproom. "We have to get a boat. We're going to get R'shiel back."

Padric never questioned Ghari's change of heart. His anguish was clear for anyone to see, and he drunkenly grabbed at the chance to undo his deed.

"We'll have to hurry. But you won't find help among this lot. The word has just come that the Defenders are mobilizing. They're all headed north to Brodenvale to pick up the troops."

"Mobilizing?" Tarja glanced back over his shoulder. That accounted for the celebration, at least. The sailors cared little for the Sisterhood, but there was a lot of money to be made transporting troops. The crews were facing a period of upcoming prosperity. The fact that it would halt virtually all other trade on the river and threaten the livelihood of countless other folk bothered them not at all. "What for?"

"To destroy us, of course," Padric mumbled. "Word is out that you are here and heading for the mountains. The entire bloody Corps will be on us in a matter of weeks."

The news concerned Tarja. He had arrived in Testra only the day before. For the news to reach the sailors in Testra, Joyhinia must have ordered the mobilization within hours of learning of their escape from the Grimfield.

The tavern door swung open and another crew entered the tavern, although they looked less enthusiastic about the celebration than the sailors who were already well into their cups. With a silent prayer to the Harshini gods he did not believe in, who he was certain must be looking out for him, he turned back to Ghari.

"I think we've found our boat," he said. "Get him out of here and meet me at the wagon."

Ghari was quickly falling back into the old habit of doing what Tarja ordered. He nodded and stood up, helping the drunken old rebel to his feet. Tarja watched them leave and then turned his attention back to the big Fardohnyan who was pushing his way through the throng to the bar. His brothers waited near the door, looking for an empty table. Tarja waved and pointed to the table that Padric had just vacated. The two men nodded and made their way across the room to him. They had not recognized him, merely taking him for a helpful farmer. Drendik was not far behind them, but as he turned to thank Tarja, his brows rose in startled recognition.

"You!" he exclaimed.

"I need your help," he said, not bothering with any preamble. "There is a Harshini girl in trouble. The Karien Envoy has her."

If there was one thing Tarja knew that would rile a Fardohnyan it was mentioning the Kariens, whom they hated with something close to religious fervor. To throw in the Harshini, whom they revered with equal passion, was guaranteed to get the riverboat captain's attention.

"The Kariens have a Harshini?" the younger sailor demanded. Although they revered them, it was unlikely the Fardohnyans had ever laid eyes on a Harshini. Unlike Padric and the rebels, however, they did not question the continuing existence of the fabled race.

"Will you help me?"

"Well it's damned certain I won't be ferrying Medalonian troops for the cursed Sisterhood," Drendik said. The Fardohnyan downed his large tankard in one go and slammed it down on the table. "Well, my rebellious young friend, let us go forth and gain the favor of the gods by saving one of their chosen ones. Do you have any money?"

Tarja shook his head and the Fardohnyan sighed. "There's just no profit in being a hero these days."

chapter 50

The Karien Envoy studied R'shiel fearfully as the ship was picked up and pushed south by the current before he turned to Elfron. R'shiel was still on her hands and knees at Pieter's feet, trying to push back waves of nausea. The pain from Elfron's staff had subsided to a vicious aching throb that pulsed in time with her heartbeat.

"What did you do to her?"

"I did nothing," Elfron said. "It is Xaphista who has spoken through the power of his staff. She is Harshini."

"But she's the First Sister's daughter! Or at least she was, until Joyhinia disowned her. Do you suppose she knew?"

"Of course she knew! Have I not been warning you that the Sisterhood is in league with the forces of evil? You are lucky, my Lord, that she did not attempt to entrap you."

If she was in league with the forces of evil, it was the first R'shiel had heard about it. Pieter looked at her again, but there was no lust or desire in his eyes. Just loathing.

"Take her below."

"We should tie her to the mast so that all of Medalon can see that we have captured an evil one," Elfron declared. "We must let it be known that Xaphista cannot be deceived."

"Don't be a fool! You can't sail through Medalon with one of their women tied to the mast! Do you want to provoke a war?"

"She is not one of their women, she is a Harshini witch," he pointed out. "Medalon should rejoice in the knowledge that we have removed a serpent from the breast of their insidious Sisterhood."

"The Harshini mean nothing to these people! They are a forgotten

race. Only in Karien, where the power of the Overlord protects us from
the thrall of the Harshini, do we remember the threat. They will not
rejoice in your triumph, Elfron, they will run you through!"

Elfron conceded the point with ill grace. "Very well then, secure her
below. But when we have left the Glass River, when we are safely through
the Fardohnyan Gulf and are back in Karien waters, then she will be tied
to the mast so that *our* people, at least, may rejoice in our triumph. My
vision was a true one. We shall sail the Ironbrook in glory."

With an imperious wave of his arm, Pieter ordered two sailors to drag
her below. R'shiel did not resist. She was still shaking and weak as they
half-dragged, half-carried her along the deck and pushed her below,
finally locking her in a small storage cabin at the end of a long passage.
Light filtered in dimly from the slatted door. Feeling her way along the
deck, she found a pile of musty smelling sacks and collapsed onto them.

Tears spilled onto the dirty sacks as R'shiel gave in to a wave of hope-
lessness. Her grief over Tarja's death overwhelmed her for a time, left her
hollow and sick. It felt like the perfect side dish to accompany the main
course of her pain. She didn't care what happened now. No suffering anyone could inflict on her could be worse than the suffering she could inflict
upon herself by simply thinking of Tarja.

R'shiel dozed for while in the small cabin, as they sailed further south.
The cabin grew uncomfortably warm as the day progressed, and she woke
up feeling thirsty and hungry, but no one came to offer her any sustenance.
She looked around the shelves in the gloom and found nothing useful.
The closet contained old sacks, lengths of rope, and several barrels of foul-
smelling pitch, but nothing remotely resembling food or water. Had they
forgotten she was down here, or was it their intention to starve her to
death? She did not think that likely. Elfron was too enamoured of the idea
of sailing up the Ironbrook River with his Harshini prize lashed to the
main mast. He would not allow her to die before then and rob him of his
triumph.

With nothing else to do and her grief over Tarja beginning to settle like
grit in a bottle of sour wine, R'shiel finally thought to wonder about Pieter
and Elfron and their strange notion that she was Harshini. It seemed so
unreal. Brak had told her a great deal about the Harshini on their journey
from the Grimfield. He made them sound so charming and elegant that she
had almost wished they still lived. His tales had drawn her out of herself,
woven a magical web of wonder over her bruised and battered soul. Until
now, she had not realized how much Brak had helped her. In the days fol-

lowing her escape from the Grimfield, she had not particularly cared if she lived or died. There had been a fear in her that she couldn't name, an unwillingness to face what she had done, an inability to even comprehend it. She had told Brak of the mural in her room, and from her description, he had been able to tell her what the mural represented. Sanctuary, he called it. A place built by the Harshini to provide a haven of peace. A place where joy and laughter filled the halls and serenity washed over the soul with every breath. She wondered how much Brak had known and how much of it he had made up. He should have been a bard.

But it seemed rather odd that the Harshini, who were long dead and gone, should suddenly loom so large in her life. First Brak had regaled her with stories about them, then Tarja had tried to convince the rebels that she was one, when he would have been much better off telling them something more credible. His folly had likely cost him his life. Now Elfron and Lord Pieter were taking her back to Karien to burn her as a witch because they thought she was one of them, too. Was it possible? Had her unknown father been a Harshini? A lifetime of certainty was threatened by the very notion. She knew her mother had refused to name her father. But the Harshini were dead. The Sisterhood had destroyed them.

It was long after dark when Elfron finally came for her. The motion of the boat had changed, and R'shiel wondered if they had pulled into the riverbank for the night. She knew next to nothing about boats but suspected that the Karien vessel must be a seafaring ship, ill-equipped to deal with the river. It was likely that the Envoy's captain was not familiar enough with the Glass River to risk sailing it at night.

In the vain hope that unconsciousness would spare her the pain of her grief, her throbbing shoulder, her dry throat, and her rumbling stomach, R'shiel was trying to sleep when she heard a rattle in the lock. She had eaten nothing since dinner at the inn in Testra. The part of her that was still grieving hoped that it would not take too long to die of thirst or starvation. The part of her that still lived craved food and water with a passion that almost overcame her grief. A spark of life burned in R'shiel, too bright to be put out by grief or pain.

Elfron threw open the door and ordered her to stand. She did so slowly, as much from physical weakness as fear. He grabbed her arm as soon as she was standing and pulled her from the cabin. He propelled her forward along the passage to another cabin with elaborately carved double doors. In his left hand, Elfron clutched the Staff of Xaphista. R'shiel glanced at it, knowing that her idle boast to herself earlier, that no pain could exceed the pain of losing Tarja, was a hollow one indeed when faced with the staff.

The cabin was sumptuously furnished. Everything—the bedhead, the chairs, the paneled walls—was inlaid with gold, and everywhere the five-pointed star intersected with a lightning bolt shone out. Even the blue satin quilt on the bed was embroidered with the symbol, beautifully worked in gold thread. The richness of the cabin was overpowering.

"You stand in the presence of the Overlord's representative," Elfron told her. "You are unclean. You will cleanse yourself and dress more appropriately before we begin." He indicated a jug and washbowl that lay on the table next to a small covered tray. Over the back of one of the chairs was a rough cassock, similar to the one that Elfron wore, which seemed plain and ordinary amid the sumptuousness of the cabin. R'shiel eyed him warily, but Elfron appeared to have no more interest in her than he would in any other animal. R'shiel did as he ordered, turning her back to him as she peeled off her clothes. Elfron continued to watch her as she washed herself with all the concern he might have shown watching a cat lick itself clean. She pulled on the rough, itchy cassock and turned to face him.

"You may eat," he told her, indicating the tray.

R'shiel removed the covering cloth and discovered a loaf of dry black bread and a small pitcher of wine. It was quite the most lavish feast she had ever consumed. She ate the bread hungrily and drank every drop of the watered wine, watching the priest out of the corner of her eye. Elfron continued to ignore her until she had finished. As she wiped the last crumbs of the bread from her mouth with the back of her hand, he nodded with satisfaction.

"You will now tell me where the Harshini settlement is hidden," he announced in the same implacable tone as he had ordered her to wash and eat.

R'shiel glanced at the staff warily before she answered. "I don't know what you're talking about."

"Lying is a sin. You will answer honestly, or suffer the wrath of Xaphista's staff."

"I can't tell you what I don't know. The Harshini are dead. I'm not one of them. I'm as human as you are."

"You are not human," Elfron declared, moving the staff so that he held it in both hands. The lantern light glittered dangerously off the precious stones. "You are the essence of Harshini evil. You wear the body of a whore, designed to tempt the righteous from the true path. Your beauty is contrived and designed solely to beguile pious men. You flaunt your woman's body and seduce devout souls with your godless magic. The Overlord spoke to me in a vision and demanded your surrender. He will not—cannot—be denied."

R'shiel stepped backward as he ranted. She didn't know if Elfron was mad or merely devoted to the point of insanity, and it really didn't matter. The end result was the same. He stepped forward and brought down the staff sharply across R'shiel's already tender shoulder. Once again the agony shot through her, forcing a scream of soul-wrenching torment. He held it there as she fell to the floor, chanting under his breath in a slow litany. R'shiel screamed and screamed until her throat was raw, and then she screamed again.

Elfron's eyes were alight with religious fervor as he watched her, his pleasure almost sexual in its intensity. R'shiel's cries were incoherent in their terror and agony as fire lanced through her body—she felt as though a white-hot sword slashed her.

"You fool! You'll kill her!"

The agony suddenly eased as Pieter snatched the staff from Elfron's hand. The priest looked down at R'shiel's sobbing, twitching body.

"Xaphista will see that she lives long enough to be sacrificed."

"Well, I'd prefer not to put the Overlord to the trouble. I said you could question her, not make her scream like a banshee. Every farmlet in a five-league radius probably heard her, you fool!"

Elfron snatched the staff back from the knight. "Why do you seek to spare her?" he asked. "Has the insidious lure of the witch overcome you?"

Pieter glanced down at R'shiel's limp, trembling body with disgust. "She has you in a thrall, more likely," the knight scoffed. "I find her repulsive. Put her back in the storeroom and leave her be. She is no use to either of us like this. Not even our people would consider that a threat." He waved his arm disdainfully toward the terrified, sobbing girl.

Elfron sniffed, bowing reluctantly to the knight's logic. "Have her removed, then."

Pieter's eyes narrowed at the presumptuous order, but he obeyed. R'shiel felt strong, rough hands dragging her to her feet and back down the long passage to her cell. They threw her in, and she landed heavily on the floor. She dragged herself over to the pile of musty sacks as she heard the door being locked. As she lost consciousness, her last thought was an idle question: *How much pain does it take to die?*

chapter 51

"id you really speak with a dragon?"

Tarja glanced at the captain. The Fardohnyan gripped the wheel of the riverboat, steering it with unconscious skill as the *Maera's Daughter* flew southward. Running with the current and under a full set of sails, the small boat was making astounding speed. They had traveled through the night, though even Drendik had balked at doing that under sail, settling for running with the current instead. As soon as dawn broke, the Fardohnyans and the rebels had set the sails, and a crisp breeze had sprung up, snapping the canvas sharply and pushing the boat on. Drendik had assured Tarja it was proof the gods favored their mission. Tarja privately considered it nothing more than luck, but he was not about to offend the Fardohnyan's beliefs.

"Yes, I truly spoke with a dragon."

During the long night and the following day, Tarja had related most of his tale to the Fardohnyans. He had finally managed to sleep earlier this morning and had come up on deck to find them much farther south than he would have thought possible. Drendik was confident they would overtake the Karien boat by nightfall. He had seen it in his travels and gave Tarja a long list of reasons why it would not move very fast, starting with the basic stupidity of its design and finishing with the incompetence of its crew. But more than anything, Drendik was enchanted by the idea that Tarja had met a dragon.

"You are truly blessed by the Divine Ones, if they allowed you to speak to a dragon," Drendik assured him. "Even our most powerful magicians only claim to have heard of them. I never met anyone who actually spoke to a demon meld before."

"Neither have I."

The big Fardohnyan laughed. "You're all right for an atheist."

"Where are we?" Tarja asked, glancing at the rolling grasslands that faded into the distance on either side of the river. The sun hovered low over the jagged purple horizon in the distance that was the Sanctuary Mountains.

"About four days from Bordertown at this speed," Drendik told him. "We should find them soon." He glanced at the setting sun on the western horizon. "They will pull into the bank for the night."

Tarja was willing to believe anything that Drendik told him that meant they would catch the Karien Envoy before he left Medalon, although Drendik's assessment was more than likely correct. Unfamiliarity with the Glass River was a prime cause of accidents on the vast waterway. Even Tarja, who had spent little time on the river, knew that.

"And when we find them? What then?" Tarja asked. "If you help us storm the boat, it will be considered an act of piracy."

Drendik shrugged. "Storming a Karien boat to rescue a Divine One would be considered an act of great chivalry where I come from." He slapped Tarja's shoulder companionably, almost knocking him down. "You are kind to worry, but we were heading south anyway. We only make this trek once a year. By next year they will have forgotten about us."

"You don't have to help," Tarja assured him. "We can do it on our own."

"What? You, the young hothead, and the old man?" Drendik said, highly amused at the idea. "I admire your courage, rebel, but not your common sense."

"Just thought I'd offer."

"That's settled then," Drendik announced, glancing at the rapidly setting sun again. "Aber! Reef that mainsail! At this rate we'll sail straight past them!"

They sailed on as darkness settled over the river and the nighttime chorus of insects struck up their evening song. The *Maera's Daughter* slipped silently through the water on the very edge of the current. Tarja glanced up at the main mast, where Aber was perched precariously, watching for the telltale lanterns. Ghari and Gazil were in the bow, watching for any sign that would betray the presence of the Kariens. Tarja stood with Padric and Drendik, who skillfully kept the riverboat hovering between the still waters of the river's edge and the powerful current in the center. They sailed on in the darkness for hours, in the same state of nervous anticipation, until Tarja was certain they had either passed the Karien boat, or Drendik was wrong in assuming they would stop for the night.

A low whistle from Aber caused them all to look up. The sailor pointed to the western bank, and Tarja quickly followed his arm. Almost too faint to make out, several small pinpoints of light twinkled in the darkness.

Drendik wrenched the wheel of the boat around toward the western bank, and Tarja cringed as she creaked in complaint. Aber and Gazil raced to set the gaff sail as Drendik cut sharply across the current, angling toward the opposite bank. They were running without lights, but Tarja was certain someone on board must see them as the current took them closer and closer. The bulk of the top-heavy Karien ship took shape in the darkness. *Maera's Daughter* seemed tiny in comparison. Drendik eased the little boat into the bank and Tarja felt it bump gently against reeds. A small splash sounded as Gazil dropped the anchor and Aber scurried down the mast in the darkness. The men gathered on the deck and looked at Tarja expectantly.

"Can you all swim?" he asked, as it suddenly occurred to him that his grand rescue would fall rather short of the mark if his small band of heroes drowned before they got to the Karien ship. A series of nods reassured him his plan was workable, and he quietly issued his orders. Aber and Ghari were to take the bow, Gazil and Padric the stern, leaving the midships for Drendik and Tarja. It was likely that R'shiel was being held below decks so Tarja and Drendik would make their way below while the others took care of any resistance above. The men nodded silently in the darkness, not questioning his orders.

"Let's go then," he said.

"You have forgotten something," Drendik reminded him. "The priest."

"What about the priest?" Padric asked. His eyes looked haunted in the darkness, as if he bore some terrible guilt.

"Kill the priest," Tarja said. "If we do nothing else, we kill the priest."

Drendik and the Fardohnyans nodded in agreement. Padric seemed equally content. Only Ghari glanced at Tarja with a doubtful look. Tarja shrugged, as if to tell the young man that he had no idea why it was so important to kill the priest but that the Harshini and the Fardohnyans both thought the world would be a better place without him.

The water was icy as Tarja slipped into the shallows next to *Maera's Daughter* and gently pushed out into the river. With a borrowed Fardohnyan sword strapped to his back and a viciously barbed Fardohnyan dagger between his teeth, Tarja swam toward the bulk of the Karien vessel. He could make out the bobbing heads of his companions as they moved toward the ship. The length of rope he carried over his shoulder was quickly becoming soaked, and he could feel it weighing him down as the river deepened near the hull of the bigger vessel. He looked up at the deck as he unhooked the rope, wondering how he could get enough swing up to hook the rope over the railing, which towered over him. A soft whistle caught his attention and he turned. As if sensing his dilemma, Aber held up the grappling hook attached to his own rope and began circling it overhead, letting a little more of the rope out with each revolution. Finally, he flung the rope up, letting the momentum of the swing and the weight of the hook carry the rope upward. It landed with a clatter on the deck and wrapped itself around a carved upright. With a silent nod, Tarja thanked the boy for his demonstration and followed suit. He winced at the sound of the hook scraping across the deck, but it seemed to attract no attention from above. Tarja tugged on the rope to assure himself that it would hold and began to pull himself up, hand over hand, onto the deck.

The main deck was deserted, which worried Tarja, as he hauled himself over the railing and dropped into a low, dripping crouch. He grasped the dagger in his left hand. He saw Drendik climb over the starboard rail and glance around, his beard dripping, a curious shrug greeting the absence of any guards.

Tarja pointed to the large carved door amidships, below the poop deck. With a nod, they moved silently toward it. Tarja glanced around again before trying the gilt handle. He cried out as a white-hot bolt of pain tore through his arm, leaving it numb to the shoulder. Almost as soon as he triggered the magical alarm, the deck came to life as a dozen or more armed Kariens emerged from their hiding places. A flare of light split the night from the poop deck. The small band of invaders backed up nervously, staring up at the specter of the Karien priest who stood on the poop deck clutching a blazing staff in one hand and holding R'shiel by the hair with the other.

"Is this what you have come for?" the priest crowed, jerking R'shiel's head back. In an instant, any lingering doubt Tarja had about the fate of the priest vanished. "Drop your weapons!"

Reluctantly, the Fardohnyans and the rebels did as they were bid. The Karien sailors rushed forward to herd the would-be pirates together as Tarja stared up at R'shiel. There were no marks on her that he could see, but she looked dazed and limp. Blinded by the magical light from the staff, it was more than likely that she did not know who her erstwhile rescuers were.

As they were gathered together, Tarja realized that Padric had not been apprehended. He was to have taken the poop deck with Gazil. Was he dead already, or had the priest revealed his presence before the old man could haul himself aboard?

As if in answer to his unspoken question, a yell came from the poop deck as Padric ran at the priest, his sword held high, aimed squarely at the priest's exposed back. The priest turned and threw R'shiel aside as he raised his arm to ward off the attack. Almost casually, the Karien Envoy stepped forward and ran the old man through.

Tarja and his companions did not waste time grieving for him. The startled priest dropped the staff and the boat was suddenly plunged into darkness. They dived for their weapons as the Kariens milled in confusion. Tarja tripped on the pile of discarded weapons. He found a sword, scooped it up with his left hand and ran it into the shadow that appeared before him, relieved that he had not run through one of his own men by mistake, when the man screamed a Karien curse. As his eyes adjusted to the darkness, he ran toward the companionway, his only thought to get to R'shiel before the priest could retrieve his staff and light the boat again. By the time he reached the poop deck, his eyes were accustomed to the dim starlight, although his sword arm still hung uselessly by his side, numbed from the magical blast. The priest was on his hands and knees, feeling about for the staff that lay just out of his reach. The Envoy was standing at the head of the companionway on the far side of the deck, fighting off a determined attack from the Fardohnyan captain. R'shiel lay near the fallen staff.

"R'shiel!"

She ignored the priest for a moment and turned toward him. As Elfron reached for the staff, she suddenly seemed to come alive. She kicked it away from him and scrambled to her feet. A Karien sailor behind him distracted Tarja for a moment. He turned, banging the railing painfully with his useless right hand and kicked the man in the face, throwing him backward into two more Kariens who were trying to follow him up the companionway. When he turned back, a blinding light split the night again, but it was R'shiel who held the staff, not the priest.

Screaming, she grimly clung to the staff, as if holding it caused excruciating pain. The priest screeched an agonized protest. With an incomprehensible cry, she swung the staff in a wide arc and smashed it against the mizzenmast.

The light from the staff died in a moment of complete darkness, then the mast suddenly burst into flame. Within seconds the flames spread along the boat in strange green lines of fire. Tarja jumped back from the rail as it flared beneath his hand. The magical fire consumed the wards protecting the ship like they were lines of lamp oil, blistering the garish blue paint and eating into the wood beneath. In less than a minute, the entire ship was ablaze.

"Tarja!" R'shiel screamed, as she dropped the broken staff, holding her burned hands out in front of her. He ran toward her, leaping the rising flames that stood between them. Only the fact that he was drenched from his swim saved him from the inferno. Drendik reached them about the same time. The Karien Envoy lay at the head of the companionway, the Fardohnyan's sword embedded in the center of his decorated armored chest. Tarja spared the captain a glance, wondering at the strength of the man. The Karien's armor might have been ceremonial, but it still took a great deal of strength to pierce it. As he reached R'shiel, she collapsed into his arms. Pins and needles attacked his numb right arm as the feeling began to return. Tarja threw his sword to Drendik. The Fardohnyan snatched it from the air and turned on the priest, slicing the man from shoulder to belly where he stood. Without hesitating, Tarja ran for the side of the boat, crashing through the flaming rail into the darkness and the safety of the river below. R'shiel, the loose cassock aflame, screamed as she felt them falling. Then the dark icy water swallowed them, pulling them down into its glassy depths.

chapter 52

In the dawn light, the smoldering hull of the Karien boat looked forlorn, floating near the shore amid the burned flotsam of what had once been a mighty, if rather cumbersome vessel. It had burned to the waterline. Another smoking pile smoldered on the shore, where the bodies of the Karien sailors had been cremated. Gazil, Aber, and Ghari spent the remainder of the night at their grizzly task, gathering the bodies from the water's edge and throwing them on the impromptu funeral pyre. The Fardohnyans were not pleased with the cremations but were willing to make an exception for the Kariens, particularly when Tarja pointed out what would happen if the bodies washed up downstream. The body of the Envoy had not been recovered. Tarja supposed he had sunk into the muddy river, weighted down by his ornate armor. The body of the priest lay separate from the pyre. Tarja would not let them burn it, not yet. They were all tired and filthy, worn out by the night's exertions and suffering the typical letdown of men who had faced death and then discovered, somewhat to their surprise, that they had survived.

Tarja scanned the western horizon again, expectantly, but the sky remained clear. With a sigh, he turned back toward the small fire that Drendik had built, away from the sight of the funeral pyre. R'shiel sat beside it, wearing the charred remains of a cassock and wrapped in a gray woolen blanket, her eyes vacant. Tarja was desperately worried about her. She had said nothing since they had dragged her ashore. She flinched whenever somebody touched her, even accidentally. Her hands were burned where she had gripped the staff, and another deep burn scarred her right shoulder.

Ghari walked up the small rise to stand beside him.

"You know the irony of all this," Tarja remarked to the young rebel, "is that we've started a war despite ourselves. When the Kariens learn their Envoy was killed on Medalon soil, they'll be over the border in an instant. The alliance is well and truly broken."

"I think Padric knew it, too," he said. For a moment they shared a silent thought for the old rebel. His body had been one of the first they recovered.

"Will she be all right?" Ghari asked, glancing at R'shiel's hunched and trembling figure.

"What happened on the boat was magic, and I don't know anything about it. Hell, I don't even believe in it." He studied her for a moment and added, "She needs her own people now."

"Did you call them?"

Tarja nodded. "Hours ago."

Ghari scanned the horizon, just as Tarja had been doing a few moments before, then he turned to Tarja. "You said it was magic? I thought the Kariens hated magic more than the Sisterhood?"

"So did I."

"Maybe it wasn't magic. Maybe it was their god."

Tarja smiled grimly at the suggestion. "Ghari, do you honestly think we would be standing here now if a god had intervened on their behalf?"

"I suppose not." He turned back to study the horizon again. "Tarja! Look!"

Tarja followed his pointing finger and discovered two dark specks in the sky, rapidly growing larger as they approached the river. A coppery glint of light reflected off the specks and removed all doubt about what they were. He nodded with relief and headed down toward the fire.

Drendik was trying to get R'shiel to accept a cup of hot tea, but she stared into the fire, ignoring him. He looked up as Tarja approached with a helpless shrug. Tarja knelt down beside R'shiel and gently took her arm. She jerked back at his touch, staring at him as if he was a ghost.

"R'shiel? Come with me. There's something I want to show you."

She stared at him for a long moment before allowing him to help her up. He led her up the small rise where Ghari waited, hopping up and down with excitement. The Fardohnyans followed them, staring at the growing specks with astonishment.

"Mother of the gods!" Drendik breathed as he realized what he was seeing. The specks had grown much larger now and looked like huge birds, their coppery wings outstretched as they rode the thermals down toward the river.

"Look!" Tarja urged.

R'shiel glanced at him and then followed his pointing finger as the dragons drew nearer. She stared at them as a tear spilled onto her cheek and rolled down toward her lip, leaving a white streak on her soot-stained face.

They waited until the dragons finally landed with a powerful beat of their wings. Lord Dranymire was in the lead, raising a dusty cloud that settled over the humans. The dragon that landed beside him was a little smaller, her scales more green than coppery, her features more delicate. The two dragons lowered their massive heads to the ground to allow their riders an easy descent. Tarja recognized Shananara riding Dranymire and was a little surprised to find Brak climbing down off the other dragon. As the Harshini walked toward them the Fardohnyans fell to their knees.

R'shiel watched the dragons, ignoring everyone around her. She shook off Tarja's arm and walked down the small slope toward the two Harshini, still clutching the blanket around her. She ignored their greeting and kept walking. Tarja ran after her, but Shananara and Brak stopped him as he drew level with them.

"Leave her be," Shananara advised. "I want to see what happens."

Tarja watched anxiously as R'shiel walked toward the larger of the two dragons. She stopped a few paces from him, seemingly unafraid, and stared up at him.

The dragon studied her curiously for a moment. "Well met, Your Highness," he said in his deep, resonant voice. Dranymire lowered his huge head toward the girl in a courtly bow.

Finally, R'shiel reached out and touched the dragon with a burned hand. As she touched him, the dragon seemed to dissolve before their eyes. One moment there was a mighty beast standing before them, the next moment it was gone, and the ground was swarming with tiny, ugly gray creatures with bright black eyes. Tarja was aghast at the sight.

"You've done well, Brak," Shananara said as she watched the demons falling over themselves to get near R'shiel, who stood frozen in the middle of the sea of gray creatures, too stunned or afraid to move. Tarja glanced at the Harshini and caught the look she gave Brak as she spoke. It was anything but reassuring.

"What's the matter?"

"Nothing, really."

"Were you expecting them to harm her?"

"That remains to be seen."

Tarja glared at the two Harshini suspiciously. "What the hell does that mean?"

"Demons are bonded to Harshini through their bloodlines," Shananara explained. "Dranymire and the demons can feel the link with R'shiel, just as she can feel the link with them, although she may not recognize it as such."

If he suspended all disbelief, Tarja found her explanation easy enough to follow. "So if she is bonded to the same demons as you, R'shiel is related to you?" he asked, not sure why that should be such a cause for concern.

The Harshini woman nodded. "So it would seem."

"Then what's the problem?"

"She's half-human," Brak pointed out, watching the girl and the demons with an unreadable expression.

"I'd already worked that out. What's the problem?"

Brak turned from watching R'shiel and the demons. "It's the family she comes from. Shananara's full title is Her Royal Highness, Princess Shananara té Ortyn. Her brother is our King, Korandellen."

Tarja was not surprised to find out R'shiel was of royal blood. It almost seemed fitting, somehow. But the thought did not seem to please Brak or Shananara very much.

"That's not the problem though, is it?" he asked intuitively.

"Actually, it is," Shananara told him. "She is Lorandranek's child."

The name struck a chord in Tarja's mind. He recalled what he had heard about Lorandranek and turned to Shananara, his eyes wide. Seeing from his expression that he had made the connection, the Harshini woman nodded.

"That's right. She is the half-human child of a Harshini King."

"Behold the demon child," Brak muttered darkly.

Brak surveyed the destruction Tarja and his Fardohnyan allies had wrought with a shake of his head. "Does the expression 'minimum force' mean anything to you?" he asked.

Tarja frowned at the implied criticism. "About as much as 'you can count on me' means to you."

"You killed the priest, then?" He walked over to the shore, where the body of the Karien priest lay. The river had washed the blood from the corpse. In death he looked barely human, like a flaccid, blue sea creature brought up from the depths.

"Drendik killed him."

"What happened to his staff?"

"R'shiel destroyed it."

Brak looked at him sharply. "She *what?*"

"She destroyed it. Smashed it against the mizzenmast. That's what set the ship on fire. How she burned her hands."

"Gods!" Brak muttered. The Harshini turned and headed toward the demons, leaving Tarja standing by the bloated corpse.

"What?" Tarja called after him.

Brak made no reply. He just kept walking.

The she-dragon was amusing herself by talking to the Fardohnyans, who stood before her reverently, like worshippers at a huge, animated altar. The demons that had been the other dragon had dispersed into smaller clusters, constantly changing shapes in a way that made Tarja's head swim. They seemed to be entertaining themselves by changing into numerous other forms, as simple as birds or small rodents in some cases. A few of the larger groups appeared to be attempting more complex forms that changed with blinding speed and were only sometimes recognizable as creatures of the world Tarja was familiar with. As they approached, a small figure detached itself from one of the groups and waddled over to them.

"Something disturbs you, Lord Brakandaran?" the demon asked. The same booming voice that had belonged to the dragon sounded bizarre coming from this grotesque little gnome. Brak bowed to the demon respectfully, which surprised Tarja a little. It was odd seeing him so humble in the presence of an ugly little imp who only came up to his knee.

"If I may seek your counsel, Wise One?"

Tarja wondered at Brak's sudden turn of manners.

"I will help if I can," the demon agreed. "What is it that troubles you?"

"R'shiel destroyed the Karien priest's staff."

"The Staff of Xaphista is not a thing to be tampered with lightly." Tarja could have sworn the wrinkled face, with its too-big eyes, was furrowed with concern. "Was the priest already dead?"

Brak glanced over his shoulder at Tarja questioningly.

"No," Tarja told them, walking forward to stand next to Brak. "Drendik killed him after she smashed it."

Lord Dranymire was silent for a moment. "She is of té Ortyn blood," the demon said eventually.

"Does that matter?" Tarja asked. There seemed to be so much that Brak and the demon knew, it was as if they were only having half a conversation, leaving out all the important bits.

"All magic is connected through the gods," the demon explained. "Xaphista is an Incidental God, but a god, nonetheless, like any other."

So what? he wanted to yell at the demon. *What difference does it make?*

Sensing his lack of understanding, Brak finally, if a little reluctantly, came to Tarja's rescue. "He means that Xaphista would have felt the staff being destroyed. If the priest was still alive when it happened, then he could have used the priest to discover the identity of the destroyer."

"So the Karien god knows who R'shiel is?" Tarja asked.

"Xaphista has probably known of the demon child's existence for some time."

"The priest's vision!" Tarja exclaimed. "Elfron said he had a vision about R'shiel. That's why they wanted her!"

"Xaphista knows the demon child is coming," the demon agreed.

"But why should that bother him?" Tarja asked. He had given up trying to puzzle out whether or not the gods existed. It was easier, at the moment, just to assume that they did.

"Because she was created to destroy him," Brak said.

"You want R'shiel to destroy a god? You can't be serious!"

"This has nothing to do with you, Tarja. If you have any sense at all, you will just walk away and leave her be. You don't believe in the gods, even though you've met one. You simply aren't equipped to handle this. Leave it to those of us who know what we're facing."

Tarja looked back at the Fardohnyan riverboat, where Shananara had disappeared with R'shiel several hours ago. The two women had not emerged since.

"I won't let you do this to her."

"The decision is not yours, human," Dranymire reminded him. "It is up to the child. Only she can decide to take up the task for which she was created."

"And what if she refuses?" Tarja asked. Brak did not answer him, but glanced at the demon who turned his wrinkled head away. Dread washed over him as he read the reluctance of the Harshini and the demon to answer his question. He grabbed Brak by his leather vest and pulled him close, until their faces were only inches apart. "What happens if she refuses?"

Brak met Tarja's threatening gaze, undaunted by his anger. "It's not up to me, Tarja. I'm not her judge."

Tarja let Brak go with a shove. "Not her judge, perhaps. More like her executioner, I suspect."

Brak shook his head, but he did not deny the charge.

chapter 53

R'shiel woke suddenly, startled and unsure of her surroundings. As she looked around she discovered she was in a small cabin on the *Maera's Daughter*. She lay back and closed her eyes with relief as visions of the previous night filled her head. Tarja was alive. Padric had died trying to undo his deeds. The Fardohnyans from the riverboat had been there, too. Drendik had killed the insane priest. And Ghari—why was he here? The swift change of circumstances left her head spinning.

"Feeling better?"

R'shiel turned toward the voice and opened her eyes. The Harshini woman was seated on the other bunk, watching over her. She had black-on-black eyes, flawless skin, and thick dark red hair. She had introduced herself as Shananara as she had led R'shiel away from the demons. R'shiel glanced down and discovered her burned hands were unmarked. In fact, her whole body felt renewed. She could not remember ever feeling so well.

"I feel . . . wonderful. Did you do that?"

"I just gave your own healing powers a bit of a helping hand."

"Thank you," R'shiel said, genuinely grateful. With the physical pain gone, it was far easier to ignore the mental scars. She pushed back the blanket and sat up, a little startled to discover she was clean, but naked, under the covers. She hurriedly pulled the blanket up to cover herself.

"You have learned the human concept of modesty, I fear."

Shananara reached into a deep bag and handed R'shiel a set of black riding leathers, similar to those she wore. "I thought you might need something to wear. We are of a size, I suspect. They should fit you."

Shananara mistook her astonishment for embarrassment. "It's all right. I won't look."

The Harshini woman politely turned her back as R'shiel dressed in the supple leathers. She had worn long concealing skirts all her life, and the velvety leather of the Harshini outfit clung to her frame as if molded to it. R'shiel felt rather exposed. When Shananara turned back she clapped her hands delightedly.

"Now you look like a true Harshini Dragon Rider!" she declared. "But for your eyes, it's hard to believe you have any human blood in you at all."

"I find it harder to accept that I have Harshini blood," R'shiel remarked with a frown.

"Your mother never told you anything useful, did she? Who your father was, for instance? How she met him? Why he abandoned her? If he even knew of your existence?"

"My mother . . . my real mother died when I was born."

"I'm sorry, R'shiel. I didn't know. Family raised you, then? An aunt or uncle, perhaps?"

R'shiel wondered how much she should tell her. This woman had arrived on a dragon. She was a member of a race that the Sisterhood had deliberately set out to exterminate. R'shiel was not certain how Shananara would take the news that she had been raised by the current First Sister.

"I was taken in by someone," R'shiel told her, evasively.

"Someone who lived at the Citadel?" Shananara asked, as she walked to the small shelf near the door and took down two goblets and a wineskin. "Don't let it bother you, R'shiel. Dranymire and the demons have felt the bond with you ever since you reached maturity. We know you lived at the Citadel. It is nothing to be ashamed of." She offered R'shiel a cup of wine. The sweet liquid slipped down her throat and warmed her through.

"I'm not ashamed of being raised in the Citadel."

"You might have been a Sister of the Blade. Now that would have been interesting." The idea seemed to amuse Shananara greatly.

"How dare you laugh at me! You don't know anything about me. You don't know who I am. You don't know what I think, or what I feel, or what I've been through! You're not even real!"

"Oh, I'm real enough, R'shiel. As for who you are and what you feel, let me take an educated guess. You were probably a perfectly normal human girl up until . . . what? About two years ago? A little brighter than your friends perhaps, quicker to learn, faster to pick things up? You never got sick. In fact, you never had much trouble with anything. Then one day, the sight of meat started to repulse you. And headaches, there would have been terrible, terrible headaches. It went on for months until finally you could not even stand the smell of meat and the headaches were so painful you could barely lift your head in the mornings. How am I doing so far?"

"Tarja told you all of this!"

Shananara shook her head. "He did not, as well you know. Do you want me to go on?" R'shiel looked away, but she continued without waiting for an answer. "Finally, your menses arrived, years after all of your friends. The headaches vanished and the smell of meat no longer made you sick to your stomach, but other strange things began to happen to you, didn't they? Your skin took on a golden cast that looked as if you'd been tanning yourself in the middle of winter. You could see auras around people sometimes. You began to feel strange, as if something far away was calling to you, but you couldn't work out what it was. Eventually, the pull became so much a part of you that you didn't even notice it anymore. Until today. Until you met Dranymire and the demons."

R'shiel felt tears pricking her eyes as Shananara described her life so accurately it was painful. There was no way she could have known any of it.

"How do you know this? Who told you?"

"Who did you tell, R'shiel? You claim Tarja told me, but you never told him, did you?"

"How could you know any of this?"

"I know because every half-human Harshini goes through the same ordeal as they approach puberty. Your experience is not unique, R'shiel. Had you been at Sanctuary, where people understand what you were going through, it would have been much easier for you. I can explain it if you like."

"Explain what?"

"Your aversion to meat for instance," she said. "Harshini can't eat meat, but humans can. It's all part of the prohibition we have against killing. The only time it seems to affect half-bloods is during the onset of puberty. Ask Brak, if you don't believe me. Like you, he is half-human."

R'shiel accepted that news with barely a flicker of surprise. She was beyond shock, beyond awe.

"And the headaches?"

"Half-human children can't reach the source of Harshini power until they mature." Seeing her uncomprehending expression, Shananara frowned. "Think of it as a door in your mind that opens onto a river of magic. Until you reach maturity, the door is locked. Opening it can be painful. I don't know why, that's just the way it is. The headaches were the result of your mind trying to open a door to your power."

"Then I really am one of you?"

"Yes, R'shiel. You really are."

"Who is my father?"

Shananara hesitated before answering. "Do you remember what Dranymire said when he greeted you?"

She nodded. "He said, 'Well met, Your Highness.' Although why, I can't imagine." Looking back, she didn't know why she had even approached the creature, or stood there surrounded by the ugly little gray monsters who swarmed over her. All she could recall was a need to reach out and touch the beautiful beast. To be wrapped in the security of the demons' affection, where she felt, for the first time in her life, that she was truly whole.

"Dranymire and his demon brethren are bonded to the té Ortyn house. They can feel the call of your blood." Shananara thought for a moment before continuing. "How old are you, R'shiel?"

"Twenty."

Shananara nodded. "That would make you born in the Year of the Cheating Moon." She rolled her eyes. "Now there's an omen, if ever I needed one! Only two té Ortyn males were alive at the time of your birth, R'shiel: my brother Korandellen, who has never stepped foot outside of Sanctuary, and our uncle, Lorandranek, whom we were never able to keep inside. Lorandranek was your father."

"Lorandranek," R'shiel said, the name sounding strange, yet familiar. "Wasn't he the Harshini King when the Sisterhood freed Medalon from idolatry?"

"When the Sisterhood freed Medalon?" she repeated with a shake of her head. "My, we have a long road ahead of us, don't we? But yes, he was King at the time the Sisterhood . . . *freed* . . . Medalon."

R'shiel pulled her feet up and tucked them under her on the narrow bunk, feeling a little more sure about herself. She knew her history. "That was nearly two hundred years ago. How could he be my father?"

"Lorandranek was nearly nine hundred years old when he died, R'shiel, and he wasn't an old man. You are going to have to learn not to think in human terms."

"I'm sorry that you find my humanity so distressing."

"Oh! R'shiel, I didn't mean it like that! You have so much to learn, that's all. But that will come with time. It's just that . . . "

"What?"

"The problem is not *you*, it's *what* you are."

"So what am I?" R'shiel asked.

"Lorandranek's heir."

"And this means . . . ?" R'shiel prompted, leaning forward a little. Being Lorandranek's heir might be a title of great importance to the Harshini, but it meant absolutely nothing to her.

"At best? That we are cousins!"

"And at worst?" Getting information out of the Harshini woman was like picking straw off a blanket.

"At worst, R'shiel, it means you are the demon child."

chapter 54

They gathered around a cheerful fire on the shore of the river later that evening. Aber and Gazil had prepared quite a feast from the boat's stores, and everyone had eaten their fill. The Fardohnyans had gone to a great deal of trouble to produce a special meal for the Harshini woman that contained no meat. For most of them it was the first substantial meal they had consumed in days. The demons were scattered around them, even more numerous than before. The other dragon had dissolved into a clutter of little demons not long after Brak and Tarja had spoken with Lord Dranymire. They avoided the humans gathered around the fire, although Lord Dranymire had sidled up to Shananara once she had finished eating and ingratiated his way into her lap, seemingly without her noticing. She stroked his wrinkled gray head absently, with the familiarity of long association.

R'shiel tried not to notice the demons and watched Tarja, wondering about him. The welcome discovery that he had escaped the noose waiting for him at the vineyard had done much to help ease the anguish of the last few days. Tarja glanced up and smiled at her distractedly.

The startling news that she was a Harshini Princess had been met with mixed reactions. The Fardohnyans had applauded the tidings and announced confidently that they had suspected as much, all along. Ghari had looked at her with wide eyes and said nothing. Tarja and Brak had seemed neither surprised nor pleased by the news. R'shiel desperately wanted to ask Tarja what he thought. However, there were more important issues to be resolved first.

"Had I known R'shiel had it in her to destroy the priest's staff, we would have risked going after her ourselves," Shananara said. The

Harshini had not taken the news about R'shiel's destruction of the staff very well at all. R'shiel wondered why it caused such a fuss. Given a chance to live the last day again, she would not have acted any differently.

"It's done now," Drendik said philosophically. "There's naught to be done but make the best of things."

Shananara nodded and turned her attention to Tarja. "I owe you thanks for what you did. All of you. R'shiel is very important to us."

"Not just to you," Tarja replied.

Shananara studied him in the firelight. "What will you do now?"

"If the Kariens invade, and it's likely they will as soon as they hear of Pieter's death, then the Defenders must be on the northern border. I have to get back to Testra to warn them."

"Why Testra?" R'shiel asked.

"The Defenders have been mobilized. By the time I get back to Testra, they should be there."

"Isn't it time to let this go, Tarja?" Brak asked with a shake of his head.

"It's my fault," Tarja shrugged. "I'm responsible for the Envoy's death. It's up to me to ensure that the Defenders are warned."

"Assuming they listen to you. As you just pointed out, they have been mobilized to hunt you down. The chances are they'll kill you before you get close enough to warn them of anything."

"I still have to try," Tarja insisted stubbornly.

"We will take you," Drendik offered, glancing at his brothers, who nodded in agreement.

"I thought you were heading home?"

Drendik shrugged. "This is more fun."

"I think you're crazy. But thank you." He turned his attention back to Brak and Shananara. "The Defenders will move in stages. There simply aren't enough boats on the river to move them all at once. Jenga will be in the advance party. The First Sister will probably follow in the second wave. There will be three companies, four at the most, in the advance party. If the rebels create a diversion, and I get to Jenga before the First Sister arrives, I might have a chance of convincing him." Tarja glanced at Ghari. "Are you with me?"

The young man nodded. "Unless you're planning to take on the entire Defender Corps single handed, I suppose I must be. But it will take some talking to convince many of our number that you haven't betrayed them. With Padric dead, there is nobody they trust left to lead them. Many of the rebels will simply give up and go home."

"Then we have to get to our people before they do," Tarja said. "And find a way to convince them that we speak the truth."

"I'll go with you," R'shiel heard herself say, unsure what had made her volunteer.

Shananara objected immediately. "R'shiel, don't be a fool! You are wanted by the Defenders and marked by Xaphista. The only place you will be truly safe is at Sanctuary. Besides, you are a Princess of the Blood. You can't go gallivanting around Medalon like a homeless orphan."

"If Tarja fails and the Kariens invade Medalon, I won't be safe anywhere," she said, her decision becoming clearer in her mind as she spoke. "Neither will you. I don't care who you think I am, Shananara. I was a homeless orphan yesterday, and despite what you tell me about who I might be, I still feel like a homeless orphan. Tarja has saved my life so many times I'm beginning to lose count. If I can help convince the rebels that he speaks the truth, then I will."

"If that does not convince you she is Lorandranek's get, nothing will," Dranymire rumbled from Shananara's lap. "Recklessness was ever a trait of his."

Brak glanced at the demon, before looking at R'shiel. "Do you understand what you are saying, R'shiel? What you are refusing?"

"I'm refusing to turn my back on a friend."

"We cannot help you if you go with them," Shananara reminded her. "And I dread to think of Korandellen's reaction when he hears that I have let you go."

"He should be delighted that I won't be around to muddy the clear line of succession." Why should she care what the Harshini King thought, cousin or not? "Besides, I have no interest in being your demon child. I don't believe in your gods, and I don't want to be a Harshini. I just want things back the way they were!"

"You want to return to the Sisterhood?" Shananara asked dubiously. "Knowing what you are? R'shiel, they would kill you if they even suspected the truth."

"And what are you offering me? What is the demon child supposed to do? Or am I just some awkward accident that you haven't figured out how to deal with?"

"I will not lie to you, R'shiel. It is not an easy path that lies ahead for you. There is a task the demon child must perform. But the decision will be yours."

R'shiel was completely fed up with being the instrument of other people's expectations. Joyhinia had stolen her from her family to raise her to be what she wanted. Now these people, who shouldn't even exist, had a "task" for her. Rebellion flared inside her like brandy thrown onto an open flame.

"No!" she said flatly.

"R'shiel, maybe you should think this over," Tarja suggested.

"Since when have you been on their side?"

"I'm not on their side. I just don't think you should be so hasty, that's all."

"I don't care what you think," she snapped. "I just want to be left alone."

"Her father to the core," Dranymire rumbled. "Lorandranek lives again."

"Do you mind?" R'shiel snapped. There was something hugely disturbing about being mocked by a demon.

"I mean you no disrespect, Princess," Dranymire said. "I admired your father greatly. He, too, despaired of being responsible for others. He did not feel himself worthy of the task. Nor was he particularly enchanted with the idea of being King. His reluctance made him a great one. Power always sits safer with those who do not seek it. I have missed him. You remind me of him a great deal."

Silence followed the demon's statement. R'shiel was aware that everyone was looking at her, and the feeling made her intensely uncomfortable. She glanced across at Tarja, who was studying her with concern.

"If R'shiel wants to come with me, then she is welcome," he told the Harshini, not taking his eyes from her. "She's right when she says I will need help to convince the rebels. Perhaps she will join you when she has had an opportunity to . . . grow accustomed . . . to her new status." Tarja glanced at Brak. A look passed between the two men that R'shiel didn't understand.

"You are risking her life, Tarja," Shananara pointed out, obviously hoping to appeal to his common sense where she had failed with R'shiel.

"It's her life to risk. You were more than happy to leave her in the hands of the Kariens, a couple of days ago."

"That's hardly fair," Brak objected.

"She's right in saying that her presence will help," Ghari added, lending Tarja his support. "Without proof, the rebels will hang Tarja soon as look at him. If we bring them the demon child—"

"*I am not the demon child!*" R'shiel declared. "Will you please stop pretending that I am?"

Shananara shook her head. "Dranymire is right. You are as reckless as your father was. You have no idea of the danger you are in, R'shiel."

"It would make little difference if she did," Dranymire observed. "She will go with her friends, regardless of what you tell her. You are té Ortyn yourself Shananara. How much notice have you ever taken of others? Even your brother? Grant your cousin the same privilege."

Shananara took in the words of the demon, then glanced at Brak with a shake of her head, before turning back to R'shiel. "Very well, if you must go with them, I cannot stop you, much that I wish I could. But I will not allow you to leave completely ignorant of your heritage. We have the night ahead of us. You will learn something of your power before you leave, I will see to that. Come."

There seemed to be as much a threat as an offer of assistance in her cousin's words, but R'shiel rose and followed Shananara into the darkness beyond the fire.

"You must understand what it is that makes you unique," Shananara told her, as they seated themselves on the ground at the top of the small knoll where she had watched the dragons landing earlier that day. "What separates you from all others, human or Harshini."

"You mean other than the fact that I don't want to be your wretched demon child?"

Shananara sighed. "You are what you are, R'shiel. Denying it will not make it go away. In time, you will come to see that you must accept your destiny, or . . . "

"Or what?"

"Or you will never be content," Shananara replied. "Now let us begin. As I was saying, your power is unique. All Harshini can tap the power of the gods. In your case . . . "

"Doesn't that make you gods, too?"

"No. It means that . . . Oh dear, this is going to take forever . . . You don't even understand the nature of the gods, do you? This is like explaining philosophy to a tree stump."

R'shiel smiled at the Harshini's frustration. "So I guess that means you'll just have to forget about me. Thanks anyway, Shananara, but . . . "

"*Sit down!*" Shananara's voice cut through her like a sliver of ice. The

Harshini might have an aversion to violence, but it seemed a bit of mental compulsion wasn't out of the question. Helplessly, R'shiel obeyed the command. "You foolish child. You have no idea of the damage you could do to yourself, let alone others. The Harshini are linked to each other through the power of the gods, and every time you inadvertently draw on that power, you risk harm to yourself and to us. The last time you drew on that power, even the gods trembled."

"The last time?" R'shiel asked, rather chastened by Shananara's outburst.

"You tried to kill someone, R'shiel. No, worse than that, you wanted to make him suffer. You deliberately set out to torment another living creature. Your human side might have thought it justified, but your actions tore through the soul of every Harshini and demon linked to that power. You cannot let that happen again. Not if you wish to live."

"Are you threatening me?"

"Of course not. I am incapable of even thinking such a thing. But there are others who are not. The demons are not bound by our aversion to violence, and their bond with the Harshini demands they protect us. If they come to believe you are a threat, then they will do whatever it takes to ensure that threat does not continue. Do you understand?"

R'shiel nodded slowly, the reality of her situation beginning to sink in with a certain amount of dread.

"Good. Now, are you ready to continue?"

"Yes." She did not want to admit it, but Shananara had frightened her.

"That's better. Now let's go back to the picture of the door in your mind I used before. That made sense, didn't it?"

R'shiel nodded.

"Well, when you reach for the power, you open that door. A normal Harshini . . . dips a cup into the river and takes the magic he or she needs for the task at hand. If the task requires more than they can channel, then they must appeal to the gods directly for their assistance."

"Is that what happened when I broke the staff?"

"Not exactly. The Staff of Xaphista is more a destroyer of magic than a weapon. The more magic you have, the more painful it is. That's why you were burned. To break it requires you to draw sufficient magic to fight the effects of the staff long enough to destroy it. What you did was no mean feat. The staff is not alive, but it can sense when it is threatened."

"You speak as if it still exists."

"It does," Shananara assured her. "Not the one you destroyed, certainly. But every priest carries a staff, and they are all as dangerous as Elfron's. Don't think that destroying one has removed the threat." She hesitated before continuing. "We are related to the Karien Priests, R'shiel. Once, a long time ago, they were Harshini, like us. Although the line is almost extinct, Xaphista keeps the demon bond alive by making his priests drink his blood during their initiation. He feeds off his believers and trust me, he has millions of them. His power rivals that of a Primal God. Incurring his wrath is not a thing you should take lightly."

R'shiel shuddered at the thought of ever meeting another of Xaphista's priests. "So what must I learn?"

Shananara sighed. "R'shiel, if we had a thousand nights like this one, I still could not teach you all you must know. You don't understand the difference between a Primal and an Incidental God. You don't understand the nature of demons, or how they are bonded to the Harshini. You don't even understand the difference between you and other Harshini."

"Well that's hardly my fault," R'shiel pointed out, a little annoyed by Shananara's despairing tone. "What is the difference?"

"The difference is your blood. Ordinary Harshini can only dip a cup into the river. You and I are té Ortyn. If we need to, we can dam the whole river and release it all at once, but unlike my brother, or me, your human blood makes you capable of using it to hurt people, to destroy. Do you understand the danger?"

R'shiel nodded uncertainly, not at all sure that she understood anything.

"I can only teach you two things in the time we have. How to reach your power and how to let it go. But you have a lot to learn before dawn. Let us begin."

By morning, the only thing R'shiel was certain of was that she would never be able to control the Harshini magic. Shananara had taught her how to touch it. Once she identified it for what it was it had been frighteningly easy to reach in, open the door in her mind, and dip into the power that lay within her. The same sweet power that had filled her the night she had attacked Loclon was waiting for her, poised to explode as soon as she opened herself to it. Her first attempt had left her almost unconscious, frightened to try again. Shananara demanded she continue, and as the long night progressed she had learned, quite painfully at times, to reach in, touch the power, and then withdraw from it, closing the door behind her. She met with varying degrees of success, ranging from a minor shiver that ran down her spine as she sensed, but could not quite grasp, the power, to a vast explosion that had destroyed the remains of the Karien vessel. Had it not been for Shananara's vigilance in turning the power toward a place where it would do no harm, she could have easily destroyed the *Maera's Daughter.* The Fardohnyans, Tarja, Ghari, and Brak had spent a nervous night, wondering where her uncontrollable magic would strike next. Even the demons retreated to a safe distance as Shananara forced R'shiel, repeatedly, to touch the source and then withdraw.

It was almost light when Shananara finally conceded that she had done all she could in the time available. R'shiel felt wrung out like an old wet sheet. Her hair was damp with sweat, her body aching in every limb. Shananara looked little better. Brak seemed to sense that they were done and walked up the knoll toward them. R'shiel was shaking all over.

"I hope you don't have to rely on your power to convince those rebels," he said. "It would be defeating the whole purpose of your journey if you blow them all into the lowest of the Seven Hells, trying to prove you're the demon child."

R'shiel did not have the energy to come up with a suitable retort, so she let the remark pass. Besides, Brak was right. The power she felt might be strong, but she had no idea what to do with it. She could not weave a glamor to hide herself, as Brak had done, or aim her power the way Shananara had been able to. All she could do was reach for it and hope for the best.

Shananara climbed to her feet and held out her hand to help R'shiel up. R'shiel dusted off her leathers and turned toward the boat, but Shananara called her back.

"R'shiel, there is something else you must be aware of."

She nodded wearily, wondering if her mind could take in anymore after the tiring night she had already endured.

"What's that?"

"Be careful of the attachments you form with humans."

Puzzled by the seemingly irrelevant advice, R'shiel shrugged. "I don't understand. What attachments? Do you mean my friends?"

Shananara exchanged a glance with Brak before she nodded. "Yes, with your friends. You are Harshini, R'shiel. You are not really human. Not completely. I don't wish to see you hurt by forming . . . attachments to humans who cannot ever truly understand us."

Not sure what her cousin meant, R'shiel had the strangest feeling that she would not like the answer if she pressed for an explanation. "I'll be careful," she promised.

"If only I thought you would," Shananara sighed, then let the matter drop.

Tarja and Ghari were waiting for them at the boat. The Fardohnyans were already aboard, preparing to cast off. She looked around for the demons and discovered Dranymire alighting with remarkable grace in the shape of an eagle, near the riverbank. She shook off Brak's arm and walked cautiously toward the demon, who assumed his true from as she approached.

"I have to say good-bye now."

"Farewell then, Princess," Dranymire rumbled.

She reached down and scratched him above the wrinkled ridge over his huge, intelligent eyes, instinctively knowing where he would like it most. He almost purred.

"If you call, we will come, whatever the reason," Dranymire assured her. "As we did for your father."

R'shiel smiled at the demon's insistence that she was Lorandranek's child. She was only reluctantly willing to concede that she was Harshini, but the rest of it was still too unreal.

"Did you really know my father?"

"Yes. And your mother, too. Lorandranek found her wandering in the mountains," Dranymire said, as if he understood her need to know. "She was very young. Younger than you are now. Your father was enchanted by her."

"Did he love her?"

"Very much," Dranymire assured her. "But he was the Harshini King. He died before he had a chance to know you. He wanted you very much."

R'shiel nodded, still not certain she accepted any of this, but a little less apprehensive than she had been. "Thank you," she said, bending down to kiss the demon's wrinkled cheek. She turned and ran back toward the boat. A small chasm of uncertainty in her mind had finally been filled.

R'shiel finally knew who she was.

chapter 55

Shananara came to stand beside her demon as the Fardohnyan boat pushed off and was caught by the current, before they could hoist the sails and turn the boat to take them up river. She idly stroked his wrinkled head as she watched them, returning R'shiel's wave.

"I heard what you said to her," she told the demon, as the boat caught the wind and began to move upstream. Brak headed back from the shore toward them, a trail of gray demons in his wake.

"Did you?" the demon asked, feigning boredom.

"You lied to her."

"I told her what she needed to hear, Shananara," Dranymire corrected, loftily. "That is not the same as lying."

"It's a very fine distinction. Why didn't you tell her the truth?"

"Much of what I told her was the truth. The gods asked Lorandranek to create the demon child. It therefore follows that he wanted her."

"Lorandranek tried to destroy her when she was still in the womb, Lord Dranymire," Brak pointed out as he came to stand beside them.

"He was driven mad by what the gods asked of him," Shananara reminded him, placing a sympathetic hand on his shoulder. "You must not continue to punish yourself, Brakandaran."

"He was still my king. Even an insane king deserves better than that."

"Lorandranek was a great king," Dranymire insisted stubbornly.

"Of course he was," the Princess said. "You must agree though, Dranymire, he spent more time trying to escape his responsibilities as king than he ever did ruling Sanctuary. And you were his willing accomplice, I might add. One noble deed does not alter that. Thanks to my uncle's madness, Korandellen was king in all but name for a long time before he inherited the crown."

"To you perhaps, Lorandranek was less than perfect, but to R'shiel he is the father who would have loved her. Would you have me hurt the child more than she has been already?"

Shananara smiled at the demon. "Of course not. I just never realized until now that you're nothing but a romantic sentimentalist."

The demon snorted indignantly. "I am nothing of the sort! Continue to insult me in such a manner, Your Highness, and you can walk back to Sanctuary."

Shananara laughed and then turned to Brak. "And you, Brakandaran? Will you finally come home now? You have found the demon child for us. Your task is done."

He shook his head. "My task is far from done, Shananara. I might have found the demon child, but in case you haven't noticed, she's sailing away from us, as we speak, into real danger."

"Tarja seems more than capable of taking care of her."

"Kalianah has made certain of that."

"Oh dear, what did she do?"

"She interfered. As she usually does. The Goddess of Love thought R'shiel might be more tractable if somebody loved her."

"And she chose a human? That's cruel."

"Maybe. He probably has a better grasp of the situation than R'shiel does."

Shananara sighed. "She is very young yet and not fully comprehending of her situation. She will come around eventually. And Tarja will see that she is safe."

Brak glanced at the Princess. "You've been in Sanctuary too long, Shananara. There's a big, nasty world out there. Tarja's got some very human ideas about honor. He is planning to take on the entire Defender Corps with a handful of hopeful farmers. R'shiel is in more danger than you can possibly imagine. You may be right, thinking she will come around, but I'm more concerned that she lives long enough to do it."

"But what can we do? We can't get involved in a human war."

"No, but I know somebody who wouldn't mind a bit. And he's quite fond of Tarja in a bloodthirsty, warrior sort of way." He laughed at her puzzled expression. "Don't try figuring it out. You simply wouldn't understand. It's a human thing."

"Just tell me if you can help them or not."

"If Lady Elarnymire and her brethren can take the form of something strong enough to fly me south, I think I can. If you could ask Brehn to stall our little band of reckless humans with some unfavorable winds, I think I can bring help in time. It will take me less than a day to get where I'm going. On sorcerer-bred mounts, help could be in Testra within a few weeks."

"Sorcerer-bred mounts?" Shananara asked. "You're going to Hythria, then? You're not planning to involve the Sorcerer's Collective, are you? Korandellen wanted you to find the demon child, Brak, not change the entire political climate in three nations. Are you sure this is a good idea?"

"No. I don't even know if it will work. But I am sure that I will have killed Lorandranek for nothing, if the child I saved by taking his life is hanged as an escaped convict, before she can do what she was born for."

Shananara looked unconvinced. "I don't know, Brak . . ."

"Let me put it this way. The gods want to get rid of Xaphista, and they can't kill one of their own kind. That's why they need R'shiel. If she dies, they will demand another demon child."

"I know that, but—"

"If the gods demand another demon child, Shananara, either you or Korandellen will have to conceive a half-human child and risk the insanity that destroyed Lorandranek. Are you sure that's what you want?"

"He speaks wisely," Dranymire agreed. "We must do what we can to protect the demon child, and if that means involving ourselves once again in human affairs, then so be it. Lorandranek never intended the Harshini to withdraw permanently."

"Perhaps you're right. Maybe the time has come for us to step forward again. Go then Brak, and may the gods speed you on your journey. I will speak with the God of Storms. And Maera. I will see that R'shiel is delayed until you can bring help."

Brak nodded and walked over to Lady Elarnymire, who chittered excitedly as he approached. She had missed him during his long absence from Sanctuary and was still in a state of excitement over his return. He did not want her and her brethren losing their concentration mid-flight. Demons in their natural form were no more able to fly than he was. He would not ask them to form another dragon. Dragons were spectacular, but they were complex creatures and hard to maintain. A large bird would be better, one with speed and agility and no desire to swoop down on a herd of hapless cattle whenever it felt hungry. He squatted down and pat-

ted the demon fondly, explained what he needed, then turned to Shananara as a rather alarming thought occurred to him.

"When you return to Sanctuary, you might want to prepare Korandellen for the worst," he suggested.

"What do you mean?"

"Well, I'm not sure how he's going to take the news that Lorandranek's long-awaited child was raised by the First Sister to be a Sister of
the Blade."

chapter 56

It took nearly three weeks to return upriver to Testra on a journey that had taken a tenth of that time downstream. It was partly the fault of the fickle river winds, partly because Drendik insisted on docking by the riverbank at night, and partly because the boat was plagued with minor mishaps that were almost too numerous to be coincidental.

On their third night out, the steering gear jammed, and it took the Fardohnyans nearly two days to fix it. After that, it was just one thing after another. A sail tore inexplicably. The hull developed a crack in the forward hold, and they began taking on water. When they got that under control, the aft hold sprang a leak. Finally, when everything on the boat appeared to be in working order, the winds dropped, and Drendik found himself sitting in the middle of a river that seemed determined to push them south with the current. The Fardohnyans dropped anchor and muttered about the gods no longer favoring them. Drendik even suggested making an offering, to appease their obvious displeasure. But nothing they did seemed to have any affect. Tarja fretted at the delay, but R'shiel found herself welcoming it. The river was peaceful, the Fardohnyans were embarrassingly solicitous of her comfort, and she was, for the moment, safe.

Ghari and Tarja had spent the first few days closeted together, forming their plans for their assault on the Defenders. Tarja was anxious to find Jenga before Joyhinia landed in Testra, certain that the Lord Defender could be persuaded to listen to him. He was equally concerned that they not force an armed confrontation with the Defenders in any great number. The rebels had courage and fervor aplenty, but little in the way of weapons or training. They were guerrilla fighters, not disciplined troops. In any organized, head-on confrontation, even outnumbered, the

Defenders would slaughter them. But once their plans were made, reviewed, amended, and then reviewed again, there was nothing left for the two rebels to do but wait, and worry, and wait some more.

R'shiel found herself with more idle time than she'd ever had in her life. Drendik needed no convincing that she was the demon child and was determined to treat her accordingly. She was allowed to do nothing for herself. The Fardohnyans insisted on calling her "Your Highness" or "Princess" or even "Divine One," which made her squirm uncomfortably. Shananara té Ortyn was a Harshini Princess—beautiful, poised, and trained to handle her magic with the delicate touch of a master. No matter how tempting the knowledge that she had a name and a family of her own, the part of R'shiel raised in the bosom of the Sisterhood did not want to accept her "fate."

Tarja appeared to be amused by her dilemma when he finally emerged from his war council with Ghari. He advised her to enjoy the Fardohnyans' attention while it lasted. R'shiel retorted that it was all right for him; nobody was trying to bow and scrape every time he tried to blow his nose. Tarja had laughed at her complaints and offered to treat her like she was still back in the Grimfield, if that would make her feel better. R'shiel stormed off and didn't speak to him for the rest of the day.

But the slow river journey sealed the final healing layer on R'shiel's battered soul as they painstakingly wound their way north. Her nightmares of Loclon and the savagery of Elfron's staff were, if not forgotten, at least no longer unbearable. How much of her newfound peace was the result of Shananara's healing, and how much was simply her own inner strength, she had no idea.

Finally, a day south of Testra, Drendik bumped the *Maera's Daughter* gently against the riverbank to allow Ghari to disembark. Tarja was sending him to Testra overland, so he could send out a call for the rebels to muster at the vineyard on the evening of the following day. Tarja and R'shiel would disembark in Testra and make their way back to Affiana's Inn, where Mahina, Sunny, and maybe Dace still waited. From there, they would make their way to the vineyard and try to convince the rebels that Tarja had not betrayed them. Worse, they had to convince them to mount an attack on the Defenders as a diversion. Although she had volunteered to go with him, R'shiel wondered if she had done it simply to avoid staying with the Harshini.

R'shiel had thought Tarja was worrying about the Kariens unnecessarily. News of the Envoy's death would take weeks, perhaps months, to reach Yarnarrow. An invasion force would take even longer to muster and cross the vast northern reaches. It wasn't until she heard Tarja outlining his plans to Drendik that she understood his concerns. The northern border was completely undefended, protected by a treaty that had been well and truly broken. It would take months to move the Defenders into position. Even if the Kariens did not arrive until next summer, Tarja worried that it wouldn't be enough time.

Ghari waved to them as he disappeared in the long reeds growing close to the riverbank. The farm of a rebel sympathizer lay less than a league from where they had left him. He would be mounted and on his way within the hour. They pushed back into the river and headed north, watching the retreating figure of the young rebel.

"Will they come?" she asked.

"They'll come. To see me hang, if nothing else."

"That's not funny, Tarja."

"I wasn't joking," he said.

It was obvious that the first wave of Defenders had arrived in Testra when Drendik eased the boat into the docks early the following afternoon. A red-coated corporal immediately hailed them. Drendik gave a wonderful impression of a foreigner who didn't understand a word of Medalonian, nodding and calling "Yes! Yes!" to every question the corporal yelled at him. Tarja and R'shiel waited below in the passage just beneath the companionway, listening to the exchange.

"Suppose they try to search the boat?"

"Drendik's an old hand at this," Tarja said. "They won't get a foot on board until he wants them to."

"I'm sorry."

He looked at her curiously. "For what?"

"For getting us into this mess. If I hadn't killed that Defender in Reddingdale . . . "

The passage was narrow and Tarja had braced himself against the movement of the boat by placing his hand on the bulkhead above her head.

"If you must blame someone, blame Joyhinia. She's the one who started it all."

"Perhaps. I wonder if she would have been so anxious to adopt me if she'd known who my father was?"

"Be grateful she didn't know. She would have slit your throat."

"Well, it must be all her fault then," she agreed wryly. "If she'd murdered me at birth, we wouldn't be here now."

"Poor little Princess," he teased.

"Don't call me that."

"What should I call you then? Divine One? Oh-Fabled-Harshini-Demon-Child, perhaps?" It was almost like the old days. She hadn't seen that mocking smile for so long. His eyes were startlingly blue in the dim light of the passage. He looked at her for a long moment then lowered his mouth toward hers. *Be careful of the human attachments you form,* Shananara had warned her. R'shiel suddenly understood what her Harshini cousin was hinting at. *To the Seven Hells with you, Shananara té Ortyn,* she thought, closing her eyes.

"The captain says it's safe to come up now."

R'shiel jerked back at the sound of Aber's voice, burying her head in Tarja's leather-clad shoulder in embarrassment.

"Thank you," Tarja said. "We'll be right up."

Aber closed the hatch behind him. Tarja gently lifted her chin with his forefinger, forcing her to meet his eye.

"R'shiel?"

"What?"

"I love you. You know that, don't you?"

"You're just saying that because you're afraid I'll turn you into a toad, or something."

He smiled. "You think so?"

"Don't you care that I'm not human?"

"You're human here," he assured her, pointing to her heart, "where it counts. Now get a move on. We'd better get up top before young Aber comes looking for us again."

She kissed him, just to be certain that he meant what he said. Somewhat reluctantly, Tarja peeled her arms from around his neck and held them by her sides.

"We have a long road ahead of us, R'shiel. Don't make it any harder."

"Do we have to do this, Tarja?" she asked. "Can't we just go away? Find a place where nobody knows us?"

"Some place where I'm not a marked man and you're not the demon child? Name it and we'll leave this minute."

She sighed. "There is no such place, is there?"

"No."

Tarja let her go and moved to the hatch. R'shiel followed him, catching a movement out of the corner of her eye. She spun toward it, but the dim passage was empty.

"What's the matter?"

"I could have sworn I saw somebody!"

"There's nobody there. It must have been a trick of the light."

"It was a little girl."

Tarja opened the hatch and stepped through. R'shiel glanced back over her shoulder at the empty passage. She was certain she had seen something. She turned to follow Tarja up the companionway, touching something with her boot on the first step. Curiously, she bent down and picked it up. It was an acorn, tied with two white feathers.

"Look at this."

Tarja looked down at the amulet and shrugged.

"It's the symbol the heathens have for the Goddess of Love."

"How did it get here?"

"It probably belongs to Drendik or one of his brothers."

She frowned, certain she had never seen any of the Fardohnyans with such an icon.

"Should I give it back to them?"

"If you want," he agreed, a little impatiently. "Come on."

R'shiel slipped the acorn amulet into her pack and followed Tarja out into the bright sunlight.

chapter 57

Tarja had never felt more exposed than he did walking through Testra toward the inn where Mahina waited. It felt like the streets were crawling with Defenders. He was certain he would be recognized, certain someone would notice them. He walked with his back stooped, a barrel of cider balanced on his shoulder, which served to conceal his face. R'shiel walked ahead of him, the Harshini Dragon Rider's leathers concealed beneath a long blue cloak. The hood was pulled up to conceal her hair and shadow her face. What had seemed like a brief ride a few weeks ago now felt like the longest walk he had ever taken. Surely R'shiel had lost her way. They must have taken a wrong turn.

Even as he thought about it, the inn appeared across the way. He could feel R'shiel relax and realized she was as tense as he was. He wanted to reach out to her. To touch her hand and reassure her. She glanced down the road and crossed it quickly, waving imperiously for him to follow. He smiled to himself as she did. R'shiel knew the habits of the Sisterhood. Tarja trailed obediently in her wake, almost bumping into her as she stopped dead just inside the entrance to the taproom.

The room was full of Defenders, officers, every one of them. Tarja saw at least four men he knew well at his first glance. Fortunately, R'shiel's blue cloak gave the impression she was a Sister, so their entrance was unremarked upon. Tarja hid behind the small barrel, wishing it were large enough for him to crawl into completely.

"May I help you, my Lady?" Affiana asked as she approached them, her eyes widening as R'shiel lifted her head and stared at her. "I have private rooms that will be more comfortable," Affiana added, barely missing a beat. "Have your man come this way."

R'shiel followed the innkeeper through the taproom, her whole body as tense as an overtightened guy rope. Tarja followed, trying to stoop as much as possible. As they moved into the hall and through to the private dining room he dropped the barrel heavily, weak with relief.

"By the gods!" Affiana declared as she closed the door behind them. "Where did you two come from?"

"It's a long story," he said, as R'shiel threw back the hood of her cloak. "How long have the Defenders been here?"

"A few days. I get the officers. The enlisted men drink in the taverns closer to the docks. Are you all right?"

R'shiel nodded. "We're fine. Is Mahina still here? And Sunny?"

"And Dace, too," Affiana told them. "When he's in the mood. Mahina's been keeping to her room, and nobody has seen her, but Sunny's been out working the docks." She glanced back at Tarja with concern. "I heard you'd been hanged. Then I heard you killed a couple of rebels and escaped."

"Almost accurate. How can I get to Mahina's room without being seen?"

"You can't," Affiana told him. "I'll bring her down. You two stay here and keep the door locked." The innkeeper slipped from the room and Tarja locked the door behind her. As soon as she was gone, R'shiel came to him and lay her head on his shoulder. He put his arm around her and held her wordlessly for a moment.

"I think walking through that taproom was the scariest thing I have ever done in my life," she said.

Considering what R'shiel had endured recently, that was saying something. He kissed the top of head, then her forehead, and then she was kissing him hard and hungrily and he was startled to discover how quickly things could get out of hand. He pushed her away with admirable self-control.

"There is a room full of Defenders out there who would very much like to kill us both. Maybe we should wait until a more appropriate time?"

She sighed and pulled out of his arms, crossing to the window to stare out into the yard. "When will that be, Tarja?" she asked. "When you've faced the rebels? When you've confronted Jenga? When you've brought down the Sisterhood? When you've fought off the Karien invasion?"

He shrugged. "I'm a busy man."

She stared at him for a moment, and then suddenly her mood changed and she laughed. "Well, you may just have to wait until I have time for you. I am a personage of some note among the heathens, you know."

"Forgive me, Divine One," he said, wondering what had made her suddenly admit to her demon-child status. She had seemed singularly unimpressed by the news up to now. A faint knock sounded at the door, and he unlocked it, opening it a fraction to look outside, then swinging it wide to allow Mahina and Sunny in.

"By the Founders!" Mahina declared. "We thought you were both dead!"

"Not quite."

"Where have you been?" Sunny asked. She glanced at R'shiel who stood by the window, her blue cloak pushed back over one shoulder. She frowned at the close-fitting leathers. "Interesting outfit," she remarked, before turning back to confront him. "We were worried sick! First you disappear, then we heard that you're dead! Then that other fella left us stranded here. Now here you are, large as life, like nothing's happened!"

"We had an encounter with the Karien Envoy," R'shiel said, glancing at Tarja. With that look, he knew she wanted him to skip the details. There was no need to tell them of Elfron, or the staff. It was enough that they know of Pieter's death and of the threat of invasion from Karien. She did not want to relive the nightmare for the sake of a good narrative.

"What sort of encounter?" Mahina asked suspiciously.

"The fatal sort," Tarja told her. "We . . . er . . . met some Harshini, too."

They stared at him openmouthed. "Harshini?"

"Have you been drinking?" Sunny asked.

"How in the name of the Founders did you stumble across them?" Mahina asked, clearly not believing a word he said. "They're supposed to be long dead."

"The Harshini came to us. It seems R'shiel is a Harshini princess."

Mahina and Sunny both turned to look at R'shiel. Mahina suddenly laughed. "And Joyhinia passed you off as her own child? Oh, that is just too much! The Quorum will have a collective fit! The Karien Envoy must have been apoplectic!"

"The Karien Envoy is dead," Tarja told her.

Mahina turned back to him, her laughter fading. "How did it happen?"

"The how doesn't matter," he said. "The important thing is that it did."

"And the Defenders are here in Testra," Mahina added, understanding the situation immediately. "Or headed this way. What are you going to do?"

"I have to warn Jenga," he told her. "If I can get to him before Joyhinia arrives. I'm going to create a diversion using the rebels."

"A diversion?" Mahina asked skeptically. "You'll need more than a handful of farmers to distract the Defenders, Tarja. Besides, aren't these the same rebels that tried to hang you only a few weeks ago?"

"I'll convince them of the truth," R'shiel said.

"You?" Mahina said with a raised brow. "I'll admit that your outfit is distracting, R'shiel, but I hardly think it's going to turn the rebels' mind from reality for very long."

R'shiel took a deep breath before she answered. "I am the demon child."

Mahina looked as if she was going to laugh at the notion, but a glance at Tarja and R'shiel stayed her mirth. "Founders! You're serious!"

"I am the half-human child of the last Harshini King, Lorandranek," she said. To Tarja, it sounded as if R'shiel were trying to convince herself as much as Mahina. "The heathen rebels will listen to me."

Mahina turned to Tarja. "And you believe this?"

Tarja nodded. "It's why the Harshini sought us out."

Mahina sank down onto one of the carved dining chairs, as if her knees would no longer support her. "Founders! I never thought to hear this in my lifetime. It's . . . I . . . I'm . . . speechless . . . "

"Imagine how I feel," R'shiel remarked wryly.

"It's so . . . " Mahina began helplessly.

"I need information," Tarja interrupted. He didn't have time for Mahina to come to grips with the truth about R'shiel.

"What sort of information?" Sunny asked. She stood behind Mahina's chair with wide eyes, staring at R'shiel.

"I need to know where Jenga is staying."

"I suppose I can find that out," she offered. Tarja was wary of Sunny for some reason he could not pinpoint, but he pushed aside his unease. The woman was a barracks *court'esa* and knew nothing of politics. But she was R'shiel's friend.

"As soon as it's dark, we'll ride for the rebel stronghold. If all goes well, we'll be back by midnight. The off-duty troops should be well into their cups by then. The remainder, except for the lookouts, will be asleep. Can you find out where the rest of the Defenders are quartered, too?"

"Aye," she agreed. "I'll do that for you. It may take me some time, though. What if I meet you on the south road at midnight? That way I can let you know exactly what's happening."

Tarja nodded at the generous offer. "Thank you."

Another knock sounded impatiently at the door, and Dace was in the room before Tarja had time to realize that he had forgotten to lock it. The boy flew at Tarja and hugged him soundly, before treating R'shiel to the same exuberant welcome.

"I knew you weren't dead!" he declared. "Didn't I tell you they weren't dead? Didn't I?"

"Yes, Dace, you said they weren't dead," Mahina agreed. "Now keep your damned voice down, before you manage to remedy the situation by bringing a whole taproom full of Defenders in here with your shouting."

Dace looked rather abashed at Mahina's scolding, but nothing could wipe the smile from his face. He immediately demanded a full and complete blow-by-blow description of their every move since they disappeared from the stables.

"I'll let R'shiel fill you in," he told the boy. That way she could tell Dace as much or as little as she chose.

"I'd best be going," Sunny said, slipping from the room.

R'shiel and Dace stood by the window talking in low voices. Tarja glanced at Mahina, who shook her head.

"When Joyhinia hears this news, she is going to rue the day she ever laid eyes on either of you."

"I think she's long past that point."

"Be very careful, Tarja. She won't make the same mistake again. There will be no trials, no court of law. If you fail, she will kill you."

chapter 58

They could see the flares from the torches gathered around the farmhouse for quite some time before they reached the old vineyard. R'shiel looked worriedly at Tarja as they rode at a canter toward the rebels, wondering what he was thinking. What would he say to them? Would he live long enough to say anything? As if sensing her concern he looked at her and smiled.

"Don't worry. I've survived this long. I'm sure I'll get through the next few hours."

R'shiel wasn't sure she shared his confidence. She glanced at Dace who rode on her left and wondered why he hadn't been in the least bit surprised or concerned by her news. His face was alight with excitement at the prospect of facing action with the rebels.

Tarja slowed their pace as they neared the first lookout, posted about half a league from the vineyard. To Tarja's obvious relief, the guard proved to be Ghari's cousin, a taciturn, hirsute man with big farmer's hands. He was not the most encouraging example of the rebellion's mettle, but he could be trusted not to kill Tarja on sight. He nodded gravely to his former leader.

"Ghari said you'd be comin' this way. You're either very brave, or very foolish, Cap'n."

"A bit of both, I fear, Herve," Tarja replied. "Are they all up at the farmhouse?"

"All them that's comin," he said with a shrug. "Two hun'ed, maybe three."

Tarja scowled. R'shiel knew that he was counting on twice that number. Tarja looked across at her and Dace. "Well, let's do it then."

He kicked his horse forward, but she followed more slowly, a little less enthusiastic about riding into the middle of three hundred angry rebels than Tarja. Dace seemed to share Tarja's suicidal enthusiasm and quickly caught up with him. She hurried her horse forward as if her mere proximity could offer him some form of protection.

Word spread quickly through the rebels that Tarja had arrived, and a torchlit clearing opened ominously before them as they rode into the yard. R'shiel didn't know what Ghari had said to the rebels before they arrived, but it had been enough to stay their hand temporarily. They were to be given a hearing, it seemed, before the rebels made their decision.

Tarja sat tall in the saddle, partly to allow him to see over the crowd and partly because he wasn't stupid. Mounted, he might have some small chance at escape if the rebels turned on him. He had insisted that Dace and R'shiel remain mounted, too.

R'shiel watched the rebels nervously. Ghari jumped down from the wagon bed under the tree where Tarja was to have been hanged so recently. R'shiel's horse, borrowed from Affiana's stables, tossed his head irritably, as if he sensed the uneasy feeling of the mob.

"Well, I've done all I can," Ghari told Tarja. "They're not happy, but they're not unreasonable. Good luck."

Tarja turned back to the rebels and studied them in silence. Many of the faces remained shadowed and anonymous behind the smoky torches.

"Tonight we unite Medalon!" Tarja said in a voice that had been trained to be heard across the Citadel parade ground. She was startled by the effect it had on the rebels. Defiant these men might be, but they were conditioned from birth to respond to authority. Tarja knew that, and was relying on his manner, as much as his words, to convince these men.

"What you think of me is irrelevant. That I did not betray you is a fact that you must accept. I didn't come here to offer you an apology or an idle promise of better times ahead. I offer you action. Medalon faces a threat from an enemy far worse than the Sisterhood. Soon the Kariens will be crossing our northern border. The Kariens will not deny you the opportunity to worship your gods. They will destroy anyone who refuses to worship theirs. The treaty between Medalon and Karien is destroyed. The Sisterhood must now bend its efforts to protecting Medalon. To do that, they need our help. Most of you profess to want nothing more than to be left alone with the chance to worship your gods in peace. I offer you a chance to act on what you profess to believe or to slink home like cowards to hide behind the skirts of your mothers and your wives."

R'shiel cringed as Tarja sat his horse in front of three hundred angry rebels and accused them of being cowards. She glanced at Dace, but the boy was as entranced by Tarja as the rebels were.

"Our northern border lies undefended while the Sisterhood moves the Defenders to Testra to destroy us. They know nothing of the Karien threat. Once they do, we have a chance to resolve this. The Sisterhood cannot support a Purge and a war at the same time."

"More likely they'll just make sure we're all dead first!" a voice called out.

Tarja glanced over his shoulder at R'shiel before continuing, as if asking her for permission for what he was about to do. She nodded minutely.

"If you won't do it for me, then do it for yourselves. For your gods. For the Harshini."

At the mention of the Harshini, someone in the crowd finally overcame their thrall to call out angrily, "We're not children Tarja! You'll not save your precious neck by spinning fairy tales! The Sisterhood destroyed the Harshini, just as they plan to destroy us!"

A murmur of agreement rippled through the mob. Tarja waited patiently for it to subside before continuing. "I do not offer you tales to entertain children. The Harshini once roamed this land in peace until the Sisterhood forced them into hiding. Medalon flourished under their hand. They are still with us. I have spoken with them. I have spoken with their demons."

R'shiel watched as Tarja's words were met with derision. She moved her horse forward and rode up beside him.

"He speaks the truth about the Harshini!" she called to the rebels. "I am one of them!"

"You're a liar!" a voice shouted angrily.

"You're the First Sister's daughter!"

"It's your fault the Defenders are here!"

"I am Harshini! I am *not* Joyhinia's child. I was born in a village called Haven. My mother was human, but my father was Lorandranek! I am the demon child!"

Her declaration was met with startled silence. Even Tarja spared her an astonished glance. In truth, she had surprised herself. She caught sight of Dace, out of the corner of her eye, riding forward to snatch a torch from one of the rebels.

He rode back and handed it to her, leaning forward as he spoke. "Hold it up and don't drop it," he whispered. With no idea what he was planning, she held the torch aloft.

"The threat of the Karien zealots is real," she continued. "I have seen their evil with my own eyes. You once revered the Harshini. The time has come for you to step forward to defend them." R'shiel could feel Dace in the background as the intoxicating sweetness of the Harshini magic washed over her. She recognized it for what it was now and was startled to realize that not only could Dace touch it, but he could do so with a finesse that made Shananara's touch feel clumsy and ham-fisted.

Suddenly the torch flared brightly, savagely, in her hand as Dace released the magic into the flame, lighting the yard as if a thousand torches had suddenly exploded into life. Her skin prickled as she felt the power, minute that it was. The circle widened as the rebels took a step backward, astounded by her display.

Tarja grabbed the moment and called out to the rebels. "Do we face this threat to our people and the Harshini, or crawl home like frightened children? I say we fight!"

Someone in the crowd started chanting "Fight! Fight!" and it was quickly taken up by the mob. Tarja sat and watched them as they yelled, although he hardly looked pleased. R'shiel lowered the torch, which sputtered and died in her hand.

"You've won!" she said, so that only he could hear. "I thought you'd be pleased."

"I've got a chanting mob, excited by a parlor trick. There's barely a man among them who would follow me in the cold light of day because he believed in what I said."

Dace rode up on the other side of Tarja. "Then let's get this done before the sun rises," he suggested with a grin.

Tarja shook his head at the boy's enthusiasm and rode forward to speak with Ghari and several other rebel lieutenants as the chanting subsided slowly. R'shiel leaned forward and grabbed Dace's bridle before he could follow.

"Who are you, Dace?" she asked him curiously. "That wasn't me, just now, it was you."

"Actually, it wasn't really me," Dace told her with a sly smile. "I stole the flames from Jashia, the God of Fire. But he won't mind."

"What do you mean, you stole it?"

"That's what I do, R'shiel. It's who I am."

R'shiel studied the boy in the torchlight. "You're Harshini, aren't you?"

"Of course not, silly. I am Dacendaran."

Seeing that it meant nothing to her he leaned across and took her hand in his. The feeling that washed over her at his touch left her weak and trembling. "I am Dacendaran, the God of Thieves."

R'shiel shook her head in denial. "You can't be. I don't believe in gods."

"That's what makes you so much fun!" He let her go and turned his horse toward the gate. "I have to be going now, though. The others will be mad at me if I get mixed up in what's going to happen next."

"The others?"

"The rest of the gods you don't believe in. You be careful now. They'll be rather put out if you go and get yourself killed."

Dace clucked his horse forward and vanished into the darkness. She opened her mouth to call him back, but he had literally vanished from sight. Dumbfounded, Ghari had to call her name twice before she even noticed he was speaking to her.

"R'shiel?"

She turned to look down at him. "What?"

"Are you all right?" he asked.

She nodded.

"Before we go the men want . . . well, they want your blessing."

"My blessing?"

"You are the demon child," he said with an apologetic shrug.

R'shiel looked up and suddenly noticed the sea of expectant faces, staring at her with a mixture of awe and fear and perhaps a little distrust.

Mandah walked forward to stand beside Ghari. "R'shiel, every one of us here has known the demon child would come one day, though I'm not sure we're pleased to discover it is you. But most likely some of these men will die this night. Would you withhold your blessing?"

"But I don't know what to say."

"Just tell them that the gods are with them," the young woman advised. "That is all they want to hear."

R'shiel nodded doubtfully and moved her horse forward to face the heathens. *Tell them the gods are with them*, she said. The only thing R'shiel knew for certain about the gods was that they were going to be rather "put out" if she got herself killed.

nly about half of Tarja's ragtag band of rebels were mounted. The rest had come in wagons or on foot to the rendezvous. Nor were they particularly well armed. Their weapons ranged from knives, rusty swords, and halberds to pitchforks, scythes, and other farm implements. R'shiel thought they looked pitiful, but Tarja assured her that the attack on the Defenders would be by stealth, rather than open confrontation.

They set out for Testra last, with the mounted men who formed the rear of the attack party. Tarja had sent his infantry ahead several hours ago. He had timed his own arrival for closer to midnight, to meet Sunny on the road outside Testra and give his final orders, based on the intelligence she provided. R'shiel watched as Tarja ordered his men with a quiet confidence she suspected he did not feel. He had fewer men than he hoped for, poorly armed, and ill-trained. Any one of them was liable to break ranks, either through fear or misguided bravery. She could tell he wished for even a handful of the superbly trained Defenders he had once commanded. The rebels were fractious, independent, and barely convinced that Tarja was not leading them into a trap. Only her faith in him let her believe that they had any chance of winning.

They reached the outskirts of Testra just before midnight. The night was dark, the moon hidden behind a bank of low clouds. The heat of the day had not been able to escape, and the night was uncomfortably warm. Sunny waved as they drew near. They dismounted and walked off the road a way.

"I found Lord Jenga. He's at an inn called the Bondsman's Friend."

Ghari nodded. "I know where it is. It's at the end of a cul-de-sac near the docks."

Tarja frowned. "A dead end? Trust Jenga to pick a place that's easy to defend. How many men are with him?"

"No more than a dozen," Sunny assured him. "Just a few officers and scribes and the like. The rest are camped on the western side of town in the fields."

Tarja nodded and turned back to Ghari and his men. R'shiel pulled Sunny aside and looked at her closely. "Is something wrong?"

Sunny shook her head. "I'm fine. All this talk of heathens and Harshini makes me a bit nervous, that's all."

"You're still my friend, Sunny. I haven't changed."

Sunny shrugged uncomfortably. "I'd best be getting back."

"I'll see you tomorrow, then?"

"You can count on it," Sunny promised.

Testra was quiet as they rode into the town. The taverns were mostly closed for the night, and decent people were well abed. Tarja sent the bulk of his troops to the field on the town's west side where the Defenders were camped, under the leadership of a tall, thin, but capable-looking man called Wylbir. A former sergeant in the Defenders, he was the closest thing to a military trained officer that Tarja had. Tarja, Ghari, R'shiel, and a dozen more hand-picked men were to move on the Bondsman's Friend. If things were as Sunny claimed, they could be in and out before the Defenders knew what had happened.

They dismounted a block or more from the inn and made their way on foot, hugging the shadows and jumping at every sound. R'shiel followed Tarja closely. He waved his men forward with hand signals as they turned into the cul-de-sac, then stopped them abruptly.

Darkened shops, obviously catering to the wealthier clientele of Testra, flanked the street. Small, discreet signs hung over several of the shops. Some of them were so exclusive, no signs were displayed at all. The Bondsman's Friend was a tall, double-storied building of red brick, with two rather imposing columns flanking the entrance. A circular driveway surrounded a small fountain in the center of the yard, which splashed softly in the still night. He studied the deserted street for a long time, before turning back to flatten himself against the wall.

"What's wrong?" R'shiel whispered.

"There are no guards."

"Is that bad?" She knew nothing about tactics, but it did not seem

unreasonable that Jenga might think himself safe in an inn in the middle
of Medalon.

"It's not like Jenga."

"Maybe it's the wrong inn?" one of the others suggested.

"Maybe it's not," Tarja muttered. He glanced across the street at
Ghari who was flattened against the opposite wall with the rest of the
men. Tarja wavered for a moment, he seemed on the verge of ordering
their withdrawal. But before he could act, Ghari broke cover and moved
toward the inn. Cursing the boys recklessness under his breath, Tarja
beckoned the others forward. There was no going back now.

They were almost at the fountain when the rattle of hooves and tack
sounded behind them. R'shiel jumped at the unexpected noise and turned
as light flared from a score of torches. The darkened inn was suddenly alive
with soldiers. Squinting in the unexpected light, she counted more than a
hundred red-coated Defenders, swords drawn, ringing the courtyard. Their
retreat was cut off by a dozen or more mounted Defenders at the entrance to
the cul-de-sac. She glanced at Tarja, waiting for him to charge, to fight his
way to freedom, or die trying. But Tarja was not looking at her. He was looking at the tall, gray-haired man emerging from the inn and the short plump
woman who walked beside him. R'shiel stood frozen in shock as the Lord
Defender and his companion walked into the light of the flaring torches.

"Don't make me kill you, Tarja," Jenga said as he stopped a pace from
the rebel leader. "There is no need for bloodshed."

Tarja met the Lord Defender's eye for a tense moment, then threw
down his sword and waved to his men to do the same. The rebels com-
plied, hurling their weapons to the ground in a furious clatter of metal
against the cobblestones. The atmosphere in the yard relaxed almost visibly as the Defenders realized Tarja did not plan to make a fight of it.

"See, I told you they'd come," the woman said. R'shiel stared at her.
"Do I get paid now?"

"A hundred gold rivets and a pardon. As agreed."

"Sunny?" R'shiel said, finally finding her voice. She was numb with
shock. "What have you done?"

"What have I done?" she asked. "I have done my duty to the Sisterhood, nothing more."

"But you were my friend!" R'shiel was suddenly afraid that she was
going to cry.

"I'm no friend to any heathen. Particularly one who's not even
human." She spat on the ground in front of R'shiel.

R'shiel raised her arm and punched the *court'esa* in the face with all the force she could muster. Sunny staggered backward under the blow, crying out in pain. She cowered on the ground, whimpering as R'shiel raised her arm to hit her again. Neither Jenga nor the Defenders made to interfere. If R'shiel could have figured out how to burn Sunny to ashes where she stood, she would have done it gladly, but she was too angry to call on her magic.

"R'shiel, no!" Tarja cried, stepping quickly between her and Sunny. He caught her wrist above her head and held it there, as she prepared to strike again. R'shiel glared at him, struggling against his hold, but he was stronger than her anger.

"Let me go! I'm going to kill her!"

"No you're not," he told her firmly, then added in a low voice meant only for her, "Look around you, R'shiel. Kill her and you'll be dead before she hits the ground. There will be another time."

"Oh? I don't know," Ghari called as a Defender grabbed him and pulled him back from the fracas between the two women. "Sounds like a grand idea to me. Let her at it, Tarja. Give the girl her head!"

"Shut up, fool," Jenga snapped, but he made no other attempt to interfere.

Still struggling against Tarja's grip, R'shiel tried to remember what Shananara had taught her about touching her magic. She couldn't break free of Tarja without it, but neither could she risk harming him by mistake. Besides, she wasn't angry with Tarja; it was Sunny she wanted to kill. His knuckles were white, and the veins along his arm stood out with the strain.

"But you don't understand . . . " she whispered. The depth of Sunny's betrayal was beyond comprehension. She wished more than anything, at that moment, that she had stayed with the Harshini. That she had never come back to discover how easily she had been duped. She slowly lowered her arm. Tarja held her for a fleeting moment before she was pulled away by two Defenders.

Sunny had struggled to her feet and approached R'shiel with a murderous look, blood dripping from her broken nose. She slapped R'shiel's face with stinging force, but the pain was almost a relief compared to the knowledge of the woman's treachery.

"Harshini bitch!"

Sunny stormed back toward the inn as R'shiel was dragged away by the Defenders. Her last sight of Tarja was of him being bound securely with heavy chains and led away to await his fate with the other captured rebels.

chapter 60

arja was separated from the other rebels and taken into the inn. He was escorted into a small dining room that held a polished circular table surrounded by elegant, high-backed chairs and ordered to sit by the Defender who had charge of him. Tarja recognized the man. He had been a cadet the last time Tarja had seen him; now he was a captain. He suddenly felt very old.

"Harven, isn't it?" he asked the young captain.

"I told you to sit down."

Tarja shrugged, indicating the chains that bound him. "If you don't mind, I'd prefer to stand."

"Suit yourself." The captain looked away, as if afraid to meet his eyes. That suited Tarja just fine. He had no wish to suffer the accusing glare of the young man. He was far too busy accusing himself.

He should have known Sunny was too much of an opportunist to be trusted. A hundred gold rivets was more than she could earn in a lifetime as a *court'esa*. In a way, he didn't blame her for choosing the reward. A fortune in gold and a pardon from the Sisterhood undoubtedly appeared a much safer option than a dubious alliance with the heathen rebels. But even had he suspected her unexpected allegiance to the Sisterhood, the fact that he had walked into a trap, while every sense he owned screamed at him that something was amiss, was unforgivable. He should have acted on his first impulse to withdraw. Thanks entirely to his stupidity, R'shiel was in the hands of the Sisterhood, and they knew that she was Harshini. The rebels had been captured, almost to a man. He had led them all to their peril while arrogantly assuming that he could win against a superior force with a motley collection of rebellious farmers armed with pitchforks. He was a bloody fool.

Harven snapped to attention as the door opened and Lord Jenga entered the room. His expression was grim. He seemed to take no joy in his victory.

"Unchain him," he ordered Harven. The captain did as he was told, then returned to his post by the door.

Tarja shed the chains gladly and this time took the seat that Jenga offered him. Jenga pushed the glass-shaded lantern on the table aside so that he could see the younger man more clearly. The shadows lent him an air of deep melancholy.

"You will talk to me this time, Tarja," the Lord Defender said. "There will be no torture. No threats. I simply want the truth. On your honor as a captain of the Defenders."

"That's a strange oath to ask me to honor, Jenga. I broke that trust a long time ago."

"Why did you come back? Why attempt such a foolish thing?" Jenga appeared more concerned by Tarja's tactical error than his desertion.

"Because the Karien Envoy is dead. We face invasion from the north, and Joyhinia is moving you away from the border."

"So you attacked me? You never used to be so stupid, Tarja."

"No. The attack was just a diversion so that I could warn you before Joyhinia got here. I hoped you'd listen to reason." How ludicrous his plan seemed now. How grandiose and improbable. Jenga was right. He never used to be so stupid.

"Did you think I would turn the Defenders around against the express orders of the First Sister to face an invasion that I've heard nothing of?"

"You'll hear about it soon enough, my Lord."

"And R'shiel?" Jenga asked. "How is she involved in this? The *court'esa* says she now claims to be Harshini."

Tarja was very tempted to lie. By denying Sunny's story he might be able to save R'shiel . . . from what? They would both be hanged as soon as Joyhinia arrived. She would not suffer either of them to live any longer.

"The Harshini are no threat to Medalon," Tarja said, shaking his head. "Quite the opposite."

"I always wondered about who she really was," Jenga said, staring at his hands, then he looked up, the Lord Defender to the core. "I assume you found them, then? The Harshini who are still in hiding? You have the location of their settlement?"

"Jenga, forget the Harshini!" Tarja pleaded. "They are not the threat the Sisterhood claims!"

"Where are they hiding? Or have you changed sides again, Tarja? Have the Harshini sorcerers addled your wits? It would account for your actions tonight, at least."

"I don't know where they are. I only met a couple of them."

"And based on this meeting with two representatives of their race, you have determined that they are no threat to us?" Jenga asked skeptically. "A sound military assessment if ever I heard one."

"The Harshini are not warriors. They're peaceful."

"Do you think me a fool? The Hythrun follow the gods of the Harshini and are the most warlike nation in the world. The Fardohnyans keep a standing army that outnumbers our entire population! These are the followers of your peaceful Harshini, Tarja. Every Hythrun warlord sacrifices living things to your Harshini gods."

Tarja wished he knew more. He wished he knew how to explain what he knew in his heart to be true.

"You're wrong, Jenga," Tarja insisted, although he lacked the words to make the old man believe him.

"Then you will not disclose the information regarding their location?"

"Not even if I knew where it was. The threat that faces Medalon is coming from the north."

Jenga leaned back in his chair. "Perhaps R'shiel will be more forthcoming?"

"Harm one hair on her head and I will kill you, Jenga."

Harven's hand instinctively went to his sword, so dangerous did Tarja appear at that moment. The Lord Defender raised his hand to halt the young captain.

"It is clear where your loyalties now lie, Tarja. I never cease to be amazed at your facility to change sides. You wondered earlier if I thought you had broken your oath. I see now that any oath is meaningless to you. You have no honor. You are nothing but an opportunist. A cold-blooded mercenary who fights for whichever side offers the highest coin."

Tarja was saddened by the Lord Defender's words, but beyond being offended by them. "If only you could see what I have seen, Jenga."

Jenga pushed himself wearily to his feet. He turned to Harven. "Take him back and put him with the other prisoners in the compound, but see that he's well guarded. They probably want him dead as much as I do, but I imagine the First Sister will want that pleasure for herself."

By midmorning, all the prisoners caught in Sunny's trap were confined to a temporary compound erected to hold them on the outskirts of the town. Although the planking that had been hastily nailed to the fences would almost certainly fall under a concerted attack, the rebels made no attempt to escape. Ringing the flimsy compound was a circle of grim-faced Defenders who were a much greater deterrent.

Just after first light, Mahina and Affiana were pushed through the gate, looking rather disheveled, their expressions more resigned than frightened. R'shiel followed, after the prisoners had been fed a thin broth and surprisingly fresh bread for breakfast. The troopers assigned to guard Tarja stepped forward to prevent her coming near, but Harven waved them back. The young captain had been surprisingly relaxed in his custodial duties. He did not seem interested in preventing contact with the other prisoners. Much to Tarja's amazement, the rebels did not hold him responsible for their current predicament. It was far easier to blame a conniving *court'esa*. Harven sensed that his charge was in no immediate danger, so Tarja had spent the remainder of the night talking with Ghari, Wylbir, and the other rebel lieutenants. The rebels had been less concerned with what had happened in the past than what the future might hold.

Tarja was certain that this time he would not escape the hangman's noose. His crimes against Joyhinia and the Sisterhood were far too numerous. The remainder of the rebels, he was less certain about. Many of them had been arrested for little more than being out in the streets of Testra after dark, armed with farming implements. Hardly the stuff of dangerous insurgents.

Mahina would probably get nothing more than a scolding, he judged. Even Joyhinia would not attempt to hang a former First Sister. Such an action would set a dangerous precedent. He was more worried for R'shiel. She had been identified as Harshini.

He stood up as she ran to him. He had not slept in two days, but the crushing fatigue he felt was almost banished by the sight of her, alive and well, still wearing those damned Dragon Rider's leathers.

"I thought I'd never see you again," she told him, as she hugged him tightly. "They asked me a few questions, but that was all."

"Me, too. But it will be all right now."

R'shiel looked him in the eye, clearly seeing the lie for what it was.

"Joyhinia has arrived. I saw them taking a carriage down to the docks to meet her when they brought me in."

"Then we won't have much longer to wait."

As if in answer, the gate swung open noisily. A Company of Defenders entered the temporary compound, spreading out to form a semicircle of red coats and polished steel.

He kissed her. It might be the last time he would ever have the chance. She pulled away and looked up at him. He could see everything she wanted to say in her eyes. Everything she would never have the opportunity to tell him. As the last of the Defenders marched through the gate, Joyhinia walked in, flanked by Jenga and Draco.

Taking her hand they walked forward together to confront the First Sister.

chapter 61

The First Sister saw them as soon as she entered the compound. Jenga stood beside her. He had probably briefed her on the ride to the compound from the docks. Draco was just as silent and withdrawn as always. Tarja worried a little about him. Would he object to anything Joyhinia ordered? It was hard to tell with Draco.

Joyhinia scowled at Tarja and then looked at R'shiel. With the knowledge of her true ancestry, it would be hard to miss her Harshini heritage. She spared a glance for the rebels, who were slowly gathering behind him, silently and expectantly, as they stepped forward. Joyhinia must be wondering what she had to do to discredit him. The thought gave him a measure of satisfaction.

"So this is what you have come to?" she asked scathingly as they stopped before her, hand in hand. "I see you have even stooped to incest."

"I'd not go down that road if I were you, Joyhinia," he advised. "If R'shiel is my sister and her father is Harshini, what does that make you?"

Joyhinia's expression darkened. Had she known the truth about R'shiel? By the look on her face, Tarja doubted it.

"I might have known you would be taken in by a Harshini slut."

"Better a Harshini slut for a lover than a heartless bitch for a mother," R'shiel snapped.

"I should have drowned you at birth!" she hissed, low enough that only those closest to her could hear. "Both of you!"

"Why didn't you, Joyhinia?" Tarja asked. "Didn't have the heart to, or was it that you hadn't added murder to your repertoire yet?"

Joyhinia slapped his face, the crack ringing out across the silent compound. His head snapped back at the force of the blow, but when he looked at her, he was smiling.

"Feeling better now?"

Joyhinia was livid as he stood there defying her. With a visible effort, she forced a smile.

"Very much, thank you," she replied. "I've been meaning to do that for a long time." She glanced back at Jenga, who stood next to Draco watching the exchange with a stony expression. "How many did you capture?"

"Two hundred and eighty-seven in total," Jenga informed her. "Including the innkeeper who was harboring them and Sister Mahina."

At the mention of her predecessor, Joyhinia looked back at the gathered rebels. Hearing her name, Mahina stepped forward.

"You are a stain on the honor of the Sisterhood, Mahina. I don't understand how you can stand there amid these criminals and still call yourself a Sister of the Blade."

"The Sisterhood's honor was in trouble the day you rose to power," Mahina retorted. "No stain I've inflicted on the Sisterhood will be noticed against the background of your grubby footprints, Joyhinia."

Rage threatened to overcome the First Sister. She had not expected to face these defiant and unrepentant agitators. She turned on her heel and walked toward the gate.

"What are your orders regarding the prisoners, your Grace?" Jenga asked.

Joyhinia stopped and looked first at the Lord Defender, then at her son and the daughter she had renounced, then at the old woman she had defeated, who was all but laughing at her. A black rage seemed to fill her whole being. Tarja could see her trembling to hold it in.

"Kill them," she ordered.

"Your Grace?"

"I said kill them! All of them. Put them to the sword!"

Jenga hesitated longer than he should have. He looked at her for a moment, wavering indecisively. The compound was deathly quiet as three hundred rebels and more than a hundred Defenders waited for the Lord Defender to give the order. The sun was high in the sky and beat down on the gathering relentlessly. Tarja could hear the distant singing of birds among the trees on the other side of the field. Jenga slowly unsheathed his sword and held it before him.

"*Kill them all!*" she repeated, just to ensure there was no doubt regarding her intentions.

"No." Jenga's sword landed in the dirt at her feet with a thud.

Joyhinia stared at the man in disbelief. "You dare question my orders?"

"No, your Grace," Jenga said. "I refuse. I'll not put three hundred men to the sword on your whim."

"They are criminals!" she cried. "Every one of them deserves to die!"

"Then let them be tried and hanged as criminals under the law. I'll supervise their hanging if they are found guilty, but I'll not murder them out of hand."

"What difference does it make, you fool! I am ordering you to pick up your sword and do as I say or, so help me, you will join them!" Joyhinia was screaming, beyond caring.

"Then I will join them," Jenga said quietly.

"Your brother will pay for your treachery, Jenga!" Joyhinia warned.

The Lord Defender shrugged. "Dayan is dead, your Grace. You cannot use that threat against me any longer."

Desperately, Joyhinia turned as the sound of another sword hitting the ground distracted her. It was the young captain, Harven, standing near Tarja, his expression serious but defiant. A few more followed hesitantly, then suddenly it seemed all the Defenders were hurling their blades to the earth in support of their commander.

Joyhinia stared at them, aghast at the implications of such treason. Tarja's expression was one of awe. He couldn't believe they had chosen to defy her. R'shiel stood close beside him, her body touching his, and she smiled.

Joyhinia turned to Draco frantically. "Draco, I am appointing you Lord Defender. Place Jenga and these other traitors under arrest and carry out my orders."

Draco hesitated. Tarja watched the man, wondering which way he would jump. Would he follow Jenga's lead and defy Joyhinia, or would a lifetime of duty override his conscience?

"As you wish, your Grace," he said finally, in a voice completely devoid of emotion.

"This is murder, Draco," Jenga told him. "Not justice."

"I am sworn," Draco replied.

"Aye," Jenga scoffed. "Just as you were sworn to celibacy, yet the proof of your oath-breaking stands before us all."

The Lord Defender pointed at Tarja, and for a moment, he didn't understand what Jenga was implying. Joyhinia seemed to pale as she glared at Draco. The realization hit Tarja like a blow. It accounted for so much. It accounted for Joyhinia's inside information, even long before she had joined the Quorum. It accounted for something else, too. Tarja knew now who had ordered the village of Haven put to the sword. He looked at the man who had fathered him and felt nothing but abhorrence.

"How many more oaths have you broken, Draco?" Jenga asked. "How many others have you murdered at Joyhinia's behest? Was she blackmailing you, too? Or are you just craven?"

Draco unsheathed his sword and held it before him. For a moment, he glanced at the son he had never acknowledged. Tarja stared at him. He had not expected to learn who his father was this day. Nor had he expected his father to be the instrument of his destruction. Draco looked away first, distracted by the thunder of hooves as a red-coated Defender galloped into the yard.

"Lord Jenga!" he cried, throwing himself out of the saddle before his lathered mount had skidded to a halt. "We're under attack, sir!"

"Attack?" he demanded. "By whom? The rebels?"

Breathing heavily from his desperate ride, the trooper shook his head. "No, my Lord, it looks like the Hythrun." The news sent a wave of disturbed mutters through the gathering, particularly among those Defenders who had just thrown down their swords in support of Jenga. "They're coming in from the south. Two full Centuries, at least. I don't know what they're riding, but they're making incredible speed. They must have crossed the river further south. Captain Alcarnen said to tell you they'll be here within minutes."

Jenga turned to Joyhinia. Tarja expected her to relent in the face of this unexpected crisis. There was no time now to apportion blame or seek revenge. Not with two hundred Hythrun riding down on them. He wondered how they had come this far into Medalon without being discovered.

Jenga bent down to pick up the sword that lay at Joyhinia's feet.

"Draco! Carry out my orders! Kill them. Now!"

This time, even Draco balked. "Your Grace, perhaps we should wait . . . "

"*Kill them!*" she screamed, her rage driving her beyond all reason.

Tarja was astounded at Joyhinia's intransigence. "Didn't you hear him? We're under attack, Joyhinia. Let the Defenders do their job."

"It's a lie! A trick! There is no attack! This is just a plot to save your miserable lives! Kill them, Draco! All of them! Kill every miserable wretch here, including those traitors who threw down their swords. Now! Do it now!"

Draco looked at Joyhinia uncertainly. The woman had stepped over the edge into blind, insane rage, and Draco may have been many things, but he was not a fool. He shook his head. "I'm sorry Joyhinia, not this time."

Looking first to Draco and then at Tarja, Joyhinia's fury knew no bounds as she saw the look of quiet triumph on Tarja's face. She screamed wordlessly, snatching up Jenga's sword that lay in the dirt at her feet and rushed at him. Her sudden attack seemed to wake the Defenders from their torpor. Tarja was vaguely aware of other shouts, other voices. R'shiel cried out. Joyhinia thrust the heavy blade forward as R'shiel stepped in front of him, taking the blade just below the ribs. Lacking the strength to run the blade all the way through the protective leather, Joyhinia twisted the blade savagely as she was overpowered.

Tarja caught R'shiel as she fell with an agonized scream, clutching at the jagged wound, dark blood rapidly spilling over her hands onto the dusty ground.

chapter 62

estra's red roofs came into view midmorning, and the sight raised Brak's spirits considerably. He was exhausted from the effort of keeping the Hythrun Raiders hidden from view. He had been drawing on his power continuously for weeks now, and the sweetness of it had long moved from intoxicating to nauseating. His eyes burned black and felt as if they had been branded with hot pokers. The trembling that had begun a few days ago was so fierce he had trouble keeping his seat. Damin watched him worriedly but said nothing. The Warlord had agreed to come to his aid, and in return, Brak had agreed to see them safely through Medalon. He had not realized what it would cost him to keep such a foolish promise.

Arriving in Krakandar on the back of an eagle larger than a horse had a gone a long way to convincing the Warlord to follow him. But ever since that day, Brak had suffered through being referred to as Divine One, men falling to their knees as he approached, and women begging him to bless their newborn babies. He accepted it as part of the price he must pay to keep his word to Korandellen.

There was no point now, Brak could see, in trying to pretend the Harshini were extinct, so he made no attempt to hide what he was. Nor had he hesitated to call on the Harshini for help. There were many of them anxious to leave Sanctuary and move openly in the world once more. When they crossed the Glass River it had been over a magical bridge constructed by Shananara and her demon brethren. On his left rode a slender young Harshini named Glenanaran. His efforts had allowed them to maintain an impossible pace. He had linked his mind to the Hythrun's sorcerer-bred horses, and through that, gave the beasts access to the magical power they were bred to channel—power the breed had been denied for two centuries.

With Testra so close, Brak finally let go of the magic, and two hundred Hythrun Raiders suddenly appeared, as if from nowhere, in the middle of the road. Their pace did not falter. It meant nothing to the Hythrun that they had been hidden from sight. They were invisible to casual observers but not to each other. Brak sagged as the power left him.

"What's wrong?" Damin asked, as Brak clutched at his pommel to prevent himself from being pitched from the saddle.

"I've let go of the glamor. They can see us now."

Damin nodded, his eyes scanning the countryside, but they were in no danger yet.

They rode on toward the town with the Glass River glittering silver on their right. Brak wondered if they would get there in time. He had no clear idea what Tarja had planned. All he knew was that it was likely to be dangerous. He had not come this far to see R'shiel destroyed. Brak slowed them to a trot as they reached the squatters' hovels on the edge of the town. Damin looked around with interest. He had never traveled this far north before.

"So this is where we will find the demon child?"

"I hope so."

"What is she like?"

Brak thought for a moment. "Like me, I suppose."

"You?"

"It's not something than can be easily understood by a human." He was saved from having to explain further by the first sign of the Defenders, although he was a little surprised they had not been noticed sooner. A flash of red and a startled yell, and the Hythrun were reaching for their weapons. "Tell your men to stay their hand, Damin. I don't want a pitched battle if it can be avoided."

"If they attack, my men will fight."

"Well, they haven't attacked yet, so give the order."

Damin frowned, but he turned in his saddle and signaled his Raiders to put up their weapons.

They rode into a town that seemed oddly deserted for the middle of the day. Although he had expected the townsfolk to run at the sight of the Hythrun, there were few folk around to notice their passage. It made him uneasy, a feeling that only got worse as they turned toward the main square and spied a fair-haired youth standing in the center of the deserted street, obviously waiting for them.

"What are you doing here?" he asked, riding out to meet the God of Thieves.

"Waiting for you." Dace looked past Brak at the dark-eyed Harshini and waved brightly. "Hello, Glenanaran."

"Divine One."

"You're heading the wrong way," Dacendaran informed them "They're all over on the fields on the western side of town. You'd better hurry, though. I think they're going to . . . NO!"

Dace vanished with an anguished cry. Glenanaran looked at Brak.

"Something has happened."

"What?" Damin demanded. "Who was that child? What's happened?"

Brak didn't answer. He urged Cloud Chaser forward at a gallop with Glenanaran close on his heels. Damin and his troop were a little slower to react, but soon the sharp clack of hooves against the cobbles sounded in his wake. Brak tried not to think the worst, but only something that touched the consciousness of a god, on a level neither he, nor even Glenanaran could feel, would cause him to retreat like that.

Brak found the compound easily enough and ignored the Defenders who tried to block his way. He galloped into the enclosure with Glenanaran at his side and skidded to a halt as the shocked Defenders suddenly realized there were two hundred Hythrun Raiders riding into their midst.

Brak flew from his saddle toward a cluster of rebels and Defenders, pushing them out of his way. His fears seemed to solidify into a core of molten lead that burned through his chest. Tarja knelt on the ground nursing R'shiel. He was covered in blood. R'shiel's blood.

"What have you done?" he demanded of the gathered humans.

No one answered him. R'shiel was unconscious, her skin waxy and pale, her breathing labored. Glenanaran pushed through to kneel beside her, and Brak felt his skin prickle as the Harshini drew on his power. The labored breathing halted and then stopped completely.

"I've stopped time around her, but it's a temporary measure only," the Harshini explained. "She needs healing beyond even our power."

They knelt in the circle of stunned Defenders and rebels. Brak looked up and saw two rebels holding back a woman whose eyes burned with hatred. Joyhinia Tenragan, he guessed. Her white gown was splattered with blood. On the other side of the circle stood the Lord Defender. Even if his braided uniform had not given him away, Brak thought he

would know him simply by his air of command. At the appearance of the
Hythrun, Jenga had began yelling orders. Defenders were scooping up
blades that inexplicably lay on the ground in front of them. As soon as
they moved for their swords, the Hythrun reacted. Short recurved bows
quivered as the Raiders waited for the order to loose their arrows into the
closely packed Defenders and rebels.

"Damin! No!" Brak called, as the Warlord raised his arm to give the
signal. Brak turned to Jenga urgently. "My Lord, tell your men to put up
their swords!"

"Who are you to give such orders!"

"I am the only hope this girl has! Put up your swords!"

Jenga made no move to comply. Damin Wolfblade had but to drop his
arm and there would be a massacre.

"Dacendaran!"

The god appeared almost instantly, which surprised Brak a little.

"There's no need to yell, Brakandaran."

"Do something about these weapons. Please."

The boy god's face lit up with glee. In the blink of an eye, every
sword, every knife, every arrow, every table dagger in the compound vanished, leaving their owners slack-jawed with surprise.

"What trickery is this!" Jenga bellowed.

"It's not trickery, it's divine intervention. Lord Defender, meet
Dacendaran, the God of Thieves. If I ask him nicely, he may even give
your weapons back, but don't count on it."

Jenga clearly did not believe the evidence of his own eyes, but Damin
Wolfblade and his Hythrun looked to be in the throes of religious ecstasy.
They would be no trouble for the time being. Brak turned back to Glena-
naran. "How long do we have?"

"Not long at all, I fear."

"Let her die!" Joyhinia screamed. "I warned you! Didn't I warn you
the heathens were still a threat! This is the price of your treachery, Jenga!"

"Who *is* that woman?" Dace asked.

"The First Sister."

"Really?" Dace walked toward Joyhinia, who fell thankfully silent,
her eyes wide with fear as the god approached.

Brak wasted no more time worrying about her. He knelt down beside
R'shiel. Tarja still held her as if he could hold her life in, simply by refusing to let go. While she was held in Glenanaran's spell she had not deteri-
orated, but his magic could not save her, merely postpone the inevitable.

"Will Cheltaran come if we call?" he asked the Harshini.

"He will come if I tell him to."

His head jerked up as the newcomer approached. Brak glanced around and discovered the humans in the compound frozen in a moment between time. Only he, Glenanaran, and Dace were free of it. Zegarnald towered over everything, even the mounted Hythrun, dressed in a glorious golden breastplate and a silver plumed helm. He carried a jeweled sword taller than a man and a shield that glinted so brightly it hurt to gaze upon it.

"Zegarnald."

"You were supposed to bring the demon child to us, Brakandaran," the War God said. "Would it have been too much to expect you to deliver her alive?"

Brak stood and looked up at the god. "You've known all along where she was, Zegarnald. You, Dacendaran, and Kalianah. Maera knew. Kaelarn must have been in on it," he added, thinking of the blue-finned arlen catch that had set him on this path. "Even Xaphista knows of her. You didn't need me. Why?"

"No weapon is ready for battle until it has been tempered."

"Is that what you call it?"

"The demon child must face a god, Brakandaran. For that she must be fearless. She must have ridden through the fires of adversity and out the other side. Otherwise, she will not prevail."

"The fact that your tempering has probably started a war doesn't hurt a bit either, I suppose?"

The War God shrugged. "I can't help it if circumstances conspire in my favor every now and then."

Brak shook his head in disgust and glanced down at R'shiel. She might be better off if she didn't survive.

"What will you do?"

"I have no need to explain myself." Brak glared at the god. He was in no mood for Zegarnald's arrogance. "You have been . . . useful . . . however, so I will indulge you. I will take her to Sanctuary. Cheltaran will heal her. Then the tempering can continue."

"Continue! Hasn't she been through enough?" *Haven't we all*, he added silently.

"She knows what she is but does not accept it. The tempering will be complete when she acknowledges her destiny."

"Well, I hope she's inherited her father's longevity," Brak snapped. "I've a feeling you'll be waiting a long while for that day."

"Your disrespect is refreshing, Brakandaran, but it tries my patience. Give her to me." There was no point in refusing. Zegarnald would see R'shiel safe, if only to ensure she lived to face Xaphista. Glenanaran hurried to comply, lifting R'shiel clear of Tarja, whose face was frozen in an expression of despair. The War God bent down and gathered R'shiel to him with surprising gentleness.

"You must ally the Hythrun with the Medalonians and move north," Zegarnald ordered. "Xaphista knows who destroyed the staff. The Overlord can use the power of the demon child as readily as we can, should he find her before she is prepared. His attempts to bring her to him by stealth have failed. His next attempt will not be nearly as subtle, and your human friends have given him the perfect excuse. So, Brakandaran, it seems you must serve me again, however reluctantly."

"Don't be such a bully, Zeggie."

Kalianah appeared beside the War God in her most adorable aspect, although she barely reached his knee. An eternity of trying had not convinced her that Zegarnald would not come around eventually and love her as everyone else did.

"This is none of your concern, Kalianah. Go back to your matchmaking. You have interfered too much already."

"*I've* interfered! Look who's talking! You're the one doing all the interfering. If I didn't—"

"Hey!" Dacendaran cut in. "R'shiel is dying, while you two stand there arguing," The gods stared at him in surprise. Without a word, Zegarnald vanished with R'shiel. Kalianah followed with a dramatic sigh. Brak turned to Dace in surprise. The boy-god grinned. "It's not often I get a chance to put those two in their place."

Brak had no chance to reply. With the departure of the gods, the humans woke from their torpor. Tarja leaped to his feet, searching for R'shiel. To him, it would have seemed as if she had simply disappeared between one moment and the next.

Tarja glared at him suspiciously. "Where's R'shiel? What have you done with her?"

"She's safe. I'll explain later."

"What is happening here?" Jenga demanded.

"I am wondering the same thing," Damin said, moving his horse forward. "What happened to the girl?"

Brak took a deep breath. This was going to take some explaining. "My Lord, I am Brakandaran té Carn of the Harshini. This is Lord Glenanaran té Daylin. And this is Damin Wolfblade, the Warlord of Krakandar. I believe you and Lord Wolfblade already know each other, Tarja."

"We've not been formally introduced," the Warlord said. "But we know each other well enough. Who harmed the demon child? Point me to her assailant, and I will make him suffer for an eternity."

"Thanks, but I plan to take care of that myself," Tarja said.

"Tarja," Jenga began. "What is—"

Tarja held up his hand to halt Jenga's questions and turned to Brak. "Is attacking us with the Hythrun your idea of helping?"

"Attacking? Captain, you woefully misunderstand our intentions!" Damin objected. "We are here to offer you assistance. Lord Brakandaran informs me there is an invasion of Medalon impending. If the Kariens get through you, then Hythria is next, specifically, my province of Krakandar, which borders Medalon. I'd far rather stop the bastards on your border, than on mine."

Tarja turned to look at Jenga. "My Lord?"

Things were happening far too quickly for Jenga. Brak looked around him, at the Defenders poised for action, the nervously alert Hythrun. Tarja standing by the Warlord, waiting for his answer. He saw Draco, his expression bewildered, standing beside Joyhinia. The First Sister stared into the sky, her face a portrait of wonder. There was something very odd about the way she smiled. Something childlike and innocent and so totally unexpected, that it made Brak uneasy. Dacendaran stood beside her, tossing a glowing ball in his hand, grinning mischievously.

"First Sister?"

Joyhinia did not respond. She seemed totally absorbed in watching the sky.

"Sister Joyhinia?"

"She can't hear you," the boy told them. "Well, no that's not true. She can hear you; she just doesn't care."

"What have you done, Dacendaran?" Brak asked sternly.

"I stole this," he announced, tossing the glowing ball over the heads of Tarja and Jenga. Brak snatched the ball out of the air and examined it curiously.

"What is it?"

"It's her intellect."

Jenga stared at the boy uncomprehendingly as Tarja took the glowing sphere from Brak. "What do you mean, her intellect?"

The god shrugged, as if it hardly needed an explanation. "It's all the bits that go into making her what she is. I couldn't steal it all; that would kill her, and I'm not allowed to do that. But I took all the icky bits. Now she's just like a little child."

"What happens if this is destroyed?" Tarja asked, holding the ball up to the light. "Will it kill her?"

"No. She'll just stay like this. It's pretty clever, don't you think?"

Tarja did not answer. He simply dropped the ball to the ground, crushed it beneath the heel of his boot, and then looked at Jenga.

"My Lord, the First Sister appears to be incapacitated," he said, as if she had come down with a cold. "We have an offer of an alliance to discuss. Would you be so kind as to act in lieu of a member of the Quorum?"

Jenga barely hesitated as he finally crossed the line into treason. He glanced at Tarja before he turned to the Warlord.

"We must talk," he said to Damin.

Out of the corner of his eye, Brak saw Mahina leading Joyhinia away. Mahina nodded patiently as Joyhinia said something to her and then giggled. She sounded like a five-year-old child. As he turned back, Brak caught sight of Draco approaching Tarja cautiously. Tarja deliberately turned his back on him and walked away. All around them, the rebels, the Defenders, and the Hythrun wore expressions of complete bewilderment.

"You're going to have to do something about the rest of the Sisterhood," Damin said as he swung a leg over his saddle and jumped to the ground. "You can't fight the Kariens effectively with one arm tied behind your back."

"I must reluctantly agree," Glenanaran added. "This moment, while historic, is only just the beginning."

"Aye," Jenga agreed heavily.

Brak was saddened by the expression on Jenga's face. The weight of his treason pressed on him, as it would for the rest of his days. For this to be resolved now he would have to do more than defy the Sisterhood; he might well have to destroy it. Dace sidled up to Brak, looking rather pleased with himself.

"Well, it looks like it will all work out for the best, after all."

Brak shook his head. "That depends on how you look at it, Dace. Zegarnald has his war and Kalianah has been able to impose her idea of order on a few hapless souls, but I'm not sure R'shiel would agree with you. Or any of the Medalonians for that matter."

"You worry too much, Brak."

"And you should stay out of things that don't concern you. That goes for the other gods, too." Dacendaran did not deign to answer, but as Brak walked away from him, the god called him back.

"Brakandaran!"

"What now, Dace?"

"Do I *have* to give their weapons back?"

GLOSSARY

ADRINA—Princess of Fardohnya. Eldest legitimate child of King Hablet.

AFFIANA—Innkeeper in Testra. Brak's great-great-grandneice.

B'THRIM SNOWBUILDER—Villager from Haven. Elder sister of J'nel. Died in a raid by the Defenders who destroyed her village.

BEK—Prisoner at the Grimfield. Sentenced to five years for arson.

BELDA—Sister of the Blade at the Grimfield.

BERETH—Former Sister of the Blade. Now a pagan. Turned on the Sisterhood following the destruction of Haven.

BRAK—Lord Brakandaran té Carn. Only other living half-breed Harshini.

BREHN—God of Storms.

CRATYN—Crown Prince of Karien. Son of Jasnoff and Aringard.

CRISABELLE CORTANEN—Wife of Willem Cortanen, Commandant of the Defenders.

DACE—Dacendaran, the God of Thieves.

DAMIN WOLFBLADE—Warlord of Krakandar and heir to the High Prince's throne. Son of Princess Marla and nephew of Lernen Wolfblade, High Prince of Hythria.

DAVYDD TAILORSON—Lieutenant of the Defenders attached to the Intelligence Corps.

DRACO—Spear of the First Sister.

DRANYMIRE—Prime Demon bonded to the house of té Ortyn.

ELFRON—Karien priest.

FARDOHNYA—Nation to the southwest of Medalon ruled by Hablet, the King of Fardohnya.

FRANCIL—Sister of the Blade. Member of the Quorum. Longest standing member, she is the Mistress of the Citadel and responsible for the administration of the Citadel.

GARET WARNER—Commandant of the Defenders. Head of Defender Intelligence and second most senior officer in the Defenders.

GAWN—Captain of the Defenders posted to the southern border to replace Tarja.

GEORJ DRAKE—Captain of the Defenders.

GHARI—Rebel Lieutenant. Brother of Mandah.

GLENANARAN—Harshini sorcerer.

GWENELL—Physic. Sister of the Blade.

HABLET—King of the Fardohnyans.

HARITH—Sister of the Blade. Member of the Quorum.

HERVE—A rebel from Testra. Ghari's cousin.

HYTHRIA—Nation to the southeast of Medalon split into seven provinces, each province ruled by a Warlord. The nation is ruled by a Cermonial High Prince, currently Lernen Wolfblade.

J'NEL SNOWBUILDER—Villager from Haven. Died from complications of childbirth without naming the father of her child.

JACOMINA—Sister of the Blade. Member of the Quorum. Mistress of Enlightenment.

JASNOFF—King of Karien. Father of Cratyn and uncle to Drendyn.

JELANNA—Goddess of Fertility.

JOYHINIA TENRAGAN—First Sister of the Sisters of the Blade following Mahina's impeachment. Mother of Tarja and R'shiel.

KAELARN—God of the Oceans.

KALAN—High Arrion of the Sorcerers' Collective in Hythria.

KALIANAH—Goddess of Love.

KARIEN—Nation to the north of Medalon. Ruled by King Jasnoff.

KHIRA—Physic in the Grimfield and a rebel.

KILENE—Probate at the Citadel.

KORANDELLEN TÉ ORTYN—King of the Harshini. Nephew of Lorandranek and brother of Shananara.

KORGAN—Deceased. Former Lord Defender. Rumored to be Tarja's father.

L'RIN—Innkeeper of the Inn of the Hopeless in the Grimfield.

LERNEN WOLFBLADE—High Prince of Hythria. Damin's uncle.

LOCLON—Wain Loclon. Leiutenant of the Defenders promoted to captain following the Purge.

LORANDRANEK TÉ ORTYN—Deceased. Former king of the Harshini.

LORD PIETER—Karien Envoy to Medalon.

LOUHINA FARCRON—Sister of the Blade. Appointed to the Quorum following Joyhinia's elevation to First Sister.

MAERA—Goddess of the Glass River.

MAHINA CORTANEN—Former First Sister. Mother of Wilem. Banished to the Grimfield with her son and daughter-in-law, Crissabelle.

MANDAH RODAK—Formerly a novice and now a pagan rebel from Medalon. Elder sister of Ghari

MARIELLE—Prisoner at the Grimfield, sentenced with R'shiel.

MYSEKIS—Captain of the Defenders stationed in the Grimfield.

NHEAL ALCARNEN—Captain of the Defenders and friend of Tarja who aids his escape from the Citadel.

OVERLORD—See Xaphista.

PADRIC—Leader of the rebels following Tarja's capture.

PALIN JENGA—Lord Defender. Commander in Chief of the Defenders. Brother of Dayan Jenga and rumored to be R'shiel's father.

PROZLAN—Sister of the Blade stationed at the Grimfield.

R'SHIEL—Probate. Daughter of the First Sister, Joyhinia.

SHANANARA—Her Royal Highness, Shananara té Ortyn. Daughter of Rorandelan. Sister of Korandellen.

SUELEN—Sister of the Blade. The First Sister's Secretary and Harith's neice.

SUNNY—Sunflower Hopechild. *Court'esa* from the Citadel.

TARJA—Tarjanian Tenragan. Son of the First Sister, Joyhinia. Captain of the Defenders.

UNWIN—Sister of the Blade at the Grimfield

WILEM—Commandant of the Grimfield. Son of Mahina and married to Crisabelle.

WYLBIR—A rebel. Former sergeant of the Defenders.

XAPHISTA—The Overlord. God of the Kariens.

ZEGARNALD—God of War.